DARKLING FIELDS
OF ARVON

Baen Books by
James G. Anderson & Mark Sebanc

LEGACY OF THE STONE HARP
The Stoneholding
Darkling Fields of Arvon
The Hidden Kingdom (forthcoming)
Ocean Isles of the West (forthcoming)

Legacy of the Stone Harp: Book Two

DARKLING FIELDS OF ARVON

James G. Anderson & Mark Sebanc

DARKLING FIELDS OF ARVON

Copyright © 2010 by James G. Anderson & Mark Sebanc

A Baen Books Original

Baen Publishing Enterprises
P.O. Box 1188
Wake Forest, NC 27588
www.baen.com

ISBN-13: 978-1-4391-3353-8

Cover art by Todd Lockwood
Maps by James G. Anderson

First printing, May 2010

Distributed by Simon & Schuster
1230 Avenue of the Americas
New York, NY 10020

Library of Congress Cataloging-in-Publication Data

Anderson, James G. (James Gideon), 1967–
    Darkling fields of Arvon / James G. Anderson & Mark Sebanc.
        p. cm. — (Legacy of the stone harp ; bk. 2)
    ISBN 978-1-4391-3353-8 (trade pb : alk. paper)
    I. Sebanc, Mark, 1953– II. Title.
    PR9199.4.A524D37 2010
    813'.6—dc22
                                                    2010005099

10 9 8 7 6 5 4 3 2 1

Pages by Joy Freeman (www.pagesbyjoy.com)
Printed in the United States of America

To Jeremy and Monique Rivett-Carnac,
in grateful tribute to a bond of friendship
tested in the wind and wave of deepest storm.
Without you this work would not have come to be—MS

With love and gratitude, to Fr. Jim Duffy,
mentor and friend, for patiently guiding
me along the songlines of my life—JA

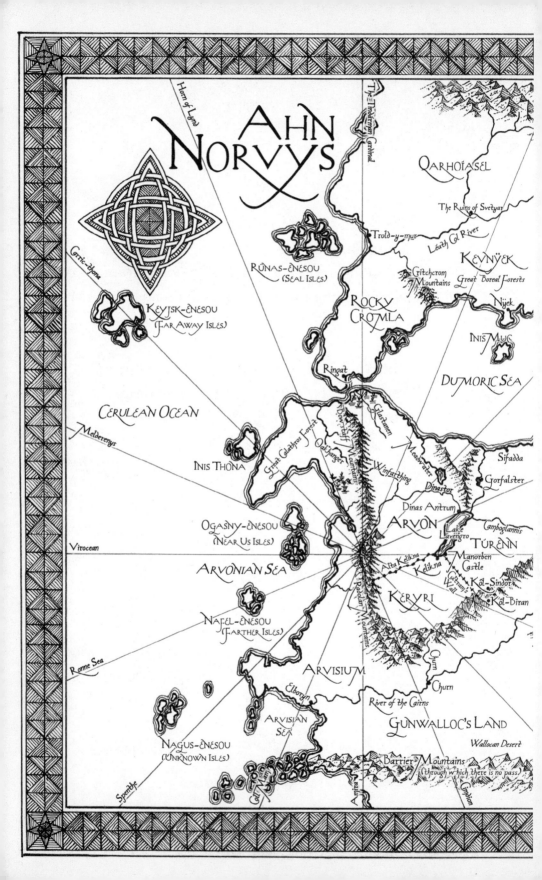

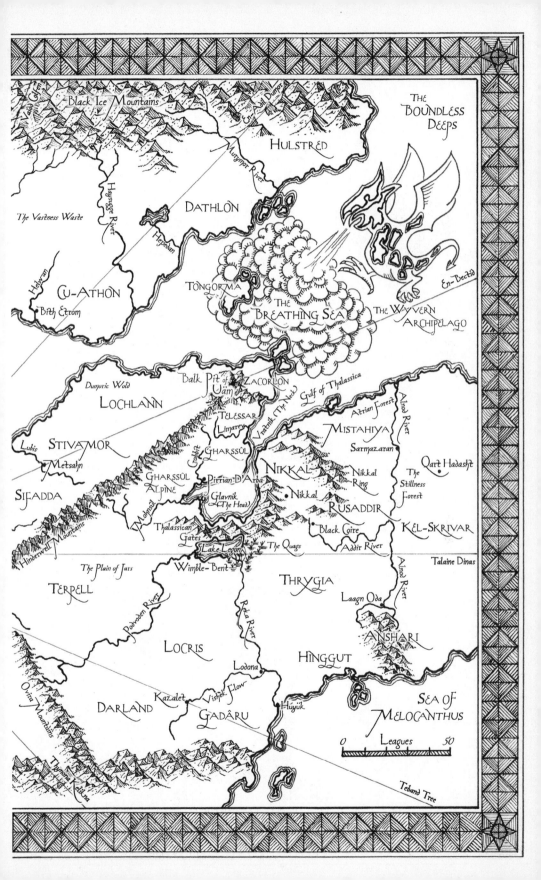

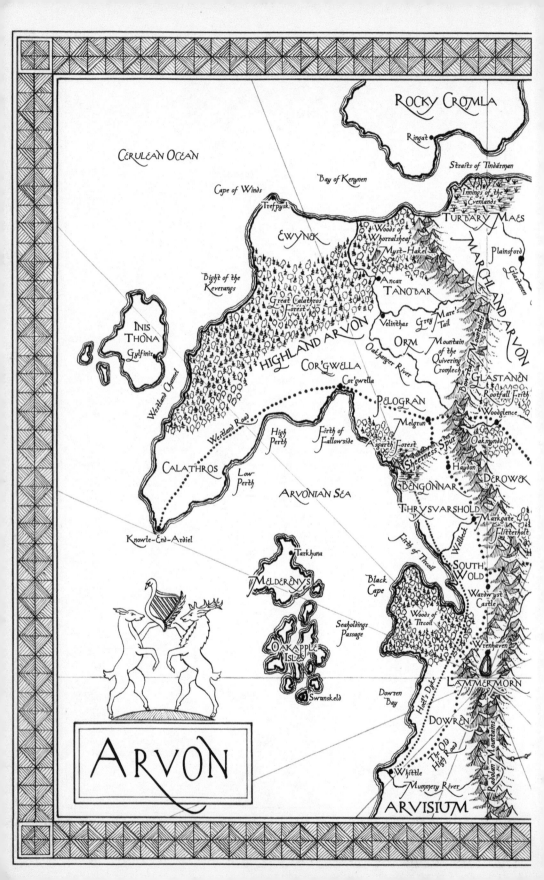

ROCKY CROMLA

Ringat

CERULEAN OCEAN

Straits of Tindárman

Bay of Kenynen

Innings of the Evenlands

Cape of Winds

TURBARY MAES

Trefpysk

Woods of Whorralsheaf

Plainsford

Glastaren

EWYNEK

Myst-Hakel

MARCHLAND ARVON

Bight of the Keverangs

Ancar

TANOBAR

Great Calathros Forest

Velinthas

Grey

Mare's Tail

HIGHLAND ARVON

ORM

Mountain of the Quivering Cromlech

INIS THONA

Cor'gwella

Oakhanger River

GLASTANEN

Gylfinir

COR'GWELLA

Cor'gwella

Rootfall Frith

Woodglence

Westland Channel

PELOGRAN

Melgrun

Oakmyndd

Westland Road

High Perth

Firth of Fallowside

Asgarth Forest

Sherness Spur

Haydon

DEROWEK

CALATHROS

Low Perth

ARVONIAN SEA

BENGONNAR

THRYSVARSHOLD

Knowle-End-Ardiel

Markgate

Glitterholt

Firth of Tircoil

Wellbeck

SOUTH WOLD

Tarkhuna

Wardwyst Castle

MELDERENYS

Black Cape

Woods of Tircoil

Wrenhaven

Seaholdings Passage

LAMMERMORN

OAKAPPLE ISLES

Dowren Bay

Hadd's Dyke

DOWREN

Swanskeld

The Old High Road

Whittle

Mummery River

ARVON

ARVISIUM

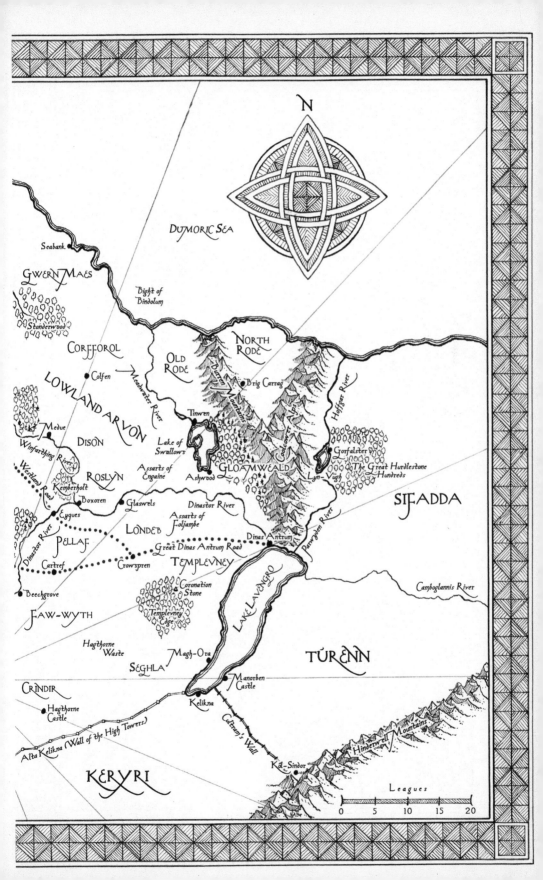

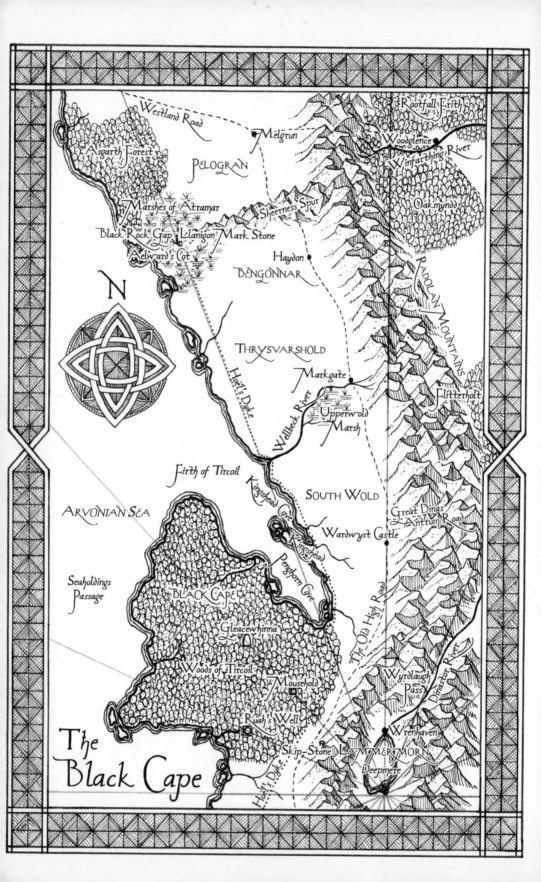

The
Black Cape

DARKLING FIELDS
OF ARVON

ONE

The clash of sword on shield rang from the grey stone walls. The noise filled the chamber, each clang punctuated by a grunt of exertion as the combatants threw their blows. A flash of steel arced overhead. The swingeing stroke met the face of a raised shield obliquely. The blade sparked and clattered across the banded surface of the oaken buckler, deflected to the side. A counter-stroke etched the air like a sliver of lightning. The opposing shield wheeled up, then shivered beneath the brunt. The fighters closed, grappling. Sword blades crossed, parted, and crossed again. For the briefest moment, steel remained pressed against steel, strength met by strength. Then each blade slid down the other until the crossguards locked. The swordsmen's faces met in a narrow space of mingled breath and the stench of sweat and battle.

In silence, the warriors held each other with a stern gaze—calculating, assessing, each taking the measure of his foe. It was the hammerson whose grim stare broke first, a sneer spreading across his bearded face. The look of derision sorted unnaturally with his clear slate-blue eyes. A strand of flaxen hair, free of the leather thong that had bound it, now stuck to the small man's sweat-soaked brow. With a throaty chuckle, he pushed the taller man away and took a step back. The two stood aloof, each in a crouched stance, each eyeing the other warily.

A sword point dipped, breaking the spell.

Kalaquinn leapt forward to meet the renewed attack. The lean, raven-haired Holdsman swept his shield left to parry the blow to his waist. In the same moment, he feinted a high cutting stroke

1

but pulled the blade in midswing towards the other's knees in a low countercut. His opponent read the move unerringly. Following Kal's feint, he slid his shield down to block the blow even as he brought his own sword into play again, aiming for Kal's shoulder. Kal twisted his body up to meet the challenge, just managing to deflect the sword with a shield edge. He launched into a return blow without pause, but, catlike, the hammerson sprang out of reach and replied with a stroke so quick that Kal had barely time to pull his sword arm out of harm's way. In the breadth of a heart's beat, Kal lunged again to the attack, forcing the small man back.

Lissome and quick, the slight figure evaded Kal, parrying with his shield, probing now and again with a sword feint as the Holdsman pressed. Suddenly, the hammerson heaved his body forward against Kal's assault, boldly stepping ahead, his shield held before him to deflect the oncoming stroke. In a blur, he ducked beneath Kal's outstretched sword arm and pivoted full around to deliver a vicious backhand blow to Kal's unguarded belly. The hammerson's sword sliced the air in a harmless arc, for Kal, just as light on his feet and anticipating the move, had spun around, whirling away from a stroke that would have surely ended the contest.

Again, the two combatants broke from the fight, staying outside range of one another to catch their breath. Sweat stung Kal's eyes. He quickly drew the sleeve of his sword arm across his face. Kal smiled. Loosening his wrist, he spun the sword blade around in a close circle by his side. Rhodangalas felt good in his grip, supple, like an extension of his arm, now strong from practice and from rest. His whole body felt strong, muscled and taut with the lithe and potent strength of a highland war bow at full draw.

Kal resumed a high guard stance with slow deliberation, shield held forward off-centre to his opponent, a gap left open between his shield and his body. Fast as a viper's tongue, the hammerson rushed to attack. What Kal's adversary lacked in size, he made up for in speed, but the hammerson did not drive his sword for the opening that beckoned between shield and body. Instead he made a quick feint toward the gap, then slashed low at the Holdsman's knees. Kal blocked with his shield, and, even as he did so, the hammerson's sword whistled around to his attacker's downthrust arm. With fluid speed, Kal lifted his shield to parry, but he was not quite fast enough to take the blow flat on its surface. The sword blade skittered across the side of the shield and grazed the Holdsman's unclad forearm, drawing blood.

"Kalaquinn!" Alcesidas dropped his sword point, lowering his guard, his face ashen. "I-I did not expect you to miss the block. You are harmed? Let me see."

"No, no. Stay yourself, Alcesidas, and your concern. I shall be fine," Kal responded with quick ease, speaking in the ancient tongue still used in this subterranean realm as he drew back from the crown prince of Nua Cearta and shrugged. He quickly examined the fresh wound, then wiped the blood from his forearm onto his tunic, still holding his sword and buckler. "'Tis no more than a scratch. You have added but a trifle to my growing collection of combat trophies."

Kal glanced from his opponent to those standing along the walls observing the contest. Though none moved, each wore an expression of worry, save for Lencaymon. The thickly built swordmaster, clad wholly in black leather, grinned as he looked on his two students. Clearly he was enjoying the bout.

"We should have used blunts!" Alcesidas stepped closer to Kal. "This . . . this was ill-conceived foolishness! Galligaskin," the crown prince called, slipping uncomfortably into the common tongue of the Holdsfolk. "The healing pouch of the Hordanu, please. Bring it. In it he will have surely some proper physic to stop the flow of blood, to heal the wound."

"Galli! Mind him not! Spare yourself the errand. Look, it is in truth but a scratch, and no longer bleeds. Stay and watch the play of sword and shield. Come, Alcesidas!" Kal slipped easily again into Old Arvonian as he grinned at his adversary. "Is your liver more mottled than those of our ignoble lowland cousins that you quake so at the sight of a mere drop of blood?" The prince's eyes widened. "Suppose you that I would slight the gift made to me of Rhodangalas?" Kal lifted the sword in his hand. "We have not yet finished our business. Come! 'Twas three touchings of the body we agreed upon, and that was but two. Now, to arms!"

Kal sprang forward and struck Alcesidas's limply held sword, which the hammerson jerked away, regaining his hold on the weapon as it was nearly knocked from his grip.

"Ah, so, you think to best a son of Magan Hammermaster?" The prince smiled and raised his blade. "You reckon not a Forgeman's mettle, young anuas! Come, then, my lord Myghternos Hordanu! Come!" Alcesidas straightened and inclined his head toward Kal in an exaggerated play of obeisance, then beckoned him with his bucklered arm. "Come, come. 'Twas three touchings, indeed, and I have but paid you two. Come, I owe you yet one more, and 'tis a debt I will soon pay." The prince straightened himself and narrowed his eyes. "Ah, do you so fear your paymaster that you sidle sidewise away from him? Stand, and I shall quickly get to the heart of the matter!" Alcesidas rapped his chest twice with the fist of his shield arm and chuckled grimly. "Come, one touch do I owe you? One touch shall I pay! Or do you, my lord Hordanu, wax overtired?"

"Methinks you wax overmuch in your speech, my lord prince. Would that you bandy blades as well as you bandy words!" A smile creased Kal's face as he held the king's gift before him, languidly tracing the air with the silver blade.

Assuming a middle guard stance, he saw the keen gleam in the hammerson's eye. The small man's ardour, his passionate demeanour, left Kal in no doubt—swordplay was a serious business in this kingdom deep beneath the Radolan Mountains, no less serious than was archery in the Stoneholding.

It was time for the third touching.

Kal and Alcesidas circled each other in a grisly parody of dance, each lifting a foot and placing it lightly behind the next to shift balance and take a shuffling step in time with the mirror image across from himself. Teeth were bared and eyes blazed. This time Alcesidas sprang to the attack, slashing high to Kal's neck. Balanced on the ball of one foot, Kal brought his right leg back a step, then leaned forward into the blow, meeting it with his shield. Then, rather than countering with a forehand blow, as his opponent might expect, in one fluid motion the Holdsman swung his sword over and around above his head, left to right, sweeping it backhand to the hammerson's body. Alcesidas read the maneuver unerringly, sliding his shield sideways to parry the blow while he brought his blade into play. Even as Kal regained his guard, the point of the prince's sword had come to rest in the hollow of the Holdsman's neck above the breastbone.

Kalaquinn's startled silence gave way to a laugh. "I yield, my friend, to your mastery of the sword. Yours is the third touching." The Holdsman bowed his head in submission and let his sword point fall to touch the flagstones, his face dripping with sweat.

Alcesidas withdrew his sword, nodding in turn to his defeated opponent.

"Well done, my lord Hordanu! Never have I seen the eldest of Magan Hammermaster so tested in a challenge of three touchings."

Kal glanced up at the swordmaster, who stood beside Galli and a handful of other applauding spectators. "You would congratulate me? I scored not one touch, not one. And 'twas merely the luck of a beginner, Lencaymon, and your peerless instruction in the arts of the sword, that saved me from an even worse bloodying." He glanced at his forearm. The fresh wound glistened, but the blood no longer ran freely.

"Nay, Kalaquinn. False modesty ill becomes you. 'Twas neither luck nor Lencaymon's able tutelage. You have an unnatural aptitude for the sword," Alcesidas said as he slumped to a bench along the wall and wiped his face with a cloth. "That I should have wounded you . . ."

"Indeed, that you should have, my lord," Lencaymon said, a tutor's reproach colouring his tone. "'Tis a testament to the sword skill you have so recently acquired, Kalaquinn, that you should have fought Prince Alcesidas such a bout and with such skill. And that you would so unnerve him in his sword handling that he would lose control of his weapon and inflict even the slightest damage on you."

"Come, with a weapon like Rhodangalas even Gammer Clout could defend herself from the mightiest of foes," Kal said, holding the sword before him so that it glinted fair in the light of the avalynnia set in niches about the small hall.

"Surely you jest, Kal. Why, Prince Alcesidas would shortly make a sieve of most any foe he might face, regardless of the blade the man bear," Galli said. Kal's companion had quickly remembered his schoolboy lessons in the old language by force of use over the past weeks in Nua Cearta.

Galli looked at the weapon in Kal's unclenched hand. His frank, open face, framed by the twining tattoo of his browmark, held an expression of wonder and enchantment as he once again had a chance to study the sword.

The weapon did indeed prove warrant to the worth of Nua Cearta's forgecraft. The bronze hilt was worked into the semblance of a hawk—both quillions of the crossguard thrust slightly forward, knuckled, then swept outward, splayed at the ends and along the rearward edges. The flat surface of each was tooled by delicate stroke to devise the shaft and vane of wing feathers. Elegantly rounding from the crossguard wings, the quillion block, which housed the shoulders of the blade, formed the head and beak of a bird of prey. The pommel, having the chamfer of a broad fan, was similarly engraved with the fine detail of broad tail feathers. Between pommel and crossguard, braided wires of steel and bronze were cross-wound over burnished leather to form the grip. Inset into the bird's head beneath a lowering brow, two small rubies, the only rich adornment of the sword, twinkled, giving the metal creature a cast of savage ferocity.

From beneath the bronze hawk's head stretched the sword blade, edges scarcely tapering down its length until rounding to meet in a point. Its mirrored surface was hollowed, a wide fuller extending from a hand's span before the hilt almost to the sword point. Here the fuller narrowed abruptly, rose to the blade's surface, and resolved into the etched heart shape of an avalynn leaf, itself a filigree of webbed veins and serrated edges. The sword's beauty, however, belied its purpose—Kal had just proven that. Clearly, despite its intricate art and workmanship, the weapon was made for war.

Seeing the expression on Galli's face, Kal lifted the blade sideways and read aloud the line in Old Arvonian that was gracefully chased within the fuller: "I am Rhodangalas, truest offspring of the craft of New Forge..." He flipped the sword over. Its reverse side was crafted in exact replicated detail—hawk's feather-graven tail and pinions, its ruby eyes, the inscribed fuller and avalynn leaf. He continued reading. "Who would wield me must be swift of limb and keen of eye and true of heart."

"Well," said Galli, tearing his eyes from the sword, "do those lines make a demand, or are they prophetic?"

Kal chuckled. "I know not. Perhaps both. All the same, it must be said that Rhodangalas is a matchless gift."

"True, and a fitting one for Magan Hammermaster to bestow upon you that are now Hordanu," Galli said. "Volodan tells me it is the finest sword that has ever been forged in Nua Cearta."

Alcesidas nodded his assent. "Here, Kalaquinn, you have earned your refreshment." He rose from his bench seat, handing Kal a tankard of ale, which he had poured from a pitcher that had been set in a broad shallow stone dish of ice-cold water recessed into the wall at waist height. The gently burbling waters appeared from a black slit just above the pool's surface, overflowing through a similar opening to disappear behind the walls of the chamber.

"I have come to look forward to these sessions, Alcesidas," Kal said as he gently wiped his blade on a cloth and lay Rhodangalas aside. Kal accepted the proffered cup, then nodded his thanks and took a long draught of the ale, savouring its cool, slaking bite.

"As have I," said the prince. "Yet I think me now, however, that it tests excessively the boundaries of good sense to fight with naked and unguarded steel. Only now do I learn how keenly you have taken to your lessons from Lencaymon. Else I would not have insisted that together we make trial of Rhodangalas sword on sword, edges honed."

Kal grunted his agreement. "I have no wish to meet an early end."

Alcesidas laughed and, tilting back his head, emptied his tankard. He sighed, then said, "Re'm ena, the next time we use blunts. Too dangerous, this."

"Dangerous? Better to call it madness. Utter madness. Such a display!" Lencaymon pursed his lips in mock disapproval beneath merry eyes as he took Rhodangalas from alongside Kal, caressed its blade, and tried its edges cautiously with a thumbnail. "Why, if Magan Hammermaster were to learn that I allowed this contest of unblunted weapons, he would feed me piecemeal to the tunnel wolves—"

"Who would surely spurn such bone and gristle, when they have gorged on Shadahr's men for better than a fortnight and a half," Alcesidas said.

"They have well-nigh scoured clean the outskirts of your kingdom, have they not—the tunnel wolves, I mean?" Galli said.

"Yes, that they have. In as short a time as it has taken Kalaquinn to become a master of the sword's art," Alcesidas said and shook his head. "The three touchings, mine, but not willingly surrendered to me, nor easily won."

Lencaymon drifted to the far end of the Hall of Arms to replace the swords in their scabbards to racks along the wall with a clatter. The gathered hammerson spectators soon began to file out of the room, each offering words of sincere consolation to the young Hordanu and less-than-sincere congratulation to their friend, brother, and prince. Even as the last echoes of laughter faded in the hall, Alcesidas sought out his bench seat again and returned to the thread of the conversation.

"It was a fortune-favoured moment for us, though doomful for Shadahr, when the wolves were loosed from their cages by his own man to raven on his forces. Now those of his men that remain fill our prison chambers to overflowing, preferring to surrender to us rather than fall prey to the horror that is the wolves. Even the mighty Shadahr has thrown himself upon the mercy of Magan Hammermaster. And in all this, no little praise is due to you, Galligaskin, for employing your native tracker's art to help us find the defects and frailties in our defences, that we might stop them up."

"So tell me, Alcesidas, when does Magan Hammermaster plan to make his embassy to the Burren Mountain forgeland?" asked Kal, settling himself on the bench beside the prince.

"Soon, very soon, I fear, Kalaquinn."

"You fear? Because of Shadahr? He may break faith?"

"No...No, not because of Shadahr. You know that the terms of his surrender were such that he bound himself under oath to my sire as the rightful king of our Burren Mountain homeland. A hammerson may wreak much toad-spotted evil, commit foul rapine and murder, but never will he yield falsely in war and battle. Even Sör the Usurper did never unbind himself in this way. No. My fear, dear friend, is of a different sort."

"How so?"

"'Tis a strange self-regarding fear—I fear...I fear that my father will succeed in reclaiming the throne of his forebears."

"I...I don't understand. You fear the success of his embassy?"

"He takes my brothers, my sister, and my mother, his queen, with him. She insists, for she knows that much may happen on account of this journey.... Oh, no, no, do not be alarmed on that count, Kalaquinn, for I am not. Both Queen Almagora and the princess are trained in the arts of war, as are all noble hammerdaughters."

An awkward silence descended upon the three, broken only by the trickling of the spring in the watershelf and the shuffle of Lencaymon as he fussed over weapons at the far end of the hall. Alcesidas shook himself free of his distracted reverie and turned to face Kal.

"I sense that this portends that I shall not see them again. Although King Magan has not said as much, his intent is clear to me. He makes this embassy not merely to make suit for peace, but to establish a lasting peace, and he takes the royal family as warrant of that. The stock of Sör the Usurper may have been malignant, as witnessed by its greenest shoot, Shadahr, but the people of the ancestral kingdom are good. They will receive their true king."

A movement at the entrance to the Hall of Arms caught their attention.

"Visitors," remarked Galli dryly. "Artun and a hammerson."

Wearing a chain-mail hauberk with a belted sword, the hammerson made straight for Alcesidas, his heavily whiskered face serious. He was flanked by Artun, similarly armed with a sword, as well as his longbow.

"My prince," said the hammerson breathlessly, bowing his head, "you must come quickly. One of our borderlanders—he is dead, attacked by tunnel wolves."

"Who?"

"Ranyeth. On his steading."

"A good man, Ranyeth. He lives near Volodan and Signy, does he not?"

"Yes, my lord. What with all the livestock that has gone missing, he went out to check his flock and was set upon."

"Alone?"

"Alone."

"Stubborn fellow," Alcesidas said and sighed wearily. "Borderland traits, I'm afraid."

"That he was, Sire, after we had followed your orders and given folk word not to venture forth alone."

"With wife and children now bereft, alas."

"It was his oldest two sons that discovered him." The armed hammerson shook his head. "Scarcely recognizable, worried and torn, his flesh and blood scattered over the grass. Not killed for hunger, but for sheer lust of blood."

"Where rests he now?"

"His remains have been brought to his home. Awylla, his wife, is beside herself. Neighbours are there now."

"Lencaymon! My sword!" Alcesidas called to the swarthy figure at the end of the hall. He pushed himself up from the bench, dropping the sweat-damp cloth on the seat behind him, and restored his empty tankard to the edge of the watershelf. "Kalaquinn, Galligaskin, you will join us? Good. Then we go."

TWO

"Too beautiful a spot for death," said Kal to himself, admiring the verdant upland meadow that banked gently to a rock-rimmed stream, the midsummer's day edging toward dusk but still mellow with the waning light of avalynn trees and the soft music of songbirds.

"Like most of our borderland places, Kalaquinn," replied Alcesidas, drawing up beside the Holdsman, his brows knit, worry etched across his face.

Kal surveyed the countryside around them. Fields and woods broke against the nearby cavern wall, which stretched up into the gathering darkness of the vaulted granite sky. At the edge of a small pasture, a knot of men stood milling about, waiting. The Holdsmen—Frysan, Gwyn, and Garis, joined now by Artun— stood taller by a head than the hammersons of Nua Cearta. Kal caught snatches of conversation carried on the breeze, the melodious texture and tone of the old language mixed with the quick consonance and resolve of the new. The native tongues of Holdsman and hammerson were mingled and used haphazardly, as the language of each had grown less and less unfamiliar to the other over the weeks of the Holdsfolk's refuge in the underground realm. Even Diggory now liberally peppered his talk with words and phrases of Old Arvonian, albeit none too delicately, as he butchered the unfamiliar syllables with his ploughman's tongue.

"Here, Artun, here's where they ambushed him!" cried Galli, who was crouched down in his tracker's stance, probing the ground with his fingers under an overhang of rock beside the stream. "Leaped on him from above," he said, pointing to the ledge, then downstream, "while others rushed him here on the flats, coming from over there . . . They were hunting him. The poor fellow never stood a chance."

"How many, Galli?"

"A pack. Half a dozen, I'd venture. Maybe more. Big brutes. This way." Galli rose to his full height, then strode on ahead, his bow held loosely in his hand. He followed the brook upstream, glancing down now and then, sweeping the ground with squinted eye in the waning light. Sometimes he slowed to study the trail over rock or where the wolf pack had taken to the stream. Often he bounded along at a long-legged lope, as if he himself were a wolf, the hammersons straining to keep up.

Suddenly he stopped. Turning, his face lit by the eagerness of a bloodhound on the scent, he motioned for the party to join him. By gesture and whispered word, Galli had the men drop to a crouch as he pointed out the direction that the wolf pack had run. The Holdsmen readied their bows, unfastened quivers, and drew arrows. There were a half-dozen muted soughs of metal on hardened leather as Alcesidas and his hammersons each gingerly slid sword into scabbard, exchanging blade for bow. Thus armed, at a word from Galli the hunters struck out from the stream, stalking across the open field, avoiding a flock of sheep that huddled, frightened and bleating plaintively, under an avalynn tree. The men clambered over a fence into a field of ripening hay.

"What's that?" said Garis in a hoarse undertone, pointing to a bloody lump in the long grass.

"Sheep's carcass," Galli said and stepped closer to examine the remains. "And freshly killed. They can't be far off." He lifted his head to scan the field.

"Do you know where they are? Can you discern their sign?" Alcesidas said.

"This way. They have gone this way." Galli continued to creep forward in a crouch, leading the others through the waving bromegrass, vetch, and clover, then pointed to a stand of looming trees. "There! That copse. They must surely lie hidden there." He slowed his pace, holding his gaze on the dark stretch of woods that crowded the open meadowland not two hundred paces away. The grove lay hard against a steep ridge, its sheer flanks barely visible under the light of avalynn trees that stood rooted tenuously in the higher footholds of soil.

"Care," Alcesidas cautioned them. "It grows darker, and so the more dangerous. We must be wary in our approach, too, if indeed the beasts lie concealed among those trees."

They stopped and peered into the veiling gloom of the woods, a shadow that seemed to deepen by the moment. It grew quiet save for the ubiquitous drone of insects. A lone bird fluted a nervous, intermittent song.

"We should send for more men, my prince?" asked Lencaymon under his breath.

"Nay, Lencaymon, 'tis too late. We are as travellers that have waded too far into a stream that needs be fordable, else we be swept away."

It was Gwyn who saw, or rather, sensed them first, pulling at Kal's sleeve in mute alarm even before they burst from the trees. Then they came—a parting of the underbrush, a formless blur, shadows melting from the inky blackness of the forest depths and resolving into distinct shapes.

"Let fly! Re'm ena, they're monstrous huge!" Kal cried.

"To arms! Form a line!" Alcesidas motioned with his freshly unsheathed sword. At the same time, the Holdsmen and a couple of the hammersons loosed the first volley of shafts over the meadow into the wolf pack.

One, then another, of the black forms slumped, writhing, to the ground.

"There's more of them than I thought!" shouted Galli as he reached back into his quiver for another arrow.

Kal felt fear sour in his gut. The wolves had halved the distance. Not only huge, they were fast, shaped to sleekness by the mountain tunnels that were their haunts. Another beast fell, its slavering muzzle twisted to a bloody pulp around an arrow shaft.

"Well-placed, Lencaymon!" Frysan cried through clenched teeth even as yet another wolf's head split, an ugly mass of bone and blood. "And Gwyn!" Frysan drew his own bow to full bend and loosed.

Still the pack flew unslowed to the attack, closing fast in the curtaining dusk, though reduced now to but a few animals. Kal could already see the fangs and feral yellow eyes of the snarling wolves hurtling towards the men.

"Draw blades!" Alcesidas bellowed, springing forward with sword drawn, followed by Lencaymon.

The lead wolf bore down on Alcesidas, who stood in the middle of the broken line of men. Bracing himself, shieldless, the prince met the mighty leap of the tunnel wolf, which flew at him, lunging for his head, jaws agape. The hammerson fell forward to a crouch and two-handed thrust his sword up into the animal's chest as it passed over him. He drove the blade to the hilt, but before he could dislodge it, he was lifted, still clinging to his weapon, wrenched backwards by the momentum of the wolf's body. As he flew, he let go the embedded sword and thudded to the ground, flat on his back, winded, dazed and defenseless. Behind him, the slain tunnel wolf sailed through the air and crashed into Lencaymon's shoulder, knocking him off stride, so that he stumbled and fell.

A second tunnel wolf followed in the wake of the first, fangs gleaming in the murky half-light, a blurred black shape.

"My prince!" There was utter panic in Lencaymon's voice as he staggered to his feet. The creature growled long and low, then coiled itself and sprang at the helpless crown prince of Nua Cearta left lying on his back.

Above the confusion of the cries of the men and the savage snarls and howls of the blood-crazed wolves, in a moment that seemed to hang suspended in time, the highland war cry resounded. The air parted with a hum as something flew past Lencaymon's right ear. The beast, midleap, let go an eerie, gurgling yelp, fell silent, and collapsed sprawling onto Alcesidas. Its forequarter was cleaved and gaping. Lencaymon lurched forward but was pushed blindly aside by Kal.

"Alcesidas!" Kal rammed his foot against the twitching black body of the wolf and drew his sword from where it had lodged in the beast, then slid its razor edge across the animal's throat. The wolf moved no more.

"Alcesidas!—Lencaymon! To me!—Alcesidas!"

Kal tugged at the sodden carcass to free the hammerson of its weight. Lencaymon laid hold of fistfuls of black pelt and, with greater strength than seemed possible for the size of the man, helped Kal heave the wolf off the prince. Alcesidas lay still, pressed into the ground, his leather jerkin fouled and reeking of blood.

"Alcesidas?" Kal said, his voice breaking. "Alcesidas!" His heart pounded from the intensity of both the action and high emotion.

The hammerson's eyes flickered open, and he groaned.

"Alcesidas!" Kal knelt on one knee beside the small man and, cradling him in his arm, helped him first to sit up and then struggle to his feet.

"My thanks—" The hammerson coughed, staggered, and recovered himself. Facing Kal, he placed a hand on the Holdsman's shoulder. "My deepest thanks, my friend."

"You are well?"

"Yes, Kalaquinn, I am fine. 'Twas a close shave," Alcesidas said, then grinned, "though closer still for the wolf, methinks."

The two men broke into laughter as the tension of the moment ebbed, leaving Kal weak and shaking.

"How do the others fare?" Alcesidas asked.

"Right well enough," said Frysan from nearby. "We've dispatched the brutes with nary a scratch to our own, and it seems there're no more."

The noises of struggle had subsided. The rest of the hammersons and Holdsmen stepped closer now, clustering around Alcesidas. In the deepening dusk, a pair of avalynn lanterns had been unshuttered, casting a pure light around the group of men. The lantern light revealed the sable corpses of three tunnel wolves, mouths open and scarlet with blood, tongues lolling, giving each the aspect of an overeager farm dog. Kal thought of Nightshade, the Clouts' enthusiastic retriever. Before his mind's eye flashed uncontrollably a series of images—the Burrows set on its hillock, white apple blossom, Marya's demure smile, the lush pastures and woodland of Mantling Moss, the greystone bulk of the Great Glence, the sapphire sky reflected crystal blue over Deepmere, a smudge of smoke against the horizon, fire, destruction, Black Scorpion Dragoons, the harrowed faces of a people in flight . . . his people . . .

As the lanterns swung around in the hammersons' grips, the surrounding darkness was pierced by yellow points of light. Kal started at a pair of lifeless eyes eerily reflecting the avalynn's gleam. A hand clapped his shoulder, and Kal regained himself, drawing a deep breath then exhaling. A skin of mead was pressed into his hand.

"Well done, my lord Hordanu," said Lencaymon, shaking his grizzled head in disbelief. "In all my years I have never seen a sword used as a throwing knife. I am amazed."

"That I am, too," said Kal, lifting the flask to his mouth then wiping his chin. "Amazed by the forgecraft of your hammersons.

The throw 'twas all Rhodangalas. Truly, with its hawk's hilt, it would seem flight is native to its design. As perfectly balanced a weapon as you are like ever to see."

"Nay, Kalaquinn," said Alcesidas, grinning. "'Tis your native skill, to which my bruised pride is witness—the way your arm is wedded to the sword. Sure and unerring. And to that I now owe you my life."

"As I do owe you mine and that of my people. We are but requited now in small wise to one another. Although uneven the balance still, for I remain deeply in your debt." Kal bowed to the hammerson prince.

"How now, uneven the balance? Friendship holds no such tally. Besides which, there is much that we have gained from your people—the art of the bow, for one, at which we were an untutored folk before you came." Wiping his brow, Alcesidas took a long pull from the skin of mead that Kal had handed to him.

"Truly spoken, my prince. There are more than a couple of our hammersons that have profited exceedingly well from the instruction given by the likes of Master Frysan here," said Lencaymon, nodding towards Kal's father, "and Thurfar Fletcher. Why, he is as adept with bow and shaft as Volodan is with hammer and—"

"Listen. Can you hear them?" Galli interrupted the swordmaster, his ear cocked. They paused in silence. A long howl rose, a hollow note sustained in the depth of night, echoing in the distance. A second voice took up the call. Then a third, closer by. The chill air reverberated with the ululation of wolfsong. The hairs prickled on Kal's neck and arms. The wolf packs were hunting.

"Yes. Let us be quit of this place. And if we are considering the balance"—Alcesidas returned to his previous line of thought—"we must not leave unmentioned Galligaskin's native gift for tracking, for this has been a boon to us as well. What tales he can conjure from a bent blade of grass or the subtle press of foot or paw!"

Kal stared into the void of night. "'Tis the wolves he tracks these days, the likes of which were never seen in Lammermorn," he said, now turning his attention back to the men beside him. "Nor here, in this haven beneath the Radolans, I would wager."

"True, indeed, and they a more dangerous and sinister foe than Shadahr and his men, who be all dead now, hunted down by their own pets, or in our prison chambers, chased there by the same," Lencaymon said.

"I see much sign of them," Galli said. "More with every passing day, Prince Alcesidas. They grow bolder, coming ever closer to Nua Cearta's outlying steadings."

"And now this savage death of one of our hammersons. The tunnel wolves are no longer content to harry just our flocks. Already our border folk live in fear, shuttered in their homes, worried for their children, weapons ever ready to hand." Pausing, the hammerson prince took another long draught of mead and passed the skin to Galli. He then made his way to the carcass of the wolf he had killed. His sword had pierced the animal through so that the blade stood point up between its shoulders, as stiff as a grave marker. Already two of the scavenger crows that had been feasting on the sheep carcasses, attracted by the stench of this new slaughter, had settled on the gory remains.

"Insolent creatures!" Alcesidas drove them away. Reluctantly, the birds abandoned their carrion, croaking, lifting themselves lazily into the night air.

He placed his heel against the limp body of the wolf and rocked it until it collapsed onto its side. The weapon made a sucking noise as Alcesidas drew it out of the creature, which made Kal, already weak in the aftermath of the fight, as the heat in his veins subsided, feel somewhat nauseous. The prince wiped the blood-smeared blade of his sword clean on the dark fur of the tunnel wolf. He then rubbed dirt off of the hilt where it had been driven into the earth by the weight of the slain animal. Holding the sword up in the lantern light, he examined it and made a thrust into the darkness, as if stabbing some unseen enemy, his brow knit with concern.

"Our patrols are stretched too thin as it is," he said. "What now? What are we to do? How shall our people work their fields? Attend to their forges? How keep guard in all the waste places where these wolves may lurk?"

Kal turned from his friend. He was lost in thought for a moment, staring into the night after the crows. "Nua Cearta needs a guardian, Alcesidas."

"Why, of course, Kalaquinn! Nua Cearta could well use a guardian. We could all well use a guardian!" In anger and frustration, Alcesidas slammed his sword into its scabbard.

"I believe I have found your guardian."

"By the forge's heat, Kalaquinn! This is not the time for riddles, nor jest."

"No, it is not. And I jest not." He turned again to face Alcesidas. "I mean, I believe I have a means to aid you in this plight." A wry smile played on Kal's lips.

"How? What do you propose?"

"That we make a little expedition to the aboveground world."

"Where?"

"The Hordanu's Enclosure."

"What! Have you taken leave of your senses, Kalaquinn?"

"Trust me, son of Magan Hammermaster. Come, we must linger here no longer. We must needs return to Sterentref in all haste and make ready. The sooner we set out, the better."

THREE

The soft light of Kal's helm-lamp caught the glint. He stooped, picked up the marble and rolled it in his fingers, musing. The crossed flecks of embedded silver flashed. It was one of Gwyn's, and a rueful reminder of the terror he had suffered, how hopeless his fall into the depths of the mountain had seemed, and how painfully alone he had felt in the blackness. Now, here in the tunnels surrounding the Cave of the Hourglass, his cries returned to him, dreamlike, as if they still echoed and re-echoed down the endless labyrinthine passageways. *If you want me to do your work, if you want me to be the guardian of your Howe, you've got to save me! Why make me Hordanu if I'm to perish here? Why make me Hordanu... Why... why... why...*

Now, here he was. He had survived. And to think it had happened scarcely three weeks ago. It was as if he had lived a whole new lifetime since then in the forgeland kingdom, revelling in the sights and sounds, the new friendships.

"Hurry along now, Kal," Frysan whispered, following close on his son's heels, with Devved behind him. "Mustn't keep Alcesidas waiting. Careful now."

The three Holdsmen stole along the remaining two dozen paces of the passage, breathless and alert for any sign of danger, and slipped out into the sidechamber where Wilum had breathed his last. A sweet hint of the aromatic oils with which the women had anointed the old man's broken head still lingered in the air. Keeping silence, they crossed the small room and entered the main chamber.

"Ah, there you are, Kalaquinn. I was about to set off in search of you." Two slight figures stood near a wall on the far side of the Cave, their surroundings and features lit by the glow of an unshuttered avalynn lantern. One turned to the Holdsmen, holding the lantern aloft. "I thought that, perchance, you had come to grief. All is clear in here, as far as we can tell. We will wait a moment. Galli and my other guardsmen are making certain the Cave entrance is secure."

Alcesidas returned his attention to the vivid murals adorning the wall. "Remarkable!" The hammerson at his side hm-hmmed in agreement.

"Yes, they are," Kal said as he walked to the centre of the chamber and kicked aside the cold remains of the fire. "Quite remarkable.... A concise history of Ardiel of the Long Arm laid out, these hundreds of years, for none to see but the one person who would know it, by virtue of his office, only too well. And much good that."

He was shocked by the sardonic edge his own words bore, and Alcesidas made no reply. He felt the dark burden of a foul mood clinging to him—it had settled on him like a black cloak as soon as he had set foot in this most secluded and hallowed part of the Hordanu's Enclosure. He chided himself for his ill-spoken words, trying to shake himself free of the irrational fear that now clutched him in its grip. Shuttering his helm-lamp, he looked up through the smoke hole and regarded the narrow tapestry of stars above.

"No sign of foe," Galli called softly and beckoned them to the mouth of the Cave, where he waited with two more well-armed hammerson guards.

After more than a fortnight's sojourn in the underground kingdom, Kal savoured the night air and the open sky. Quite a task it had been persuading Magan Hammermaster and Alcesidas that they should make this foray into the upperworld. But the respect they afforded him as Hordanu had won the day. That and his assurance of a sure remedy to the fearsome incursions of the tunnel wolves.

"No need for helm-lamps or lanterns out here," Galli said. "They will only draw attention to us. There is light enough by which to see."

A gibbous moon cast its soft glow on the lintel of the Cave of the Hourglass. Kal considered again the verses in Old Arvonian etched deeply into the rock beneath the chiselled images of the sea-girt island and fantailed bird, spectral in the white moonlight. Alcesidas stepped up beside him, disturbing his reverie.

"What do you look at there?"

"Read for yourself. Perhaps as a hammerson you will discover some meaning that has escaped me."

Alcesidas turned his eyes to the lintel and began to read the verses aloud.

> "O Son of Prophecy, know surely that thy quest
> Shall not be satisfied nor brought to end
> When to the newfound place of Vali's final rest
> Thyself shall come and wearily attend...."

Alcesidas stopped in thought for a moment. "Who is this 'Son of Prophecy'?"

"Would that I knew. I asked Wilum the same, but he gave me no answer."

The two men stood in silence. Then Alcesidas finished reading the lines in an undertone, as if to himself.

"Well, that makes things no more clear. Save for the piece..." He raised a finger to point along the last lines of the cryptic verse. "Ah, there. 'Great woes by thine own kingly heart.' The Son of Prophecy must be a personage of blood royal. Think you this be the Prince Starigan that Wilum charged you to find?"

"It may be, Alcesidas. That much has occurred to me, but I know not."

"It would seem an arduous and comfortless task allotted to him. A bleak prospect, to be sure. And the allusion to Vali the Betrayer, whose memory rests uneasy with us—"

"I know not. I know not. 'Tis but pointless prophetic doggerel scratched here by some witless ancient—" Kal cut himself short as he rounded on Alcesidas. The prince looked at him with evident concern. Kal's tone softened. "Forgive me, my friend." He dropped his chin to his chest and closed his eyes. "'Tis all so murky...Too hard to decipher and understand. These lines make your Riddle Scrolls seem like child's play." Kal smiled weakly, lifting his head.

"It would appear that this 'Son of Prophecy,' whoever he may be, is not the only one that labours under a heavy burden."

Kal turned away from the Cave of the Hourglass and faced the night that spread out before him over the Stoneholding.

"Yes, Alcesidas, I am overwhelmed. My heart misgives me. I knew that I must revisit this place, but in so doing I fear I have lost the peace garnered in your underground haven."

"Well, it would seem that all that has been accomplished in coming to this place is to have fired your spleen and weakened your temper."

"'Tis not this place that fires my spleen, but remembering that goads my heart." Kal heaved a deep sigh and looked down to where the clutch of men stood waiting not a stone's throw away on the trail leading to the Well of the Seven Springs. "I am reminded of the urgency of my folk's plight. We have—I have—been lulled, perhaps, by the sweet narcotic of welcome and safety, distracted into a forgetfulness of our dire urgency. I feel now, in revisiting this place . . . I know not rightly what. Disquieted, for certain." Despite the warmth of the night air, Kal shivered involuntarily. "I apologize, Alcesidas, for my melancholy. But, come now—let us move on to the Seven Springs below. I would look upon my home and native country one last time. Then we shall make for your hidden realm once more."

Alcesidas looked relieved as they made to join the others on the path. "It is good," he said. "The sooner we are quit of this whole place, the better. By the hammer and tong, Kalaquinn, a hammerson is an ember out of the fire in your aboveground world. But I wish you would make clear what your purpose is. I fail to see how this aids us in our plight against the wolves."

"Be patient, friend. A short while yet and all will be clear, I hope. You shall be pleased, if my plan is not misconceived, and I believe it is not."

Kal turned his attention to the small group of men they were approaching and called, "All is well, let us make our way down to the—"

"A gathgour! Look!" Galli cried, pointing to a cleft high among the rocks.

"Where?" Frysan spun around, peering up the mountainside, even as he reached over his shoulder to pull an arrow from its quiver and nock it to the bowstring.

"I see nothing," said Devved, cuffing Galli in the chest. "Clout, you're starting at stone shapes and shadows."

Galli shot a glance at the big smith. "No. I saw it just up there."

"Bah! We should have brought your uncle Diggory along, Galli.

At least he was carried away by something more solid than his imagination," Devved said, stifling a chuckle.

A hammerson guardsman moved to open the shutter of his helm-lamp, but his hand was stayed by one of his fellows.

"No, it's not Galli's imagination," said Kal in a low voice. He scanned the looming rocks, frowning. "Make no mistake. They are there."

"Re'm ena, I'm right," Galli whispered hoarsely. "There, look, a gathgour—and another one. I knew I was right."

Far up the rocky slope, the muted forms of two large creatures wavered and swayed uneasily. Frysan flexed his bow to full bend, but it was Galli who, in one swift, fluid movement, plucked an arrow from over his shoulder, drew, and let fly. The arrow rattled and clattered among the stones.

"Hold," said Frysan, releasing the tension from his weapon. "Hold. You'll nought but waste your shafts in this dark. They're too far off to make a fair mark."

"Aye, they keep their distance. They're wary for some reason. It may be this they fear." Kal opened his satchel and drew forth several sprigs of rowan, dried leaf and berry still clinging to the twig, each bound by thin strips of leather. He held them out, turning to the group of men. "Here, each of you must take one of these. Wear it around your neck."

Alcesidas and his men each held a rowan talisman, looking to Kal and then to one another. With dawning comprehension, they followed the Holdsmen's lead, each removing his helm to hang the sprig around his neck.

Swords drawn and bows fitted with arrows, the small group now moved on down the path. Every man cast glances up the mountain-side to where the gathgours cowered, watching, until the animals were blocked from view as the party rounded a bend in the trail.

With Galli in the lead, alert for sign, they traversed the side of Mount Thyus, threading their way down a narrow, stone-strewn defile of uneven ground and close-winding turns. Kal stiffened as they passed a gap in the rocks. A night breeze touched his face from the open flanks of the mountain. As if still carried on the night breeze, he imagined that he could hear the alarmed voices of his fellow Holdsfolk and the coughing bark of gathgour.

About a mile farther along the trail, they left the confines of the pathway and stepped into the full light of the moon illuminating a long, sloping field that lay before them. They could now just discern the distant drone of rushing water, Skell Force tumbling into the small lake below. They quickened their steps down the alpine meadow's gentle incline towards a low stone wall, a half circle bounding the Well of the Seven Springs against the hillock from beneath which it rose. Near the centre of the wall there was a narrow break, and through this opening water rushed, flashing silver into a tight, stone-lined channel set deeply in the ground and edged by walls half the height of those enclosing the Well to which they abutted. Down the gradually widening flume, the water coursed in a torrent towards the plunging waterfall that was Skell Force.

"Wait!" Galli held Alcesidas back. "Something's wrong. Can you smell that?"

"Aye . . . Yes, I do."

"And a sound. . . . I thought I heard something, but faint. From over there." Galli pointed to the far side of the Well, screened from view by the brow of the knoll and the low wall extending beyond.

"Do you see anything?" Frysan pressed forward beside Galli and peered down to the Well himself, where crisp black shadows stood out starkly against the meadow awash in moonlight.

"No, not a thing. . . . But something's amiss."

"We must scout. Slowly. Careful. Keep weapons in hand," whispered Frysan.

The group fanned out and began stalking down the field. Minutes later, they skirted a weathered ledge of rocks that protruded from the hummock of land overshadowing the deep springs. Here the men followed the arc of the wall around the Well in single file. The smell grew stronger. Mingled with the sweet scent of crushed grass and early summer's meadow flower borne on the slight wisp of breeze was a raw, foul, musky smell, and a deeper odour underlying that: the sick, coppery stench of blood and death.

"Re'm ena, what's this?" Frysan was the first to advance, overstepping the narrow watercourse, sword held out before him, staring wide-eyed at the horror that met him. "Black Scorpions!"

Then they all saw it, a scene of carnage, bodies and armour, spears and swords strewn in bleak disarray, clearly visible in the cold moonlight.

"By the avalynn! What has happened here?"

"Gathgours, Alcesidas. They were attacked by gathgours. Here, see?" Galli said as he stepped forward, pointing his sword at a long-limbed body that lay tangled in a heap of Scorpion corpses, its grey fur caked with blood, its slit-eyed face, even in death, contorted by a ravenous, feral snarl. There were three gathgours lying slain that they could see. The reek of the creatures was choking, more so even than the stench of slaughter that stained the night. Most of the men had covered their faces, burying their mouths and noses in their sleeves and turning away to find cleaner air.

Alcesidas commanded that the helm-lamps remain shut. The flash of their movement would be a beacon, surely attracting the attention of anyone, or anything, nearby. Instead, he half opened the shutters to the steady light of his lantern.

The bodies were scattered around the remains of a large campfire. Three tents, torn to shreds, lay flattened nearby. The gear and supplies of their former occupants were strewed about, among it the heavy mail armour and weapons of Black Scorpion Dragoons. Galli cast about the camp, trying to glean from the grisly discovery what meaning he could.

Kal, in a daze, stood blindly staring at the legs of a soldier sticking out from beneath the canvas wreckage of a tent. He became aware of Galli beside him, who was explaining how the attack must have happened at night, probably the night before, and that the gathgours had caught the soldiers unawares. Galli was telling how the Black Scorpions had obviously tried to fend off the beasts. Despite claiming three kills of their own, however, the soldiers had been overwhelmed. Then Galli mentioned the wounds—great gaping wounds where the flesh had been stripped to the bone or torn, exposing mutilated viscera. Some of the soldiers were half eaten. One body had been dragged away, the twin heel marks scoring the ground and ending where one of the beasts had hefted the corpse's bulk onto its back. The creature's footprints were more deeply impressed into the ground there. Kal saw before his mind's eye Diggory bouncing like a rag doll over the hunched shoulder of a stooped and loping figure.

A sound like a moan escaped the broken remains heaped nearby. Galli started in sudden fear.

"It's one of the men. He's alive," Frysan said, moving behind Galli. "He's pinned under a gathgour. Still gripping a dagger. Come, help me free him, Devved. You, too, Galli."

When Frysan drew closer, the wounded man made to lash out

at him with the blade. He groaned deeply at the effort. His arm swung out and fell listless to the ground, his hand lolling. The knife twitched in his grip.

"By the lifting, that Scorpion's got some sting in him yet," said Devved as he wrenched the dagger from the wounded man's fingers. Carefully, they freed him, disentangling limb from limb until at last Devved was able to lift off the heavy weight of the gathgour. He flung the creature aside as if repelled not only by the creature's stink but also by the suggestion of mortal danger still clinging to its thickly corded muscles, glistening fangs, and lifeless, staring slit-pupilled eyes. Frysan and Galli laid the soldier down by the circle of charcoal and blackened wood that had been the campfire. Kal stepped closer, looking down at the man. Blood seemed to cover him from head to foot. It was nearly impossible at first to tell where his injuries lay.

"'Tis his middle. He has been gutted," Alcesidas said, his face grave. "If not for the weight of the gathgour pressing on him, he would surely have bled to death."

Kal cringed at the sight of the wound. Entrails, soft, pale pink, and now streaked with red, as the blood began to ooze again, pushed through the rent cloth of his tunic where the gash was deepest. The man's eyes flickered open, unseeing, and a gasping moan escaped his lips.

"Water. Fetch me some water," Kal said, and one of Alcesidas's guards promptly handed him a skin. Kal pressed it carefully to the wounded soldier's face, wetting his mouth, until, like a suckling, the man sought out the skin with his lips. Kal lifted the skin, letting water slosh in the man's mouth and over his cheeks and chin, until at length he began to swallow, half choking, taking weak, shallow draughts.

"And woundwort," Kal continued, lifting the skin away. "I need some woundwort to pack his wound and staunch the bleeding. Devved, I saw a clump of it by the big boulder we passed near the Well. Do you know where I mean?"

"Yes, but . . . Why bother? He'll not survive. And besides," Devved said, his voice becoming hard-edged, full of remembering and loss—wife, children, home, "he's just a canker-hearted swine, our sworn enemy. And mine mortal!"

Kal turned to look at the big man and said gently, "Go, do as I bid, Devved. We will tend to the living while we may."

"Aye, Devved. 'Tis a poor time to quibble with the Hordanu," said Alcesidas.

A muscle flexed above Devved's jaw, his honest face etched by the potency of the feelings he fought to master. "All right, then. As you will," he said and turned on his heel.

"Thank you, Devved. You're a good man," Kal said after him.

"From what I can tell, it seems they were attacked sometime the previous night." Galli squatted, speaking to Kal in a low voice across the chest of the wounded soldier.

Kal nodded. "Aye, so you said."

"Came at them in the dark without warning. And the gathgours weren't the only ones feeding. The birds have been at them, except for our friend here. He kept them away with his knife, I suspect, else they would have pecked out his eyes. And the gathgours... Well, I count it a full squad of Black Scorpion Dragoons by my reckoning, posted here by Ferabek to keep watch and prevent our escape, no doubt. Seven dead, one of those dragged off, and two who fled in terror. That way, towards the Stairs." Galli rose to his feet. "And there's a dead Telessarian as well on the edge of the camp. One of the first to fall."

"The poor fellow must have been parched. But look, he's reviving now," said Kal as the stoutly built Gharssûlian emitted a loud groan of pain and struggled to focus his eyes. At the same time, he twisted his body in an attempt to move, but only managed to worsen the flow of blood from the wound across his stomach.

"Easy, easy. Lie still, man. You are badly hurt," said Kal, his voice firm but hesitant, as he searched for the right words in Gharssûlian. "And you're not like to survive, unless Devved hurries with that woundwort," he muttered to himself in his own tongue.

"Come, son. Truth be told, he's not like to survive regardless," Frysan said.

"Aye, but still, I must try."

Devved returned a few moments later, his hands full of dew-moist plant tops. Kal took the herbs, crushed them, and gingerly began pressing the pungent leaves into the wound, trying to stem the increasing flow of blood. The man shrieked into the night, his limbs convulsing in agony. His screams reverberated off the mountain face and across the upland field.

"We might as well use a horn, amble over to that wall there, and announce to the whole world that we're here," Devved said sullenly, glowering. Others glanced about, squinting into the moon-cast shadows of the outlying rocks. Kal finished dressing the wound.

"The blood continues to seep. 'Tis a mortal injury, Kalaquinn," Alcesidas said.

"Yes, yes. It is of no use," said Kal, shaking his head in resignation, regarding his blood-soaked hands.

The screams abruptly subsided. The dying man grew still, his breathing heavy and laboured, as if he was garnering his strength. His eyelids flickered open. His gaze swam, his eyes weaving back and forth before coming to focus on Kal. For a long moment the soldier looked at Kal; then, as if noticing him for the first time, the man narrowed his eyes and pulled his lips back over stained teeth clenched in a snarl.

"C-curse you! . . . Curse you!"

"So much for gratitude," remarked Devved, understanding the sentiment if not the Gharssûlian's words.

"You die, man. You are dying. Do you understand? Dying," Kal said. There was a quiet desperation in his voice that silenced Devved and the others who stood watching. "I am Hordanu. Fortune has brought me to your side in this your hour of greatest need. I can sing your Prayer of Passage. I can ease your crossing of the Birdless Lake. Let me help you. The time remaining to you is short."

The soldier's mouth worked like that of a fish lying on a river bank, opening and closing, gulping at the air soundlessly. His eyes rolled back in their sockets and then returned to stare at Kal. Then he whispered, in a voice strained and breaking, "I would rather . . . would rather the dreosan gnaw my guts. . . . I spit on you, Hordanu."

The dying man drew a sharp breath, then pursed his lips to heave a gob of spittle at Kal. But his body rebelled at the effort, and in a final bid to cling to life forced him to cough weakly. There welled from his mouth a gush of blood and saliva, spilling down his stubbled chin. His throat rattled as breath escaped him. All hatred spent, his pupils widened and his head fell drooping to one side.

"He makes his own crossing," Kal said, looking up at his comrades. "I tried. He is dead. May he find what peace he can."

Kal reached over the dead man and drew a limp arm across

the still body, then lifted the other likewise. The hands folded on the soldier's chest obscured the crumpled insignia of the dread scorpion. He seemed even in death to cling to it. Kal pushed himself off the ground.

"What shall we now, Kalaquinn?" Alcesidas said, fingering his rowan sprig. "What is your purpose? There is naught else we can do here. And here we stand exposed to gathgours and other unseen enemies."

"Let us bring the others. Lay them here, beside him."

"But, Kal," Devved said, "we stand in danger here. His cries will bring the gathgours. Or his fellow—"

"Just do it! We haven't time to bury them, nor fuel to burn them. But we will do what we can. Now go."

Galli was the first to respond, striding away to the edge of the encampment. As the other men dispersed in silence to do Kal's bidding, Galli returned carrying on his shoulder the dead Telessarian tracker. He lowered the weight to the ground, then took a step to the side and bent over to pluck a flowering head of Eveningstar that had escaped being trampled. He touched the pale flower to his own forehead, then laid it across the dead man's forehead, so caked with blood that the birthrite tattoo could scarcely be discerned. "Let thy browmark be thy warrant," Galli intoned over the Telessarian, then turned quickly away to help the others.

Kal had the bodies laid neatly abreast of each other, covered with the torn canvasses from the tent and weighted down by the arms and armour of the Gharssûlian warriors. He knew it would do little to protect the dead from predation by vulture and carrion crow. Or, worse still, that of the gathgour, although Galli averred that the creatures had not returned to the site since the slaughter—perhaps they preferred fresh kill. Still, the act did something to assuage the sense of duty the living here in this place felt towards the dead, and an uneasy peace rested once again on the group.

The gathgours they dragged to the outer edge of the field, where the high stone ramparts crested the lower face of Mount Thyus. From the parapet of rock that enclosed the meadow, the mountain fell sheer hundreds and hundreds of feet to the black forest below. They threw the fetid carcasses down from the look-out gap in the wall.

The lookout was close by the Stairs of Tarn Cromar, the sole way down into the valley of the Stoneholding. Galli pointed out the tracks of the two Black Scorpions who had escaped the slaughter by the Well, fleeing past the lookout and down the Stairs. "They bolted like frightened rabbits. We've naught to worry from them. And I see no other sign of danger," he explained above the steady drone of Skell Force as he peered out into the darkness though the opening.

"Galli, I want you to light me a small fire, just enough flame to smudge the air with smoke. Put some grass on it."

"But, Kal—"

"No questions. Devved, help him. We're safe enough here. At the first sign of danger, we can bolt back to Nua Cearta. It's close enough."

Kal strode to the lookout. With Alcesidas and Frysan by his side, he surveyed the moonlit landscape below. There the waters of Tarn Cromar glistened against the darkness of the surrounding woods, and beyond that, far away, the faint glimmer of Deepmere's unsettled surface. Kal stood staring as the minutes passed. No one dared break his meditation.

"Nothing. There is nothing—no light, no fire, no sign of human life," Kal said quietly, then shifted his gaze to the skies above the flanks of the mountain. "Now, I wonder if he's anywhere about?"

The slight breeze bore a whiff of the fire that Galli had kindled nearby from remains he had retrieved of the camp's fire. Kal glanced over his shoulder. The small blaze crackled merrily. "Grass, Galli. Grass," he said.

Soon the air was thick with the pungent sweetness of smouldering grass. Alcesidas frowned with impatience. He and Frysan looked at each other.

"Now, Kal, what—"

Frysan had turned to speak to his son, but his words were cut short by a whistle, ear-piercing and close at hand. Kal had his fingers to his mouth, his head cocked back. The sound he made mounted heavenwards, cleaving the night air. It was a thin, shrill shriek that slurred downwards, then, just as quickly, rose in pitch, until it fell off again in a long, descending trailer. Kal withdrew his fingers from his mouth and paused.

Alcesidas and his fellow hammersons regarded the young Hordanu with wide-eyed alarm.

"By the forge, Kalaquinn, between that noise and your smudge, you are sure to bring every gathgour on the mountain down upon us. Not to mention enemy soldiers."

"Dhu...," Frysan said to himself. Then, turning to Alcesidas, he spoke so all the hammersons could hear. "'Tis the cry of a fellhawk that he imitates. He summons his pet."

"There he is! Look!" Galli pointed out from the gap in the wall to the silhouette of a great bird wheeling through the air, climbing towards them on the horizon, wings beating the night air above the forested slopes below.

"'Tis a monster! You have conjured the night drake in your folly!" Alcesidas stiffened, drew back a step from the embrasure and Kal, and made to unsheathe his sword.

"Stay your hand, Alcesidas. Peace. There is no need to fear." Kal sought to reassure the hammerson prince; then once again he raised fingers to mouth and shaped the fellhawk's cry.

"Come, Dhu, come." Kal raised his arm and hailed the fellhawk, his voice low and urgent.

The bird drew closer, growing larger and larger, an awesome sight, its sleek black body and huge span of wings now clearly visible as it approached Skell Force. It now emitted the same piercing wail. Still rising, it flew over the waterfall. The men crept back from the lookout, keeping their eyes trained on the bird as it glided, circling in the sky, and swept down towards them, scattering sparks from the fire with the draft of its wings as it overflew the group.

"That blasted bird! I'll never get used to it," Devved said as he ducked.

In a flurry, the fellhawk alighted on the wall near Kal. Alcesidas cringed and kept his distance, his fellows closing ranks alongside him.

"Come, Dhu. Come to me. Here's a tasty morsel," Kal whispered, opening his night pouch. From it he pulled a small bundle and unwrapped a piece of meat the size of his fist, which he held out at arm's length. Majestic in profile, the fellhawk jumped down from the rocks, wings half unfurled, and hopped, bobbing, to Kal. It plucked the meat from Kal's hand in a huge curved beak below a proud brow and fierce eyes, and swallowed the flesh with a toss of its head. The bird stood as tall as any of the hammersons. Kal stroked its glossy black head, speaking soft soothing words. Frysan and Galli joined him, a step ahead of Devved, while Alcesidas and the two hammersons warily looked on.

"Draw closer, Alcesidas. Dhu won't harm you. He savours human contact, when it's friendly—"

"Savours human contact, hmm...My fear is that he may savour human flesh."

"No fear, my friend, no fear." Kal laughed good-naturedly at the small man's apprehension. "I have nurtured him from a fledgling. It is company he craves. That is why I had Galli light a fire to help draw him to us. You, too, Devved, you have met Dhu before. You must show our hammerfriends that there is nothing to fear."

"Aye, nothing," Devved said, now standing with Frysan, though his tone betrayed him.

"Truly, Kalaquinn, you are a font of strange and unexpected wonders." The prince eased his way closer to Kal and to the fellhawk, impelled by curiosity. "Incredible!" he said as he took measure of the bird. "He must have a span the height of three of the tallest of you anuasoi!"

"You may stroke him, Alcesidas. Come, he will not harm you." The small man inched forward his hand to touch Dhu's smooth breast, then withdrew it again quickly, glancing at the fellhawk's hooked beak.

"Again. Stroke him again, my prince."

Once more Alcesidas stroked the fellhawk's glossy feathers, but this time he let his hand linger.

"Aye, don't worry. He enjoys being stroked," Galli said as he, too, placed a hand on the bird, then moved away to the opening of the lookout.

Soon Alcesidas was sweeping his hand softly down the fellhawk's sleek plumage. As he repeated the gesture, Dhu lowered his head and lifted his shoulders, gathering himself together. The great bird began to thrum contentedly, a deep, rolling rumble in its gullet.

"Re'm ena! Never have I seen Dhu thus aptly gentled. Not even by you, Kal," Frysan said.

"Yes, 'tis amazing to behold. It must be that you two see eye to eye in some wise, Alcesidas," Kal said, laughing again. "'Tis fitting then that you should be his new master."

"New master? By the forge, what mean you?" Alcesidas started, pausing midstroke, and looked at Kal.

"We shall bring Dhu back with us to Nua Cearta. It is not right that he should be masterless in your fair kingdom." Kal opened his night pouch again and rummaged in it.

"Back to Nua Cearta? Why?"

"Because you and your folk are in sore need of a guardian, and Dhu has a taste for wolf's flesh—"

"I can see movement below, just down from Tarn Cromar. Human figures...a small patrol, maybe," Galli said as he turned away from the break in the wall.

"Hardly surprising. This place is not safe, and we've made our presence known," Frysan said. "We must leave quickly. How do you propose to take Dhu with us, Kal?"

"With this..." From his night pouch Kal extracted a brown leather sack. "A makeshift hood I scrounged from the tannery of the royal household in Sterentref." He quickly pulled the sack over the fellhawk's head. The fellhawk had straightened himself and stopped the low, monotonous cooing, its hypnotic spell broken by the new urgency.

"Now that his eyes are covered, he will settle down again. Like any hawk," Kal said. "And the sling, Galli, the sling that I asked you to bring?"

"Here."

"Quickly, unroll it. Come, Devved, help me lift Dhu onto it. We'll bind him in it. He'll be a light load for two of us to carry. He's all feather."

The great hawk submitted readily enough to the touch and voice of his master as it was laid down and gently tied into the broad canvas. Frysan and Devved picked up each end of the sling.

"Now, to Nua Cearta," Kal said, and the group turned and began striding up the meadow's slope to the path that would lead them back into the safety of the hollow mountain.

FOUR

"A most intriguing idea, Master Kalaquinn. Most intriguing."
Meriones regarded Dhu with an approving eye. All the same, the
stern-faced bard took care to keep his distance from the fellhawk.

"Well," the king said with raised brow, leaning on an ornate
staff of office, "to gain such praise from the redoubtable Meriones,
one can be sure it is a plan with much merit. Indeed, methinks
our venerable bard has in Dhu finally met his match, a creature
with a more forbidding mien than his own." King Magan's beard
shook with good-natured mirth, his remark teasing a reluctant
smile from Meriones.

Unhooded, Dhu preened himself, perching on the roost that
carpenters of Nua Cearta had hurriedly built in a secluded meadow
at the edge of the training grounds near Sterentref. The jangle of
sword and shield drifted in the lazy summer air, vying with the
drowsy hum of cicadas.

Kal pushed against the post and crossbar of the perch, testing
its strength. "Well-wrought, this roost for Dhu that your doughty
craftsmen have constructed on such short notice. 'Tis surpassingly
well wrought, Sire. Elegant and well fitted to its intended purpose,
like everything else I have seen in your kingdom."

"There is much, I am sure, that your folk could teach us,"
Magan said.

"And are teaching us, Sire," added Meriones. "The bowyers and
fletchers of the Stoneholding are without peer. Much of their craft
and bow skill have we acquired these past days."

"You are most gracious, Meriones," Kal said.

"My lord Myghternos Hordanu," said the king, "I have sent word throughout Nua Cearta to all my subjects that yon great bird is a gift from you, that he will cause no injury to them or their flocks, and that he is to be neither hindered nor harmed in his coming and his going."

"My deepest thanks, Magan Hammermaster." Kal bowed to the king, then turned his attention to making a final adjustment to one of the jesses that bound Dhu by a leash to the crossbar on which the bird stood. Fussing impatiently with the leather straps, he estimated once more how much leeway the fellhawk would need.

"Alcesidas is come, Sire," Meriones said, leaning towards Magan and pointing to a wagon that trundled its way towards them.

The king shifted his weight and gaze, still clutching his staff of office, which had struck Kal as slightly absurd, its heavily carved, gilded, and jewel-adorned surface a stark contrast to the simple russet tunic and hose in which the diminutive monarch was attired.

At the approaching creak of wagon wheels, Kal straightened and looked up from his task. Quickly, he knotted the jess, stroked Dhu, and strode to where the two draught horses had halted.

"Briacoil, one and all!" Alcesidas greeted them with a nod and wave from the driver's bench. Beside him sat the carter, his hands clutching the reins.

"Briacoil. You did my bidding, I trust?" Kal said as he looked into the box of the cart.

Alcesidas stood from the bench and jumped into the box of the cart, where he pulled back a heavy sheet of oiled cloth. Kal clambered onto the cart and squatted beside the prince.

"Freshly killed and dressed. As you requested." Alcesidas said, looking pleased with himself. At their feet lay two long sable carcasses, a pair of tunnel wolves, neatly gutted and not long dead.

"It is well, Alcesidas. Indeed, you must add provisioner to your list of talents and accomplishments," Kal said, grinning.

"Nay, you have not me to thank."

"How so?"

"There were no fresh kills reported. We were at a loss. All the wolfmeat we had ready to hand was already fouling and fetid. And you made it clear that Dhu is no mere carrion bird. So a hunting party, Galli and Lencaymon, accompanied by Gwyn—"

"Gwyn?"

"Indeed, Gwyn. By the forgefire, the fellow would not be

gainsaid. I had come to yon field of arms to confer with Galli and Lencaymon early this morning. The two of them were contesting one another, and that with ardour, at the archery butts. And 'twas no longer a one-sided affair, as it has been these three weeks past. Lencaymon was using one of the new bows that our bowyers have crafted according to your highland wisdom. Never have I seen him so hot and eager. In any case, I explained to the two of them our quandary, how urgently you required unspoilt wolfmeat. I had hardly spoken but that the two of them volunteered to track and kill a tunnel wolf for our purpose. Gwyn was there as well, close at hand, himself exercising his sure eye and surpassing bowman's skill to the gain of our hammerfolk. He made clear his desire to join Galli and Lencaymon in their hunt. And he did so with such insistence that I dared not brave the storm of protest if he were denied."

"You must learn to exercise a firmer hand, Alcesidas, else Magan Hammermaster make Gwyn prince in your stead," Kal said and exchanged amused smiles with King Magan. He stood and leapt over the wagon's side to the ground. "Now, Alcesidas, if your carter can bring the wagon closer to Dhu's perch, it will save us some lifting." Kal walked to where he wanted the wagon to be unladen. The draught horses shied from the great bird, stamping their feet and shaking their manes, but the driver managed to calm the team by soothing word and expert touch, and shortly succeeded in drawing the wagon up to where Kal stood waiting.

Kal grunted with exertion as he pulled first one and then the second carcass off the wagon and onto the ground but a few yards from where Dhu roosted impassively on his perch. "By the avalynn, Alcesidas, we needed not two tunnel wolves. Dhu may be a large bird, but there is flesh enough here to sate the night drake for a fortnight."

"For that, you may thank Gwyn. For no sooner had Galli and Lencaymon sighted a pack of tunnel wolves than did Gwyn let loose, twice, in quick succession, making his mark both times. So were two wolves killed."

"Ah, well, 'tis better too much than too little."

Relieved of its burden, the wagon moved off, and Kal knelt beside the dead wolves.

"He will eat what I have prepared—in this manner, meat in the pelt—so long as it is fresh and from my hand. Thus does he learn what he is to hunt on his own," Kal said to the men gathered close by. "Granted, in the past it has usually been smaller game—rabbit, hare, fox, and the like. Though he will hunt deer upon occasion."

Now he gestured to the black carcasses and summoned Dhu. The fellhawk hopped down from its perch and across the grass, still leashed to the roost.

"Come, Dhu, come. Come and feed. It is as fresh as a kill of your own."

Dhu cocked his head to one side then darted his beak down, plunging it into the neck of a tunnel wolf. He placed a jessed foot upon the carcass and tugged at it, lifting the lifeless head. Kal winced. The wolf's fangs gleamed wicked and sharp, menacing even in death. Pulling against his talons' grip, the fellhawk tore the black pelt, exposing the red flesh of the animal's forequarters, the fatal arrow wound now visible as a circle of black congealed blood. Bobbing, the fellhawk ripped at the meat of the carcass in quick, convulsive motions, gorging himself, his cruel hooked beak becoming crimsoned, wet with blood.

"It is best this be done when Dhu is hungry," Kal said, "ravenously hungry, as he is now."

"And what shall we do next, Master Kalaquinn?" asked Meriones, who turned away from the spectacle in distaste.

"We shall let Dhu have his fill. Leave him 'til the morrow to acquire a taste for wolf's flesh."

The party withdrew, skirting the training grounds, where hammerson and Holdsman practiced their battle craft, the staggered staccato of sword on sword ringing in the air over the field. Farther away, just on the edge of hearing, were the archery butts. At this distance, each arrow's flight was followed a second later by a gentle whistle and thwack. There were women on the field, too, clothed in simple garb suited to the work of swordplay. A handful of taller women, women of the upperworld, had only recently been introduced to the implements of war, evidenced by the awkwardness with which they wielded the weapons. The hammerdaughters, who tutored and sparred with them, were apparently as adept in the arts of combat as they were in the arts of the hearth and home. There was not the least snicker from the few men who stood by watching the clumsy display of the Holdsfolk, but only a sober silence, broken by the occasional word of encouragement or instruction.

As Magan Hammermaster passed by, the small knots of people paused in turn from their work, bowing in respect to their king. Each was met with a nod, a smile, or a word of greeting from the monarch. Kal could sense a growing urgency in the realm, heightened here on the training grounds. It was a sense of anticipation, of excitement and apprehension. Kal wondered if it had to do with the recent incursion of Shadahr's forces upon Nua Cearta, or the more recent predations of the tunnel wolves. Perhaps the impending foray that Magan would make into the hammerfolk's homeland under the Burren Mountains weighed on his people. Or perhaps it was a more personal urgency that affected Kal, the growing need he himself felt to be setting out upon the next leg of his own journey, he and his own folk, in their flight from their own homeland.

Ahead of him, the king had fallen into deep conversation with Alcesidas, and Meriones, left to his own thoughts, had drifted behind the royal pair. Kal hastened his step.

"My apologies, Master Meriones," Kal said, as he drew abreast of the hammerson bard. "I do not wish to disturb your reverie. However..."

"Hmm?" Meriones glance up at Kal. "Ah, my lord Hordanu."

"May I have a word with you? I would seek your guidance, your counsel."

"Of course, of course. I am ever at your service." The bard bowed his head ever so slightly, his stony expression unchanged. "In fact, it has been upon my mind to speak with you myself."

"Perhaps now is the opportune moment?"

"Yes, perhaps." Meriones shifted his gaze to the king ahead of him. "Let us first beg our leave of Magan Hammermaster. My lord!" Meriones hailed the king, who turned to look at them. "My lord, by your leave, Master Kalaquinn and I will part company with you and make our own way back to Sterentref."

The king did not bother to reply, but simply lifted his hand in recognition of the bard and returned to his conversation with his son.

"Hmm." Meriones stopped walking. "My lord the king makes preparation to leave Nua Cearta," he said in a low voice. "It sits heavy with him." Kal had grown accustomed to the small bard's impassive nature. It was the man's tone, now, that disconcerted him. There was much weight in what the bard said, and much more, Kal knew, in what remained yet unspoken.

Meriones pointed to a side path just ahead of where they stood that veered away into the shaded depths of a small wood. "Come, let us walk this way," he said.

The two men walked in silence, their path leading them through a stand of sizable oaks and beech, until they came to a wrought-iron bench set beside the footpath.

"Let us rest awhile, Master Kalaquinn," the small bard said as he drew his robes up behind his knees and sat. He gestured for Kal to take a seat beside him. "Come, come, my lord Hordanu. What then is this matter which you wish to discuss with me?"

"You are familiar with the ancient texts, are you not, Meriones? With the *Criochoran*, and the *Master Legendary*?"

The small bard shifted in his seat and raised an eyebrow.

"Yes, yes," Kal said, flustered, "Of course you are—"

"Peace, my young Hordanu." Meriones placed his hand on Kal's arm, the corners of his mouth lifting in a slight smile. "Yes, I am quite familiar with these ancient texts. Our forebears brought copies of these from our Burren Mountain homeland. These form the larger part of the trove entrusted to the bard of the hammerfolk, these along with the Riddle Scrolls, with which you are now familiar." He patted Kal's arm, then withdrew his hand. "'Tis the *Chronicles of the Harmonic Age* to which I have been more recently introduced, since your most unexpected but welcome arrival in Nua Cearta. These I have studied with great interest in light of recent events."

"And what do you make of recent events? Wilum spent much time trying to ferret up some meaning from the ancient prophecies. He said that much of their content had come to pass with the invasion of Lammermorn and the fall of the Great Glence. I think, however, that much of what he knew was lost with his passing before he could tell it to me."

"Come, come, Master Kalaquinn. You do yourself a disservice. You possess a far deeper knowledge than you would admit even to yourself. Such is evident to me from our conversations, and from the prophecy contained in your own Lay of Investiture."

"And that is itself dark to me as well."

"These are dark days for Ahn Norvys. Ferabek's arm is long. It reaches even into the sheltered peace of this mountain realm of ours." Meriones fell silent for a moment, then looked up at a sparrow that had alighted in the tree beneath which they sat and had begun to sing. "Ah, yes!" he said. "Look you, Master Kalaquinn, how this little minstrel calls us to be mindful of the true nature of things—no matter how dark be the days, there is ever hope. This is the larger meaning of events, both in their presaging and in their fulfillment. Indeed, hope often shines brightest and strongest when matters seem the darkest. So did you sing in your own Lay. 'Yet hope! For hope is life's bequest, emboldening the meekest breast,' and 'A tristful heart doth hope emboss with mettle when all seemeth loss.' Very seldom do we grasp the full significance of matters as they are unfolding, and seldom even in their completion. This we do know, in truth, both of us, that we must never lose hope, otherwise we forsake that which surely is, in favour of that which is not."

"You begin to sound like Master Wilum," Kal said.

"Which I take as a great compliment." The bird flitted away into the branches of another tree, and Meriones returned his full attention to Kal. "However, unless I am mistaken, 'tis not the prophecies of the ancient texts alone that trouble you, my lord Hordanu."

Kal shifted on the bench, then stood and paced across the path, his hands clenched behind his back. "You are shrewd, Master Meriones." Kal chuckled to himself and turned to look at the small bard. "As I revisited the Cave of the Hourglass, I read again an inscription carved over the entrance. 'Tis written in Old Arvonian. I do not know why it has unsettled me, but it has."

Meriones nodded, his eyes closed. " 'O Son of Prophecy,' " he said, " 'know surely that thy quest shall not be satisfied nor brought to end—' "

"You know it?"

Meriones looked up at Kal. "Prince Alcesidas mentioned to me that you were disquieted by the inscription. I, too, have visited the Cave of the Hourglass—" The bard lifted a hand to forestall any questions. "I assure you, it was only out of necessity that I did breech the hallowed boundaries of the Hordanu's Enclosure, an act for which I crave and humbly beg your forgiveness, my lord Myghternos Hordanu."

Kal smiled at the small man's deference. "There is no need for forgiveness, Master Meriones," he said. "The times are such that some ancient traditions must naturally yield to necessity. As Master Wilum himself said about the Enclosure, 'There comes a time when you have to bend the rules to serve the common good.' "

"I trespassed there only in an attempt to untangle what meaning I could of the events that have overtaken all of us," Meriones said. "For what affects you, affects all of us, all peoples of Ahn Norvys. 'Tis in my heart that you may play a larger role in this than you or I suspect. Indeed, it may be, given the events foretold in the ancient writings, which do now seem to be fulfilled in the destruction of the Great Glence, that these are the times of the last days spoken of by Hedric in the *Criochoran*. Moreover, it occurs to me that you yourself may be the 'Son of Prophecy' spoken of in the Cave inscription."

"Me?"

Meriones nodded.

"The Son of Prophecy?"

"Certainly, it lies well within the realm of possibility that such is the case. Perceive it in the light of your own Lay of Investiture, for that, indeed, sheds more light on the matters at hand than do the ancient texts. If we do in fact stand upon the very threshold of the last days, as it would appear we do, then you are a young anuas of inestimable importance in the grand scheme of things. Here, look at this. I have had it written down for you." Meriones produced, from among the folds of his robe, a parchment carefully folded in quarters. "Set down at the moment of its recitation by one of my scribes. Selvyn, be he hight—but that matters not." He waved his empty hand as he offered Kal the parchment in his other. "Here, read again. Your own words tell of the events as they are, a recounting of events as a fulfillment of prophecy, and more importantly they speak of what it is that you must next do...." Kal looked up sharply. Meriones continued as he also stood. "That is to journey. 'Tis this that puts me in mind of the possibility of your being the subject of the inscription, the Son of Prophecy himself."

"The Son of Prophecy..." Kal held the folded page without opening it. "But what—how do you arrive at this conclusion?"

"Possible conclusion," Meriones corrected Kal as he held his hand out in invitation for the two to continue along the path. "Your own Lay of Investiture, despite its many riddling lines, makes this much obvious—these are the direst days to visit Ahn Norvys in ages, possibly the direst since Ardiel banished Tardroch at Velinthas. Yet in the teeth of these dark events, that are the consummation of much that has been foretold, you are the hope that Wuldor, in his wisdom, has chosen to give us, and you are the fruit that will nourish hope in these most desperate times. You are Hordanu. As such, you are, in truth, the Son of Prophecy, Kalaquinn."

"But the inscription speaks of the Son of Prophecy as one of royal blood."

"Ah, but is it the blood or the heart of which is spoken? 'Great woes by thine own kingly heart shall be endured, amidst the time-lost realms, far from the fields of 'pressed and joyless Arvon,'" Meriones quoted as he stopped walking to face Kal, placing a hand on his arm again. "And yours is a kingly heart, Master Kalaquinn, kingly in grace and graciousness, as I have witnessed. Furthermore, it will needs be kingly in courage to undertake the venture that must be undertaken, and undertaken soon."

"But, Master Meriones, would not Starigan more likely be the Son of Prophecy, he having a kingly heart?"

"Well it may be, Kalaquinn. In fact, it may well be Starigan and you both. Often prophecy has a double edge, and can cut both ways." The bard took Kal's elbow and turned him back to the path. "And this brings us to the matter that has been on my heart to discuss with you, Master Kalaquinn. The Lay which is written on the page you hold makes clear the task that must be engaged by you yourself. There is much tangled meaning in your Lay of Investiture, Master Kalaquinn, but this much is immediately clear, and forgive me if I do not put too fine a point on it, my lord Hordanu—the Sacred Fire must be rekindled in the Clanholding of Lammermorn, and while the crown prince of Arvon, first of princes in Ahn Norvys, remains lost, still, you have the Pyx of Roncador, necessary to secure the kindling Spark. To find the prince, this is your first task, then, with him, to journey to the Balk Pit of Uäm. Again, forgive me my bluntness, but it weighs ever heavier upon my heart. Ahn Norvys waits for you to begin your work as its Hordanu. What is at hand, this must be done." Once again, Meriones paused from walking and faced the Holdsman. The small bard's eyes flashed with a passion that Kal had never seen before on the man's usually inscrutable face.

"You must leave, Master Kalaquinn. At the risk of being impudent, I must tell you, my lord Hordanu, no longer may you remain sequestered in the hidden belly of Folamh. Time will not wait for you. The seasons of the upperworld turn. Your task awaits you to take it up. It behooves me to urge you to embark upon your journey. You must leave, else you stand in default of the demands of your own hordanic lay, which obliges you to make a start on this dire path."

Kal glanced down at the page in his hand and carefully unfolded it. A flowing script filled the page with the words which had, unbidden, welled from his very being in the great Hall of the Stars. But who was this posturing little man to challenge him like this? Anger bloomed in his chest, hot and suffocating, then passed as quickly. It was true, he knew it. He could not avoid what he knew to be inevitable.

"I fear you are correct, Meriones, and I thank you. I believe that this is what I myself have been wrestling with of late, and the source of my recent distemper, to which Alcesidas was witness. Your words prick my heart...." Kal's eyes fell to the ground at his feet. He sighed heavily and looked again at the page in his hand. "Yes, Meriones, the time rapidly approaches. Though my heart misgives me, it is strengthened by your counsel. Your words are a goad to my resolve."

"Then I am well pleased, my lord Myghternos Hordanu."

"But the task seems so very daunting that it would appear to be without any hope of success."

"So it would appear, save that you yourself are the very hope of success. 'Now know wherein this hope lies fay—not in the Harp, but hands that play; the one who sings, and not the Lay; mark, it is he who sings today, for I Hordanu am.'" Meriones smiled and tapped the parchment in Kal's hand. "Your own words."

The two began to walk along the path again in thought. The woods thinned and ended, giving onto a broad meadow that bordered the stone dwellings of Sterentref.

"'Tis entirely appropriate," Meriones said, breaking the silence as the footpath lead them into the meadow, "that Wuldor would deign to have one so young carry the burden of these times. Yours is a path that is not enviable, Master Kalaquinn. Were I a younger man, I might well throw in my lot with yours, but such is not my state nor my duty. I must stay with the remnant of the hammerfolk here in Nua Cearta, even as Magan Hammermaster strives to bring unity once more to the peoples below the mountains. So you, Master Kalaquinn, must do everything you are able, even to the last ounce of your strength, to make one all the realms of Ahn Norvys. 'Tis within your office and within your power to do so, provided you rely upon the virtue of your office, the strength afforded by Wuldor, and the friend-fast bond of fellowship with those that he has placed in your path, even if they journey with you only a short while."

"Would that my people could enjoy the security of Nua Cearta," Kal said, "even while I embark upon this next venture. Though Galligaskin informs me of their present comfort and peace among the people of the hammer in this subterranean realm, I sense their restlessness growing as well. In fact, while Galli has suggested that the Holdsfolk remain here, I fear that this is simply not possible." Kal glanced at Meriones, who maintained his customary stony expression. "Not that I question the peerless generosity and kindness of the hammerfolk. No, it is rather that the remnant of Lammermorn must make their own way in Wuldor's providence. You and I, and both of our peoples, have some role to fill in the ensuing months."

Meriones lifted an eyebrow at Kal and nodded his assent. "There is wisdom enough in your words," he said. "While all people of Ahn Norvys are now your people and in your custody, the remnant folk of Lammermorn, being the remnant of the folk of Lammermorn, have a particular and uniquely important role to play in the unfolding of things. Their fate is without a doubt inexorably tied to yours as the Hordanu. They are the remnant of the chosen of Ahn Norvys. You must make ready to go, now that the people are rested. Their path must take them out of Nua Cearta, and you must lead them hence."

"And where am I to lead them? Where shall I go?"

"What did Wilum tell you?"

"Not enough," Kal said with a dark chuckle.

"If Wilum was half the mentor to you that I suspect he was, then he would have made it plain to you. Did he not?"

"Yes, but how am I—"

"Trust in yourself. And trust in your office. Steel yourself, Master Kalaquinn, my lord Myghternos Hordanu, and take but the first step upon the path that lies before you. Every journey, even the most difficult and dire, is taken one step at a time."

"So, what lies before me?"

"Indeed, what lies now before you?

"The Marshes of—"

Meriones lifted his hand to stop Kal, and gently shook his head. "'Tis best that you do not tell me. Tell no one but your closest and most trusted companions. 'Tis far safer that way. The fewer who know, the fewer can tell."

Kal sighed, then lifted his head and squared his shoulders. "Then I shall make ready to go."

"It must be so," Meriones said.

"Yes, yes. I must confer with Magan Hammermaster."

"And soon. And, if you have not yet done so, you must recount the events that have befallen your people, all of them, before time dulls the edge of your remembering. Such is your bounden duty as Hordanu, to append your own narrative to that of your fore-bears in the *Chronicles of the Harmonic Age*, particularly as that age begins to falter. I shall return the texts to you immediately."

"I thank you, Meriones, heartfully, that you bring me to mind of my duty."

"But, my lord Hordanu, while you are duty-bound, be not bound by duty. Rather, embrace your fate freely, unhesitatingly and unflinchingly, with all the passion that is proper to your youth and innate disposition. Kalaquinn, be Hordanu. Study your Lay of Investiture. The ancient texts may expose the past, but this"—Meriones tapped the page in Kal's hand—"this illumines your future, and that, I believe, of all Ahn Norvys. But enough for the nonce. I have said my piece, presumptuous as it may have been of me to speak my mind. My thanks to you for hearing me. Now, come, let us to Sterentref."

FIVE

Dusk was falling in Nua Cearta as the small party meandered back across the training grounds to where the great bird was perched. They had separately enjoyed the sleepy leisure of a summer's afternoon, but come the evening, Magan's curiosity had brought them together again. The field of arms lay deserted. The air was filled now with the ringing of the crossed swords of mirthful wit. Much to Kal's amusement, the hammerson king and his bard once again heaved and parried the blows of good-natured jest—Magan's keen jibes were each well met by the staid, almost morose, constancy of the stern-faced bard. The king had proven to be an incorrigible tease. Kal had grown comfortable in his presence; indeed, he found he had become quite fond of both Magan and his advisor.

A keening cry rose above their banter.

Meriones stopped short and held back King Magan, gripping him by the sleeve.

"Hark! What is this?"

"Fear not. 'Tis only Dhu," Alcesidas said, evidently amused at the look of alarm etched across the bard's face. "But his cry is changed. Something is amiss?"

"You have a good ear, Alcesidas. You will make a fine and attentive master to Dhu. He grows restless on his roost and desires to be quit of it. Come, let us to him quickly."

Again the fellhawk shrieked—a short, piercing note, importunate and insistent. Kal broke into a jog, leading his companions across the rest of the training ground. Soon the bird came into

45

view, bobbing on its perch, half lifting dark wings from its sides, shrugging its shoulders as if giving air to a bemused consternation over its state of confinement. Again, Dhu tilted his head to the dark void above and emitted another shrill cry.

"Upon my hammer, Kalaquinn, you were right. One tunnel wolf would have been enough," said Alcesidas, breathless behind Kal as they eased their pace and approached the fellhawk.

On the ground before Dhu lay the stripped corpse of one of the two great tunnel wolves. White bone, stark in the ghostly, faltering light, protruded from beneath a tattered pelt. The second carcass remained largely untouched. Already it had begun to spoil and attract flies.

"It is as I said. He will glut on fresh meat but leave the rest as carrion. All the same, he must have been famished, else he would not have eaten as much as he did. But now he grows restless and desires to take up the hunt on his own." Kal reached up and ran his hand down the fellhawk's chest, croodling to him softly. Dhu stooped his head and caught one of Kal's fingers gently in his curved beak.

"Yes, Dhu, yes. All right, then. You shall have your freedom."

The Holdsman bent his hands to the nearest of the jesses, even as King Magan and Meriones caught up and rejoined them, remaining at a distance beyond the range of Dhu's traces.

"By your leave, Sire," Kal said, glancing over his shoulder at the king leaning heavily on his staff, "now that Dhu knows that tunnel wolf must be his quarry, I shall set him free to roam the vaulted skies of your kingdom."

"You may do as you see fit, my lord Hordanu." The king nodded his assent. The fellhawk cried again and, spreading its wings, flapped twice, straining upwards, ungainly on the crossbar.

"Easy, Dhu. Stay yourself. You must give me a moment yet to unbind you."

Alcesidas stepped up to the perch and began to stroke the fellhawk, speaking gentle words of reassurance.

"Many thanks, Alcesidas. Re'm ena, but you do have a way with this bird." In the growing gloom, Kal's fingers fumbled at the knots that bound the leather traces to the jesses.

"There, we are done. Now, on your way and good hunting, Dhu. Go on now. Off you go... You must step back from him, Alcesidas, else he will stay fixed to that post as surely as if he were still bound to it." Kal laughed.

As Alcesidas moved away, the fellhawk unclenched his talons from the crossbeam and lifted himself into the gloaming with great wing beats. Alcesidas and Kal both shrank back instinctively, brushed by the billowing wind from Dhu's wings. So, too, did Magan and Meriones.

"The wingspan, Sire, 'tis a wonder. 'Tis wide enough to easily compass three, nigh four hammersons standing one upon the other, and to spare." Meriones's head rose back, as did the others', marking the black form's mounting progress. They watched Dhu climb gracefully through the twilit sky and wheel away above the field of arms in the direction of the borderlands, until at last he faded into the growing darkness and could be seen no longer.

"What excitement this fellhawk of yours will stir in Nua Cearta, Kalaquinn. 'Tis good that our people are well warned," Alcesidas said.

Meriones still stared after the fellhawk, long lost to sight, with knitted brow and tightdrawn lips. Turning to Kal, he said, "My lord Hordanu, are you certain that yon monster will molest neither folk nor flock?"

"Rest easy, my good bard. No harm will come to them, of that you may be assured. As for the deer in His Majesty's royal chase . . . Well, I can offer no surety that—"

"How so? What mean you?" King Magan raised his voice in dismay.

"Fie, Kalaquinn! 'Tis a poorly turned jest at Magan Hammermaster's expense," the prince said in a tone of feigned disapproval.

"It would seem our good Hordanu knows you all too well, Sire," said Meriones, the hint of a smile playing across his face. "I doubt me not but that Queen Almagora has plied him with endless tales of your deeds as a huntsman. Or, at the very least, her deeds as a huntsman's wife, striving in valiant effort to break her husband of his—what would she say? . . . Obsession? Compulsion? What say you, my lord prince? . . . His passion?"

Magan chuckled at the jest, then grew suddenly quiet at a thought.

"Mayhaps my erstwhile deeds as a huntsman, should there be no more game," he said. "Who knows but that the tunnel wolves have already emptied my chase?" As quickly as a puff of summer cloud blots then unmasks the sun's bright face, the king's anxiety passed, and his tone lightened again. "And doubtless, my lord Hordanu, you are not wholly unaware how dear to my heart also are the pleasures of mead." The king winked and placed a hand on Kal's arm, smiling broadly. "Come, let us back to Sterentref, and to the Alechamber. 'Tis fit—our meed, one might say—that we should raise a bumper or two and slake our thirst."

That evening, in the cosy confines of the Alechamber, panelled in oak and dimly lit by half-shuttered avalynnia and a small fire in the hearth, it was Magan himself who regaled them with tales of his exploits in the King's Chase. Frysan and Galli joined them there, as did Gwyn. The other Holdsmen and a collection of hammersons sat talking in knots around the small hall. Narasin's voice lifted above the drone of conversation in point of some practice of husbandry, while Thurfar evinced by animated gesture the art of the archer at the butts. In a corner, Devved leaned his heavy frame on the thick oaken board in front of him as he bent his head to one side, attentive to the talk, no doubt of smithcraft, that engrossed the three hammersons with whom he sat.

Kal slowly drank in the whole of it, his gaze shifting among the assembled folk. A depth of cheer took possession of him. He sighed contentedly, lifted his tankard and pulled at the ale's warming spice. He returned his cup to the table and his attention to the prince beside him. Alcesidas's bearded face broke into a beaming smile. He thumped Kal on the back, then slammed his fist on the table. Meriones broke midsentence from the story he was telling as he and his listeners turned to look at the prince.

"A song!"

The room grew quiet at the disturbance.

"A song! Come, Master Kalaquinn, you who art Hordanu, sing us a song to dress the meat of our merriment! A song, I say!"

"No ... no, Alcesidas—"

"What? No? What say you, friends?" Alcesidas pushed himself up from the table and stood leaning on his knuckled fists. "Shall we have a song? What say you?"

The room erupted in clapping, laughter, and calls for Kal to sing.

"Come, my lord Hordanu, what say you now?"

Kal rose slowly from his seat with mock weariness and discomfiture, and again the hall burst into acclaim. Then he lifted his hands.

"Very well, very well, if you insist. What shall I sing?"

The question elicited a series of suggestions from the gathered Holdsmen—some met with cheers, some with abuse, all of which seemed to amuse the hammersons to no end. From the opposite side of the Alechamber, Diggory guffawed loud and long, giving vent to a mirth that could be matched only by the king's. Kal smiled and winked and again raised his hands in an attempt to quell the boisterous crowd.

"I shall sing...I shall..." He paused, twice interrupted, then began again. "I shall sing for your pleasure a finely turned lay... as I am, after all, Hordanu—"

A fresh chorus of cheers arose amid the clank of raised tankards. Kal laughed.

"It is a lay in the mode of our upperland home," he said and waved a hand to forestall yet another round of approbation. "And while it may not, truth be told, befit the royal company in whose august presence we find ourselves this evening"—Kal nodded to the king and his sons beside him—"I think it more than befits the occasion. It is a lay wrought in the tongue of our native Clanholding of Lammermorn, and yet I have little doubt that you, our fine hammerfolk brothers, who have proven yourselves so adept at acquiring mastery of all our upperland skills, shall find little difficulty in tuning your ear to its tune and training your mind to its meaning—"

"Less talk, more song!" a voice broke out from the crowd.

"Yes, yes, yes. So we come to it. Galligaskin, a beat, if you please."

Galli began drumming his hands upon the table as Kal made his way to the centre of the room.

"Faster, Galli! 'Tis a jig!"

"But you said it was a lay," someone cried.

"And so 'tis. I am Hordanu—I sing only lays. Faster, Galli!" Kal winked, grinning at his friend.

The rhythm of the drumming increased in speed as Kal began to tap his feet from toe to heel and turn in a slow circle, his hands upon his waist. Soon the cadence was caught up by clapping hands and stomping feet.

Kal raised his voice and said, "'Tis a lay...'Tis the 'Song of The Three Maidens.'"

Diggory practically squealed his delight as he giggled. "Aye, 'tis my favourite," he said, looking around at his tablemates. "The three bonnies! How I do love them!"

With that, while his feet flew, and all about him his fellows clapped and whistled, Kal began to sing.

"Three damsels come daily, to me they sing gaily,
Three maids of whom I've had my fill!
Three beyond compare—the one, she is fair,
And one dark, and one darker still.

"The fair one is bitter, the darker, her sister,
Is heavy, the third carries a bit.
By these three I've been ruined, made many-a-day truant,
From good work, and good reason, and wit.

"Yet I laugh, 'Ah, my pretties, 'tis such a sad pity,
Ye've robbed me of wife, house, and purse!
I've nought ye t'offer from out my life's coffer
Save for my good heart and my mirth.

"And it saddens my heart, that by nature's cruel art
I'm not framed as I ought to be,
With but one mouth and two hands, I'll ne'er fully command
At one time the lot of you three!'

"Ah, this my dire state! And this my grim fate!
But I am resigned to my lot.
One after another, they'll help me recover,
For I am a merry old sot!

"So come, fellows, and hearken, by the tun or the firkin,
For I know that you know beyond doubt
That nought brings as good cheer as good comp'ny
     and beer!
So let's drink to Ale, Porter, and Stout!"

In the last line of the song, Kal snatched a clay mug from the hand of a nearby hammerson, raised it in salute, then drained it to the lees. The song thus ended, the fluid rhythm of Galli's drumming was soon drowned in cheers and applause. Kal bowed, restored the now-empty mug to its laughing owner, and then returned to his seat. He was met by the enthusiastic praise of Magan, Meriones, and Alcesidas, together with Magan's other son, the young prince, his own father, Frysan, Galli, and the others at table with them.

Soon another song was sung, then another, and so an exchange of song ensued between hammerson and Holdsman, each sharing the hearth-spun wealth of his world with the other. Alcesidas was pressed into singing, albeit with little reluctance on his part. Even Magan sang a snippet, a ditty that won him a loud tribute of praise, certainly due more to his rank and the influence of an evening's ale consumption upon the assembly than to the merit of his performance. Meriones demurred from singing, insisting that the tenor of the dirges he knew would ill fit the blithe spirit of the evening.

Songs eventually gave way to tales, and tales to talk. Magan returned to reliving memories of the chase as the night wore on, and Kal listened with interest.

It had been some weeks since the king had indulged himself in the hunt. The King's Chase was bodeful ground now, too dangerous to tread, given over to the tunnel wolves, for it was a naturally enclosed area of dense forest and thickets that delved the mountain beyond the very borderlands of Nua Cearta, full of dens and hollows. In its remote wildness, it was the perfect place for breeding game, but also a natural haunt for the tunnel wolves.

The company had thinned as people took their leave by ones and twos of the king and his party. The eyes of those who remained grew heavy-lidded, and the banter fell off. Heads nodded with weariness. Finally, as he returned for a second time to the story of a near-fatal encounter with a boar, even Magan found himself unable to fend off a yawn. This provoked a succession of gently stifled yawns around the table.

"...there is not a beast more fearsome than was that one," Magan went on, "not even your vaunted Boar, Ferabek, my lord Hordanu—but, alas, clearly I have turned bore unto my guests." He yawned again, his words becoming laboured. "The time has come, methinks, to adjourn this audience."

The king struggled to his feet. Turning, he noted the vacant space beside him on the bench. "I see that Meriones has already slipped away. Ever the wise man, he."

Gwyn, who had fallen asleep, his head nudging a tankard on the table, had to be roused and helped to his feet.

"Come along, lad. Give me a hand with him, will you, Galli?" said Kal.

With sluggish steps the men left the hall and sought their bedchambers, eager now for nothing but the softness of pillow and sheet and sleep.

SIX

Kal had risen early, prompted by a nagging restlessness, well before the first blush of dawn light rose from the avalynnia scattered throughout the underground realm. He had tossed and turned, unable to fall back to sleep, staring into the darkness until he finally resigned himself to climbing out of bed and dressing. Fumbling in the darkness, he managed to unshutter an avalynn lamp, then dressed himself and moved to the window. He drew back the curtains and looked out into the utter blackness of the Nua Ceartan night, a blackness punctuated by nothing more than a handful of pinprick lights scattered throughout the city spread beneath him. The upperworld landscape, he knew, would be bathed tonight in the soft silvery glow of a full moon; but here, the impenetrable inkiness veiled everything and seemed strangely suffocating to him. Kal pulled the heavy curtains closed again.

He carried the lamp to the writing table in his chamber and began to pore over the ancient lines of *Hedric's Master Legendary* and the *Criochoran* in a desperate bid to assuage the growing malaise that plagued him. Meriones's remonstrations presented themselves time and again to his mind as the night slipped away. Eventually, Kal drew out the latest volume of the *Chronicles of the Harmonic Age,* which had been returned to him the previous afternoon. This he placed on the table in front of himself and thumbed through until he arrived at the final few entries. Here, Wilum's graceful script had become increasingly spidery, as if the hand had been moved by a mind ever more harried and under duress, compelled by a growing alarm at the significance of events only half recognized and half understood.

Kal reread his master's words. The last few entries had been penned only hours before their flight from Wuldor's Howe. Kal could hear the old bard's voice in his ears as he scanned the lines, the snippets of prophecy set alongside the account of the events that finally led up to the fall of the Great Glence, interspersed with Wilum's own convictions, musings, maunderings, fears, and faint hopes expressed in the face of the impending disaster that he alone seemed to have recognized. Kal read his own words and those of Galligaskin Clout set down on the page as Wilum recounted their brush with the lowlanders above the Shaad overlooking the Great Glence. The Hordanu's suspicions and speculations had been fairly accurate, but little did Wilum know at the time of his writing just how soon his predictions would come to pass, nor how complete would be their fulfillment.

It was in the middle of these entries that Kal recognized Wilum's first intimations about invoking the Right of Appointment. It was evident in the old man's writings that he admired Kal and held his young assistant in high regard; but it was only now that Kal saw the significance of what Wilum had been doing in those final days and hours. He had been purposefully arranging for the preservation of the office of high bard in the person of Kal, only events had overtaken Wilum more precipitously and more intensely than he had anticipated.

Kal finished reading the final entry, then closed his eyes. Wilum's face came to mind. Kal thought of the flight across Deepmere in the borrowed boat, the depth of blueness in sky and water, the cold touch of the golden Talamadh in his hands, the coolness of Wilum's hands over his own, and the words of the Debrad he had sworn. He would never fully comprehend the significance of the words—that would take a lifetime, a lifetime of being Hordanu. Kal sighed deeply and opened his eyes to stare at the avalynn lamp, which glowed, unwavering, in the darkness of the room. At length, he broke from his reverie and turned the final page of writing over, revealing a blank sheet. This he flattened with his hand, then removed from the desk drawer a small stoppered pot of ink and a quill, which he sharpened. He sat with the quill poised over the page for some minutes, collecting his thoughts. Then, bowing his head, he began to write.

*HERE BEGIN THE ENTRIES OF KALAQUINN WRIGHT IN THE
CHRONICLES OF THE HARMONIC AGE, THE FIRST BEING AN
ACCOUNT OF HIS OWN INVESTITURE AS HIGH BARD AND THE
DIRE EVENTS RELATING TO THE FALL AND DESTRUCTION OF
THE STONEHOLDING.*

I, Kalaquinn, of the Arvonian Clanholding of Lammermorn,
son of Marina, herself daughter of Cealya and Marrdoch, and
of Frysan the wheelwright, once Royal Life Guardsman under
Colurian, High King of Arvon, and himself son of Brescia
and Nathaer, do here enter my name and accounting in these
the Chronicles of the Harmonic Age, *on this the last day of
wane-spring's month, known in the Old Tongue as Tramys, the
Month of Fire, thirty days from the Candle Feast, twenty-one
days from the Fall of the Great Glence, in this the 3019th year
of the Great Harmonic Age, inaugurated by the first singing of
the Lay of the Velinthian Bridge by Ardiel of the Long Arm,
First High King of Arvon, to the holy tones of the Talamadh,
the harp most sacred.*

*I, Kalaquinn, do here enter my name and accounting by
warrant of the office I hold, the office of Hordanu, the office
which was conferred upon me by Right of Appointment at the
hand of Wilum, my predecessor, son of Annath and Wilthar,
the office which I agreed to accept out of bounden duty to my
folk by way of my Debrad sworn and sealed while in headlong
flight upon the waters of Deepmere, the office to which I attested
by my Lay of Investiture, sung while in exile in the forgeland
kingdom of Nua Cearta, beneath the Radolan Mountains,
domain of Magan Hammermaster, whose protection and generous hospitality I yet enjoy, even as I pen these words.*

*I, Kalaquinn, do set ink upon this page in my own hand.
In the wisdom of Wuldor, though undeserving and considering
myself ill-suited to the task, I have been chosen to be High Bard
of all of Ahn Norvys, Guardian of Wuldor's Howe, Keeper of
the Sacred Fire of Tramys, and Master of the Holy Talamadh,
ninety-seventh Hordanu in succession from Hedric.*

*I am humbled that, unworthy as I am, I should be included
in the esteemed company of these my forebears, that my name
should appear in a list alongside theirs, and that my words
should be appended to theirs as a continuing testament to the*

mindfulness that Wuldor bears towards Ahn Norvys. May he always direct my hands, my strength and my heart so that I may never give him cause to regret his choice or disown his chosen Bard.

As my first entry in these collected writings of the Hordanus, I here give an accounting of those few folk of the Clanholding of Lammermorn that survived the ravages of The Boar and the events that have ushered in the darkest days since before the Great Harmony was ever spun over this world, since before even the veiled time of the echobards, days of a darkness the likes of which have not been seen since The Great Undoing.

Apart from the betrayers Kenulf, son of the late Thane Ayllin Strongbow, his cousin, Enbarr, his retainers Nechtan and Dellis, and the black-hearted Relzor, all of whom have fled to the skirts of their liege and master, Ferabek, and the Hordanu, Wilum, who died at the hand of Relzor in the Cave of the Hourglass, there survive the following persons, who yet abide in the hope of Wuldor's kindness:

+ *I, Kalaquinn Wright, Hordanu;*
+ *My mother, Marina, her man, Frysan Wright, wheelwright and once Royal Life Guardsman, and their son, my brother, Brendith;*
+ *Goodwife Gammer Clout, her man, Diggory, a farmer, together with their daughters, Marya—who holds my heart—Marrisya, and Heathal, as well as their nephew Galligaskin;*
+ *Riandra Woolage, her man, Narasin, a farmer, and their sons, Artun and Garis;*
+ *Fionna Fletcher, her man, Thurfar, a bowyer and fletcher, and their daughters, Laesia, Giarra, and Bytha, and their son Gwyn;*
+ *Devved Smith, a farrier and blacksmith, together with his son, Chandaris;*
+ *Rindamant Lakesward, her man, Athmas, a fisherman, together with their daughter, Mikail, and sons, Petrys, Joranth, and an infant son yet unnamed, as well as Rindamant's mother, Charyll;*
+ *Gara Shepherd, her man, Manaton, a herdsman, together with their daughter, Laloke, their son, Hannon, and an infant son yet unnamed.*

This is the remnant of the Stoneholding—of more than fourteen hundred folk, thirty-four souls remain.

I hope that Master Wilum's intention in seeking out Aelward was for him to offer us some counsel, for, beyond getting my people to the safety of the Marshes of Atramar and into Aelward's care, I have no idea as to how I should proceed with the rest of my mission. I trust that Aelward, whoever he may be, can provide me further guidance.

The Sacred Fire is extinguished. It must be rekindled before the turn of the seasons occurs once more and it be time again for the Candle Feast. However, the sacred spark that kindles the Fire can only be acquired in the Balk Pit of Uäm, which lies more than two hundred leagues away. Further, the Balk Pit can only be broached by one of Ardiel's very own blood. So, I must discover the whereabouts, in all the broad reaches of Ahn Norvys, of Prince Starigan, then, with him, go to the Balk Pit. All this with Ferabek growing ever more powerful and his forces on the move everywhere. And the Talamadh, the holy binder of heaven and earth, is lost. It must be recovered. And still the Great Harmony grows ever weaker, as the world plunges into dark chaos—and I am Hordanu. I am overwhelmed.

I am overwhelmed by the unknown road that stretches before me. But, in this, as it is in any thing—be it the grandest undertaking or the most commonplace and meanest of tasks—every journey is taken in pacing strides, one after the other. So I shall first bring the remnant of the Stoneholding to Aelward, then with his counsel will I set out to find the prince. Beyond that, at present, I can design no further.

I know not what dangers, what trials and adversities loom ahead on the veiled pathways of the future. But, though death lurk in wait, this is the course that lies before me, and this is the road I must venture. I entrust myself and my quest to the wisdom of Wuldor and the care of the anagoroi. May he ever hold me in his watchfulness.

So ends my first entry into the Chronicles of the Harmonic Age. *I trust it will not be my last.*

⁓

Day had dawned in Nua Cearta, and light now spilled through a gap in the curtains over the window. Bleary-eyed, Kal cleaned the quill and ink pot, restored them to the desk drawer, and pushed himself up from the table. He shuttered the glowing avalynn and closed the heavy leather binding cover of the volume in which he had written.

After washing his face, Kal felt somewhat refreshed and awake; however, his disquiet had not yet completely coalesced into resolve. He would speak to the king later in the day, he thought to himself; he must. He moved to the window, drew the curtains aside, and opened the casements. The soft inflow of light from the avalynn trees planted in the courtyard was still a marvel to him. He lifted his gaze and looked up towards Sterenhall, rising from its rock-founded terraces as if holding up the sky with its glence dome. He wondered how Dhu was faring, whether he had made the right decision in bringing the fellhawk from the upperworld to Nua Cearta, but that was just one of innumerable thoughts and questions that swirled through his mind. He sighed and lowered his gaze to the broad courtyard outside his window again.

At King Magan's insistence, the young Hordanu was lodged in a guest room of the palace itself, which lay at the heart of Sterentref, the town seat clustered around the royal enclave. The place teemed with stables and shops, armouries and forges—an abundance of forges. It seemed every hammerson was a master smith—a forgemaster, as they termed it. Indeed, they reckoned everything in terms of their smithcraft. It was their constant point of reference.

There were other dwellings, too, in Sterentref, including the guesthouse where Kal's mother and father and brother and the rest of the Holdsfolk were lodged. It stood at the far end of the central courtyard, which was beginning to stir with life. Already two hammersons, Magan's guardsmen, were filling pitchers for their morning ablutions from the fountain that dominated the centre of the concourse, its high-flung waters tumbling down into a square pool edged with smooth stone slabs to knee height. A third figure, taller, one of the Holdsfolk, came into view—a young woman clad in a cream-coloured tunic, clasping a smaller jug. Her footfall seemed hesitant. Kal leaned nearer the window ledge and stared down for a moment, trying to make her out. She drew closer, circling the fountain towards the near side of the water pool, and looked up to the window of Kal's chamber on the second story, fastening her gaze on it . . . on him. Now he knew who it was, not from her features, too indistinct from this distance, but from the way she carried herself. It was Galli's cousin, Marya.

At a loss, Kal averted his eyes and turned quickly aside from the open window. He stood for a moment in thought, composing himself, considering how greatly things had changed for him and for Marya. Their old life in the Stoneholding seemed an ever-receding, distant dream, a life as neighbours, as friends, a life as...

Well, he had hoped it would become more, but that had all changed. Besides, he could do nothing about it here and now, so it did not really warrant pondering. At least it would accomplish no good to mull on it. Despite the pang of guilt he felt at the thought of Marya left standing, staring at an empty window, he pushed himself away from the wall beside the window and paced across the room to his bed. Hastily, he dragged the coverlet over the mattress, then turned and left the chamber.

The faint fragrance of freshly baked bread drifted through the halls. It stirred his hunger, and lured Kal down marble corridors and staircases to the palace kitchens, where he took a breakfast of still-warm bread and cheese with chilled apple cider pressed only the evening before. While he ate, he quietly watched the bakers, following them with his gaze and exchanging morning pleasantries with them as they stoked the oven fires and set about mixing and kneading dough for the many loaves that would be needed in the royal household that day.

Still chewing from a thick slab of bread slathered with honey, Kal left the kitchens and climbed to the spacious entrance hall of the palace. Its pillars rose to a vaulted ceiling, which arched then swept down to sidewalls hung with an array of beautifully wrought implements of both peace and war—poleaxes and swords, ploughshares and coulters, firedogs and grates, hauberks and helms. There was also the handiwork of the hammerdaughters, finely woven tabards and tunics, along with banners representative of the various crafts in Nua Cearta. Licking his fingers clean of honey and crumbs, Kal lingered for a time in the hall examining the work of the hammerfolk, until, at length, he realized that others were close by. He turned to see the palace steward supervising the placement of a new banner on the wall across from him.

For a while, he stood by, silently watching the steward and his two workmen. Kal felt a warm flush of pride, for on the banner, against a field of green, surmounted by a range of mountains, was an archery butt bristling with arrows, arrows fletched in the manner of the Stoneholding. Which is to say, the manner of Thurfar Fletcher, for he had been the sole fletcher in the Stoneholding and a master of his art. Kal grinned to himself as the steward finally approved of the banner's placement and, with his two subordinates, turned and departed. Soon the place became busy with the coming and going of palace life. Kal decided it was time he leave the hall himself and go outside.

As he wandered across the vaulted chamber towards the rear of the palace, he paused to admire a tapestry on the wall next to doors that gave onto a courtyard. It set the theme not only for the hammerfolk king's royal abode, but for the hammerfolk themselves. A rich, earth-toned tapestry, it depicted a flaxen-haired hammerson, girt with leather apron, standing before his blazing forge by night. The man lifted from the forge's fire a sword, its blade aglow and ready to be tempered, annealed. The tapestry was one of the first sights that Alcesidas had shown him in Nua Cearta, a masterpiece woven long ago by exquisitely gifted hammerdaughters in the Burren Mountain homeland of Alcesidas's ancestors. It had been brought with them to Nua Cearta. Alcesidas had spoken of it as an heirloom of inestimable importance to his people, for it was a constant reminder of both the past and the future, a reminder that they were a people of the forge destined to be tempered and shaped by the trials and challenges of a new life far from their homeland. Not at all unlike the folk of the Stoneholding, mused Kal, thrust out of their mountain redoubt, forced to embark on an ominous new adventure beyond the comfortable familiarity of their clanholding. Perhaps that was why they had experienced so much fellow feeling among the forgefolk, such affinity with them.

Kal felt a twinge at the thought of the parting that must come, and must come soon. It spurred him from his reverie, and he strode across the slate floor towards the rear of the entrance hall. He passed through a broad set of doors to a square filled with stalls and shops, now milling with hammerfolk, men and women, bustling about their tasks. Here and there, still a wondrously distinctive sight for a Holdsman, avalynn trees gave forth their light, stronger and more intense than he had expected, until Kal realized to his surprise that it was already pushing midmorning.

He fished into his pocket for a coin with which he bought an apple from one of the stallkeepers, a wizened old man hawking his wares, a delightful little girl in tow. Kal gave the bright-eyed hammerdaughter an affectionate chuck under the chin, then bit into his apple and wandered into the Ward of the Forgemasters. The air carried the sweet tang of horse manure, for here, hard by both forge and farrier, there were stables, themselves crowded by the stalls, booths, and market stands of merchant and craftsman. Kal regarded the blacksmith shops of the Ward, all marked with the colourful insignia of the most respected trade in Nua Cearta. They were hot and noisy hives of activity, the armourers and smiths beating out metal and driving rivets with their hammers.

"By the Stone, Volodan, will wonders never cease? The craft, the workmanship! Truly you are all masters in Nua Cearta. Not a journeyman among you." Devved's voice rose unmistakeable above the din. It came from the other side of a shop front open to the traffic of passersby.

"Look, Volodan, there is the Hordanu. Master Kalaquinn! Bria-coil! Here, you must come see this. Here, here we are." Having caught Kal's eye, Devved waved, beckoning him.

Kal sidestepped a wagon heaped high with coal and entered the workplace of one of the armourers.

"Briacoil, Devved. And to you, Volodan." Kal nodded to each of them and to a third figure, to whom he proffered a similar greeting, a sinewy hammerson clad in a soiled leather apron, his thin, heavy-browed face smeared with grime. The smith inclined his head shyly.

"This is Kesontor, Master Armourer," said Devved. "Look what he's made. The workmanship!" Devved pointed to a chainmail hauberk draped over an anvil. "Come, feel it, lift it. Never before in all my days have I seen its like—"

Volodan burst out laughing, recovered himself and said, "Forgive me. We have visited half the forges in Nua Cearta, so many that my head reels. So many that I have lost count." Volodan chuckled again. "Just as I have lost count of the number of times I have heard those same words coming from his lips. 'Never before in all my days have I seen its like.' You should hear yourself, Devved. Like a child in a room filled with new toys."

"Why, it is so light, so smooth to the touch. Like cloth, not rings of steel," Kal said, fingering the coat of mail Devved had handed him.

"Nor better nor worse than the work of any of my fellow forgemen," said Kesontor, abashed by the attention he was receiving.

"Not true, Kesontor. 'Tis indeed better by far than most of our forgework. The work of a master among masters. You were my finest student," Volodan said. "I have never been sadder to lose an apprentice than when I lost you."

"My thanks, Volodan," Kesontor said, nodding to his former master. "'Tis no small praise coming from the lips of Nua Cearta's finest forgeman. But you understand my meaning."

"He means that all the forgework in Nua Cearta, even the craft of lacklustre forgemen, is of a quality that far surpasses what we have aboveground," Devved said, his enthusiasm waxing again. "They have a way of smelting that is of their own devising, one that makes for a harder, lighter steel than anything I have ever seen." Devved laughed at himself. "I do it once again, Volodan. But it is true! So true! I would never have thought it possible, but I begin to gain a notion of how it is done. There is so much to learn, and Volodan has offered to teach me, to make me his apprentice. This is fortunate, no?"

"Yes, fortunate indeed," Kal replied. His flat tone betrayed his misgiving.

"You sound uncertain, my lord Hordanu," said Volodan, eyebrows lifting in surprise.

"No, not at all. I do not mean to give offence. We owe you much—too much, I think at times. Our people grow . . ." Kal paused, searching for words, burdened by a growing disquiet.

"'Tis nothing, such instruction as I can give," Volodan said, and smiled broadly. "A trifle as compared with the lessons in archery and bow skill your folk have given us. Thurfar Fletcher—well founded is his naming—he teaches our hammersons the art of shaping both bow and arrow." The hammerson winked at Devved. "We have never seen the like of his work—"

Galli burst into the shop. "Ah, there you are, Kal! I've been looking all over the place for you. King Magan's guardsmen and Alcesidas have, too. It was the costermonger's little girl said you'd come this way."

"Why? What's the matter?"

"It's Dhu. He's made his first kill. A farmer from the borderlands witnessed it firsthand. Came straight in to report it. And one of the hammerson border rangers saw the whole thing too, but he stayed back, keeping his station, standing watch, as by orders bound. Re'm ena, Kal, the whole kingdom's on about the news."

"It was who, Galligaskin? Do you recall the name of the farmer, by chance?" Volodan asked.

"Nor...Nor-something. I do not rightly remember."

"Nordisst? It was Nordisst?"

"Indeed! That is the name!"

"A solid, dependable fellow, and a respectable forgeman. He has a farm in the valley next down from ours. You have met him, Devved. His was one of the forges you desired to visit."

"Indeed, I remember him."

"Kal, you must come now," Galli said. "Magan Hammermaster awaits you."

"Aye, Galli. Kesontor, Volodan, Devved, briacoil. I will take my leave of you."

"My lord Hordanu, I am honoured that you would attend my shop," the smith said and bowed.

SEVEN

The two Holdsmen found King Magan and Alcesidas in the sprawling courtyard before the main palace doors. The place was filled with commotion, a crowd of people abuzz with talk, gesticulating towards the arched and turreted roofs of Sterenhall.

"Look, Kal, up there." Galli pointed to the heights of the domed building that rose to meet the granite roof of the cavernous landscape.

"Dhu," Kal said softly. "But why the excitement?"

The fellhawk stood perched high above the courtyard, its wings tucked close to its body, peering down on the throng. As Kal and Galli jostled their way towards the king, they realized that the attention of the people was divided, shifting between the great bird and an open patch of ground in front of the king. When they reached the spot, there lay the carcasses of two tunnel wolves, black fur mottled with thickly caked blood from horrific wounds.

"Two of them? Where did the second one come from?" Galli asked in surprise.

Alcesidas beckoned, lifting his voice above the noise of the others. "Ah, there you are, Kalaquinn!" Beside the prince stood a middle-aged man with a crag-worn face, dressed in homespun and fidgeting nervously with his hat. "Come meet Nordisst and hear the tale he has to recount."

"Indeed, what a tale," echoed Meriones.

"Indeed, what a bird!" King Magan exclaimed. "Already there are two horrors the fewer since you set him free to roam our skies." The king's eyes strayed up again to the turreted abutments of Sterenhall.

"Aye, that's our Dhu!" Narasin said in the common tongue, proudly stepping out from the crowd of onlookers that ringed the mangled remains of the tunnel wolves.

"How so? What has happened?" Kal asked.

"Please, Nordisst. Explain again, for the sake of my lord Hordanu, the events that transpired this morning."

"As you wish, Sire." The farmer bobbed his head to Magan. Then, with his eyes fixed to the ground at his feet, wringing his hat in earnest, he retold his account.

"I arose early this morning, sooner even than the breaking of the dawn. Leaving my wife and little ones abed, I roused my eldest son. I was keen to check on my flocks in their pasturage, for I had heard the wolves howling in the night. We armed ourselves, my boy and I, with the best steel from my forge. My son donned a bow and quiver, newly fashioned by yon anuas." Nordisst paused, his gaze briefly seeking out Thurfar, then dropping again to his feet. The farmer spoke slowly, choosing his words with care.

"Our farm lies on the very frontier, hard by the walls of Nua Cearta. We carried lanterns, the two of us, and made our way through the ploughlands close by the house, walking out to a sheltered meadow where we had left one of our flocks folded. 'Tis the most isolated place on our steading, but good pasture and protected by our best ram and by stone walls built in long times past. As dawn broke and we drew near the place, we met one of the rangers stationed by our parts. With him was the anuas here, Garis." Nordisst stopped twisting his hat long enough to lift an open hand in the direction of the young Holdsman now standing beside his father, Narasin, and Artun, his brother. Garis smiled broadly, understanding the gesture if not the words. "He has stood watch with the rangers on the frontier these past few nights. Like me, the ranger and Garis were drawn by the terrible howling, now grown many times louder and more menacing, and closer, too, coming from trees along the far end of the pasture. We moved to the stone fence by the sheepfold. As we climbed over the wall"—the farmer flattened his hand and made a steep swooping motion—"there came a wild shriek unlike anything that I have ever—"

"You should have seen Dhu, Master Kalaquinn," Garis said, unable to contain his excitement and prompted by the farmer's gesture, which he understood better than the farmer's words and now imitated. "He simply fell from the sky! It was—" He was cut short, chastened by a scowl from his father.

"It's all right, Garis. Clearly you were impressed." The young Holdsman brightened at Kal's words.

"Yes, indeed, it was a sight! But forgive me..." The young man tipped his head to the hammerson farmer and lifted his empty palm to encourage the farmer to once again take up the telling.

Nordisst returned his attention to Kal, raising his gaze from the ground, and continued. "Looking up, I saw yon great bird swoop down screaming from the sky, dropping fast as a stone. As I topped the fence, I was chilled to see black shapes bounding across the field towards my poor, bleating sheep. Tunnel wolves, a good half-dozen of them, the lead wolf outpacing the rest. It all happened so quickly. The lead wolf slowed a step and lifted its head. At once that bird dropped like a stone onto the wolf's back. It drove the creature into the ground, even as it plunged its talons into the wolf's back. When the wolf strove to turn its head and bite its attacker, the hawk kept one foot planted while it seized the wolf's muzzle with the other and with a jerk snapped its neck. The wolf went limp, dead."

A murmur passed through the assembled folk. The story had clearly lost none of its power for being now twice, thrice, even four times told.

"The hawk stood on the carcass and screamed at the wolves that followed, spreading its wings wide. It was something to behold, the change in the wolves. From fierce beasts of prey they changed into tuck-tail whelps and slunk away like shadows to their caves. I would not have believed it possible." The small farmer shook his head in wonderment, then looked to Garis, nodding for him to take up the account.

"What happened after the wolves retreated, Garis?" Kal prompted in the common tongue.

"Well, as a Holdsman, I'm more accustomed to Dhu. So I'm not so afraid. I run down ahead from the stone fence into the fold. The sheep are still frightened and cowering, except for the ram." Nordisst smiled, as Garis raised his fists to his temples, and dropped his head in imitation of the beast. "He lowers his head and advances a few steps from the flock when he sees me. Dhu had quietened down, all right. The wolves had turned and fled. Nordisst and Lesk—the ranger that was with us—they are chary about getting any closer to our bird. And I should not blame them. We shared the same dread back in the Holding when Master Kalaquinn first showed his nestling.

"Anyway, when I bid him leave the dead wolf and take to the air, he obeys like I was his master. Leaves us there with the carcass at our feet and flies off. Then we decide that, as this is probably Dhu's first kill in Nua Cearta, we ought to bring it back to Sterentref, a trophy for Magan Hammermaster. So we four load the tunnel wolf onto the farm wagon Nordisst went to fetch and bring him here. Lesk remained at his post, on patrol in the borderlands, as were his orders. But no sooner do we arrive back and lay the beast down here in the shadow of the palace than all eyes are on the sky in amazement, hammerfolk and Holdsfolk alike, pointing and shouting. There is Dhu again, a second wolf gripped hard in his talons like a rag doll. So then he swoops down over the crowd and lets go the second wolf, dropping it atop the first, neat as you please. And then our bird, well, he flies up to that turret where he is now perched." Garis looked up at Dhu, a grin on his face.

"My thanks, Nordisst. 'Twas a well-told and welcome tale," Kal said, then turned toward his fellow Holdsman and added, "As was yours, Garis. A good telling—but for one very important detail."

"H-how so?"

"Dhu is no longer our bird." Kal now turned to the gathered people and switched again to speak in the language of the hammerfolk. "He has been made gift to Magan Hammermaster and the folk of Nua Cearta. With Dhu on the wing, our friends may beat back this plague of tunnel wolves."

"Indeed we shall, my lord Hordanu. My heart is filled with gratitude to you on behalf of my people." Magan bowed, then initiated a round of thunderous applause. As the clapping subsided, he spoke again.

"Our bird"—a grin played across his face, and he winked—"shall be known henceforth as Dhu Wolfhammer. Alcesidas, see that yon turret is given over to him as a mew."

"My thanks to you, Magan Hammermaster, for providing Dhu with such apt ground in which to fill the measure of his skills as a hunter. It seems your bird has taken to his role with a dauntlessness that befits his new masters."

"Well and smoothly spoken, my lord Hordanu!" Meriones's stern countenance broke into a broad smile. "'Tis not to be wondered that the Test of the Riddle Scrolls was but a gentle prod to your quick wit and ready tongue."

"Indeed. Perhaps too often too ready a tongue." Kal paused; then, turning to Magan, said, "And now, Sire, I would ask a boon."

"Come, let it be spoken, my dear Kalaquinn."

"I request an audience with you and Meriones in private, Sire. As soon as may be conveniently occasioned."

"Easily done, my dear Kalaquinn, and willingly, too. But do unfurrow your brow. Methinks that these great events of recent happening do neither arouse nor increase your cheer, but rather serve only to compound some unspoken burden you carry upon your heart."

"Indeed, you speak truer than you may know, and it is of this burden that I would speak to you."

"Then, come. We shall retire to the palace library. I think it my favourite place in all my realm. Like Meriones, I savour its atmosphere of parchment and polished oak." The king clapped his hands. Then, placing one in the crook of Kal's arm, he began to direct the Holdsman towards the palace. "What better place to open a bottle of Regnal in the company of friends—nay, rather boon companions. And would that all my boons were so agreeably dispensed!"

In the high-ceilinged bookchamber of Sterentref, King Magan pressed a delicate crystal goblet half filled with red wine into Kal's hand. "Come, my lord Myghternos Hordanu," he said. "You have brought a great gift to our people. We must raise a glass in grateful celebration."

Flanked by Meriones, the king directed Kal to a comfortable chair in a carpeted alcove with soft-grained wainscotting that set it apart from the rest of the palace library, where in contrast neat shelves stuffed with leather-bound tomes stretched from floor to ceiling. Here, stained-glass windows above the wood panelling gave a warm colouring to the midday light that streamed in from the outside and fell across the reading stands and soft, deep chairs. A fire crackled merrily in a small stone hearth set deeply in the back wall of the reading room.

Kal sat upright on the edge of his seat, resisting its easy contours. Restlessly, he cradled his glass while King Magan and Meriones each took a crystal goblet from the sideboard and settled in two high-backed chairs opposite him. The bard sniffed at the wine in his fine-stemmed glass like a dark moth testing the nectar of some dainty blossom, then held the glass up to the light with a knit-browed look of appreciative scrutiny.

"To the folk of the Stoneholding"—Magan lifted his glass—"and to Dhu Wolfhammer, and to you, my lord Myghternos Hordanu."

Meriones broke from his studied appraisal of the wine in his still-raised glass. "Indeed, my lord, to the Hordanu's weal. May he and his people be held in the eye of Wuldor and know always his gentle hand."

Kal, too, raised his glass, inclining his head with an uneasy smile. "And to you, Lord Magan Hammermaster, together with all the forge-folk. And to you, Meriones, their most esteemed bard." Kal's voice was strained, his mirth forced.

In unison they each placed glass to lips and sipped gently at the rich red wine.

Magan exhaled with satisfaction. "Regnal Five. Our finest vintage," he said as he rolled the stem of his wine goblet between his thumb and fingers, admiring its contents.

"Without a doubt, Sire, but Regnal Six and Seven come close, I would wager. Those were good years—the early days of your reign. Amazing to think that you were scarcely older than Alcesidas is now. A mere babe," Meriones said, nodding to the hammerson prince, who had slipped quietly into the room. Alcesidas grinned back at him impishly and poured himself a goblet of Regnal from the bottle on the sideboard, then turned to stand beside Kal's chair.

"I apologise for my tardiness. I had to see to Dhu Wolfhammer's new lodgings. Here is to a long and fruitful fellowship of our peoples." Alcesidas lifted his glass, tilting it to each of the others in turn. The room filled with the tinkling laughter of the crystal goblets as their rims met.

"Something is amiss, my lord Hordanu?" asked Magan, lifting a bushy eyebrow. "Indeed, your manner ill suits our spirit of conviviality. Perhaps the Regnal Five is not agreeable to your palate? If so, we will unstop a bottle of the Six, or the Seven—I shall call for a footman."

"No, no, my lord. I do not mean to be rude, nor to cause offence. 'Tis a fine vintage..." Kal rose to his feet and paced the few steps across the room to where the small fire burned.

He fidgeted with the crystal ridges of his glass, staring into the flame and ember. "But even in its joy, my heart remains heavy."

"Heavy? How be this so?" The king leaned forward in his chair, his brow furrowed with concern. Meriones had followed Kal's movement with his gaze and now stared intently at him.

Kal sighed, then said, "Because the time has come, Sire, for us to take our leave of Nua Cearta and our hammerfolk friends."

"Why so? I do not understand. We have failed you as hosts? Our ways are different. Irksome to you in many ways, one cannot doubt. It comes from the long centuries we have lived in isolation from the upperland world, from the rest of Arvon. But we have learned so much from you and from your folk. You have added an untold richness to our lives. But, come, my dear Kalaquinn, if you could but bear with us—"

Meriones had placed a hand on Magan's arm. A ponderous silence ensued. At length, Kal lifted his eyes to the diminutive monarch and smiled wanly.

"Nay, my good King Magan," Kal said, "'Tis not as you suppose. Rest easy. Your hammerfolk are matchless in their hospitality, without peer as hosts. I dare any man, aboveground or below, to deny it is so. You have given us safe haven in the midst of a fearful storm. And we have learned so much from you as well, more knowledge than you have gained from us. In many ways our people's fate is bound together with yours, and in some ways it is not. You seek to bargain for peace with your Burren Mountain cousins, while I know I must embark on the path that stretches out before my feet and leads away from this sanctuary that you have provided us."

"He speaks true, my lord Magan," Meriones said, regarding Kal with a look of sober concentration. "In this happy meeting of our two peoples, we have each of us grown forgetful of the duties to which he is bound by his office. He is Hordanu of all Ahn Norvys, and in a most perilous time, with burdens and responsibilities that call him forth from our humble caverns to embark on an enterprise of fretful extremity. In truth, my lord, we may not—nay, we must not tempt him from his destined course."

"But surely, my lord Myghternos Hordanu, if it be that you must leave and go about what tasks you will, still your people may remain here with us. It may be so?" Magan's expression of concern resolved into one of grim determination. "Indeed, yes.

Indeed, they shall enjoy sure safety in my domain from the broken peace into which you would venture. It shall be so!" Magan averred with such forceful gesture that the wine slopped over the side of his goblet, spilling onto the floor.

The Holdsman turned and faced the three noble hammersons. He bowed his head slightly and said, "I am certain that nothing would please our folk more than to rest secure here in Nua Cearta enjoying your boundless hospitality as your forge-fellows, partaking of your board and drinking deeply of your wisdom. You are the guardians of such craft, such knowledge, such a wondrous way of life. Take Devved, for example." Despite his dark humour, Kal chuckled.

"What would he not give to spend the rest of his days striking the anvils of your smithies, exploring their workings, learning their art, sharing a tankard with your splendid forgemen. And as for the others? Well..." The tension had lifted from his voice, and Kal smiled again. He paused to sip from the Regnal, savoured its age and smoothness. "But now, alas, we have imposed quite long enough, even if it be a happy and welcomed imposition, upon your hospitality."

"How so, Kalaquinn?" Alcesidas said, the blitheness fading from his eyes, his jaw set. "Our hospitality is not something we portion out like some close-fisted and niggardly shopkeeper haggling over a chipped chamber pot. Your folk may remain with us no matter how long, even to their children's children, for you are as kin to us." Almost imperceptibly, the prince's chin quivered.

Kal's throat caught. Smiling, he lifted his arms wide and stepped towards the hammerson prince. "And you are as kin to us, Alcesidas. To me you shall always be both friend and brother, bound by ties stronger even than ties of blood." Kal's eyes welled with tears, and they embraced each other.

"I am deeply touched," the young Hordanu continued, breaking from Alcesidas and turning to the king and Meriones, the hand which was unencumbered by the wine glass remaining still on the prince's back. "But howsoever much we are welcome here, we are yet the remnant folk of the Stoneholding, with a warrant in the wider world, a warrant and a fate that outreaches our sojourn in Nua Cearta. Happily, our paths have merged and run together for a span, and our paths will doubtless cross again. But until then we must continue on the separate journeys that have been set before our peoples. Nonetheless, my lord Magan, this does not mean that I shall not remain forever in your debt. For as long as I hold breath, you and your forgefolk shall have a place of grateful honour in my heart."

"As you shall in ours," the king answered. "The doors to our realm stand open to you always as home haven in fair weather and in storm, in weal and in woe."

"I thank you once more, Magan Hammermaster." Kal bowed to the king. Then, straightening, he emptied his wine glass and pursed his lips appreciatively. "No, no, Alcesidas." Kal waved off the prince, who made shift to retrieve the wine bottle from the sideboard. "If I take one more sip of your Regnal, I shall never summon the resolve to leave your wondrous kingdom." Kal laughed. "'Tis potion strong enough to beguile a man from his bounden duty."

"Ah, I see, Kalaquinn," said Alcesidas with a wink. "We are a folk too ill-favoured to gain your settled residence here. Evidently our Regnal has charms that we lack."

"You retemper my meaning with your ready wit, Alcesidas. If we make not haste with our preparations to leave Nua Cearta, you shall soon have your hammerfolk spurning me for a hopeless ingrate."

"Impossible, my lord Hordanu!" roared Magan. "Pay no heed to Alcesidas."

"Spurned? No fear of that," Meriones agreed.

"There, Kalaquinn, you have turned my own sire against me. And Meriones. I am outnumbered and overruled."

"Indeed, Alcesidas," Kal said, "if I so affect your state, then you will be glad to see the last of me."

"By the forge, Kalaquinn, who now retempers meanings? No, my dear friend, know for certain that I shall miss you deeply. But how soon must you leave us?"

"I would leave two days hence. Would that it suit you, my lord Hammermaster."

"Suit us? Absolutely not," Alcesidas replied in mock horror. "Never would suit us better. But we will make shift, Master Kalaquinn, we will make shift. Far be it from me to argue with my lord Myghternos Hordanu."

"Far be it from you indeed," King Magan said, glancing at his son. "Far be it from any of us. Rest assured, Kalaquinn. We shall see that you and your people are well provisioned for the journey you must make. Alcesidas, you will make the necessary arrangements. See to it carefully. And Meriones, attend to whatever needs my lord the Hordanu may have himself. You are a bard—you will know best how to provide what he requires."

"Yes, my lord."

"My land and my people remain at your disposal, my lord Myghternos Hordanu. Whatsoever you request, it shall be yours. And not only that, but we shall have a proper leave-taking, with a feast the likes of which these forgeland caverns of Nua Cearta have never witnessed, nor are like to witness for ages to come!"

The vast chamber of Sterenhall rang with the noise of merrymaking. Indeed, the revelry had grown like leavened dough, swelling until it outgrew the confines of the great bowled structure, spilling over into Sterentref. Every window was thrown open to the gentle night air, and every window glowed with the soft warmth of avalynn light. From each flowed and rippled the sound of festivity—voices raised in laughter and song, the clatter of crockery and the muted thud of mead and ale mugs lifted in cheer, the background wash of conversation, and a dog's barking, which was soon met by that of other dogs within other windows. And there was music—high-pitched pipes swirling around the rhythmic thrum of drumbeat, the quick whine of fiddles and low drone of the viols, cymbals' tamp and clash, bells' chime, and the feathered strum and pluck of the harps.

It was the music that, to his mind, had swept Kal out of the immense doors of Sterenhall like a great and gentle wave, washing him tumbling to rest upon the upper tier of the terraced fundament of the Hall of the Stars. Here it bathed him, as he sat looking out into the darkness, washing over him before it plunged, splashing down step over step to the shadowed town below, richly embroidering the black velvet silence of the Nua Ceartan night.

True to Magan Hammermaster's word, the celebration was magnificent. His generous providence for the leave-taking feast was second only to his providence in preparation for the actual leave-taking. The feast had begun in earnest early in the afternoon, although a steady stream of people had been arriving from all directions since just after dawn, revelry spontaneously erupting wherever the stream gathered into a pool of carousing hammerfolk. Now the celebration was at its height and would no doubt sustain itself long after the Holdsfolk had bidden goodnight and retired to seek their rest before the morrow's journey. Indeed, Kal anticipated that the celebration would continue for days after he and his people had bidden their final farewells and departed the sequestered peace of Nua Cearta and the fellowship of its folk.

Rumour had spread of Magan's own journey, a journey to the hammerfolk's homeland and of his suit for peace. In fact, it was common gossip that the king intended nothing less than the restoration of the Ancient Forge-throne to its rightful lord—Magan himself. The whispered hearsay seemed annealed into fact by the rapid mustering of forces for the Royal Guard ordered by the Throne only yesterday and also by the further bit of news, let slip from the unguarded tongue of a young captain to his beloved, that the Guard would march out from Nua Cearta not two weeks hence. All this, together with the fact that no effort had been made to quench the rumours, was reason more than enough to fire the hammerfolk's appetite for revelry and merriment.

Kal chuckled to himself as he leaned back upon his elbows and looked out to the far-flung steadings whose lights glittered like earthbound stars beneath the pitch-black void of the cavernous sky. Magan had surely kept at least half his word about the party—none finer had ever been seen. But if he were successful in his quest in the Burren Mountains... Well! The upperworld realms would shudder and quake from the riotous celebration that would then take place, rumbling below their very feet. *Magan Hammermaster! Your present jollity will seem but a quaint and quiet dinner party—*

"Kal?"

The Holdsman started from his musing and sat up.

"Kal? Is that you?"

A woman's voice drifted to him, floating on the music. Before he could turn, a hand came to rest on his shoulder.

"Marya!" Kal recognized the voice in that moment, even before he turned to look at her face.

"I thought I saw you leave. Are you all right?"

"Yes, yes, I'm fine. I simply needed to take some air." Kal scrambled to his feet and brushed the grass from his clothes. "Magan's graciousness this evening is a very rich repast—one can only enjoy so much before needing a brief respite to cleanse the palate."

Kal lifted his eyes. Before him stood a young woman. Her flaxen hair, dressed in flowers and sprigs of sweet herbs in the fashion of the Stoneholding, was wound in thick tresses, bound by ribbons, that met at the nape of her neck and flowed down her back. She wore a dress, beautifully made, the handiwork and gift of the hammerdaughters. The dress was elegant, full in the sleeve and in the skirt, the bodice following the gentle curve of the girl's waist and torso. And the fabric was of a blue so pure... Kal felt a shiver down his spine, and his stomach knotted. Her eyes were the same colour. He could not see them in the faltering light, but he knew the colour—the flax-flower blue, as if the upperworld sky had stooped to kiss the earth and left something of itself upon retreating to its rightful place.

"I-I... You look beautiful tonight. That's a lovely dress."

"Thank you, Kal." She held him in her gaze.

"I saw you the other morning.... In the courtyard, by the fountain. I was in my chamber. I saw you from the window. I-I'm sorry I didn't greet you."

Kal realized that he sounded sheepish, like a schoolboy fumbling in response to a question, and he chided himself for the artlessness of his words. He felt the awkwardness of that last meeting compounded in this one. He had ignored her, deliberately gone out of his way to avoid her these past weeks, though not for any lack of affection for her. Of that much he was sure.

"Is it true that you will not travel with the rest of us tomorrow?"

"Aye, Alcesidas has counseled that out of respect for my being Hordanu, it would be best for me to follow after the main body of the Holdsfolk to ensure the safety of the office. While Alcesidas assures us that his scouts have found no sign of immediate danger, he says he cannot know with certainty what threats may lie on the other side of the Radolan Mountains. Out of respect for his counsel and for his father, who agrees with him, I will obey his wish."

The young woman kept him fixed in her gaze. Strains of music from the great hall filled the silence left in the wake of their words.

"Marya—"

"Kal, why have you not spoken to me? You hold back from me. I thought we were... Have I done something to offend you, Kal?"

"Marya, come, let us sit down. There is a bench over there by that garden. Please, sit with me."

The two walked stiffly along a short path that led to an ornately crafted wrought-iron garden seat beside a neatly trimmed flower bed. Kal lifted his arm to place a hand on the young woman's back as they walked, but he thought better of it.

As they turned to sit down, Marya's face was caught in the glow from Sterenhall's windows. A tear stood poised and swollen, high on her cheek, then broke and traced its way to her chin. She quickly wiped it away with delicate fingers.

"I'm sorry," she said, shaking her head gently and turning away from his gaze.

"No, Marya, it is I who am sorry." Kal paused and sighed, then shifted on the bench and faced her. He placed his hands palms up on his knees before himself. "May I?"

Marya nodded, and Kal took her hands in his.

"Marya, please forgive me. Please rest assured that you have done nothing, ever, that has caused me any offence. Quite the contrary. You have always and ever been a cause of great and abiding joy to me. I, however, have caused you offence. I have been self-absorbed and inconsiderate, neglecting you in a way which you could only interpret as my feeling disdain for you. Please know that there is nothing further from the truth." Kal paused and looked into her face.

"Oh, Kal, you have been worried, harried by so many concerns." Marya's voice was soft with emotion. Her words fell like heavy snowflakes tickling Kal's skin. She turned Kal's hand over in her own and stroked the back of it with her fingers, tracing the line of sinew and knuckle. He could feel his resolve slipping. "Even if we have not spoken, I have seen it in your eyes. You laugh with joyful voice, but your heart, your heart... And I fear, Kal, I fear what my heart tells me."

"It is true, Marya, it is true. I have been overwhelmed by the events of the past few weeks. We all have been. But I, I who was but a simple homespun Holdsman, aspiring to nothing more than being a wheelwright in my father's place, I have become Myghternos Hordanu, with none of the traditional glory of the office, but, instead, a greater portion of its burden of obligation and responsibility than is meet. Our world, as we ever knew it, has been turned upside down, and it will never be the same. But my world—well, it is almost beyond fathom. I have been very confused as of late, but something has been growing in clarity within my heart, as if I now begin to come to terms with who I am, and what I have become, and what I must do.

"But in my time of confusion, sadly, many have been hurt. Those closest to me in the worst ways. I have repaid the love of others with what I know must appear to be thoughtlessness, or worse, indifference.

"And you, dear Marya, may have borne the brunt of it. I honestly didn't know how to address . . . well, what to do about us. And so I simply ignored it. It was wrong of me, and I beg your forgiveness. Please, Marya, forgive me."

"Yes, Kal, of course I do. But, Kal, I need to know, do—"

"Do I love you?"

Marya nodded once, slowly.

"I had intended to ask Goodman Diggory this fall for your hand in marriage, and, were circumstances different, I would do so still. But now we come to the crux of it. Perhaps this has been the very reason for my hesitation to face you these past many days. Perhaps I feared to say what I now know I must. I have loved you, Marya. But now my love for you is an appetite I must not feed."

Marya stifled a sob and pulled her hands free from Kal's gentle grip, burying her face in them.

"Marya, I'm sorry. Again, I beg your forgiveness. I am Hordanu. I am Hordanu of all of Ahn Norvys, and as such there is much that I may not and, indeed, cannot determine for myself. My path goes out into a very strange world, and where it leads I know not, other than that it leads into sure and real danger. I have been summoned by the powers of providence, indeed, by the fateful voice of Wuldor himself, to attempt deeds that I fear may prove to be more dangerous than you or I could possibly imagine. And to wrest from the future's cold grip even the remotest chance of success in achieving great deeds demands great sacrifices. And chiefest of these, that taking most toll of me, is you, and my love for you. I go out on a quest from which I will likely not return. You must remain with the Holdsfolk. These are your people. They are no longer mine. I beg your forgiveness for this cruelty."

Kal leaned forward as he stood to leave and gently kissed Marya on the forehead, then whispered to her, "If you have loved me, love me no more."

EIGHT

The narrow passage rose at an even grade, its close darkness broken only by the gentle gleam of helm-lamp and filled with the sound of staggered footfalls and laboured breathing. Kal and Gwyn kept a close step behind Alcesidas. The two Holdsmen had followed him through the long tunnel that had originated in a hillside on the steading of Volodan the forgemaster, which lay deep in the borderlands of Nua Cearta.

Unlike the occasions of their journeys to and from the Cave of the Hourglass, there had been no steep pitches to scale, no narrow ledges to traverse, no fathomless pools to skirt, only a steady plodding climb. It was a straight-run passageway, hewn uniformly from the rock, without branching side paths to break the monotony of the lightless gloom. Like a tomb, the place had pressed on them with a feeling of confinement, in stark contrast to the brightness and beauty of the forgeland kingdom hidden in the heart of the mountain from which the tunnel led.

The tunnel broadened abruptly into a chamber. Alcesidas paused at the foot of a set of broad stone stairs. "We are nearly there," he said. In the feeble glow of the helm-lamps, Kal could discern that the stairs spanned the breadth of the chamber. On either side, the short flight of steps was flanked by a solid mass of stone that rose plumb to meet the square-hewn underside of Mount Thyus and ran to an unbroken stone face that blocked their path just beyond the top of the stairs. This was the end of the tunnel, and apparently a dead end.

"Come," the prince bade his companions as he turned and

ascended the stairs to a landing, his helm-lamp pooling its light before him. They faced the rock wall. Its surface, at one time chiseled and worked to a smooth finish, was now cracked and fissured and marred by the heavy hammer strokes of hurried stonework. Alcesidas bent down and seized a protruding knob of stone.

"Let us shutter our helm-lamps and keep silent vigilance. Once the portal swings open, I shall make certain the way is clear. Follow me closely." Alcesidas remained stooped over, his hand on the knot of stone, and, as the lamps were shuttered, the place turned pitch-black. Kal heard a low rumbling. A faint light broke the darkness. One behind the other, the three inched through a narrow gap, their shoulders brushing against rock. They became visible to one another again as they stepped clear into a larger cavern. Shadow-ridden light filtered into the space weakly from an opening some fifty paces beyond. The opening was obscured by ragged, unworked pillars of stone that rose, tight-standing, from the hard rock floor to a roof that was half again as tall as the two Holdsmen. There was a sweetness to the air of the cave. Kal breathed deeply. They had reached the outside world at last.

Alcesidas put a finger to his lips and motioned to Kal and Gwyn, bidding them stand fast. Slowly, the hammerson prince stalked towards the light, creeping from pillar to pillar, until Kal and Gwyn could no longer see him. Then, after a few moments, he came into view again, walking towards them openly and in plain sight.

"This way, Kalaquinn! Come Gwyn! No sign of danger." Alcesidas called, beckoning with his hand for them to join him.

In a few moments, the three stood just inside the mouth of the cavern, drinking in the freshness of the open air, scanning the terrain outside.

"A perfect bolt-hole," Kal said, looking back over his shoulder into the murky cavern that served as a portal from the underground world to this open spot perched on the western flanks of the Radolan Mountains.

"Yes, a most curious natural structure. It serves to hide the entrance to the tunnel," Alcesidas said. "As I mentioned before, the tunnel was built many generations ago, but it was sealed off again as my people forswore the wayward upperworld realms and took to themselves. Sealed off so far back in the history of the hammerfolk that the tunnel itself passed out of common memory, until Meriones's predecessor discovered reference to it in a forgotten parchment."

"Years ago, when Magan Hammermaster was but a babe, so I am told," Kal said. "It was very clever of the king and Meriones to keep knowledge of the passage such a closely guarded secret, allowing its entrance to remain blocked, inaccessible to friend and foe alike."

"'Twas no great secret," Alcesidas said, fetching an uneasy glance at the sky outside, so different from the solid firmament of Nua Cearta. "We have always found it a comfort to know this way into our domain was closed. Surely you noted the fresh stonework as we entered the tunnel. That end was sealed as well, sealed under the order of my grandsire, and has remained sealed, until now, when need has arisen for a straight and sure means of passage to the upperland world." The crown prince returned his attention to the Holdsman at his side. "But know this, Kalaquinn, by the anvil and the forge, as long as you shall live, and your successors after you, this tunnel will remain open, as will my forgeland kingdom of Nua Cearta, in warrant and proof of a lasting friendship."

Gwyn nudged Kal and pointed to a circular smudge of charcoal to one side of the mouth of the stone chamber. Kal was happy for the interruption. He had begun to grow uncomfortable at the extravagant flourishes of emotion to which the hammerfolk seemed wont. While he appreciated the sentiment's underlying truth, its excesses had become increasingly cloying.

Kal stepped to the remains of a campfire and turned up its black dust with the toe of his boot. "Someone's laid a fire here, I see."

"A good two weeks old, it seems, from report of our scouts. No directly pressing threat to us. All the same, 'tis a baleful sign, one which bids us use caution."

"Indeed, we must, Alcesidas. It is, as you said, a treacherous path from here," Kal said, surveying the slope that fell away before the cave, rocky and precarious. "Open and exposed, in plain view of any lurking foe. Yet, despite the danger of being seen, 'tis well that the body of Holdsfolk went while yet there was some daylight by which they could mark their footing. It looks a more daunting course than was even the Ellbroad Bridge."

"Aye, there stands not a chance that it could be traversed under cover of night," said Alcesidas, "leastwise not without grave mishap. Especially not with children in company."

"I hope they are safe."

"Ease your mind, Kalaquinn. They were well escorted. Lesk and Hannereg, our finest scouts, accompany them. Aided, too, by your own men, Galligaskin among them. Come, let us meet them as planned down below. But I warn you, this, the first part of the way, is the most perilous."

They stepped outside the shelter of the overhanging rock and for a moment paused to blink at the wavering sun, which hovered near the horizon to their left. Pine forests pricked the flanks of the Radolan Mountains and fell away to hills and plain and the not too distant ocean. Behind them, south by west, these same mountains spread their rugged profiles into the offing in broad ranks that bellied out like a ship's full sail into the hinterland of highland Arvon.

Once again, Alcesidas took the lead. They ascended first along a rock-strewn path that took them above the cavern that concealed the portal to Nua Cearta. As they climbed, Kal realized that the great stone that formed the roof of the cavern was a smooth, nearly perfect oval slab of rock that jutted from the side of Mount Thyus, supported by the rough pillars beneath it.

"Perfect for a giants' game of 'a duck and a drake and a half-penny cake,'" muttered Kal.

"How is that, Kalaquinn?" asked Alcesidas, looking back over his shoulder.

"The slab over the cavern there. 'Tis shaped like a skip-stone."

"If only you were a giant." Alcesidas smiled. "A good name for the place, though. The Skip-Stone."

Their path now hugged the mountain. Its sides sloped steeply to a cliff's edge that dropped to a tangle of thickets and forest below. This part of Mount Thyus rose barren and without veg-etation, except for the wiry tussocks of grass where they trod, a place too lofty and windblown to allow bushes or trees a roothold. Kal kept his eyes fixed to the trail at his feet. The ground was scuffed, the hardy turf bent. It would not take an experienced eye to recognize that a crowd of people had passed this way. He cast a glance at the sky, looking for a cloud in hopes of rain to wash away telltale sign, but there was none.

The men kept silent as the path wound its way down the stark upper slopes and broadened, losing steepness. Taller grass and low-slung bushes now dogged their steps. In places the ground grew sodden underfoot. Here fresh footprints marred the soft earth. Kal shook his head grimly. Even a blindfolded, city-bred Dinasantrian would be able to read the sign. He found himself haunted by a fleeting shadow of dread, hoping fervently he had made the right decision when he insisted that his people take refuge in the Marshes of Atramar rather than letting them remain in the safe haven they had found in the forgeland kingdom.

In the fading light, they stopped to survey a quiet vale hidden in an overgrown rift. Running water tinkled lightly nearby. Leafy aspens whispered softly to mottled ranks of birch and fir. Following the murmur of the water, they came to a hill fountain that bubbled from a natural wall of loosely locked stones, spilling into a pool edged with banks of water mint not yet dressed in its pale amethyst bloom. At the men's passing, the bruised herb incensed the night air by the water's edge.

"Lesk? Are you there?" Alcesidas stopped and called out in a soft voice.

"We are here, my prince." The ranger emerged on the other side of the pool, from behind a great boulder resting against the crumbling mountainside. By his side was another hammerson scout, likewise clad in green, rendering them both virtually indiscernible in the faltering light of the upland glade.

"Kal, is that you?" said a third figure, a taller man, who stepped out now close on the heels of Lesk and his fellow scout.

"Galli! Briacoil! Is everyone safe? Who have you brought with you there?" asked Kal as yet another man stepped out of the gathering gloom.

"Briacoil, Kal. Galli insisted I come along. Said you might need an old soldier to keep you out of harm's way," Frysan hailed his son. The party of men that had stepped from cover now walked around the small tarn.

"How goes it, Lesk? All is clear?"

"As far as we can tell, my prince. But caution is in order."

"They have been here, Alcesidas," Galli said. "But the sign is old. It would seem that the enemy have abandoned their search for us hereabouts. Still, it would be foolish not to tread carefully in these woods."

Kal felt Alcesidas's unease abate somewhat at the report, as did his own. The prince had laid aside his bow and helm and now stretched himself prone on a smooth rock that overhung the pool beside the spring. Scooping up the cool water into his cupped palms, he slaked his thirst and sighed contentedly. "Ah, Kalaquinn, a fine mountain-filtered brew. And it goes down better than a draught of the Hammermistresses' choicest bragget. By my hammer, 'tis drink fit for a king!"

"Or a hammerson prince and heir apparent," said Kalaquinn.

"I had not thought it would be such hot work getting your precious self out of Nua Cearta," rejoined Alcesidas, wiping the dripping water from his whiskers with the back of his sleeve, rising as he did so from the stone slab to make way for his companion.

"Nor I, Alcesidas. Gwyn and I were hard pressed to keep stride with you. There must be gathgour in your ancestry somewhere." Kalaquinn stepped onto the rock and stooped, loosening an emptied drinking gourd from his belt. Having slaked his thirst, he refilled the gourd and passed it to Gwyn.

The forgeland prince chewed thoughtfully on bites of a tharf cake he had procured from the highland codynnos slung over his shoulder. He rummaged again through the haversack and produced two more of the rye and barley cakes. He offered these to Kal and Gwyn with outstretched arm, then turned to take his rest on a boulder well-cushioned with moss.

"Remember, Kalaquinn, if you are ever sore beset and need to return untimely to our kingdom, seek out the Skip-Stone. Could you find the place again, had you not me as your guide?"

"I think so. Using landmarks as a guide," said Kal, pointing with his tharf cake, nodding back towards the heights that lay east of them. "That bulging nose of rock beneath that icefall—that marks the north face of Thyus."

"Indeed, Kalaquinn, find Thyus and you will find the Skip-Stone." Alcesidas rose from his rocky seat and stretched his limbs.

"Well, now, my dear Holdsmen, 'tis time for us to be on our separate ways, else the light shall fail us. I must return now to Nua Cearta to aid Magan Hammermaster in the preparations for his own departure. I am fearful of what fate the future may bestow upon us and our underground kingdom. The times are grown dark, my lord Myghternos Hordanu." Alcesidas, his eyes grown solemn, turned to face the black-haired Holdsman and placed a hand on Kal's arm. "All the same, I know not why, Kalaquinn, but there is something about you and your manner that instills in me hope. I wish it were possible for my path to run in course with yours. To find Prince Starigan. Rekindle the Sacred Fire. And who knows? From there, with the newfound prince for us to hang our fortunes on, we might make a start. We might push aside the darkness, just as Ardiel did, when he was called and when he gathered his comrades around him."

"I am sorry, too, that duty calls you homewards," Kal said, placing a hand upon the prince's shoulder.

"And you, too, are called, Kalaquinn, of this I am sure, and you shall have your comrades, too, and would that I were included in their number." The prince turned to address the others. "Now I bid you goodspeed, brothers. May you and your folk prosper!"

Alcesidas embraced each of the Holdsmen in turn, exchanging warm words. He turned last to Kal, whom he held fast for a lingering moment, then released.

"Briacoil, my lord prince. May you walk ever held in Wuldor's eye." Kal touched the palm of his hand to Alcesidas's forehead.

The hammerson prince bowed, then turned away with his two scouts to climb the sloping meadow. At the very moment when he was about to slip from sight into the twilit cover of a copse of alders, he looked back, gave a last wave and an elegant bow from the waist, then turned and was gone.

Kal followed Gwyn, led by Frysan and Galli, along the well-trodden game trail. The camp of the Holdsfolk had been pitched in the shelter of a broad gully that held an ancient overgrown trackway known as Eyke Sarn, as had been decided by Wilum while escaping across Deepmere. Kal recalled from his study of the ancient maps during his sojourn in Nua Cearta—maps that Galli had hauled over his shoulder out of Lammermorn, and which now rested in the oiled canvas sack in the encampment of the Holdsfolk—that Eyke Sarn twisted its way down from the ruins of an old and no-longer-distinguishable glence. According to Galli, the glence had become the home to a family of hard-working beavers, plaited over with a generous quantity of sticks and mud and stranded in a flooded stretch of bottomland. The remnant Holdsfolk were ensconced in a depression surrounded by alders and brambles just a stone's throw from the beaver pond.

Evening drew ever closer. The sun threw long shadows across the rough terrain. It cast the pines and spruce spread out below them in a dusky bronze haze. The rising wind, heavy with the scent of evergreen, felt cold on their faces. It rustled through the stand of aspen and birch that girdled the hidden hollow. Above the whispering of the wind, a solitary loon cried its haunting complaint from a lonely alpine lake. In the deepening murk, they clung to the beaten path, entered a thick swath of upland forest, then emerged again onto a high-grassed meadow.

On the verge of the falling meadow, Frysan came up short and put his hand to his lips, bidding them keep silence. There was movement ahead—a parting of the brush at the edge of a covert that lay below them. Three elk emerged, spooked and running fast, their creamy rump patches fluttering in the breeze. Then, startled by the eddying backwash of man scent that came from the Holdsmen standing uphill but downwind of them, they wheeled and disappeared down a wooded slope below the clearing. Something had flushed the elk from cover.

Kal felt the light prickling awareness of an unseen presence and carefully unslung his bow, holding it ready in his hands. The others had done the same, each peering into the thickening twilight. No one dared speak. A branch snapped, and something grunted sharply. Thrashing though the woods from which the animals had bolted, a dark shape emerged. The four Holdsmen edged their way towards the partial cover of a large clump of juniper. The figure drew clumsily away from them through the undergrowth that fringed the clearing. Kal marked its progress down the shoulder of the slope.

The Holdsmen dropped into a crouch and crept closer through the tall grass. Now the figure could clearly be seen, a man dressed in colours that blended with the woods. They stood too far away yet to make out his features. Whoever it was, he showed curiously small concern for stealth. When he did turn to examine his back trail, he did so with clumsy haste. It seemed that he was travelling from the vicinity of the Holdsfolk's camp, although he had not been on the beaten path of the game trail. They dared not call out a challenge, for fear that the man proved to be foe rather than friend.

The man dipped from sight beneath a crowning ridge. Frysan stayed his three comrades with a commanding hand. They waited a short while to determine whether there were others following in his wake. All remained still. Frysan waved them forward and took the lead in following the man's trail. Their path began to descend rapidly, winding its way around scarps and boulders and dense copses. The fellow was certainly moving fast, slipping from them recklessly through the gloomy woods. An owl hooted fiercely and wheeled in flight across the face of the darkening sky.

The Holdsmen pressed on in an attempt to gain ground and catch up with the fleeing man. Struggling through briar and thicket, they too were no longer worried about making noise. It would be lucky if they didn't break their necks, thought Kal. All the same, he trusted his father's sure foot, his instinctive feel for the terrain and its pitfalls, even in the declining light.

In a few steps, they emerged from the trees and undergrowth, as the terrain levelled off in a small clearing before a steeply curved and imposing bluff. The bluff rose dark and immovable from the spine of the mountain, closing off the area before them. Set into this wall was a blacker space, a cave opening, which yawned in the uncertain murk and gave the impression of extending far back into the escarpment. At their feet, a small stream ran past them through the sheltered meadow. It broadened out, as it brushed past the leading edge of the bluff to their left. There, the brook lost itself amid a tumble of rocks that crested the edge of a ragged talus slope at the far end of the cliff face and fell burbling down the mountainside. The man, their quarry, was nowhere to be seen.

Senses alert, the Holdsmen stepped into the flow and waded carefully through the stream, its ice-cold water tugging at their ankles. Gwyn grunted softly and motioned for them to come and look. He had found tracks on the far bank, tracks leading from the soft soil of the brookside in the direction of the cave. Kal's eyes fixed on the opening in the cliff face.

He stiffened, sensing an almost imperceptible flicker of movement in the recessed darkness. Something lurked in the veiling shadows. There was a scuffling sound and a faint glint of reflected light that glimmered, disappeared, then gleamed again. Something emerged from the cave in awkward jerks, a blackness resolving out of the blackness, thickening and taking shape. The thing lurched forward, struggling out of the cave, and Kal could now clearly see leathery pinions that, in fits, half-extended then folded back against a massive black-furred torso. Beside him, Kal heard Frysan catch his breath.

"The night drake..." his father whispered, as the four men dropped to a crouch. At a gesture from Frysan, the men fanned out, each finding what cover he could. A figure sat bolt upright on the creature's back, goading the beast in their direction through the dusk. There was no mistaking the profile; Kenulf was mounted on the night drake, wrestling to stay seated in his saddle as the beast lumbered forward. Kal could hear him talking, but whether to himself or to his terrible mount, he was unsure. It was impossible to make out all that the traitorous Holdsman was saying, but Kal could discern, through the tone of imprecation, certain words and phrases as the impassioned voice rose above the noise of the monstrous creature.

" Ferabek . . . Enbarr . . . no more . . . I found their nest, I did! . . . me, a fool? . . . Thrag, we catch them, we will . . . Ferabek, when . . . kill them all . . . Enbarr . . . me? No more!"

Kal glanced at his father. Frysan held a hand raised then placed a finger to his lips. In silence, he reached over his shoulder and drew an arrow from his quiver. The other Holdsmen followed his lead. "Must stop him." Frysan mouthed the words to his companions on either side of him. The creature had lurched clear of the cave opening and now stood erect not twenty-five paces away, its bulk blocking a clear view of its rider.

"Up, Thrag, up!" the man commanded, his voice quavering. The night drake lowered its immense shaggy head, swaying it from side to side. "Quickly now! To air!" Kenulf cried. The beast blew a gust of steam from its nostrils into the cool dusk air. It pressed its body closer to the ground, then lifted its black muzzle, testing the scents carried by the evening. The creature's long ears lifted, and it took two ponderous steps forward, sniffing to the left and right. The beast was terrifying. Kal's stomach churned cold, his palm slick with sweat on the grip of his bow. Kal glanced at his father again. Frysan remained frozen in place.

"Up, I say! Up, Thraganux! Up!" Kenulf cursed the creature in an attempt to make it do his bidding. The beast bent its head around, snorted at its rider, then drew itself together and thrust upward with a mighty leap, hammering the air with its powerful wings.

The night drake rose higher, Kenulf now visible clinging low to its back. Frysan drew the arrow on his bowstring and let fly. The shaft sailed over the creature's shoulder, narrowly missing its cringing rider. Frysan broke cover as he drew a second arrow.

"Stop him! Bring him down!" he yelled, but before any of the Holdsmen could release a shaft, the creature wheeled low over them and screeched, a piercing cry splitting the air. Kal staggered and fell from a blow of the creature's wing. Beside him, Frysan had been flattened to the ground. Gwyn and Galli also dove to the ground as the night drake passed inches over their heads, churning the air with its wings, lifting itself and its rider up over the trees behind them. Again the clearing was charged with the beast's shrill scream.

Kenulf glanced back over his shoulder at the men, his look of surprise quickly giving way to one of mocking contempt.

"Too late! You're too late!" Kenulf screamed from the back of his frightful mount. "Now I've found your nest! There'll be no more running! No escape!"

"Shoot! Now! Bring it down!" Frysan cried, nocking another shaft to his bowstring. Frysan's arrow followed close on Kal's, but the creature was screened by the crowns of the trees encircling the clearing, and the shafts were lost amid the branches. The night drake wheeled away towards the talus slope. The Holdsmen dashed forward in pursuit, trying to keep pace with the beast's flight. The creature's movements were quick and erratic.

"It's too hard a target!" Galli yelled, fumbling with his arrow as he ran. Kal and Galli came to a halt beside Frysan at the edge of the level clearing, their attempt to close the gap on foot now thwarted by the treacherous pitch of the slope.

"Too far, it's too far off. Hold. Save your arrows," Frysan said, releasing the tension from his bow. "It's out of range. It would take a—"

Raucous screeches pealed through the air.

"It's been hit. Look!" Galli cried.

The night drake wavered in its flight, then steadied. At their backs they heard the twang of a bowstring. The beast reeled.

"Again! It's been hit again!" cried Kal.

Its rider pitched in the saddle, but clung tenaciously to the monster's back.

"Re'm ena! Well done, Gwyn!" Frysan turned to see the young Holdsman standing at their backs, reaching for yet another arrow from his quiver.

The night drake slowed, hung suspended in mid-flight for a moment, then screamed, a sound more horrible and eerily high-pitched than before. The beast wheeled in the air, goaded by its master's high pitched curses, and pounded the purpling sky with its black wings, still hovering in flight. It quavered, rocked in the air, then dove, plummeting like a stone from the sky, until it was lost from sight behind the trees, leaving behind only Kenulf's terrified screams echoing off the mountainside.

"Is it dead?" Galli asked, when stillness had resettled over them. "You must have hit it at least once, Gwyn. Did you kill it?"

Gwyn raised two fingers, a stern expression on his face.

"Twice? Still, would that kill it?"

"It fell fast," Frysan said. "I can only hope that its rider didn't survive the fall. Come, we must find it if we can. Kenulf must not escape. It's clear that he has found our encampment. Come." The four men started clambering down the stone-strewn slope. To their right, the broken brook chattered and babbled among the stones.

It was rough going, and more than once, Kal slipped in the gloom, scraping the skin off the heels of his hands as he tried to steady himself against the rocks. Frysan set a brisk pace, Galli following close behind him. The old soldier had said that it was imperative that they discover Kenulf before nightfall, though to Kal's way of thinking chances of that were slim at best.

The Holdsmen paused at the brink of a precipitous fall in their path. Kal surveyed the vast tracts of shadow-cast forest that lay stretched out over the sides of the mountain. Night was falling fast. It would not be long before the mountainside and all on it would be lost to sight. Frysan and Galli started down over the edge, and Kal fell in line. Behind him, Gwyn grunted as he scrambled over and around the boulders that lay scattered over the steep slope. Kal glanced back up at him. The young Holdsman stood rooted in place, his face expressionless, staring straight ahead into the gathering gloom over the mountain. Slowly, he turned around and looked back up the slope.

The creature had appeared from nowhere. It stood towering over them on the crest of the slope but a few paces away, where Kal himself had stood not moments before staring out into the vacant air. The beast glared at them, its head lowered, muzzle wrinkled, and lips curled back, exposing long, dagger-like fangs.

"To arms!" Kal cried. "To arms!...to arms..." His alarm echoed over the rocky face of the mountain. The creature cocked its head sideways for a second, then growled, pulling its lips further back in a snarl.

Somehow, Kenulf had circled them. Now, the man smirked at them from the back of the night drake, as he levelled his crossbow at Kal over the shoulder of the beast. There was the sharp smack of the weapon being shot and, in the same instant, Kal felt the air part beside his head. The missile narrowly missed him, clattering off the rocks behind. Thragunux leaped from where it clung to the rocks, its membranous wings outstretched. Gwyn loosed an arrow at the creature as it fell on the Holdsmen, but the creature lurched and the shaft went wide, tearing a hole in its wing. Galli, too, shot an arrow, his lodging in the monster's chest. In that moment, Kal dropped his bow and drew Rhodangalas. The night drake's scream pierced the gathering darkness as it lifted a massive taloned foot to seize Gwyn. The young Holdsman stumbled backward away from the creature, loosing another shaft into its thick body even as he fell, tumbling like a rag doll, down a stone face, collapsing on top of Galli and Frysan in a heap of arms and legs.

The night drake's talons bit into the rock where Gwyn had stood and left three long white scratches on the stone's surface, as it drew its empty claws back. The creature lifted its head to the sky and shrieked, filling the air with its fury at having missed its quarry. In that moment, Kal leapt forward, clambering up the slope under the black mass of the night drake, and thrust Rhodangalas deep into the monster's chest. The beast recoiled from the bite of the blade, pulling himself free of the sword. Blood spilled down the length of the blade and spattered on the ground. The night drake glared, wide-eyed, at Kal, before it screamed again, its cry of pain blending with one of horror from its rider, who still clung to its back. Kal fell to the ground, seeking cover among the rocks, as the beast shook its head wildly, then pushed itself into the air, retreating from the Holdsmen with heavy wingbeats.

From beneath him on the slope, Kal heard bowstrings smack against forearms. Kal glanced down at his companions. They had recovered themselves and sent a flight of arrows speeding through the sky at the creature's retreating form, but these fell wide of their mark. Gwyn shot again, and missed again. Frysan stayed the young man's arm from pulling a third shaft. The night drake continued to draw away from them in unsteady flight, still filling the mountainscape with otherworldly echoes, although now it was losing speed and height. In the gloam, the creature careened wildly for an instant and then plummeted from the sky like a ship's anchor dropping unfastened from its windlass. Kenulf's cries could also be heard, cries of raw terror mingled with the ghastly screams of the wounded beast, while both man and mount fell earthwards into a tangle of trees, hidden there out of sight.

NINE

Kal and Galli were already scrabbling down the slope, drawing a line on where they had seen the creature drop. Its laboured screams could still be heard, though less fearsome now and more plaintive, as if the terrible monster quailed at the cold approach of a reality even more terrifying than itself. The men followed in the direction of these sounds. The screams grew less frequent and then ceased altogether. Stillness fell on the lonely mountainside.

The Holdsmen pressed on through the forest.

They saw it in the deepening gloom—a dark, inert shape draped over the crowns of three or four swaying birch trees and an aspen that bowed and creaked under the weight. It hung suspended over the shelving floor of the forest. A shallow catching wheeze filtered through the trees, sounding out the creature's death rattle. The breathing stilled and left in its place a wet sound of steady dripping like a trickling spring. The night drake bled heavily. Its blood, drained of all colour in the deepening shadows, drizzled with a dull steady patter onto a large boulder, where it pooled in a black puddle.

The four Holdsmen approached the spot slowly.

"Do you hear that?" Galli said, halting at the snap of a twig and the quiet rustle of parting brush barely audible above the breeze in the leaves.

"Aye, Galli. There's something out there in the woods," whispered Frysan.

"But growing fainter," Kal said, stepping forward to peer around the blood-stained boulder, Gwyn close by his side. "Moving away from us."

Even as Kal stared into the dark void of the forest depths, Gwyn grabbed his arm, tearing him from where he stood, pulling him violently away from the boulder. Above their heads, tree branches groaned and shook. The great dark mass of the night drake had begun to stir.

"The thing's still alive," shouted Kal, scrambling for cover behind the trunk of a large birch, Gwyn still holding him fast by the arm.

"It's coming down! Stay back!" Frysan yelled.

The trees overhead creaked, tilting their burden still more precariously out of level. The creature's head lolled, rolling sideways, and a branch bowed, then broke. The night drake slid crashing through the leaves and branches and thudded to rest in the undergrowth. Slowly, Kal crept towards the gory mass splayed across the forest floor. He drew Rhodangalas from its scabbard and gripped the hilt tightly in both hands.

"Careful, Kalaquinn!" Frysan called out and followed, his own sword drawn.

Kal drew near the night drake. Its teeth were bared and sharp as needles, its muzzle flared open to the gums, and its eyes stared, glazed and lifeless. But despite the cruelty of its features, Kal saw that the beast had a handsome face, a long, almost elegant snout, not unlike a wolfhound's, curving, aquiline, to a raised brow, which was crowned by two large tapered ears. The air hung heavy with the metallic tang of blood. He circled the black mass warily, pricking its shoulder with the tip of Rhodangalas to made certain it was dead. A saddle remained strapped fast to the creature's back, stout leather bands encircling the beast's girth above and below where crumpled wings met torso. A heavy belt dangled limply from the saddle horn. Kal gingerly laid a hand on the night drake's flank. Its body was entirely covered in a heavy black fur, glossy and soft to the touch. It struck Kal as strangely unbecoming the savage ferocity of the creature; in fact, were the monster a more familiar animal, Kal would have been tempted to bury his face in the silky pelt and rest there, drawing comfort from the creature's warmth.

The others joined him by the carcass. Kal placed the point of Rhodangalas on the night drake's chest and, leaning on the hilt, drove it, twisting, deep into the beast. A wheeze escaped the dead body, as if the malevolent spirit of which this beast was but a minor manifestation had fled the corpse to return to the realm of the dreosan from whence it had come.

"No sign of Kenulf," Frysan said.

Kal started at the voice and turned away from the night drake. "N-no. And no mark of injury or sign of blood on the beast's back, either."

From somewhere deep in the woods, a branch cracked, its loudness muted and distant.

"That's him. It must be. He's survived," Galli said. "He jumped, or was thrown—hush!" Galli cocked his ears, straining to listen, then relaxed his attention. "I can't hear any more. Too far."

"But we must capture him. We must stop him before he reports that he's found us, else they'll place a steel-meshed net around these hills to catch us," Frysan said.

"And make our chances of reaching safety slim at best. More like nonexistent," said Kal. Gwyn bobbed anxiously beside him.

"You mean we should set off on his trail now, Frysan?"

"Aye, now, Galli. We can't afford to wait 'til dawn." Frysan's face was set and grim. "It's clear that Ferabek gave Kenulf command of a back party—as much to be rid of him as to make him feel useful, no doubt. Left him behind to patrol these barren flanks. And by sheerest luck, he found us!"

"Which means that there's some sort of base camp..."

"And no telling how far or how close it may be," Frysan said.

"Would that we had avalynn lamps," Galli said. "It would be so much easier. I still don't understand why Magan didn't let us take one or two for the journey."

"No need to understand anything," said Kal. "For the hammerfolk, the avalynnia are a sacred hallmark of their kingdom. More sacred to them even than is their forgecraft. As far as they're concerned, the avalynn is not meant for the upperland folk, and that's that."

"Aye, do not call Magan Hammermaster's generosity into question," Frysan said.

"Come, Galli. We waste precious time," Kal said. "It should be as nothing for you to follow Kenulf's tracks. He's no woodsman. He won't get far."

"True enough." Galli chuckled. "Kenulf has a hard enough time finding his way out of the Sunken Bottle six nights out of seven. All right then..." Galli dropped to the stooped stance of the tracker. "Stay here a moment...." He glanced at Gwyn. "All of you. Give me a chance to find his trail, and then we'll set out after him."

The last smouldering embers of daylight were fast being snuffed under the gathering cover of night as Galli struck out into the surrounding woods. Dimly, Kal could discern his movements, erratic yet fluid, as he swept the forest floor, looking for a stirred leaf, a faint impression in the ground, scuffed and exposed humus, a broken twig, or bent underbrush—anything that might indicate the direction of Kenulf's flight.

No sooner had Galli disappeared into the forest gloom than he was calling out to them. Kal, Frysan, and Gwyn hurried to where Galli stood looking up.

"See! Here's where he fell from the night drake. He must have jumped from its back. Happily for him, his fall was broken by this fir tree. Look at the broken branches. He picked himself up here, and hurried off this way. Do you see the crushed undergrowth here?" Galli continued to speak as he turned and led the way deeper into the forest. "And here, the overturned leaf mould—there's a snapped twig . . . And see, this bramble caught his leg. It's bent back against his trail. . . ."

Kal could see next to nothing. By now night had fallen and the darkness had deepened. Galli chattered on quietly to himself, chronicling their progress. The others kept silent, tramping behind Galli on a level course. They fought their way over deadfalls, struggling awkwardly to keep from being impaled or gashed by bone-dry branches, which, on the occasion of a missed footstep or a fumbling grasp for handhold, cracked loudly when they snapped.

They descended a ravine, groping in the dark for purchase to keep from slipping. Reaching the bottom, they followed it down the mountainside, until its sides grew shallow then disappeared. The trees thinned and gave way to a narrow clearing falling away to their left, littered with a haphazard scattering of rock. Below, there spread the cold black surface of a small lake. As the Holdsmen stepped into the clearing, lit dimly by the rising moon, Galli raised his arm as a sign for them to halt.

"Careful. He's somewhere close at hand," Galli whispered and edged forward, pointing to freshly bruised stalks of grass where a foot had fallen. Kal had advanced behind Galli no more than a step or two when a sharp snap rent the still night air—the unmistakable sound of a loosened crossbow string followed a fraction of a second later by the whistle of a quarrel.

Even as the quarrel smacked off a rock at his back, an arrow sped past him from behind. Kal spun his head around to see Gwyn standing upright, his bowstring still quivering.

"We've got to get to him before he can span the thing again!" Galli shouted, already at a flat run, leaping forward down the open field. Kal saw Galli bounding, rushing zig-zag towards a man standing slack-limbed in the moonlight.

Behind Kal, someone groaned.

Kal turned back again. Frysan, last in the file of Holdsmen, leaned heavily against a boulder, his head bowed. Gwyn had dropped his weapon and stood now beside Frysan, supporting him. Frysan pushed the boy away.

"Go, Gwyn! You, too, Kal! Leave me! You've got to stop Kenulf," said Frysan through clenched teeth as he clutched at his tunic high on his chest, a black stain oozing from beneath his fist. Reeling unsteadily, Frysan turned and seated himself, his back against the rock. Kal hesitated. The coarse, ugly fletching of a crossbow bolt protruded from between Frysan's curled fingers at his left shoulder.

"Go, I say, both of you!" Frysan said again. "Go now!"

"Kenulf's been hit!" Galli called out to them from below. "There's blood on the ground here."

Kal looked at Frysan again, then turned and ran the sloping length of the field, Gwyn close on his heels, to where Galli stood peering down towards the black surface of the tarn.

"Gwyn! You would make your father proud!" Galli clapped the mute boy on the back. "And fast! You could have had no time to see him before you drew and let loose. How did you know he was hiding there? Watch your step, Kal. Watch the edge. It's a steep drop."

"But what happened? Where is Kenulf now?"

"As far as I can tell, he's there somewhere." Galli pointed down the embankment. "Look here. After he was hit by Gwyn's arrow, and hard enough to make him drop his crossbow, he stumbled back. It's easy to see from the trail of blood here," said Galli, sitting on his haunches and pointing to dark stains on the ground. "He had no other path of escape—"

"No other path of escape..." Kal said, then looked back across the field. "Reckoned he'd have to make a stand here or let himself be taken."

"Aye, he must have known we'd be following him, gaining on

him. It was just a matter of time. He panicked. Tried to ambush us, and took an arrow in the attempt. Then he staggered, two... three steps, wounded, and over the edge here." Galli had risen and followed the blood on the grass to where the ground dropped off into darkness.

"Anything to get away from us."

"Aye, he knew the stakes. At all costs, he wanted to escape being captured."

Kal stared down the tangled bank, lit only enough to invest the uncertain shadows with a sense of fathomless danger.

"He's down there somewhere," Galli said, his eyes squinted.

"Aye, Galli. How far away is that water?" Kal pointed to the oily black sheen in the distance.

"A goodly bow's shot, I'd guess. Perhaps a furlong."

"We should find him, make sure he can do us no harm."

"Are you mad, Kal? And break our necks in this dark? Odds are he's more dead than alive. Leave him be. He's in no shape to do us harm."

"But he may try to attack—"

"He won't. He can't. Not after that wounding. And without a weapon?" Galli picked up the lowland crossbow with a look of disdain and heaved it into the darkness. It crashed to rest in the undergrowth.

Kal looked up sharply. "Why'd you do that?"

"Useless to us without bolts," Galli said. "An ugly weapon anyway, like everything from the lowlands. Kenulf, you black-hearted traitor!" he muttered through clenched teeth into the night.

Kal stared into the darkness and at the water below. He shook his head slowly. "I don't know, Galli. We have to be sure he can't—"

"All right, all right," Galli said. "Perhaps in the morning. It would be foolishness to look for him in the dark. We'll look for him in the morning, though I doubt that he'll even be alive by then."

"You reckon Kenulf will be dead by morning?"

"If he isn't already."

"My heart misgives me, Galli. You are sure?"

"Sure, I'm sure."

Kal turned away from the edge. "All right, then," he said. "Let's get back to my father, quickly."

"Gwyn's gone back already, I think. What's the matter?" Galli said.

"He is wounded also."

"Wounded? By whom?"

"Kenulf...and misfortune."

They ran across the clearing to where Frysan lay on his back. Gwyn knelt beside him, working the keen edge of a hunting knife around the shaft of the quarrel jutting from the older Holdsman's shoulder.

"Ha-have you scor...Have you scored it?" Frysan asked in halting syllables.

Gwyn nodded.

"Deeply?"

Gwyn nodded again and laid the knife aside. Frysan exhaled slowly with relief as the young Holdsman let go of the shaft. His head rolled to the side, aware of Kal and Galli beside him.

"Did you get him?" he asked.

"He went over the bank at the end of the field, but he's dead. Mortally wounded, at least," Galli said. "How do you feel?"

"Like I've been shot with a crossbow bolt." Frysan grinned, then grimaced in pain, sweat standing out on his forehead. "Kenulf, the bungler. The only way he could hit his mark was to have a boulder get in his way." Frysan's eyes returned to the boy leaning over him. "All right, Gwyn, now break off the fletched end." Frysan stifled a groan as Gwyn gently seized the shaft of the dart and broke it with a quick snap.

"Good, Gwyn, good..." Frysan half choked on the words, then, panting, looked back at his son. "Kal, help him. The point is not all the w...all the way through, but the barbs are caught. You'll...you'll have to push it through and draw it out...out my back. Gwyn, give me the butt end."

Gwyn pressed the broken fletched shaft of the quarrel into Frysan's left hand. Frysan raised it to his mouth and placed it, rattling, between his teeth. He nodded.

Kal rolled his father onto his side and gently pried the fingers of his right hand away from the broken stump of the bolt protruding from high on his breast.

"Now," Kal said and placed his weight against the jagged wooden shaft, pressing it until his hand lay flat against his father's chest. Frysan clenched down on the shank between his teeth and shook his head, but made no sound. Kal felt the stump disappear from under his hand as Gwyn, using the edge of his tunic for purchase, pulled the barbed iron point free of Frysan's flesh and drew the shank through his body. Blood rushed from the two wounds that the heavy arrow had made in entering and leaving Frysan's body. The wounded man loosened his jaw, letting the dented wood fall to the ground. Noiselessly, he mouthed the words "Good" and "Thank you" and then slipped into unconsciousness.

"We must staunch the bleeding," Kal said.

Already Gwyn was tearing strips of cloth from his tunic to stuff over the wounds. As he looked up at Kal and Galli, anxiety etched the boy's face.

"Good, Gwyn. Galli, you stay with him, help him." Kal stepped away from them as he spoke, making for the near verge of the clearing where a tangle of weeds grew. He searched hurriedly for hedge nettle and, finding a plant, stripped it of its foliage. With fists full of the herb, he ran back to where his father lay.

"He's one tough man, but he's bleeding badly," Galli said as he crouched beside Gwyn, each of them fussing over a wound with pieces of now-sodden cloth. "I can't see. It's too dark, and there's too much blood."

"Here, let me take over now," said Kal. Gwyn and Galli made way for him. "This may stop the blood better. Woundwort." Kal peeled away the blood-soaked cloth and carefully packed first one wound then the other with the delicate leaves. Frysan groaned, still unconscious. Kal paused, then continued his task. The flow of blood was lessening.

"We've got to stay here tonight. He can't be moved."

"What if I went back to the tunnel and tried to fetch Alcesidas?" Galli said.

"It's too dark. And too dangerous. He cannot be moved, and the hammerfolk, for all their wisdom, have no knowledge of herb lore or leechcraft that I lack. They cannot help us. Right now, we'd best stay here together, light a fire, tend his wounds, and make camp."

"But we're exposed here. There's no telling who may be about. We can at least move into the forest a bit—right there. There's a good spot." Galli pointed to a hollow at the edge of the moonlit clearing. It was sheltered by trees. And it was close by.

"All right then, Galli. You go ahead and get a fire going over there. Carry our things with you. Gwyn and I will carry him over," said Kal. Galli snatched up weapons and codynnos, slung what he could over his shoulder, and loped away.

"Gwyn, you stay here with him for a moment."

Kal rose to his feet again and stepped to a nearby balsam fir that had found root amid the rocks. He pulled his hunting knife from its sheath and pricked three large blisters on the trunk. He scraped the thick resin onto the blade, and, cupping a hand beneath it, he returned to the wounded man and applied gobbets of the gummy liquid to the wounds, fixing the plugs of hedge nettle. This seemed to stop the bleeding entirely.

"Now, carefully, Gwyn, you take his legs."

Minding the wounds, Kal lifted his father with Gwyn, staggering a bit under the awkward weight, and carried him some thirty paces to the depression. Galli had drawn flint and iron from his night pouch, together with a small tinder horn. He had struck a spark and fanned a curl of smoke into an eager flame, which he now fed with dry kindling and deadfall wood. Galli had already cut and prepared a bed of soft fir boughs, upon which Kal laid his father down.

While Galli built the fire, Kal and Gwyn cut boughs and undergrowth with their swords. They banked up the sides of their hidden hollow, making a low circular wall of brushwood around the lip of the depression in an attempt to make the small fire less visible to any enemy who might chance to come upon them.

When they had done this, Kal returned to his father's side and, in the wavering light of the campfire, attended once more to the wounds. The bleeding had started again, but not heavily, and Kal soon had the dressings repacked and bound in place.

He sat back quietly for a moment, watching the balanced ebb and flow of Frysan's breathing. "It's a bad wound, but I don't think it's mortally serious," Kal said.

"You tended him well, Kal, very well. You're every bit as good a leech as Wilum ever was," said Galli as he and Gwyn warmed their hands before the licking flames.

Kal shook his head slowly.

The fire provided a welcome focus of light and heat, but in its glow Kal was shocked to see how pale and drawn Frysan's face had become, the keen, frank moulding of his nose and cheekbones now shadowed with pain, his thick hair sweat-soaked and limp.

Kal and Galli sat in silence, staring into the flames. Gwyn stood, took out his sword again and busied himself cutting boughs to use for bedding. A short while later, he returned and sat on his heels by the fire. His stomach growled loudly.

Kal sorted through his codynnos and pulled out the last tharf cakes they had been provisioned with by the hammerfolk. He passed these to his companions, holding one for himself, which he bit into and chewed disinterestedly. The cakes they washed down with what remained of the springwater they had taken on parting with Alcesidas. This served to blunt the edge of Kal's hunger, but the cakes were few and the water little. They had not planned on being separated from the main body of the Holdsfolk for more than an hour, or two at the most. The others would be wondering what had happened.

"What are we going to do, Kal?" Galli asked.

"We'll have to decide in the morning. It all depends on how he's doing. If he's better, we may be able to move him, join the others. We've done all we can tonight. For now, let's get some sleep. If you take the first watch, I'll take the middle one. I can check my father's wounds then. And Gwyn, you'll take the last watch."

Kal pushed himself off the ground, looked at Frysan once more, and then settled on the sweet-scented bed of evergreen that Gwyn had made for him beside the fire. He lay on his side. At his feet, Gwyn already breathed the slow, rhythmic measures of slumber. Across the dwindling flames from him, his father lay, a dark lump, unconscious and unmoving. As sleep pulled at his eyelids, Kal saw Galli's lithe bulk, crouched, banking the coals of the fire with a stick, now rocking back on his heels, standing, pacing to a tree on the edge of the camp, sitting with his back resting against it . . . his bow across his knees . . . four arrows stuck in the ground beside him . . .

Something poked him. Light grew—his eyes were closed, but he could see it flickering. Kal opened his eyes. Flames licked around a piece of branch wood on the fire. He rolled onto his back. The moon shone through the trees overhead. From its place in the sky, Kal could tell that little more than an hour had passed since he had fallen asleep. His eyes closed. Something poked him, harder.

"Kal."

Galli's insistent whisper made him open his eyes again.

"Kal. Wake up. Something's out there."

Kal sat bolt upright, swung around, and shook Gwyn.

"Kenulf?"

"I don't know."

"Scorpions?"

"I don't know, Kal."

The dancing flames cast eerie wavering shadows all around them on the leafy walls of their encampment. Galli sat, wide-eyed, an arrow nocked to his bowstring.

"It was a noise from out there," Galli whispered hoarsely and pointed towards the clearing. Kal had lifted his own bow, fixing an arrow to it. Gwyn had done likewise and crouched peering through the barrier towards the place where Frysan had been shot.

"What did you hear?"

"I don't know.... It sounded almost like humming."

"Humming?"

"Aye, humming. Like someone softly humming a tune."

"Do you think it could be Kenulf?"

"I don't know ... It sounded almost like whoever it was wanted to be heard—"

"Indeed, I wanted to be heard!" a voice said from behind them.

The three Holdsmen leapt to their feet and spun around, three bows drawn to full bend. There—caught in the light of their fire, looking down at them over the tangled boughs of their fortification, their three arrows trained on it—was a face.

TEN

The face did not belong to Kenulf. It was a Telessarian's, a brow-mark twined over a deeply tanned forehead.

"Peace, my lord Myghternos Hordanu, forgive me for startling you. I wanted to be heard, not shot—"

"Who are you?" Kal demanded. The Telessarian's voice sounded soothing, placating. Ferabek had Telessarian trackers among his troops. They would be looking for the Holdsfolk. And Kenulf might have escaped death and sought the aid of his black-hearted confederates. Trackers would be among them. Kenulf might be standing right behind this man, right there in the veiling darkness, right now.

"Who are you?" Kal demanded again. His arm began to burn from holding his bow at full draw. The man's face was weathered. Crow's-feet branched from the corners of his clear eyes. Kal could see them plainly in the firelight, grey eyes that twinkled with a soul-borne vitality and wisdom.

"Peace. My name is Broq. I wear the pios. I am a bard."

Kal watched as the man lifted his head slightly, and there, at the man's throat, glowing golden in the firelight, was the image of the Talamadh, a small harp-shaped brooch that clutched the man's cloak around his neck.

"Broq, a bard—How do I know that you do not lie?" Kal said. Gwyn grunted and took a shuffling step forward, bending his bow even more.

· The Telessarian's eyes shifted. He looked at Galli.

"Brother of the wood, peace. May the sun kiss your brow."

Galli started. He looked at Kal, confusion and surprise on his face.

"Brother of the wood, peace. May the sun kiss your brow," the Telessarian said again. Conviction and purpose coloured his tone.

Galli looked back to the man. His arrow point wavered.

"B-brother...Brother of the sun, p-peace. May the wind rest upon your shoulder," Galli said.

"Brother of the wind, peace. May the rain never be tears," said the Telessarian.

"Brother of the rain, peace. May the woodland ever be your home." Galli's response was swift this time, and his grip upon the bow and taut bowstring began to relax.

"Brother of my brother, peace, and may you also there dwell." The Telessarian bowed his head and touched his browmark with his first two fingers, then extended his hand towards Galli.

Silence fell upon the men. Kal looked at his companion sideways over his shoulder. "What was that?" he whispered hoarsely.

Galli slowly released the tension from his bow and removed the arrow from the string. He held both the weapon and the shaft in his one hand.

"It's all right, Kal," Galli said, bowing his head and lifting two fingers to his brow. "He is who he says he is." Galli stretched his hand out towards the Telessarian, who nodded and smiled.

"Galli, what's going on?"

"Kal, it's all right. He made the pledge of peace. It's...it's like the Test of the Riddle Scrolls, but Telessarian. No true son of the woodland can exchange the pledge of peace and be untrue in his heart. Please, lower your weapon. You, too, Gwyn. His peace is sincere."

Kal hesitated, then slowly unbent his bow, as did Gwyn. Kal's shoulder ached. He nodded and stepped aside. Broq stepped into the ring of firelight in the hollow. He was dressed in green hose and blouse covered by a leather jerkin. Over this he wore a cloak of the same green as his leggings, fastened at the neck by the pios. The brooch glistened even more brilliantly now, close to the fire, and Kal instinctively reached up to his own throat and clasped his pios.

"My thanks, Galligaskin," Broq was saying. "And to you, Master Kalaquinn, again, I proffer my apology and goodwill, as well as the hearty greeting of your mother and your people."

Kal looked up sharply at Broq.

"Yes," Broq continued, "I have come from the camp of the Holdsfolk in search of you. Your arrival was overlong in coming. We assumed some mishap must have befallen you, and I see that it has. That must be Frysan who lies there."

"Aye, it is," Kal said. "He was wounded by Kenulf—by a traitorous Holdsman wretch. But his wounds are tended and bound. He will not die."

Broq's eyes rested on the still form of Frysan for a moment. "Kenulf?"

"Aye," said Galli. "He ambushed us, but has paid dearly for it."

Broq lifted an eyebrow. "Kenulf... Yes, I saw him."

"You saw Kenulf?" Kal exclaimed.

"Aye, that I did—which reminds me...," Broq said, slipping the quiver from his shoulder and removing three arrows. Though they had been cleaned, blood still stained the wooden shafts. "These must belong to you. They are fletched in the same manner as the one that you held aimed at my eye for so long. I had a good chance to examine that one." Broq smiled and handed a pair of arrows to Gwyn. "Two there were in the back of the beast, a third was left broken in its chest. It is good that that creature is dead. I hope there is no other of its kind.

"And this," he said, looking at the arrow in his hand, "well, Kenulf was attached to this."

"Kenulf is dead?" Galli said.

"Yes, if indeed that was he in whom this arrow stuck, and I judge that it was. It was a good shot, Master Fletcher," Broq said, handing Gwyn the third arrow. "A very good shot, indeed. You caught him through the heart. He was dead before he fell to the ground, before he had even staggered over the bank." Broq turned his attention to Kal, then Galli. "He lay not two paces over the edge, caught up against a stone, concealed by the grass and the dark of night."

Broq looked back to Gwyn and, pointing to the arrows in the boy's hand, said, "These, you shall find, are precious. Do not waste them. Do not use them wantonly. And never leave them unretrieved if you can help it. Now, may I look to Frysan? We should leave if we can."

Kal and Galli moved aside for the Telessarian, who strode to where Frysan lay and knelt on one knee beside him, lifting the cloak with which they had covered him. He examined the injury with practised fingers, nodding his head in approval.

"Whoever dressed this wound did a fine job of it."

"There you go, Kal. Like I said." Galli smiled at his friend.

"But he's unconscious. And running a fever." Broq placed a palm on Frysan's brow and glanced up at Kal. Firelight played on the Telessarian's face, etching in shadow a frown of concern. "We must wait 'til morning before moving him. He'll need a good night's rest. For now, we will remain camped here." Broq rose to his feet.

"Who are you? How did you find us?" Kal said, his words edged with impatience.

"A moment, Master Kalaquinn. Let not my arrival be an occasion for you to let down your guard. From what I have been able to learn, the woods hereabouts are clear of the enemy. Still, Kenulf's presence leaves a nagging doubt. While Ferabek has withdrawn the most part of his troops from the highlands, he is no fool. He's clearly left a rearguard to forestall the possibility of your escape on the windward side of the mountains. I suggest that a guard be posted while we talk."

"Very well, Broq," Kal said, eyeing the Telessarian warily. "Gwyn, what say you to standing watch now?" The young Holdsman nodded and walked with bow in hand towards the tree at the edge of the clearing where Galli had positioned himself earlier.

"Mind you keep your eyes trained on the forest, lad, not the fire, else you'll see naught in the surrounding darkness," Broq said to the boy. Gwyn stopped in midstride and turned. He nodded again in quick acknowledgement and retired to his watchpost.

With a sigh, Broq lowered himself cross-legged to the ground before the campfire, then undid a waterskin that hung from his belt and lifted it to his mouth. From a dwindling pile of fuel, Galli threw a few gnarled pieces of deadwood branch on the fire, sending up a swirl of orange sparks and rousing the flames. Then he, too, sat by the crackling fire and poked at the embers with a stick.

Kal had fixed the stranger with a grim stare the whole while. He stood, his arms folded, across the rekindled fire from Broq. Galli glanced up at his companion.

"Kal?" he said.

Broq lifted his eyes to the Holdsman across from him, then let his gaze drop again to the fire, shaking his head slowly, a wry grin creasing his face.

"You are a suspicious lot, but perhaps it is best to be so. It was

Aelward who sent me to find you," said Broq, his hands holding the skin of water. "Aelward Lamkin, the Flockmaster of the West, 'him as lights shepherds home and carries the dropped foals.'"

"Re'm ena! Do not speak in riddles." Kal's hand fell to the hilt of the sword by his side. "Do not try my patience, Master Telessarian—"

"Stay your hand, my lord Hordanu. Know that I would have you cut, bled, and trussed ere you drew that blade. But know also that I have come in peace and friendship to your aid, to assist you in any way that I am able. What may I offer you as pledge of my true intent?"

"Stay, Kal, stay. Have no fear. He speaks in truth. He's a friend," Galli said, dropping the stick he held and scrambling to his feet, facing Kal.

"Indeed, my lord Myghternos Hordanu. Make no mistake. As a bard, I pledge my life in your service, as does Aelward." Broq rose from the ground and inclined his head in a gesture of deference, while the fingers of his right hand strayed to the glinting pios brooch.

Kal sighed heavily and eased his stance. "My apologies, Master Broq. I trust your good faith, not least thanks to your brother and my friend, Galligaskin." Kal placed a hand on Galli's shoulder, then sank to sit on the ground. The two others also sat. Galli took up his stick again and resumed poking at the fire.

"It's just that Wilum, too, mentioned this Aelward fellow," Kal continued. "And in like manner, through hints, and that only at the last, when disaster had already overtaken us."

"But, Kal, even Wilum seemed uncertain and said he didn't actually know who Aelward was," Galli said.

"And, to tell the very truth, nor do I, strange as it may seem," said Broq, unfolding his legs and leaning forward before the fire. "Know first and foremost that I serve Aelward as a wise and ageless master. But until you meet him yourselves... Well, let what I have said be enough."

"Aye, good then, Broq, let it be so." Kal nodded his assent. "Wilum said that he and Aelward communicated with each other—"

"Used pigeons to send messages to one another," Galli said, shifting a log and sending up another shower of sparks.

"I would not do that, Galligaskin," Broq said, glancing up at the young Telessarian. Galli dropped his stick.

"He said he'd been waiting for word from Aelward for some

time," Kal continued. "It was overdue, and Wilum was worried. Then he sent that last message, sent but never received. In it, Wilum told Aelward that the Holding was lost."

"A fact that we learned by other means," Broq said. "Hosts of enemy troops combed the highlands searching for you and the Holdsfolk in the wake of the assault. News has spread quickly, news of the Hordanu's death and the fall of the Great Glence. Gawmage now trumpets his victory and that of his liege lord, proclaiming 'the end of the old order.' And the Talamadh. The Talamadh has been paraded as a victory trophy in Dinas Antrum."

Kal shot a pained glance to Broq, startled, as if he had been pricked by a pin. Broq caught Kal's look, nodded, then returned his gaze to the fire.

"And Aelward has also learned that Messaan, the Mindal's lapdog and false Hordanu, intends to sing the orrthon to its accompaniment in a grand spectacle when the final highland clanholdings are brought to heel and Ferabek returns to Dinas Antrum."

The tidings hung heavy over the group.

"But how did you know where to find us?" Kal asked, breaking the silence.

"Aelward was also aware of the secret path leading from Lammermorn. Indeed, Wilum had mentioned it to him as a possible way of escape in a time of calamity. With this in mind, Aelward sent me to these parts to lie in wait and watch for you and help you out of danger. In my watchful roamings, I discovered the encampment of your folk even before they had arrived. The folk of Folamh are more adept at stealth in their caverns and tunnels than they are in the aboveground woodlands. It is good that there were no Black Scorpion Dragoons around, for I tracked the scouts with little effort and found the place they had prepared for the remnant folk of Lammermorn.

"When I came upon the encampment of the Holdsfolk, I managed to convince them of my good faith. But that only by the very skin of my teeth, I might add. You are, indeed, a suspicious lot. Especially you men. I'd give more for your womenfolk. At least they're canny enough to tell the difference between friend and foe. It was a young slip of a girl named Marya that won the rest of them over for me. Starting with your mother, Master Kalaquinn."

"No doubt Gammer gave you a good tongue-lashing for your efforts before she was convinced," Kal said with a chuckle.

"Gammer? Ah, yes, Goodwife Clout. In her might be found the Holdsfolks' fiercest means of defence." Broq smiled. "They are a good people and showed much concern for you. When you were late in arriving, they feared some mischance had befallen you. I took it upon myself to seek you out." Broq paused in his talk for a moment, and the snap and spit of burning wood filled the silence before he continued. "But now, Master Hordanu, what plan have you in mind for your people?"

Kal shifted on the ground, then looked at Broq. "Wilum suggested we make for the Marshes of Atramar and Aelward's Cot," he said. "We will follow that course."

"A good plan. It is a good plan, and one of which Wilum informed Aelward, and with which Aelward concurs. There is a problem, however. South Wold and Thrysvarshold are still heavily garrisoned with enemy troops. Among them are no small number of Telessarian trackers. Aelward has decided that the surest way for you to reach the marshlands is by ship rather than overland."

"By ship?"

"Indeed, by ship, Master Kalaquinn. One awaits us at Kingshead Cove, a small sheltered inlet that lies out of the way just north of the Black Cape."

"Aye, I remember Kingshead Cove from the map."

"Good. Aelward has arranged passage up the western coast of the highlands to a landing place close to the Asgarth Forest on the far side of the Sheerness Spur, near the marshlands. That way, we'll sidestep the places of highest danger."

"Sounds like an excellent arrangement, don't you think, Kal?" Galli said.

"Indeed, it does. We're in your debt, Master Broq."

"No, do not thank me. You may thank Aelward when you meet him. Besides, it'll be no safe and easy journey. Reaching the Cove itself will require some care, what with children in tow and a wounded man, too." Broq glanced to where Frysan lay. "There's no telling what dangers lurk even in these remote upland places. As I said before, Ferabek has undoubtedly left a rearguard. The situation is uncertain. Which is why it is time to retire. Tomorrow brings a long day and unknown perils. We'll want to return to your people at dawn's light. The sooner we make our way to the Cove, the better."

"But what about the watches for the remainder of the night?" Galli said.

"I'm better rested than are you," said Broq. "I will relieve Master Fletcher and keep this watch. You three may take your sleep. Rest while you may. You will need it."

"Wake me for the third watch," Kal said. "I'll take it 'til dawn."

Kal felt a gentle tugging at his shoulder. It felt like he had only just fallen asleep, huddled in his cloak next to his father. He became aware of the intense warmth of Frysan's body beside him. Remembering the urgency of the last time he had been woken during that night, he opened his eyes.

"Come, Master Kalaquinn. Wake up."

It was Broq.

"It's Frysan. He has taken a turn for the worse. Just now."

Kal heard low moans and mumbling beside him. Staggering to his feet, Kal rubbed his bleary eyes. The fire had subsided to coals. The air felt chill. Glancing up to the sky, he could tell from the position and pulsing brilliance of the Longbowman that the second watch of the night had ended.

"The arrow point. Do you still have the quarrel?" Broq asked as he knelt hunched over Frysan.

"What?" asked Kal, still groggy, as he placed more wood on the campfire, coaxing it into flame.

"The one you pulled from him. I must see it. His fever is worsening. He burns to the touch, and I fear that he begins to rave."

"The quarrel? I . . . I can't remember. It was Gwyn. He pulled it out and—"

"Was he careful? Did he cut himself on it?"

Kal stood mute for a moment. "I don't think so. . . . I don't know. He didn't say anything."

On the other side of the fire, Gwyn stirred, opening his eyes, then cast aside his cloak and fumbled for his night pouch. Galli, now woken from his sleep as well, slowly propped himself up on an elbow, watching from his bed of boughs.

Gwyn struggled to his feet. Before him, in his right hand, he held the broken dart that had pierced Frysan, still wrapped in the torn cloth in which he had placed it. He turned quickly to bring it to Broq and stumbled.

"Slow down, lad. Don't let one of those barbs nick you, if it's what I think it is. Pass it to me. . . . Carefully. Very slow and easy," Broq said. With delicate fingers, he lifted the wickedly shod arrowpoint from Gwyn's hand. "You didn't cut yourself on this, did you? Even a scratch?"

Gwyn shook his head.

"That is no small wonder, no small wonder."

Broq brought the thing close to his nose and sniffed at it warily. Then, bearing it at arm's length before him, with the three Holdsmen following uncertainly at his heels, he walked to a nearby boulder caught in the ring of firelight. He placed the quarrel in a shallow depression formed naturally atop the rock. From his skin he poured some water into the bowl, submerging most of the arrowhead.

"As I thought. Sumokhan," Broq muttered.

"What do you mean, 'sumokhan'?" Kal asked.

"It's a mortal festering poison, odourless and tasteless. But look how it turns water cloudy on contact. A sure test of its presence."

"You mean to say that Kenulf used a poisoned arrow?" Galli said.

"Yes, or rather that he poisoned the arrow. Sumokhan is a frightfully potent substance to work with. Too potent. Often does more damage to the one using it than to an enemy." Broq turned an eye on Gwyn. "Wuldor smiled upon you, lad. A mere scratch can be deadly. I've always held that only a fool uses sumokhan."

Frysan moaned again, more loudly. Kal turned back to his father's side, a step ahead of the others.

"If I were you, I would discard that codynnos of yours." Broq continued speaking to Gwyn. "You were very fortunate not to be harmed." Broq stepped away from the boulder towards the fire and with a flick tossed the broken quarrel into the glowing embers as though dispatching a venomous serpent.

"What shall we do now?" Kal asked tensely, leaning over his father. "How can we help him?"

"There's not much we can do. Let the poison take its course. Sometimes a stricken man may survive the ravages of the fever," Broq said.

"But not often. Is that what you're saying?" Kal said. His voice quavered with frustration and grief.

"It depends on his constitution."

"What are his chances, then?"

Broq faced Kal, looking at him squarely. "I've heard report of only one man who has survived. From what I was told, he spent days like this, in a fever, hovering between life and death."

"Is there no remedy?"

"None."

"Nothing we can do? Nothing at all?" Kal's tone betrayed his growing desperation.

"Make him comfortable. A cool compress will drain the heat and—"

Gwyn had drifted to their side and was resting his hand on Kal's arm, looking at him intently.

"What, Gwyn? What is it?"

Gwyn reached to where Kal's codynnos lay on the ground, drew it towards himself, then lifted it and handed it to Kal. Kal took the leather satchel, unbuckled its straps, and opened the flap. He looked inside the codynnos and then back at Gwyn with a puzzled frown.

"What do you mean, Gwyn? Here, you show me." Kal handed Gwyn his night pouch. The mute lad rifled through it and extracted a parchment sheet, giving it to Kal and laying aside the satchel.

"The map Wilum gave me?"

Gwyn dipped his head, urging Kal to open it.

"It's a map of Arvon," Kal said to himself as much as to anyone else, unfolding the broad sheet and looking to Broq. "We spread it out to dry in the palace library after my near drowning in Nua Cearta. I think Gwyn's spent as much time looking it over as I have."

Gwyn crowded close to Kal, grabbed hold of an edge of the opened sheet, scored with creases where it had been folded, and jabbed at it with his forefinger.

"What is he pointing to?" Broq asked, leaning forward.

Kal peered at the map. "The Woods of Tircoil on the Black Cape," Kal said. Gwyn tapped his finger insistently on the parchment, and Kal looked more closely. "It's the ancient ruins of Ruah's Well, I think. Yes, he's got his finger on Ruah's Well."

Gwyn withdrew his hand, grinning.

"The springwater at Ruah's Well...," Broq said, rubbing his chin with a hand. He seemed lost in thought for a moment, then said, "Centuries ago, the spring was renowned for its healing waters."

"For Frysan's wounds?" Galli said.

"Yes, indeed—if the Well hasn't fallen into complete ruin and its spring dried up. Its waters were once a wonderful health-giving remedy for the sick and infirm, and might still be. But it lies far off our path, a good day's journey from here, deep in the forests of the Black Cape."

"Wilum spoke of the Woods of Tircoil," Kal said. "A dark and dangerous place, by his account, filled with things unnatural. Waldscathes, he said, and who knows what unnamed perils. You remember that, Galli."

"Aye, that was something of what he said that kept my attention."

Broq shook his head. "No. Even I myself have never really ventured there," he said. "In my scouting and watching, I've skirted the Woods of Tircoil, but never have I entered far into the forest. Odd to think that there was a time in the past when Ruah's Well was a much-frequented place. But in the years upon years, the Woods have grown thick over the Black Cape, and a darkness deeper than the Woods broods over it. I doubt that one could even get close to the Well, let alone find its ruins. No, abandon that notion. It would be an impossible venture and foolhardy to even consider."

Gwyn shook his head, pushed himself off the ground, and went to stand beside Frysan. The wounded man's face was ashen, sweat-soaked, and twisted with pain.

"No," Kal said. "No, it cannot be. I can feel it. There must be a way. We have no choice. Without it, he will die."

"But my lord Kalaquinn," Broq said, his hands thrown up and his brow raised in anxious concern. "Your folk await your presence and my guidance for the journey to Kingshead Cove. Every moment that we linger brings fresh danger of discovery. This reckless undertaking that you propose will cause a delay of two days, two days at least, while I journey to Ruah's Well, or what might be left of it, and back again. No, it's madness. No, no, Kalaquinn." Broq shook his head gravely. There was no gainsaying his logic—his tone made that clear. Kal's brows furrowed in thought.

"No, I know I must do something. I cannot let him die."

"At what cost, Kalaquinn? At the cost of your people? Your father is a man of no little hardihood. Aelward still speaks with admiration of his exploits in Dinas Antrum as a Life Guardsman." Kal looked at Broq with surprise. "Yes, Aelward knew of your father many years ago, during the desperate time of the uncrowning. There's iron in his bones and sinews. You must trust that he stands a better chance than most men of surviving the effects of sumokhan."

"No, Master Broq. Galli and I, we'll carry him to Ruah's Well while you and Gwyn return to the camp of our folk. If fate is kind, the three of us will meet you at Kingshead Cove by way of Hoël's Dyke."

"What madness you speak!" Broq stood, his fists clenched by his sides. "How do you think to bear a sore-wounded man by stretcher through the unknown dangers of the Black Cape? And what is more, you are my lord Myghternos Hordanu, with a duty as High Bard towards all of Ahn Norvys. To endanger yourself like this and set Aelward's designs at nought—"

"It must be done, Master Broq. It shall be done. I will not be hindered in my purpose. In these times, my appointed role is rife with danger, whether I depart now with you or undertake this side journey. If I turn aside from this smaller task and forestall its success, I know in my heart that I cannot expect to accomplish the foreordained tasks in the larger mission I have been given. Besides all of this, as Hordanu, I am a healer, and I would betray my calling were I not to seek out any means possible to heal the one besides the many."

Broq sighed, turned away, then turned back again and stooped by the fire. "Very well, then. I see that your mind is set," he said. "Allow me, if I may, to suggest some small changes to your plan. It may afford you a slightly better chance at success, as unlikely as I think that may be. Let me and Galli bear Frysan by stretcher to the camp of your folk and from there make haste with them to Kingshead Cove. I'll need Galli's brawn for this. Meanwhile, you and Gwyn can proceed, as you proposed, to Ruah's Well. After you've fetched a skin or two of healing water, you can meet us at Kingshead Cove. Here"—Broq pointed to the place on the map—"in three days' time."

Kal folded the map along its worn pleats carefully and, reaching for his codynnos, stood. "If Gwyn and I are not at Kingshead Cove three evenings from now, leave without us. Take the people, board the ship, and leave."

Gwyn now stood beside Kal, his bow in hand and his quiver on his back.

Broq's shoulders rounded in resignation, and he shook his head. "Be it as you wish." He untied the flaccid half-filled waterskin from his belt and handed it to Kal. "You will need this."

Galli threw off his cloak and scrambled out of his tunic. He folded the tunic, stuffed it in his codynnos, and threw the codynnos to Gwyn. "And you'll need that. More than I will, anyway."

The boy smiled and slung the satchel over his shoulder, so it hung beside his quiver.

Kal stepped to where his father lay, knelt, and placed a hand on the man's fevered brow. He muttered something with a bowed head, something inaudible to the others, then rose again.

"We will leave now."

Kal turned to Galli and clasped his forearm. "Take care of my father, Galli. Take care of him."

"I will, Kal."

"Briacoil, Broq the Bard," Kal said, turning to face the Telessarian. "Watch for us before the setting of the third day's sun."

"One last word of counsel I would speak, Kalaquinn," Broq said. "Be mindful that the pios remains a potent image of the Talamadh. And though it be lost, you are still its keeper. But reveal this to no one, for by good fortune our enemy must be unaware that the office of Hordanu has survived, and this may, indeed, work in our favour. Guard the secret of your office with utmost care. Play the part of bard, but let the part of Hordanu remain hidden until we consult Aelward."

Broq placed his fingers to his browmark, then extended his hand to Kal. "Briacoil, my lord Myghternos Hordanu. May you walk this path kept ever in Wuldor's eye."

With that, Kal and Gwyn turned away and stepped through the barricade of branches and out of the sheltered hollow into the spectral darkness of night to follow the pale westering moon.

ELEVEN

Kal stopped to consider the two branching paths in the pale moonlight. Each of them appeared to lead down the mountainside. The air was heavy with the earthy reek of dew-sodden moss and lichens. It was dark, too dark to be tramping this high and unfamiliar terrain, perilous enough in full daylight—but at night? Even with Gwyn by his side, he felt a pang of loneliness and fear, wishing Galli could have come with them to lead the way. Already he and Gwyn had encountered natural obstacles that had lost them precious time. They had been met first by a sheer bluff that rose towering over them, blocking their path, and then by a swamp, impassable and seemingly endless, that filled a rift in the mountains and forced them to retrace their steps. Still, Kal knew that if they kept on the downslope they would eventually reach the Old High Road and from there Ruah's Well. Kal peered again down one path, then the other.

"Re'm ena, it's like these mountains have a mind of their own, always herding us north. At this rate we'll end up in the heart of South Wold before we ever reach the Old High Road." Kal stepped onto the trail descending to their left. "Well then, Gwyn, we'll go this way. Veer to the south."

Before Kal could venture more than a few steps down the path, Gwyn pressed forward and laid a hand on his arm, shaking his head and pointing the other way.

"What?" Kal said. "The other path? That makes no sense."

Gwyn remained undeterred. Keeping a firm grip on Kal's sleeve, he tugged him, stumbling, to the other path, until they met an

114

outcrop that narrowed the way, eventually forcing the trail over a stone lip, where it fell away amid a tumble of rocks down the steep slope.

"All right, Gwyn, leave off!" Kal pulled back, shaking his arm free. The young Holdsman released his companion and jumped down to the solid ground below. There he paused and beckoned Kal to join him. A light gleamed in Gwyn's eyes, a glint of vitality and alertness that Kal nearly mistook for amusement.

"I must confess, Gwyn, you do try my patience at times." Kal clambered down to where Gwyn stood grinning. "Go ahead—you lead, then. You seem to know where we're going better than I do."

Gwyn turned, and Kal fell in behind him as the boy shambled along the path. Their course meandered gently across a grass-covered flank of the mountain, steadily angling its way northwards, but descending all the while. By slow degrees, the shapes of stock and stone seemed to materialize from the veiling darkness. A murky light began to seep onto the sloping hillside. Kal looked back up into the Radolans. At his back, a grey glow cast Thyus and its companion peaks into soft relief. Dawn stood close at hand and would soon creep, flesh-coloured and streaked ruby, across the eastern sky.

Somewhere behind him, high on the mountain slopes, the vestiges of the population of Lammermorn would even now be readying themselves for their own flight down the mountain. He plodded on in silence, following the ungainly form of Gwyn. Perhaps this very trail, this ambling footpath that they now trod, would be the path that carried the Holdsfolk to safety, the path that felt the heaviness of their footfalls. He thought of them, their faces drifting before his mind's eye—Galli, Devved, Marina, his mother, and his brother, Bren, Gammer Clout and Diggory...Gara, Manaton, and their children...Narasin and his boys...Marya, sad, lovely Marya...his father lying wounded and unconscious...and Broq....

Broq! There was something that unsettled him about the man, although he couldn't quite put his finger on it. Yet in all, Broq was a bard, had won Galli's confidence, and had been sent by Aelward, or so he claimed. And what choice did he have but to trust the fellow? But still, something nagged him about the man.

Kal was roused from his musings by a sudden turn in the path. No obstacle checked the gently winding progress of their way, and yet the faint trail broke sharply to the left and fell, cutting straight over the rise and fold of the foothills. Below them, the path disappeared into a burgeoning stand of birch and scattered pine. The two Holdsmen followed the path until it met the edge of the birch wood. Here they stopped, each unshouldering his codynnos, seeking out what dry place they could find to rest.

The silence Kal found oppressive, and the dawn's dampness pervasive. He shivered as the sweat cooled on his neck and back. He hunched over, elbows on knees, and looked across the trail at Gwyn. The boy nibbled contentedly on the soft end of a stalk of grass and gazed back up into the mountains. Despite the gangly awkwardness of his limbs, Gwyn had proven, over and over, his stalwart hardiness. Kal admired the boy. He was in possession of a strength belied by his mute cumbrousness, a strength that was beyond physical.

"So much for marbles, eh, Gwyn?"

Gwyn smiled at Kal, grabbed the hilt of the highland short-sword at his hip, and drew it up several inches in its scabbard then slammed it back into place.

Kal chuckled, but it was a quick laugh devoid of mirth.

"Aye, no more games and play for you, lad. It's all sword and bow now. What strange bend in life's road has brought us here? Re'm ena, but it's cold." Kal pulled his cloak close, clutching at it around his neck "I just hope this path gets us—"

A chord burst into the cool dawn air like a trill of morning birdsong but more vivid and less expected, its tone light and delicate. Kal jumped to his feet, his right hand clutching the small golden harp that pinned his cloak. Gwyn stared into the empty air around them, his face alive with amazed delight.

"The pios! I touched its strings and...and this—" Kal ran his finger across the four slight wires on the harp-shaped brooch. Again, sound, ethereal and sublime, sprang from the pios and hung suspended and sustained in the air around them. Kal could feel it enveloping him. It was a warmth. He could sense it as a vibrant colour, or rather, as a wash of all colours, like a pulsing light augmenting the brilliance and intensity of the leaves, the trees, and rocks, of the sky and grass, unveiling each hue and tint as an undimmed essence. And in the pure tones, all other sounds were caught up in mellifluous accord, resounding, a harmony of birdsong, insect drone, and the rustle of the birch leaves above. Time seemed to stand still. And then, like a wave, the sensation passed.

For a long moment, Kal said nothing. Then, with his thumb and fingers, Kal plucked the delicate strings one at a time in a slow, ascending arpeggio. Unbidden, a flow of words spilled from his mouth. He sang. Words framed lines, and lines verses, as a song sprang spontaneously to his lips, tripping from his tongue.

> "From fastness falls a winding way that wends
> And, skirting stony face and flank, descends.
> Through foothill, forest, field, and fen, it weaves,
> Until, at length, to truer course it cleaves.
> A song-spun way, of Ardiel, a trace,
> A grace-fraught stain of victory, a chase
> Unyielding in its gain, its strain, its might.
> Though hidden in the dusky dawn's wan light
> Upon its very verge, we take our rest
> And by its winsome melodies are blessed.
> Despite the chill of morning mist's grey veil,
> And shadows that begrudge the dawn its hale
> Arrival, hailing dark's demise, the heights
> Will flash in thousand thousands spectral lights,
> Will sound in thousand thousands golden tone,
> Will feel the thousand thousands strength of stone,
> Will scent as thousand thousands springborn flower,
> Will spark the mind and heart with ancient power..."

Gwyn stood enrapt by the soft melody, his eyes fixed, still staring into the middle distance as Kal withdrew his hand from the pios and the music re-echoed and dissolved into the dawn.

"I know the tune!" Kal cried, breaking the stillness that had fallen over them "It's a turusoran, a journey song. It's Carric-thona. I know the tune well enough from the Lay, even though these words are strangely unfamiliar. We're on a songline, Gwyn. It's as Wilum said. We're on Carric-thona! Here, listen again." Once more he began to pluck the strings. Once more a clarity suffused the air, limning the trees and rocks with a bracing sharpness of detail. It stemmed from a source that was fresher and clearer than the rising tide of morning light. Again he began to sing the journey song, letting the melody unfold through one verse, then another and another.

> "Let ancient power amend our thoughts and wills,
> And mend our bodeful hearts, and heal our ills.
> And bend our feet upon the straighter track,
> The song-graced way before, all woe to back.
> But for the nonce, shall we our leisure take
> Amid the slender forms of this birch brake.
> Then hie we hence, our journey to renew
> Upon the woodland walk, through woodland-rue,
> Amid the paling birch that line the way,
> Until birch brake doth break onto a grey
> And mist-enshrouded lea, ablaze in bloom,
> O'erlooking forest tracts awash in brume.
> Our course declines to bend by lake and bluff..."

Kal ceased singing. "Did you listen closely to the words, Gwyn?" he asked even before the reverberating strains had entirely faded from hearing. "A journey song." He shook his head. "If we follow Carric-thona, we'll get to the Old High Road, all right. But you knew that already, didn't you, lad? You knew which turn we needed to take."

Wide-eyed, Gwyn pulled a face and shrugged.

"Aye, you. Come now, Gwyn, don't play as if you didn't know." Kal lowered his brow and shook his head in feigned disapproval, then turned, picked up and shouldered his codynnos, and clapped his companion on the back.

"Well then, let's be on our way.... How was it? 'Amid the paling birch that line the way, until birch brake doth break onto a grey and mist-enshrouded lea, ablaze in bloom...'"

Gwyn nodded, grinning broadly.

"Good. Then we're off," Kal said as he and Gwyn took to the path once more, heading into the airy wood.

The sun rose higher, heralding what promised to be a clear and bright day despite the ruddy streaks that blushed the sky's eastern face. Much of the terrain, however, still lay in the grip of mountain shadows, awaiting the sun's waxing strength. From the trees, they stepped onto an upland meadow awash in dewy wildflower. From the top of the grade, they could see formless garlands of mist drifting up from fog-bound hollows to wreathe the crowning tops of the forests spreading out below them. A tree swallow glided trimly above their heads, its cheerful song overlaid by the harsh caw of a crow.

Their path traversed the meadow, following the songline as it dropped to thread a narrow defile between a sedge-lined tarn and a high apron of rock. Because the turusoran of Carric-thona described it as a point of vantage, they clambered up its shelving side to the crest. The western horizon unfolded and lay open before them.

"There..." Kal pointed to a grey-brown ribbon running away to the north. "There's the Old High Road. And the ocean...on the far horizon there, that band of deep blue—that's the Cerulean Ocean. And there's another roadway beyond the Old High Road, but more overgrown. You can only see it here and there. Hoël's Dyke, I'd wager."

Kal continued peering squint-eyed into the distance. His voice grew more serious.

"Human traffic. There are people on the Old High Road, and in ranks. Do you see them, Gwyn? Moving too fast to be on foot. Mounted troops. On their way north towards South Wold. Foe, not friend, don't you think?"

Gwyn frowned his agreement.

"We'll have to be careful, then, when we reach the roadway."

Gwyn's frown grew deeper, and he pointed to a vast expanse of woodland, thick with impenetrable purple shadows, the canopy of an immense and ancient forest that lay beyond the long, thin strands of roadway.

"The Woods of Tircoil. Aye, Gwyn, I feel it, too. But there lies our way. Somewhere down there is Ruah's Well." Kal's eyes swept over the southern margins of the strange old forest. "But the way to the road from here looks easy and clear. In fact, if we follow Carric-thona for the first bit, straight along there..." Kal pointed, waiting for Gwyn to look where he indicated. "Then, you see, the high ridge the trail must climb? We could leave the songline, go straight along the base of the ridge instead, due west, easy going straight out to the Old High Road. And right where trees press closest to the road. Good cover. We'll cross there, then head south in the cover of the trees to the southern reaches of the Woods of Tircoil. Ruah's Well is in there, along a songline, Melderenys, if I remember aright. And we know how to find a songline now, don't we, Gwyn? Come, let us be off again."

They descended again to the path and hurried along. The morning wore on, and, before midmorning they had travelled without difficulty a good league's distance. They had left the arrow-straight path of the songline halfway along, striking out directly towards the Old High Road, beating a trail at the foot of a humpbacked ridge thickly set with stout oak and beech that swept down to the roadway itself.

They continued beneath the high-spreading limbs of the wood, following game trails where possible, until, gradually, the ridge to their right began to lose something of its aspect. Eventually, the ridge fell into a sloping hollow, from which an embankment rose, shaded by trees from the sun that blazed now overhead.

"Very quiet now, Gwyn. We must be careful. The road's right up there," Kal said. They stole their way towards the rise, keeping to cover. Kal paused at its base. "We'll want to cross it now, if we can, and head south."

Up the shoulder of the bank they crept, to the very edge of the Old High Road. Trees and underbrush crowded the uncobbled shoulder of the Road on either side. The air was still and drowsy with the hum of cicadas. Dust motes hung suspended over the roadway, caught in the shafts of sunlight that pierced the foliage overhead. To their left the Road swept towards them from a thinner scattering of trees in a dogleg turn from the south, while to the right it continued straight, as far as the eye could see, through an open stretch of ground that pushed the surrounding trees away from the Road's embankments.

For a long moment, they listened and watched. Then Kal motioned to Gwyn, and they dashed across the cobblestones to the other side. They ran south through the cover that hugged the margin of the Old High Road. On the southern edge of the greenwood, which gave way to slight stands of slender birch and aspen, they paused again, taking stock of the situation from behind a large oak footed by undergrowth that afforded a clear line of sight both up and down the roadway.

"We'll try to follow the Road now, but not so close. It'll be a fair hike to reach the way to the Well. I hope it's still there," Kal said. He shifted uneasily. "Strange to think that the Woods of Tircoil are so close, and soon we'll be—"

Gwyn cocked his head and put a finger to his lips. He cupped his ear to listen. Kal stiffened and made certain he was hidden from sight.

The sounds came nearer, became more distinct—the uneven clop of many hooves and the jangling clatter of tackle and weapons heading their way from the bend in the road to the south. A column of mounted soldiery hove into view. The two Holdsmen dropped to the ground. The line of horsemen rode past and into the shade of the trees overhanging the Old High Road. From where he lay, not half a dozen paces from the edge of the road, Kal could see the horses' hooves beating the cobbles, and men's boots in stirrups, dust-covered from miles of travel, and the occasional hem of a grey cloak. All else was blocked from view by the leafage beneath which he and Gwyn cowered. The column had all but passed by them.

"Halt! Halt! We stop here." The Arvonian words that broke the peace of the cool shade were forced and thickly accented.

Kal bade Gwyn with a gesture of his flattened hand to remain still. Very slowly, he raised his head and ventured a furtive look through the leaves and brambles from behind the oak. It was a company of horsemen, some two dozen of them, cloaked in grey hodden over grey tunics and boiled leather cuirasses, lightly armed with pikes and swords, as well as bows. All were highlanders, Southwoldsmen, except for a trio of swarthy barrel-chested men at the head of the column, each wearing mail, helm, greaves, and a scarlet surcoat emblazoned with the black scorpion. Kal suppressed a shiver. The three of them swung down from their mounts while the Southwoldsmen milled behind them in the roadway. These kept their distance from the Dragoons and, one by one, began to climb stiff-limbed from their horses.

Two of the grey-clad men lagged even farther back in the very rear of the mounted troop, reining in their horses level to where Kal and Gwyn hid among the trees. They talked in low tones to each other, their highland brogue unmistakable.

"By the welkin, it's about time we pulled up for a spell!" said a robust dark-haired man, who leaned forward in his saddle, swore, and spat loudly onto the dry cobbles beside his horse. His broad florid cheeks and chin were shadowed by a scraggly growth of dusky stubble. "We ride hard, and, as it is, we'll be lucky to reach the Crossed Daggers before midnight. And it's off again amorn, before even cockcrow!"

"What do you want, Tam? Our kind and good taskmasters need a rest. After all, they've ridden from before dawn," the other high-lander replied sourly, arching his back in the saddle, stretching. "Wouldn't want to tax them overmuch." He was a somewhat older man, but still in the flush of youth, tall and lean. As he turned to look behind him down the road, Kal saw that the man had a narrow, sallow face framed by curling reddish muttonchop whiskers. He looked fraught, but it occurred to Kal that this might have been the cast most common to his countenance, features etched and set in lines of worry. The lean man returned his attention to the three soldiers at the head of the company. "How many times will these idiots have us ride this road?"

"Bah!" growled the dark-haired man. "Who knows? As thick as birch stumps, the lot of them. Look at that one, there. Did you mark how he sits his horse? He'll have broke that poor nag's back ere we're quit of them."

"Aye, so you've said afore. 'Got the seat of a tilt-yard dummy.' So you've said about them all."

The lean man's horse tossed its head while, farther up the road, other horses stamped restively. Their riders stood beside them, gripping their reins, occasionally speaking an inaudible calming word.

The dark-haired man leaned forward once more and stroked the neck of his mount. "I tell you, the horses don't like it. Why did they order us stop here? Too close to that accursed forest."

"One can hope that if the waldscathes come, they'll take the Scorpions first. They're meatier than any of us." A thin grin creased the lean man's expression, then vanished as suddenly as it had appeared. "One can hope."

"Aye, one can hope," the dark-haired man said, then cleared his throat and spat again on the ground. "One can hope that the lot of them rot. The whole stinking lot of them. I've about had my fill of them, the vile Gharssûlian hag-seed, commanding us about in our own holding. Who brought us to this pretty pass?"

The lean man shook his head. "You've said afore."

"Aye, who was it, then?" the dark-haired man ranted, ignoring his companion's gesture of warning. "Who was it welcomed the Scorpion whoresons into South Wold? And with open arms—?"

"Hold your tongue, Tam—"

"Who was it? None other than our own—"

"Hold your tongue—!"

"—proud and independent Baron Nuath, staunch leader of his people, lapdog to the mighty Boar."

"Hold your tongue, man! Are you mad?" the lean man hissed angrily, glancing at the main body of his fellow Southwoldsmen. "You know there are spies. Everywhere. And you, you hurling insults around like a boy tossing stones at a hornet's nest."

"But think of it. I tell you, things aren't right." The dark-haired man's tone softened. He seemed to appeal now to his companion's sense of justice. "Things are not right. Look, here we are, ordered about by these outlander pigs, trotting all over South Wold trying to chase down what? A handful of survivors from Lammermorn?"

Kal's neck bristled as the man spoke, his arms and legs cramped from lying still, tense, alert. He could feel Gwyn beside him.

"Survivors? Do you really think there were survivors? Do you really think the pigs would let any escape?"

"What nonsense do you talk?"

"And here they have us hunting for them, them that were like us—highlanders. Highlanders, I tell you, sold out to the Boar by their own, by Strongbow. And how long 'til the pigs turn on us? How long, eh? How long 'til it's our necks stretched on the block? And it's Nuath, I tell you, Nuath that's sold us out!"

"Shut your trap, Tam. You'd do well to shut your trap!" The lean man reined over his horse into a sidestep until he faced his comrade. His face had grown flushed. "You know full well that you've no choice in this matter, not unless you fancy your Bridura in widow's weeds, with your little ones as orphans. You've no choice. And nor have I."

"Bah! I tell y—"

"Enough!" The lean man raised his open hand. "I can't say that I don't agree with you, Tam. I can't say that I don't. But you and your notions. They'll get you in a spot of trouble one of these days, in a bad spot of trouble." The lean man shook his head, then turned his horse and spurred it forward, mixing with the others. Most of the Southwoldsmen were now afoot, savouring the shade. Some stood talking amongst themselves, others sat leaning against trees, and three or four knelt on the cobbled trackway playing at dice. None of them seemed keen to draw near the Black Scorpions, who glowered at their highland conscripts with ill-disguised contempt.

Now was the time to creep away. Kal's limbs loosened as he

prepared to back off slowly. He returned his attention to the dark-haired man just as the man swung a leg over the back of his horse and, with a creak of leather, dropped lightly to the ground, cursing under his breath all the while. Kal froze. The man stepped towards the edge of the road, threw the reins around a sapling, and started into the woods, lifting the hem of his tunic and unlacing his breeches.

Kal lowered his head, hoping that he had completely drawn his cloak over himself and hoping that Gwyn had done the same.

The man strode crashing through the undergrowth towards Kal and Gwyn until he had come to the great oak behind which they lay. This he leaned against as he relieved himself loudly, sighing.

From the corner of his eye, Kal could see the man. Kal closed his eyes. "Thou, Wuldor, art great... Thou, Wuldor, art great... Thou, Wuldor..." The lines from the Great Doxology whirled through his mind as he lay there. It seemed interminable. Then the man finished. Kal heard him, opened an eye, and saw him. He stood there, adjusted himself, and relaced the front of his breeches, then turned, stopped, turned back, peered into the woods, grunted, and thrashed his way up to the Road.

They had been seen. Kal was sure of it. They had been seen, and in a moment two dozen horsemen would be upon them.

The dark-haired man had retrieved his reins, taken his horse by the bridle, patting its neck, then walked without haste down the cobbles towards where his fellows were gathered.

He had to have seen them. Kal lifted his head again, puzzled. Or perhaps, by some chance, he hadn't. Or then again, perhaps he had and was letting them slip away. Either way, now was the time to run. Behind them, the woods were thick with undergrowth. It would be nearly impossible for a horse to manage. Any pursuers would have to make chase on foot. If he and Gwyn could slip into the heavy growth, they just might stand a chance.

The two Holdsmen eased their way farther into the copse and crept westward away from the Road, watching every step, keenly aware of every sound. The woods, however, were not deep. After some fifty paces, they came to the far edge of the trees and found themselves on the verge of a large field, filled with tall grass and brush, dangerously exposed to view in every direction except north. In that direction, ranks of trees rose on a gentle slope, an unbroken flank of the copse.

"That way," Kal whispered, pointing north. They would have to go parallel to the road, past where the soldiers still rested in the shade. "It's the only cover. We'll put some distance between us and them then double back, west then south. Quiet now, as you value your hide."

Nerves taut, Kal stole one last glance back over his shoulder. Through the screening leaves, he could discern the fragmented forms of the horsemen beginning to mount again and form a column. Though the men still talked, he could hear nothing more than the pitched whinny of a nervous horse. He nodded to Gwyn and, leaning forward, began slipping his way through the woods, guarding his footfall against every rustling leaf or snapping twig. Gwyn remained close on his heels. Once more, Kal marvelled at the deftness with which Gwyn was capable of moving. They crept farther up the rising wood. To their right, on the Old High Road, now nearly a hundred paces from them, the company of soldiers began to move again. Kal heaved a sigh of relief. That had been a close-run game—too close.

Kal took another step, and a drumming flurry erupted at his feet. The air exploded in front of him. He recoiled from the blur of grey-brown that flew up in his face and staggered back onto a fallen branch that cracked under the weight of his step. The flushed grouse wheeled away up the slope.

Kal whirled around. There, through the trees, he saw that the column had stopped. And there, as if framed by the leaves, a lone horse stood on the road, its rider in clear view, red-clad and staring hard at Kal. Shouts filled the air, a hard-edged guttural voice, sharp and commanding. A horseman reared on his mount, turned and plunged headlong into the woods, only to be thrown from his horse as the beast got entangled in the scrub. Other soldiers had dropped from their horses and were running into the woods, hacking their way with swords through the undergrowth.

"Gwyn! Run! This way!" Kal seized his companion by the shoulder and jerked him up the forested hillside.

"Halt!" The shouts multiplied behind them. "Halt! Halt!"

Breathless, Kal glanced back and saw a clutch of Southwolds-men swarming through the woods, slashing, shouting, pointing up the slope, their excitement overborne by the gruffer voices of the Scorpions who goaded them. Kal's heart pounded as they clambered up the steepening ground. Around them, arrows sliced through foliage and thudded into trees. They would cross over the wooded ridge ahead, then try to lose their pursuers in the countryside beyond.

North. They would go north. That was where Carric-thona lay. It couldn't be far...Carric-thona...a songline, and a songline meant safety—that's what Wilum had said. If they could just reach Carric-thona again....

Kal crested the ridge and spun around, looking for the other Holdsman. He had lagged behind, struggling up the hill, dragging his leg slightly.

"Hurry, Gwyn!" Kal stretched out his hand to the young Holdsman, who fought his way up the last few feet to grab it. Together, the two threw themselves headlong over the brow of the hill and out of the line of sight. They tumbled several paces down the opposite slope, then scrambled to their feet and rushed down the ridge, angling their way westward to the left across its flank, fighting the undergrowth.

Kal slipped and narrowly missed impaling himself on a bone-dry limb, jutting sharp as a spear point from a fallen tree trunk. He stopped for a moment, leaning against the deadfall, his chest heaving. Gwyn pulled up beside him. Behind and above them, the soldiers crashed through the trees, fighting to gain the ridge. Kal grasped the brooch at his throat with one hand, while the shaking fingers of his other sought the strings of the pios and plucked them—nothing. All he could hear was the thin ting of the wires, his and Gwyn's laboured breathing, and the approach of the soldiers. A head appeared over the ridge, then another.

Clumsily, Gwyn clambered over the log, pressing forward keenly on the downslope. He turned into a well-trodden game trail, like a hound on the scent. Now it was Kal who found himself struggling to keep up. Down the trail they flew. Again, arrows clattered among the trees behind them, but not as near. They had stretched their lead.

The falling woodland levelled somewhat. The oaks and beech gave way to thin groves of aspen and birch. They ran down through a maze of staghorn sumacs into a grassy field that stepped down into a further long hollow, then swept up the side of a facing hill. They stopped. Kal looked for a bolt-hole, some means of slipping away. He made to turn aside into the bordering woods. The deep cover offered some hope of escape, but Gwyn ran ahead full tilt into the open field.

"Not that way! No! Gwyn! Not that way!"

Gwyn paid no heed to Kal's cry, but continued to speed down into the valley.

"Fine. Here we go, then," Kal said to himself through gritted teeth, and ran, trying to keep up with the boy. But Gwyn pressed on, putting distance between them. As he ran, every now and again, Kal brought his hand up and ran his thumb across the strings of his pios. For his efforts, he got never more than a feeble and tinny thrum. Kal thought his lungs would burst.

Finally, he caught up to his companion, panting like a bellows, halfway along the uphill slope of the field. Gwyn had stopped at an outcrop of rock terraced into the hillside. Crowning it was a solitary tree. Across the dell, the soldiers spilled out of the woods and into the open. Somehow, Kal and Gwyn had managed to outpace the soldiers and put nearly two furlongs between them. But now they were in the open and had been seen. The soldiers rallied, pointing across the shallow valley. From the woods came horsemen, ten—eleven of them. The horses each turned tight circles on the edge of the field, tossing their heads, then, as one, rounded and began to gallop down the field, followed by the soldiers on foot at a run.

Panic gripped Kal's gut. He gasped for air. Beside him, Gwyn smiled. Kal's mind reeled. How could the boy smile? Smile, as if not a thing in the world was wrong? The horses thundered down the field. Already, arrows streaked across the sky. They would fall short, but the next flight would not.

Kal felt trapped, not by the enemy bearing down on him, nor by the bank of stone at his back, but trapped, as though he was submerged in honey, with limbs leaden, and time slowing, slowing, painfully, to a standstill. In his eye, Kal beheld the whole— Gwyn's full-toothed grin, the arrows in midflight, the horses and their riders, the Southwoldsmen and Scorpions on foot, the blue sky overhead, an elm limned against it, and the Talamadh...the Talamadh...

He lifted a hand heavily to the figure of the harp at his neck and played a listless finger across it. Like a rose releasing its fragrance, or a fountain its crystal waters, a chord burst forth from the pios and hung suspended in the air around the two Holdsmen. Kal felt all the hair on his head stand up as a strange stillness settled over them.

In the field before them, the horses' legs stiffened and their hooves churned the sod as their riders reined them up short. They stamped and turned in their places. Soon the men on foot had caught up with them, the lot of them shouting in confusion. Over the sound of disorder, a Gharssûlian's voice grew louder, yet remained indistinct. Moments passed one to the next as the soldiers' confusion increased.

Kal looked to Gwyn, his own expression of awed confusion reflected in the boy's. The resonant tones still echoed, and Kal struck the strings again. The sound swelled like a rising breeze.

The men in the middle of the field thronged, arguing, pointing up along the grassy side of the slope, scanning its brow and the wooded verges on either side. To the front of the group moved a mounted figure, dark-haired and leaning forward in his saddle. He brought his horse around, his back to Kal, to stand in front of the Black Scorpion Dragoons, one on horseback and two on foot. He spoke with them, gesturing emphatically. He pointed diagonally across the rising grassland towards the forest to the north, then dropped his arm. The Gharssûlians looked one to the other, then barked sharp orders and moved obliquely across the field in the direction the horseman had indicated. The Southwoldsman wheeled around on his horse to the back of the forming column, and, as he did, Kal recognized him as the dour-faced man he had overheard on the Old High Road.

Kal and Gwyn watched, numb with shock, burning with relief, as the column, horses and men, trotted up the field to the left and began to disappear into the woods. As the last few Southwoldsmen were about to enter the trees, Kal saw the dark-haired man pull up his horse and turn to face the outthrust rock under which he and Gwyn stood. The horse fidgeted beneath its rider, tramping the grass. The man looked at the Holdsmen, then bowed his head, spun his horse around, and was gone. Kal could have sworn he saw a smile on the man's face.

Kal and Gwyn stood alone on the hillside. Over them, the air released its hold on the tones, and the sound of the pios faded and was gone.

"Carric-thona...," Kal said.

Gwyn grinned again at Kal and winked, then turned and clambered up onto the rocky shelf over which grew the tall elm.

"Aye, Gwyn. Good idea. We'll stay on the songline"—Kal pointed northwest along the grassy rise—"and move away from our pursuers. Let's go now."

Kal and Gwyn scrambled on a slant up the last of the hillside, following, as nearly as Kal could figure, the lie of Carric-thona. They crested the hill and dropped into a depression out of view of the long field and the path the soldiers had taken behind them. Kal slowed his pace as they threaded between towering pillars of stone that ringed the hollow and topped the ridge like the battlements of a castle.

"Time to check our song map again, Gwyn," Kal said as his fingers sought the little harp. He plucked the strings in steady rhythm as he walked, and, again, words and melody sprang to his lips.

"A solitary elm stands o'er this vale,
Vale Mengoleth, as hight by men of old.
Upon its crown, a crown—no gem, no gold—
But stone, and stony flies the raven, black,
Above the way, which drops to quarry track.
Its broad'ning flight, rough hewn, descends, until
Alighting by a cool wellspring; 'twill fill
Its cold and stony bed unto the brim..."

"Down there!" Kal cried and scrabbled down a bank of wiry grass rooted in loose gravel to a large boulder, its top lying flat to view. On it was painted a black raven, faded by the weather of years but too obvious to miss. Just below it, a trackway cut across the hillside. Kal and Gwyn followed this. It plunged into a deep, broad pit with high sides of chiselled rock, then emerged only to drop again into a further depression, a small spring-fed pond at its centre.

"Now bends the way to overslip the rim
And rising fall. But mark, by ancient craft,
The song-sung path runs true, an arrow shaft
Unto its point hard-set upon the spine.
Here 'bout, the rod is fletched in feath'ry pine,
And at its balance crosses with the bow,
Where bear and buck and boar are wont to go.
Then flies the bolt o'er fen and face and field,

Until beneath the black escarpment yield
To plummet to the ground by ancient track
And enter there the Tircoil forest black.
And thence four easy furlongs to the Heath,
Sequestered peace and from the depths relief.
Beyond this glade, there lies a goodly cot..."

The track continued, well trodden, through a stand of tower-ing pines and onto a narrow grassy plain. They recognized the orienting landmarks, following always the ruins of a tall watch-tower that sat directly before them on a distant dark-faced ridge, tapering like a stiff finger pointing to the sky. Once, traversing a long curve of rolling hills, they startled a bear, sending it sham-bling out of their path into the forest. On the crest of the hill, Kal looked back towards the heights. He scanned the way they had come for signs of pursuit, but saw none.

They pressed on in an unswerving line across terrain at times flat and easily travelled, and at times rugged, steep, and treach-erous. Now and then a trail would angle into the way they trod and follow it for a time before veering away in the face of some obstacle or rough ground to follow a less difficult route. The Hold-smen, however, held their course without deviation, ever keeping the watchtower before them, until it loomed over them, perched atop black cliffs. From the base of the cliffs, they descended.

They came to stand on the ancient thoroughfare of Hoël's Dyke, its broad flagged surface in disrepair and mostly overgrown but still proof against the vast forest that encroached the ditch on its western edge.

"A well-built roadway this, to have broken the tide of the Woods of Tircoil for so many centuries." Kal stooped and ran a finger along the seam of age-worn paving stones perfectly cut and jointed, yet remained careful not to disturb the lichen, moss, and forest debris that covered most of the surface of the road and that might show sign of their passage.

There was no telling how far behind them the Black Scorpions and Southwoldsmen might be, or what other foemen might chance upon their trail. They had sidestepped the threat of Kenulf, only to raise the alarm farther along their way. The intensity of the chase earlier that day had left little doubt that he and Gwyn had not been mistaken for unwary woodsmen gathering faggots for the hearth. No doubt, the woodland and countryside of all of South Wold, and, indeed, of every one of the highland clanholdings west of the Radolans, were under the rule of Ferabek's troops, and every man, woman, and child would have been accounted for. Any travelling stranger would be a wanted man. But maybe this was to their benefit. Perhaps their having been discovered might provide the distraction necessary to divert attention away from the Holdsfolk and help their passage go undetected.

Kal stood and looked into the ancient forest beside the old road. Great boled trees stood spaciously apart, their branches interwoven in a high dense canopy of green, its shade too deep to permit undergrowth on the forest floor that receded, gently rolling, into the cool depths. The forest's darkness was broken only by the occasional thin shaft of sunlight that pierced the deep shadow far back among the trees, each illuminating a small patch of woodland grass or flower. It seemed hardly likely that such an apparently pleasant place should harbour anything as dire as the terror that was supposed to be the waldscathes. Such a place would surely be inhospitable to such a sinister reality.

"The dread Woods of Tircoil. This is them. It doesn't look so bad."

Gwyn, his wrist cocked over the hilt of his shortsword, gave him a look askance.

"What? Waldscathes? I'd chalk that up as an old wives' tale. Does that fireside story still scare you, lad?"

Gwyn didn't change his expression, but looked again into the Woods.

"Aye, well, I'm not entirely settled on that matter yet myself." Kal knit his brows in thought, then squinted into the sky overhead. The sun shone warm with a drowsy summer's heat.

"We've the better portion of the day left to us, Gwyn, and a fair hike yet to reach Ruah's Well. Down Hoël's Dyke to the songline of Melderenys, and from there we strike a distance into the Woods. What say we take a rest?"

Gwyn looked alarmed. He gestured back the way they had come, grimacing.

"Not here. I don't mean here. Let's follow Carric-thona a little bit more. Just four easy furlongs—but half a mile—to a quiet glade, as in the journey song."

Gwyn's look of alarm didn't lessen.

"We've nothing for it. We have to enter the Woods sooner than later. Why not here? Along the songline? We'll ease our limbs at the glade without fear of capture. If the Southwoldsmen are anywhere about, they won't dare come into the Woods of Tircoil."

Gwyn still frowned, and now shook his head slowly.

"We'll keep to the songline, Gwyn. You've seen its power. No need to worry about waldscathes, not on Carric-thona, not in broad daylight. Besides, it's only a short distance, and it'll give us a chance to shake off possible pursuit."

Gwyn sighed and shrugged, slid his bow from his shoulder and checked how its string sat in the grooves of first one tip and then the other. He bounced the bow in his hand at the grip, reached over to the quiver on his back, drew forth an arrow, and nocked it to the string. Holding his weapon, he moved towards the far side of the causeway.

Kal stepped behind the younger Holdsman and paused to strum the pios. He smiled in approval, the notes hanging sweet in the sun-charged air. They were still on the songline.

"Go on. I'm right behind you."

Gwyn stepped down the breastwork of the Dyke to an even stretch of forest tenanted by enormous oak trees, gnarled and wizened, like old men with unkempt mossy beards. Not a few dozen paces into the Wood, they were surprised to discover that the line they walked had become a clear and heavily travelled game path. Animals of all kinds had left their tracks in the soft soil. Kal chuckled; Galli would have been beside himself at the wealth and variety of spoor.

The Holdsmen walked in silence for several minutes. Kal savoured the cool stillness of the Woods, particularly after the early start that morning and the terror that followed. A rest would be welcome, but they could not stay their journey for long. Thoughts of his father haunted him. They would rest—they needed rest—and then they would seek out the Well.

Deeper into the Woods, the path widened and descended to skirt a large pond lying blue under a break in the forest's roof. The pond's banks were grass-covered and fringed by large clumps of lily and violet. On a branch overhanging the placid water, there perched a kingfisher. It rattled out a greeting to them as it waited for a telling ripple or stir to dive for its meal. Across the water, maples in flower scented the air with sweetness.

Beyond the pond, the ground lifted and sunlight filled a large opening in the forest. A fawn frisked and gambolled atop a low earthen bank, then bolted when it sensed the approach of the two Holdsmen. Kal and Gwyn entered a lush meadow that rose gently to a facing hillock, its tall grasses furrowed by the continuing path.

"The Heath," Kal said, low-voiced. He hardly dared break the spell woven by the lazy drone of bees high among the pale flowers of a great lime tree at the edge of the grass.

"There is no danger here." Sighing with relief, Kal lowered himself onto the soft cushion of grass growing thick beside the path. He lay on his side, propping his head on his hand. Gwyn joined him. They lounged and savoured the warm sunlight that flooded over them. Kal lay back and closed his eyes. Several minutes had passed before Kal sat up and rummaged through his codynnos for a tharf cake that Broq had given him, half of which he handed to Gwyn.

"Well, we've lingered long enough. Long enough, I hope, for the Southwoldsmen to have given up the chase, if, by chance, they even got as far as Hoël's Dyke. Whatever the case, we've got to get back on the road, back to the Dyke, and then to the Melderenys songline." Kal pushed himself to his feet. For a moment he regarded the facing hill, so low that it was scarcely more than a mound.

"I wonder what lies farther down this songline."

Giving way to the impulse of curiosity, his hand strayed to the pios. His voice rang clear in the summer air, swelling in common measure with the lines sung earlier in the day. He recognized the words he sang, and yet they seemed unfamiliar, somehow new to him.

> "And from the sleepy languor of the Heath,
> This way will wend unto sequestered peace.
> Beyond this glade, there lies a goodly cot,
> Its keep and keeper by the world forgot.
> 'Tis Mousehold hav'n, quickset by laurel 'round.
> And yew, and privet, morning glory crowned..."

The sound of another voice drifted to his ear, so subtle that Kal hardly noticed it at first, blending with his song and the chorus of insect and bird. It had taken up the words and melody of the song, even as Kal sang them. He glanced at Gwyn. No... Impossible... The mute Holdsman returned Kal's look of shocked puzzlement.

"...Enclose bejewelled beds of lily, rose,
Shy violet, and columbine. Here grows
Lace maidenhair...

Kal had stopped singing, but the song continued. He recognized the voice as that of a woman, rough, almost gravelly, but not unmelodious. It carried a strange suggestive power. She had taken up the burden of the turusoran. Her voice came from up ahead, where the path that they had been treading disappeared beyond the gentle rise in the near distance.

"...and marigold, 'mid pale
and purest banks of lily-of-the-vale.
'Forget-me-not,' the graceful bluebell rings,
'Nor me,' the sorrel wood-sage mother sings."

Already Gwyn was running, overleaping the little stream that purled across the field. Kal followed, no less drawn to whoever it was that was singing Carric-thona.

Kal topped the rise, stopping beside his companion, and gazed down into a small clearing ringed around by a low greenwood hedge. In the middle of it was set a charming, half-timbered cottage, roofed with thatch and overflown by myriad twittering swallows. The singing had stopped. Before the cottage was the tilled soil of a small wicker-fenced kitchen garden surrounded by banks of well-tended flower beds. There, hoe in hand, stood a white-haired woman, wiping a hand on her apron. She was evidently not that old, for she had a straightness of posture that belied age.

"Come." She beckoned to the Holdsmen, smiling.

They descended the short slope and stepped through a gap in the waist-high hedge. The woman was of average height, of solid frame but not stout, dressed in a plain brown kirtle of braided wool that reached down to her ankles and was drawn tight at the waist by a light beige hip girdle under a garden-stained apron. Her hair, like silvered drifts of snow, was strangely at odds with the unwrinkled softness of her cheeks and brow. Falling down to her waist, her hair was held in place by a floral circlet of honeysuckle. With its high cheekbones and smooth forehead, her face was striking, not quite beautiful by normal reckoning but possessed of a chiselled perfection that spoke wisdom as well as a deep sadness that seeped like tears from her bright grey almond-shaped eyes.

"I...We..." Kal fumbled in his attempt to establish cordial terms. He remembered Galli's pledge with Broq. "Peace, Mother of the Wood...," he ventured.

The woman smiled again and said, "And peace to you, little son. What brings you to Mousehold?"

"Wise Mother," Kal said, "we seek Ruah's Well."

The woman leaned her hoe against the woven willow twigs of the garden fence and looked again at Kal.

"Ah...," Kal continued, "for the healing water. For my father.... He was poisoned by an arrow dipped in sumokhan. He's very ill and like to die without it."

The woman remained silent for a moment, then looked at Gwyn.

"You are mute in voice, but not in heart...nor in deed. It is good. Guard him well." Gwyn bowed his head and, unbidden, drew aside as the woman stepped forward and took Kal's hands in her own. As she held them, she looked into his eyes and glanced down at the pios.

"You are a bard," she said.

"I am."

"A bard, yes, yes." She held his hands fast, looking into his eyes. "That, yes, but much more." She paused, closed her eyes, then lifted Kal's hands, pressing them to her lips, kissing them softly.

Kal stood in stunned silence. "But how...What...Who are you?"

"What I am is of small account. Who I am you shall learn soon enough. You have come to Mousehold"—now at last she released Kal's hands—"on the songline Carric-thona, and I know that Nuath's men search for you. I know that, if you are to save your father's life, you cannot linger here."

"Which way is best from here to Ruah's Well, Wise Mother?" Kal asked.

"Retrace your steps to Hoël's Dyke, and from there travel south to Melderenys. Once on the songline, you'll find Ruah's Well sure enough. You'll find that the way is clear of the enemy. You'll have no problems." The mysterious woman had confirmed their original plan. Her tone of reassurance brought warmth and peace to Kal's heart.

"Wait here and I'll send you on your way with fresh provisions," she said and hurried into her cottage. Kal looked at Gwyn and shook his head in amazement, then let his gaze roam over their surroundings. On the right side of the cottage there grew a stand of birch, beyond which loomed the ruins of what, at one time, must have been a glence, the stones of its dome collapsed, flanked by a tower in similar disrepair. A score of questions thronged Kal's mind as he waited.

The woman returned. "You have many thoughts. Stay your curiosity until there is time, which now there is not," she said as she approached them again. She carried a platter of oatcakes, which she offered them, and which they stowed in their night pouches. "Content yourself to know that I am not unknown to Aelward."

"A friend?"

"Indeed a friend, Myghternos Anadem." She took his hand once more in hers, an earnest sparkle rekindling in her eyes. "A friend in your need. Now, may Ruah guide your steps."

TWELVE

"I'd say we've walked a full three leagues," Kal said, adjusting Rhodangalas at his hip, as he lowered himself to sit on a stone by the edge of the track. He slipped the codynnos from his shoulder and, placing it on his lap, drew a sleeve across his sweaty brow. "It can't be much farther." He gazed down the road that lay ahead of them to the south, where it took a gentle dip and made a sweeping turn. It lay peaceful in the afternoon sun.

So far, the journey had been uneventful. They had travelled quickly, hugging what cover was afforded by the shoulders of Hoël's Dyke. As they walked, the raised wagon track had broken occasionally from its otherwise uniform span, broadening for a space. Many of these places were little more than a slight widening of the flagged surface, enough to allow carts of old to pass one another, their wheel hubs narrowly clearing. Other places, often shaded by the spreading branches of some ancient tree, had obviously been intended as rest stops for the travellers of centuries past. By the wayside at one of these spots, there had been the remains of an old stone byre. Gwyn had scrambled about the building's wreckage, exploring, while Kal studied the map yet again. In another place, there stood the crumbling remains of a stone and mortar water trough that at one time had been filled by a spring, now long dry. What was left of the trough was filled with tall grasses and overflowing creepers.

Kal looked up from the road ahead to the verdant roof of interwoven branches above him. Here, where they had stopped, four immense ivy-clad oaks stood evenly placed, two on either side of a generous expanse of flagstone. Beneath the overarching limbs, Hoël's Dyke lay in deep shade at four times its normal breadth, wider by far than any other place they had encountered along the forgotten road that afternoon.

Kal pulled the map from his codynnos, unfolded it, and scrutinized it. After a moment, he tapped its surface and glanced up to where Gwyn nosed about between the huge oaks on the west side of the road.

"Melderenys, the songline. I figure that it can't be far off," Kal said and returned his attention to the water-stained parchment. "It can't be far now."

Gently, Kal refolded the map and restored it to his codynnos. In its stead, he pulled out the pios. He turned the tiny harp in his hand, contemplating its golden surface, its curves and lines. He had unclasped the pios from his cloak when they had left the old woman's cottage. It had seemed prudent to keep the brooch hidden. No telling who they might encounter on the road, and in open sight the thing was a dead giveaway. At the foot of one of the trees, Gwyn had drawn his hunting knife and was cutting away creepers with determined effort.

"What's that, Gwyn? What have you got there?"

Kal snatched up the satchel from his lap as he stood and strode across the track. The ground between the trees was solid, flagged like Hoël's Dyke, except more crusted with debris and age, and uneven, hardly visible as a roadway. Here and there, tree roots had heaved the surface of the ancient trackway, the jagged edges of broken flagstone cutting the bed of moss and leaf mould.

Kal came up behind Gwyn, who knelt, tearing at the vines with his hands, clearing the surface of a stout slab of black marble, which had been pushed off true and cradled in the time-swollen roots of a tree. Incised into the slab, though still partly obscured by lichen, was a series of interlaced squiggles in a row across the black face of the stone. This was surmounted by a graceful double curve ending in a swirl, clearly suggesting the arch and stoop of a deer's back, neck, and head.

"Water..." Kal ran a finger over the etched waves and flicked a patch of lichen away. "And the deer... Ruah's Well. It must point the way. The songline—we're on Melderenys!"

Already, Gwyn had descended out of the shade of the oaks and onto a scrubby patch of ground. Kal turned to follow him. The way was thickly overgrown with briars and brambles that tore at their legs, but remained paved and solid underfoot, leading straight away from Hoël's Dyke into the Woods of Tircoil.

"There was a road here, Gwyn, a road that people took to reach the Well," Kal said, catching up to his companion on the ancient path now overshadowed by the Woods. "It should lead us right there. No need for the pios to check our way." Kal gripped the brooch hard in his fist for a moment then refastened it to his cloak.

The forest appeared as it had before; broad expanses of deeply shaded woodland spread beneath a heavy-pillared sylvan roof. Straight along the path they continued, and, while at times an aged tree would lean heavily over it, never did the path have to stray from its course to avoid one. Gradually, the great trees thinned, and the land grew more wild, coarse with scrub. Here and there, a sarsen stone stood tall by the way, like a dark and silent sentinel.

The path descended to the edge of a vast swamp fetid with gas that bubbled pungently from an ooze of stagnant water. Dead trees thrust their broken limbs into the sky like bony, white-robed dancers frozen midstep. Here the path mounted a raised bed and continued unswerving across the centre of the bog until it rose again into woodland still shaggy and unkempt, and gained height, rising towards a ridge among blue wooded hills.

From the crest of the ridge, the land fell away before them into the narrow end of a long valley walled by the thick-wooded Tircoilian hills. They stood high above the valley floor, which undulated gently down its length over low hummocks that in the distance shouldered their way back under the mantle of forest stretching towards the coastal plain. Far away, the valley's steep sides lessened in height and eventually fell into the forested hills that lay hazy and purple on the narrow horizon.

Below them, the path dropped into the valley. Except for the occasional coppice, the woods had retreated, leaving the roadway clearly visible, a ribbon in an emerald sea of grass. A stream snaked its way back and forth among the low hills, twice cutting across the path, which then rose onto a knoll crowned by a group of standing stones. Kal pointed west, down into the rift, where the molten light of the afternoon sun was held as in a long vessel.

"There, that's it. That's Ruah's Well!"

Their pace quickening, the Holdsmen descended the road, now cleanly flagged, no longer a mouldering ruin. Here and there, in the broad expanse of sloping downland, stood spinneys of white birch that overshadowed narrow defiles and brooks, most scarcely more than rills, which tumbled like liquid silver from ledge to ledge down the sides of the valley, sometimes spilling into pools overhung by wildflower and grasses.

Silverweed now crowded the trackway, its yellow flowers scenting the air, as the path bottomed the valley and mounted an arched stone footbridge that overstepped the clear stream. The flagged path continued through lush flatland, bridged the stream again, and mounted the hill upon which stood the stones.

The view from a distance had been deceptive. The hill was high. Upon it rose stones of a massive size, standing in an open area that must have been nearly a hundred paces across, thick with low-growing sod grasses and offering a lordly view of the valley behind them. The stones were smoothly hewn, all of them roughly the same size. A rank of stones stood in a straight line across the edge of the hilltop. Both ends of the row cornered and ran to a closing rank, forming a great square. Within the square, a ring of the tall stones stood in a circle of the same width as the square.

Kal and Gwyn followed the track and entered the structure in the middle of the line of stones, where the sides of both circle and square met, through a portal comprised of two immense pillar stones surmounted by a shorter lintel stone. Directly ahead of them loomed another portal, constructed in like manner of two pillars and a lintel. Again, to their left and right, where circle met square, were lintelled openings in the otherwise unbroken lines of free-standing megaliths that towered, solemn and immovable, like giant guardsmen posted to keep watch on an outlying battlement.

Kal stepped farther into the structure. His eyes widened with realization. The openings were not aligned to the cardinal directions but rather lay along the songline of Melderenys and at right angles to it. This structure, this ancient portal to Ruah's Well, was built something like any glence in Ahn Norvys was supposed to be—according to a glence mark—oriented to the Great Glence itself. Wilum had taught him that once. Kal remembered the old Hordanu bemoaning the fact that, in recent centuries, glences had been erected that lay, as only the Great Glence should, along the cardinal directions dictated by the pole star and the rise and fall of the sun rather than according to a glence mark for which the Great Glence itself was the focus and anchor. Yet another indication of the waning of order in the twilight of the Harmonic Age, Wilum was wont to say.

Of course, every songline would naturally form a glence mark, except that this structure would have been built in the mists of time, by the echobards themselves, before ever there was any glence mark or songline—before the Great Glence was conceived in thought. Kal considered the fathomless mystery of the place.

In a stupor, he gazed about the squared ring of stones as he and Gwyn wandered into the structure. The floor of the edifice was flawlessly cobbled, and at its centre was inlaid the same pattern of hind and water that they had noted earlier on the stone marker. Here, however, the pattern was formed in brilliantly coloured stones—glistening azures, indigoes, and violets set among snowy whites and silvers.

Kal stood in the very centre of the inner ring of stones and turned in a slow circle. His hand strayed to the pios at his throat, and he delicately plucked the strings. As before, a resonant chord sprang from the tiny harp. Syllables swelled in the young Hordanu's throat, then burst from his mouth—syllables he didn't recognize, forming words he didn't recognize, in a language he didn't recognize—save for one word. One word, repeated and becoming the only word ringing among the stones: "Ruah ... Ruah ... Ruah ... Ruah ..."

The tones resounded and faded as Kal stopped singing. Beside him, Gwyn spun around, then stood stock-still, his gaze riveted on the western wall of the edifice. Out of the corner of his eye, Kal caught a hint of movement, the suggestion of a ghostly white shape gliding indistinct behind the stones and slipping out of view over the lip of the knoll.

Kal and Gwyn rushed through the portal before them, passing through it onto a terrace bounded by an ivy-veiled low stone wall. They found themselves standing atop an escarpment, the knoll falling sharply to a grove of mountain ash that crowded a pool. The overhanging trees obscured all but the surface of the pool. In the pool, Kal saw reflected a spectral image that stooped to drink, then lifted its head to look up at the two Holdsmen before disappearing beneath the trees. A feeling played delicately along the nape of Kal's neck and spread down his spine, a strange tingle of hopeful expectation. In the space of a heartbeat it was gone.

"Ruah ...," Kal breathed.

To their left, through a break in the low wall, was a set of stone stairs that led to a landing, then broke to the right, falling across the face of the escarpment.

"This way, Gwyn," Kal said in little more than a whisper.

The grey slate steps were encrusted with moss and lichen. On either side of them ran intricately worked iron railings, rusted but still sound and solidly fixed into a series of flanking stone pillars. Each pillar was carved square and smooth, the inner face of each displaying the same weathered representation of hind and water.

Down the stairs they descended until they reached another landing. Here the stairs doubled back and continued to the left until ending in a small meadow nestled in a hollow made snug on three sides by wooded slopes bathed in late afternoon sunlight. Before them lay the pool bordered by mountain ash, its surface a shimmering sheet of gold, disturbed only by a lone swan that glided stately on the water.

"Gwyn. This is it. This is Ruah's Well," Kal said with hushed voice, regarding the pool. The Well was contained by a low curb of mortared stone covered by a smooth capstone of slate. Kal leaned over the wall. The water of the Well had the aspect of crystal and receded into a depth of blackness. Farther away from him a stony bottom appeared, sloping sharply upwards as the pool shallowed. A good part of the Well lay hidden from view, enclosed by a cavernous grotto in the bowels of the very same hillside upon which they had stood among the standing stones. He moved to the right, away from the steps, following the curve of the wall. The cave's opening was framed in purplish-blue and white by a densely woven checkerwork of columbine that filled every crack and ledge that could hold soil and root.

The two Holdsmen walked beside the pool on a broad walkway of pebbled stone that led into the hillside. Now they stepped from sunlight into the gloom of the cavern. Rather than a murky dankness, however, the two were met by a bracing splash of running water that freshened the air of the broad cavern, while a soft watery light seemed to cast a glow over the place. Gwyn leaned over the low stone wall and touched the surface of the water.

The light seemed to emanate inexplicably from the Well itself, not from the outside. Stranger still, in this sunless cavern grew a startling profusion of columbines, decking rocks, over which a little rill of water splashed and gurgled into the pool from a broad shelf set in the back of the grotto. There on the shelf, standing rampant in the gentle flow of water, was the life-size figure of a hind sculpted in softly phosphorescent white marble, her moist nostrils flared and her head lifted. Kal pressed past Gwyn and clambered over worn rocks to the statue. It was an exquisitely fashioned piece of work, so clean-limbed and majestically supple, so filled with glowing gentleness, that she appeared poised to spring into movement and life. The light in the cavern seemed to flow from the statue itself, and yet, when he stretched out his hand and brought it to rest on the figure, the cold white stone changed hue and darkened, as if his hand cast its shadow upon the marble surface, blocking the light. As he removed his hand, the stone appeared to glow again.

There was a splash behind him. Gwyn had shed his cloak, weapons and codynnos, thrown aside his tunic, and leaped into the pool. He lay in the water, rolling in it, sucking it up through pursed lips, swishing it in his mouth, as if it were a fine vintage. Finally, he sat up in it, washing his lame foot.

Kal smiled and returned his attention to the white stone figure and the ledge upon which it stood. Behind the statue, he could see a deeper depression funnelling to a hole beneath the water's surface. Over it, the water stretched and swelled with movement as a spring bubbled up from unknown depths below. This was the very source of Ruah's Well, forever replenishing its healing flow. Behind the spring, at the very back of the grotto, was a further shallow overhang of rock, worn smooth from the coming and going of countless people over the centuries. Here the path ended. Kal stepped onto the smooth stone and knelt, cupping his hands to scoop up the Well's water. Kal sipped at the clear, cold liquid as it dropped from his fingers in a cascade of crystal droplets. Stooping down farther on hands and knees, he immersed his face in the pool and drank deep draughts of the water. It had an icy sweetness, more savoury and refreshing than any water he had ever sampled before, even water from the clear mountain springs of the Stoneholding. It was as if he was drinking the very essence of water, water so pure that it spilled forth light much as the white marble form of Ruah in this grotto seemed to do.

Having had his fill, he unfastened the two waterskins he had brought and began to fill them, dipping them in the water one at a time. After he had stoppered them and reattached them to his belt, he sat back on his heels, kneeling, and closed his eyes. He let the peace of the Well engulf him. It felt like a spring flooding him from within. For measureless moments, his spirit stepped beyond the portals of time and space, and he saw himself on the crest of a lofty promontory amid a wide blue expanse of ocean, his eyes trained on a hill in the distance, atop which stood a milk-white hind. She bowed. Blazoned in the sky over them were a glinting golden harp and a beautifully crafted sword.

He became aware of strong guttural noises. They mixed oddly with the vision. Kal frowned, and the vision faded. He opened his eyes and turned his head back to see Gwyn, who stood dripping wet, knee-deep in the pool, his face twisted with effort as he tried to frame sounds with his broken voice and misshapen tongue, trying to find the words that had failed him since birth.

Kal rose to his feet and walked down to his friend. With wet hands, Gwyn wiped tears from his face. He pointed first at his lame foot and then his lips. In a slow, poignant gesture, he held out his palms and shook his head.

"I'm sorry, Gwyn. I'm sorry. It doesn't always happen that way. Ruah's water always heals, but not always as we would hope and wish it to."

Gwyn's gaze fell despondently.

"Gwyn, look at me." Slowly the mute Holdsman lifted his head again. Kal looked deeply into his eyes, holding them fixed. "Listen to me. You must listen to me. You have gifts." Kal nodded to him gravely, their eyes still locked. "Extraordinary gifts. Gifts not given to most other men. As I am Lord Myghternos Hordanu, you must believe me. It is truth." A tranquil calm descended on Kal, even as the pain faded from Gwyn's eyes. "There is a depth of peace and wisdom in you. And even more so now are the peace and wisdom of Ruah with you."

Gwyn's face brightened as he turned his gaze to the soft form of the hind and nodded in turn.

"Healing of the body may not have been your lot. Trust that it is for the good and serves Wuldor's intent. And know, Gwyn, that while you may not have been strengthened in limb and voice, you have been strengthened nonetheless, and in ways vastly more important. Now, let's get out into the sun before you catch your death of cold."

Kal helped Gwyn step over the pool's wall. The mute Holdsman picked up his tunic and pulled it over his head. Then, having retrieved his cloak, codynnos, and weapons, he led Kal into the daylight.

In the open area before the cavern, Kal was surprised to discover that it was now late afternoon, for the sinking sun had begun to overhang the treetops on the western slope of the hollow. Shadows would soon spread over the pool and the foot of the stairs. It was time to return to the Holdsfolk, time to find his father.

Having drunk of Ruah's water, Kal felt a powerful surge of energy and alertness. He fairly bounded up the stairs to where the standing stones towered over the escarpment.

"You're not chilled?" Kal asked when they reached the terraced landing before the western portal. Gwyn shook his head. His clothes were quickly drying in the late spring breeze.

"Good. We'll double back on Melderenys to Hoël's Dyke. If we travel quickly, we can make it to Mousehold before the light is gone. We can spend the night with the wise woman there. It's not at all far off our way. We can set out for Kingshead Cove at first light."

They paused for a moment among the stones fixed above Ruah's Well, then turned and hurried out along the flagged trackway down across the bottomland and up the valley's sloping end. At the top of the ridge from which they had first beheld the site of Ruah's Well, they paused again to catch their breath. With a last look down towards the Well, they resumed their journey back to Hoël's Dyke and entered the Woods once more. Before long, they came to the bog over which the path crossed on its raised bed. The Dyke now lay little more than half a league away.

"Did you hear that?" Kal held up his hand and stopped in midstride. They stood halfway across the bog. Gwyn looked at him and threw his head back, raising a loose-fisted hand to his mouth.

"Aye, Gwyn. Hard to make out, but I think you're right. A huntsman's horn." Kal cocked his head and listened, but heard nothing more.

"We'd best tread carefully."

They walked on for a bit, all but clearing the swamp, when to their ears came the sound again of the huntsman's horn, one long winding, now much more distinct and from the direction of the Dyke.

"That way." Kal's features grew sombre, thoughtful. "Somewhere up along Hoël's Dyke." After a moment he shook his head decisively. "You know, Gwyn? I think we'd be foolish to continue this way to Kingshead." Kal glanced up at the sky. "The day's wearing on. Darkness will fall fast in the Woods. And it would be difficult to hide from pursuers in the dark along Hoël's Dyke. By day, too, for that matter. I think we should return to Ruah's Well. We ought to be safe there for the night. The Southwoldsmen won't venture this side of Hoël's Dyke. They wouldn't enter the Woods of Tircoil, not even in the light of day. I've an idea we'd do better to strike across country tomorrow, at first light, through the Woods to Mousehold—"

Even as they heard the winding of the horn again in the distance, another more ominous sound fell on their ears. A long note rose, hollow and sustained, closer to hand in the Woods, from somewhere up the songline's path directly in front of them. It took Kal but a moment to place the feral cry, and, as he did, he turned to Gwyn. There, in the young Holdsman's face, he saw reflected his own white fear. The howl subsided, only to be taken up afresh by a second creature, farther away and to the north. Its cry was echoed by two others to the south of the path.

Kal needed to say no word. Gwyn had turned heel, putting his back to Hoël's Dyke, bent on regaining the only conceivable place of safety available in these Woods: the hallowed ground of the Well. Kal took flight also, and the two Holdsmen pressed across the swamp at a jog. At his waist, the water skins sloshed and jostled as Kal ran, as did his codynnos, the bow and quiver, and Rhodangalas in its scabbard. Kal felt encumbered, awkward, and unable to put distance between himself and the unthinkable terror at his back. Still the horns winded, and still the wolfsong rose in reply. Kal chuckled to himself grimly. At least the Southwoldsmen would hear the same howls and, out of fear, would not dare to trespass the boundary of these mysterious Woods.

Trotting heavy-footed behind Gwyn, Kal approached the edge of the bog. Though it was still hours from nightfall, the Woods gave the curious impression of being already cast in the shadows of dusk. A purpling gloom seemed to pool beneath the trees that verged the broad marsh and into which the path ran rising again into the forest. Kal threw a glance over his shoulder, and there, on the raised trackway on the far side of the fetid bog, he thought he saw a form, man-sized and stooped, lift its head, then turn and lope away into the trees. . . .

Or perhaps it was just a will-o'-the-wisp, some errant trick of light and mist and marsh gas in the gathering shade. Kal shuddered uncontrollably. It was nothing, he told himself, shrugging off the prickling chill from his shoulders and arms. Nothing at all.

Kal picked up his pace until he drew abreast of Gwyn, who now shambled quickly up the long slope ascending the ridge.

"The howling's stopped."

Gwyn looked to Kal and nodded but did not slacken his pace. "Do you think it was the..."

Again Gwyn nodded at Kal but made no sound. Kal found his companion's silent intensity unnerving. At the same time, he could think of nothing to say that might dispel their mounting trepidation, and so they plodded on up the hill, hearing only the steady drone of insects and the scuff of their footsteps on the flagstone.

Atop the rise, the sky broke blue through the curtain of trees in the gap where the path crested the ridge and fell into the valley beyond. There sunlight gilded the ancient flags of the track, bathing them in soft warmth, streaming down the path towards the two Holdsmen still steadily climbing the hill. As Kal looked up the path, a deer stepped onto the road at the very crown of the hill, its graceful form silhouetted by the westering sun, dark against the sky. It paused, a forefoot raised, and slowly turned its head to look down upon the two men. After a brief moment, the elegant creature broke its gaze and sauntered away from them down the path, the sun blazing white on its back and sides as it disappeared over the brow of the hill.

Kal choked a cry and spun his head around to look at Gwyn. Beside him the young Holdsman walked on, his eyes fixed on the trackway before his feet, unwitting and unaware. But Kal had seen her. Indeed, he had seen her. He felt relieved of the accusing doubt that the watery reflection in the pool may have been only tempered by his fancy. But now... No, it was her! It had been her then, as it was her now! And she would guide them to safety. Kal laughed and slapped his companion on the back. Gwyn shot him an expression of mild shock, then smiled nervously.

Topping the rise, Kal surveyed the valley. There stood the pillared structure above the Well, the path running to it up the knoll. There lay the stream, sparkling in the late afternoon sun, a myriad other runnels and rivulets chasing the steep hillsides to join it. There stood the coppiced woods of aspen and birch and the vast field of green, but nowhere was there sign of the white hind. Kal shrugged. His newfound peace remained undisturbed.

"We'll make for the standing stones," he said to Gwyn. "The hill gives us a clear view in all directions. It will be a clear night tonight, and with a good moon... for the better part of it, anyway."

In a matter of minutes, the Holdsmen had traversed the distance to the hill beneath which, on the side opposite them, was nestled Ruah's Well. They trudged up the rising ground. The sound of the horns had long since faded from hearing. Whether it was because of distance or because the Southwoldsmen had stopped winding them, Kal couldn't tell.

The two of them decided that they would forgo a fire that night. It would be warm enough, and a fire could only serve to attract unwanted attention. Kal thought it wise, however, to lay the makings of a fire in readiness by the mouth of the grotto, one that could be quickly kindled. In the event that something should besiege them in the night, they could easily flee down the stairs from their post, strike the tinder, and seek refuge in the cavern. Only two things did Kal know about waldscathes, the only things that Wilum had been able to tell him—they were to be feared by man, and they feared man's fire. Kal could only hope that, should this threat from the Woods prove to be more than simply fanciful legend, a ready fire, good shelter, and the protection of pios, songline, and Ruah would suffice as a defence.

After readying a large fire and stacking an ample supply of dry wood near the mouth of the cavern, the two supped on oatcakes and draughts of cool water taken from the Well. They were thankful enough for the oatcakes the wise woman had sent with them. If she had hoped that they might return to Mousehold that evening, then she had provisioned them with more than they needed for the day's journey. Doubtless, they would be even more grateful for her generosity come morning.

Twilight came quickly to the valley, despite its being clear and open. It was as if the valley was inescapably joined to the darkness of the Woods of Tircoil simply by virtue of its being nestled in the Black Cape. Kal and Gwyn stood on the terrace of the hill, looking out towards the setting sun. Even as it was, there had been few words spoken—Kal saying little during their preparations and meal, and Gwyn withdrawing all the while deeper into his mute silence—and yet a heavier stillness and quiet fell upon them. Kal's was the first watch, and, as the sun grew large and orange on the narrow horizon afforded by the valley's gorge, Gwyn removed himself from the point of vantage to one of the stony columns and sat down. Placing his weapons and baggage beside him, he leaned against the tall black stone, pulled his cloak over himself, and bowed his head. Within a few minutes, the young man was asleep.

THIRTEEN

The sun set, red and wavering, and gave the sky over to the stars. A swollen moon was poised to break into the eastern sky, but it would be an hour or two until it did. As the darkness deepened, Kal paced back and forth through the standing stones, looking first to the west then to the east, then to the west again. There was little to see in the blackness footing the knoll. The crickets maintained a low buzz in a million rhythmic chirps, and fireflies dotted the night, their lights waxing and waning like lazy green sparks. The forested hills surrounding the valley were indiscernible save as an inky, irregular stain along the horizon that blotted out the stars. Kal studied the sky, tracing with this eye the disjointed starpoint figures of the Raven, the Ploughman, the Stag, and the North Crown, set with its polestar jewel. He caressed the delicate form of Alargha, the Swan, with his gaze. He thought of the feast with Magan and his hammerfolk in the Great Hall of the Stars, then let his mind wander where it would.

Soon the sky over the eastern end of the valley began to glow with the approach of the rising moon. He watched its silver face break above the forest and climb over the trees. The moon flooded the valley with a pale and misty glow. What fears his imagination had presented to his waking mind were banished by the lambent beauty of the landscape before him. He crossed again through the western portal and leaned over the terrace wall but could see nothing of the pool below.

Behind him, Gwyn coughed in his sleep. More than once the huddled form had stirred and moaned in the grip of some dream. The young Holdsman had slipped onto his side, his knees pulled up to his chest. No longer the bumbling boy, Kal mused, looking at him. Gwyn's adolescent awkwardness was fading and being transmuted into sinewed brawn and a self-assurance that Kal found increasingly disconcerting, all the more so given his friend's muteness. But change had come fast in the circumstances of recent happenings—a change that affected them all, himself included.

Kal looked again to the moon caught between the standing stones. It had risen higher in the sky. Soon he would wake Gwyn and let him take a turn at watch. Sleep pulled at Kal, and his eyelids grew heavy. He walked again through the circle of stones, trying to shake the cobwebs spun by weariness from his head, not wanting to slip in his vigilance...needing to remain alert... only a few more minutes...

Kal's eyes snapped open. He was still standing, but he had dozed off. Something had woken him—a horn. Its harsh note faded in the distance and fell silent. It sounded again. Kal peered up the path into the darkness of the Woods of Tircoil. These blasts were closer than the ones that had turned them back from Hoël's Dyke. They sounded like they were coming from the path leading to the Well.

Kal ran to wake up Gwyn and, kneeling by the young man, gently shook him awake.

"Quiet, Gwyn. They're coming."

Gwyn lifted his head, then sprang to his feet, snatched up his sword belt and began to buckle it around his waist. Kal retrieved his own weapons and gear and joined Gwyn, who had walked over to the eastern side of the knoll. A horn winded again. Kal scanned the walls of the valley. He hadn't reckoned on this. The slopes would be difficult to climb in full daylight, but at night and in the panic of flight it would be well-nigh impossible.

"From the sound of it, they can't be far off Hoël's Dyke..."

Again came the faint but insistent blast of a horn. Kal recognized something about the sound, something familiar in its unfamiliar tone. His eyes widened in recognition.

"Gwyn! That's no highland hunting horn. It's Gharssûlian—of course! The Southwoldsmen would not brave the Woods on their own, but if you set a troop of Black Scorpions at their heels...We've got to get out of here. We've got to lose them in the Woods. If we can make Mousehold..." Kal grabbed Gwyn by the arm and pushed him into a trot down the path they had already three times travelled. "Listen, we have one chance, and one chance only. We can't climb the sides—too steep. And we can't walk farther down the valley, or we'll never get out. So we run this way—" Again a horn was winded; then, as if in response, a wolf's howl rose eerily.

Gwyn tore his arm out of Kal's grip and stopped dead in his tracks. He pointed up the path, shaking both his arm and his head.

"I know! I know! It seems madness. We've got to run towards them, faster than fast." Kal's fear became choking, and he grabbed Gwyn again, pushing him along. "If we can make the ridge, we can escape into the Woods between the ridge and the swamp and make for the old woman's cottage. They may follow us on the path, but I don't know if they'd dare go into the Woods themselves at night—and I know what you're thinking, but I'd rather take my chance with the wolves, or waldscathes, or whatever, than the Scorpions. Now run!"

With that, the two Holdsmen galloped down the path, Kal carrying in his hands the water skins. On they bolted, then up the long slope leading to the lip of the valley's eastern end. The horns sounded repeatedly, their blasts drawing rapidly nearer as the two men closed the distance with them. Wolf howls, too, laced the night air, rising and falling. From where, Kal could not discern—they seemed everywhere. As they reached the crest of the ridge, hearts pounding and chests heaving, another sound met Kal's ears. It was the baying of hounds.

"Lymers!" Kal cried, his panic near complete. "Th-they've brought dogs! Into the Woods, Gwyn, as you value your life!"

Gwyn pointed at Kal's throat and arched his fingers, drawing them back.

"What! The pios?" What was the boy thinking?

Gwyn nodded, pulling his fingers past Kal's throat again.

"No, no, it won't work!" Kal screamed. "They found us again, and now they have dogs.... Just run, Gwyn! Run!"

Off the road and into the trees Kal thrashed, Gwyn close on his heels. While the path had been bathed in moonlight, the woods were veiled in thick darkness. The tree trunks loomed out of the blackness at him. Kal could hear the horns, the hounds, the wolves, and he could hear Gwyn careering through the undergrowth behind him.

A root or stone caught Kal's toe. He stumbled and pitched forward onto the forest floor, then saw an explosion of white fire as his head hit a rock. He pushed himself off the ground, feeling around for the lost water skins. Something trickled from his hairline down his temple. He was bleeding. His hand fell on a lump, cool, soft, and swollen. One skin was intact. Kal's hand brushed over leaf, twig, and stone. He found the other skin. It was torn and lay limp on the wet ground. Gwyn rushed past. Kal threw himself scrambling back to his feet, nearly buckling at the bolt of pain that shot from his left knee. He gritted his teeth and hopped, stumbling back to a run, but could barely make out the bobbing form of Gwyn not two or three paces in front of him.

It seemed to Kal that the darkness deepened even further as they ran. Time blurred. Had they run for seconds? Minutes? Or even longer? Up and down slopes, clambering over deadfalls and across narrow cuts and runnels in the forest floor—running, ever running. In the lightless forest it was impossible to tell, and impossible to know in which direction they were moving, except that the baying of the hounds remained ever at their backs, so that they must be heading roughly north.

He had panicked, he realized, and panicked badly. Now, in the midst of their flight, he could see it clearly. There was not a chance that they would ever find the old woman's cottage—Mousehold, she called it. And a mouse hole was what they needed! Now they would be caught, and whatever was left of them unmauled by the dogs would be crushed by the hunters. That would make an end of it....Why had he bolted? The pios and songline had proven themselves once already. But there had been the horns, Gharssûlian horns. That meant Scorpions. And the hounds meant Telessarian trackers. And the wolf howls meant—

"Stop it, Kalaquinn!" he chided himself. "Keep it together! Don't lose your head!"

But it was so black. And the wolves' howling seemed to grow pervasive through the Woods, coming from all quarters and from every distance. From the hounds' baying, Kal knew that the dogs and men were gaining on them. Mixed now with the barks were the shouts of men. The horns had ceased sounding. There had been so many horn blasts. Why...? Unless—yes! They had used the horns to frighten their quarry, to flush it out and put it to flight. And, oh, but it had worked! They must have mustered a force along Hoël's Dyke earlier in the day and then come in force at night. And now the hunters were on the scent and closing—they had left the path and were tracking them through the Woods of Tircoil.

Fear clutched at Kal's throat. He reached up with his hand and touched the pios. If only he had stayed at the Well. His fingers jerked across the strings as he ran. The wires tinkled mutely. No music came from the little harp, and no song came from Kal's mouth. His fingers jerked again across the wires.

In front of him, Gwyn's black form melted, disappearing into the thick curtain of night enshrouding the forest. Kal caught sight of him again for a moment before he was once more swallowed in darkness.

"Gwyn! Gwyn!"

Kal could hear his companion running ahead of him, though he seemed farther away.

"Gwyn! Wait for me! Don't lose me!" Kal heard the strain of panic in his own voice.

His forehead still bled freely down his face. His head pounded and his knee burned. He was growing desperately tired, burdened by the weight of hopelessness as much as by his baggage and gear. Rhodangalas seemed to catch on every branch and bush he passed, as did the bow over his shoulder. On his back, his quiver and codynnos thumped him more and more heavily. He clung to the remaining water skin with both hands, which made it all the more awkward to run.

"Gwyn!"

No response.

"Gwyn! Wait!"

Ahead of him loomed only silence.

"Gwyn?" Kal called out, still running ahead. Panic bloomed afresh in his breast and rose cold and acid in his gorge.

Like a man floating half-submerged in water, Kal felt disjointed from his surroundings in the darkness and aware of nothing but the steady slam of his heart in his ears and the sound of his own quick sucking breaths.

Still he ran.

"Gwyn! Where are—"

Kal ploughed into something and was knocked to the ground. The water skin flew from his hands and splattered on the forest floor out of his seeing. A black wave of despair swept over him—the water was all lost. Kal lay on the ground. Beside him, Gwyn struggled to his feet. He had run into his companion. In the dark, Kal saw Gwyn stand and peer into the night surrounding them. The baying of hounds was even closer and seemed to be coming from both behind and in front of them. The young Holdsman beside him held out an open palm as a sign to be still and listen. Kal pushed himself to his feet, disoriented. Perhaps he and Gwyn had run in a circle, or the Scorpions had chased them into a trap or had split forces and flanked and caught them. The possibilities whirled around in Kal's mind.

Kal shook his head, trying to clear it, and then listened intently to the sounds in the forest. While the wolf howls had, strangely, all but ceased, hounds encircled them now and were not more than a fifty paces away. From the insistent sound of the whining barks, Kal knew the dogs were leashed and restrained by their keepers—and if men held the dogs howling around them back, then Kal and Gwyn were hemmed in by Black Scorpion Dragoons.

Out of the corner of his eye, Kal saw the flicker of movement as Gwyn reached over his shoulder and silently drew an arrow. This he set to his bowstring, bending the highland bow to full draw. The young Holdsman stood, feet planted firmly apart, awaiting the inevitable.

Kal unslung his bow, quiver, and codynnos and tossed these aside. His right hand slid to the hilt of Rhodangalas, and he silently drew the blade out of its scabbard. Even in the dearth of light, the sword glistened feebly. Kal sidled behind Gwyn and stood with him so that, back to back, they faced the unseen threat which encircled them. The two Holdsmen peered tense and alert into an impenetrable darkness filled with the hungry baying howls of the dogs and the unheard and unseen presence of their masters. In but a moment, the dogs would be loosed, and then the Scorpions would be upon them. It was simply a matter of time.

Like the precipitous crash of thunder from a midnight storm, the sound of wolf howls broke anew. It was the sound of wolves on the hunt. Kal knew this from Nua Cearta, and they were upon them from every direction. In that moment, even the hounds faltered in their baying, then redoubled their cries. The wolves' howling turned suddenly in pitch and tone and fell to angry growls and snarls. Amid the din of the ravening wolves rose the cries and yelps of both men and dogs, and, below that, sickening wet noises. It was unmistakable. Kal swallowed hard against the knot in his throat, staring into the pitch darkness before him, to his left, and to his right. From all around came the fell sounds of slaughter, barely veiled by the night. The air hung heavy with the acrid smell of fear and blood. And still the wolves snarled.

As quickly as it had begun, the confusion of noises ended. A dead silence fell over the two men. Kal's ears were ringing in the stillness, his breath catching in fits and starts. Against his back, Gwyn's own back trembled. Blackness enveloped them. Kal felt the blood draining from his fingers as he gripped Rhodangalas in a white-knuckled clutch . . .

And waited.

FOURTEEN

Seconds passed into minutes, and minutes stretched into an eternity as the two men stood peering into the veiling blackness of the Woods. Kal could perceive nothing—no noise, no movement, nothing other than the tense quiver of his own muscles and those of the young Holdsman standing at his back.

The sounds of carnage had crashed over them with the suddenness and violence of an unseen breaker, then ebbed as quickly, leaving only the undertow of sheer and utter terror. Kal imagined from the noises that both the pursuers and their dogs had been overwhelmed and destroyed. And there was little doubt in Kal's mind as to who—or, rather, what—had been the agent of that destruction. The blade of Rhodangalas shivered in Kal's quaking sword hand. With his left, he reached to clasp the comforting shape of the pios at his neck.

How long had it been? How long had they stood there, still and silent in the void of night, watching and being watched? At his back, Kal felt Gwyn ease his tension on the bowstring. Even in the shock of the moment, when a body discovers untapped sources of strength, the constant strain of the weight of a highland bow at full bend would be exhausting. And how long had Gwyn held it drawn taut? Kal felt Gwyn ease his pull further. The young Holdsman shook uncontrollably. Panic and fear were yielding to raw exhaustion and with it the numbing allure of resignation, surrender, and ultimately the cold cradle of death. They could not hold out much longer. Twice was it? Or three times that, in the span of one midnight to the next, they had been on the brink of obliteration, only to escape by the very skin of their teeth—until now.

The waldscathes encircled, a silent menace. Against the black curtain that surrounded him, Kal could envision every miscreation and monster of his childhood imagination. Every image he had ever conceived of Hircomet and the fell host of dreosan or their misbegotten progeny now danced before his night-blinded eyes. These were the faces the waldscathes wore, and these were the faces that would soon, very soon, rush howling out of the still darkness to tear him and Gwyn to pieces.

"Hail, Tobar"—Kal barely breathed the words—"Mighty One, be at our side . . . Scourge of Evil"—the words of a different night, a different woods, under a different moon—"Destroyer of Darkness, King"—the words of a child at play, now words of childlike petition—"of Freedom, Wuldor's pride . . ."

In the darkness of the Woods, just to the right, Kal heard a scuffling, a scratching. Something moved there. The sound grew steadily louder, then ceased. An instant later three harsh, rasping strikes sounded, each met with a small explosion of sparks close to the ground that showered and scattered on the forest floor not ten paces away. Gwyn spun around. A small fire sprang to life, and from it a larger licking flame was ignited and borne aloft. A torch, held high, its yellow-orange tongues casting wavering shadows among the tree trunks. Pine pitch sputtered and crackled as a second and third torch were kindled in the air from the first, on either side of it. Then, like a grassfire skipping before the wind, balls of flame burst to life as more torches were lit in an encircling chain of fire, ringing them in blazing arms that ran in both directions and met behind them.

Light flooded the Woods within the circle of torches. There must have been more than fifty of them, and among the weaving shadows beneath the upheld torches stood a line of wolves—each standing stooped upright and the size of a man, each snarl-mouthed with fangs bared, each staring with leaden and lifeless eyes.

Gwyn had pulled his bowstring taut again, training his arrow in a slow swing on the creatures surrounding them. Kal gripped Rhodangalas, tracing the empty air with its point, looking to the right and left, awaiting the onslaught. In the light and in the face of an enemy unveiled of shadow, Kal felt fear resolve into courage. He and Gwyn would die, he knew that, but they would die side by side, and they would die fighting.

"Woa-ho! What have we here, brothers?" A huge voice broke the stillness, followed by a ringing peal of deep laughter that erupted in the forest to Kal's left. Kal and Gwyn turned to face the voice.

"What have we here? Two rabbits running from the hounds, only to be caught by the wolves, eh? Should have stayed in your burrow!"

Again, the trees shook from the thunderous laughter that rose and fell in the darkness outside of the circle of firelight. The ring of torches and their bearers parted, and through the gap stepped an enormous figure, a giant of a man clothed in wolf skin, the long twin braids of his red beard falling over a grey fur-clad and barrelled chest. Atop the thick thatch of red hair on his head perched the stiffened face of a silver wolf, its sleek pelt hanging over the man's shoulders and down his back. The creature's hind paws and tail touched the ground—it must have been a massive wolf.

The man carried in his hand a dagger, a crude-looking blade, which he wiped on an already blood-sodden sleeve. The man's ruddy face bore a broad grin and eyes that flashed and danced.

"Did we scare you, then, little brothers?"

Kal blinked in confusion and disbelief.

"Come, lads, show your true selves!"

Around them, the ring of men began to straighten, raising their heads, each one lifting and letting fall to his back the wolf's-head visor he wore. There were men of all ages among them, some older and some no more than boys, younger even than Gwyn. All of them, however, had a look of savage earnestness in their eyes, a look not belied by the grins that many showed at their leader's jest, and a look that made it clear that, while these were men of mirth, they were also men not to be meddled with or taken lightly.

"Have you had your fill of fear? Enough then! Call me 'friend,' for I am Gelanor, bravest, truest, proudest, and—"

"And loudest!" one of the men standing in the ring yelled. This was met with a shuffling banter of amusement among the others. The big man smiled even more broadly, twirled the knife in his hand and, in a single fluid movement, slipped it into a leather sheath at his waist.

"And first"—Gelanor continued unperturbed—"first of these, the Wood Maid's men, who are all, to a man, at your service."

He placed a hand on his hip, held the other before him, and bowed grandly.

This quick turn of fortune left Kal weak, and he fell to one knee, leaning heavily on his sword. He vomited and remained bent over, heaving for breath.

"What? You are not pleased to see us?" Gelanor said, straightening, his laughter joining that of several of his men. "Come, Feylon! Water for my lord Bard. And some for his nervous friend. Here, Bowllyn—step lively, now!"

Kal nodded to the man who handed him a water skin. He filled his mouth, spat, and then drank greedily of the water. His burning thirst slaked, he paused and returned the skin to its owner. Wiping his chin on the back of his hand, Kal rose shakily to his feet. He slid Rhodangalas into its scabbard and turned to look at his companion. Gwyn remained fixed in place, ignoring the outstretched water skin, bow still bent and arrow point quavering, his face blanched. Kal rested a hand on Gwyn's arm, and the young Holdsman slowly lowered his weapon, his eyes blinking back tears.

Kal faced the big man and stooped his head. "My apologies... And my thanks to you, Gelanor, and to your men."

"Bah! Think nothing of it! It was no more than was asked of us. And no more than ought one bard do for another, eh?" Gelanor said and winked as he pointed to the pios pinning Kal's cloak, then lifted his woolly chin to point to a glinting pios buried deep in the grey fur at his own throat. "Nay, no more than ought one bard do for another, little brother!"

The big man stepped forward and clapped an enormous hand on Kal's shoulder.

"Come," he said, "come, be at peace. In Wuldor's pity and by Ruah's guidance, you are safe. But, now, pardon me for but a moment."

Gelanor turned away from Kal and Gwyn. In a fog, Kal listened as the big man dispatched various groups of his men to deal with the corpses of both dog and man. Kal realized that the surrounding ground must be strewn with gore and the bodies of those that had pursued them into the Woods of Tircoil. He was thankful that what he did not wish to see was hidden yet in darkness beyond the reach of the torchlight, and he refused to follow with his eyes the torches that were plucked up and carried into the Woods in all directions as men hastened to do Gelanor's bidding.

Kal became aware of how badly his head throbbed. His knee ached and burned as well. Beside him, Gwyn had collapsed to the ground, sitting as though his legs had buckled under him. Someone had pressed a water skin into the young man's hands, but this he held, unnoticed, as he stared vacantly into the dark Woods.

Kal lifted a trembling hand to the side of his head, gently fingering across his brow. He felt a long gash and withdrew a hand crimsoned in blood. He instinctively backed away from the dripping fingers held before his eyes.

"Ho, little brother! It's a mighty blow that's cracked your egg. Let me look to the shell." Gelanor stood in front of Kal and placed a hand on his back, stopping his retreat. The big man must have been observing him for a while, for he held a wet cloth, which he lifted to Kal's head, and wiped away the blood from his face. Turning the rag, he blotted along the wound. He had a surprisingly delicate touch, but still Kal winced. Gelanor pulled back his hand.

"Come, come, little brother," he clucked. "There's more leak than break. Not all that bad. Nothing a patch of green pitch can't mend." The big bard now pressed a thick paste onto Kal's head none too gently with his thumb as Kal winced again. "There, that'll hold. Though, by the look of it, the egg's yet a bit scrambled!" The big man chuckled. "A good thing the hen still scratches, eh?"

"Thank you." Kal lifted his eyes to Gelanor's face. "Thank you."

His knee still pained him, but, by a surreptitious glance, Kal determined that his leg was not cut, bleeding, or broken, marked only with a bruise he could suffer for the time being and tend to himself when time permitted.

Gelanor had moved on to Gwyn and taken a quick survey of the other Holdsman to ensure he was in one piece and sound, and, satisfied that he was, stood again and faced the two men.

"Well, now, if you're both fit and able, we've a walk ahead of us to get to Mousehold afore—"

"Mousehold?" Kal said.

"Aye, Mousehold."

"Where the old woman lives?"

"Aye, the Wood Maid. And, if I were you, I'd not be calling her 'old woman,' leastwise not to her face."

"But who is she, the Wood Maid?" Kal asked, looking at the big man. "And who are you?"

"Well, now, that's two questions, little brother, and no doubt those two will spawn many more, whole families, I'd wager, before they're through, as is the way of things." Gelanor winked, and his braided beard shook with his laughter. "Aye, as is the way of things! But come, let us be on our way now. We'll talk as we walk."

Kal turned to retrieve the gear he had lost during the attack only to find the pelt-covered form of one of Gelanor's men standing near him, already holding the codynnos, bow, and quiver. The man stepped forward and handed these to Kal, as if in anticipation of the Holdsman's desire, and Kal slung them over his shoulders. Beside him, Gwyn had been likewise re-outfitted with his belongings and stood dazed but ready to depart. Kal was aware of a weight missing from his belt.

On the ground before him lay the rent skin. Beads of water near it were still held cupped in what few upturned brown leaves had escaped being trampled in the passage of so many feet. Kal crouched down slowly and lifted a leaf, its quivering burden golden in the torchlight. He tipped the leaf and rolled the heavy drop onto his open palm, where it broke apart and dispersed between his fingers. He wiped his hand on his tunic and stood.

"Aye, little brother, I noticed that in the scare you broke water."

Kal frowned at the quip, at Gelanor's grinning face, and at the chortles that sprang up among the men who overheard.

"But the water is the reason we came here!" Kal said hotly.

"Aye. It's the reason most come here. Or so did in ages past."

Kal rounded on the big man. "Well, it's the reason I made this hateful journey, and I need it."

"A hateful journey, is it?"

"Yes, detestable! So, while we're here anyway, could we not go back to the Well and get more water? As I said, I need it."

"Aye, could do, could do . . . but won't," the big bard stated flatly.

"But I need it!"

"Well, then, let's to Mousehold and see what the Wood Maid says about that." Gelanor set his jaw and thrust his chin forward, his braided beard jutting out sharply.

"You do not know who I—"

"Nay, I can't say that I rightly do know who you are. What I do know is that we saved you from a spot of trouble and that now—right now—we are heading back to Mousehold to see Katie Woodencloak. So, will you walk, or do I have to carry you?"

Kal saw the hard glint in the man's eye and knew it was futile, even dangerous, to press the point any further.

The bard spun around, the silver wolf's tail and legs swinging behind him. With a sharp sweep of his hand and a barked command, he ordered his men to begin walking. Kal fell in beside the big bard, and Gwyn shambled in behind. Kal shot a glance up at the bard. Though he still scowled, the cast of Gelanor's countenance soon softened. His was like a clear summer sky on a breezy day in which any aberrant puff of cloud is soon swept away.

As they walked deeper into the Woods, the torchlight pooled around them on the forest floor, breaking against the blackness beyond. Kal saw no sign of bodies, but here and there blood stained the disturbed leaves and broken twigs and brush. There was no doubt that butchery had taken place here.

Soon, however, they were pacing through clear forest, a column of torches snaking through the Woods before and behind them. In the soft light, Kal saw that once again great-limbed and huge-boled trees spread over the spacious forest floor, as when they had first entered the Woods and also along Hoël's Dyke. After little more than a minute's silent trudging, Kal ventured to make conversation again with the man.

"To see Katie Woodencloak...? Who is she?"

"Katie Woodencloak? Aye, to be sure, she's the Wood Maid. A spirit younger than any of us, and a wisdom more ancient. Beyond that, you'll have to ask her yourself, little brother."

"We're going to see her?"

"Aye, to Mousehold, to see the Wood Maid, as I told you...." The big man eyed Kal sideways. "So, your egg did get scrambled. Or perhaps a wee bit baked?"

"And she's the one that we met? The woman who gave us the oatcakes?"

"Aye, so I'd imagine, so I'd imagine. Especially if they were the finest oatcakes you've ever eaten in your life! She's a cook! She's a cook—the finest!" He looked over his shoulder to the man walking behind him. "Mind you echo that not to my Ellyn, else no meat I'll meet at my table for a long while!"

"No, Gelanor, for sure, I'd say naught of the kind," the fellow said, shaking his head, then broke out laughing. "Might say something of the like, though!" His mates joined in the banter at the big bard's expense.

"Ach, go on, the lot of you! Enough that I've got to chief you, but to put up with your giggling jibes the while. Why, it's enough to—"

"To make you weep, Gelanor?" another man taunted. "Eh, big man?"

The banter thickened among the men behind Gelanor, the men ahead turning to look back and smile.

"Bah!" Gelanor growled, feigning irritation. Then turning to Kal, he said with a wink, "Pay them no mind, no mind, else they'll drive you out of it."

"What of the waldscathes? The terror of the Woods? Are they real?"

"Waldscathes? Aye, little brother, they are real," Gelanor said soberly. "To be sure, they are. And a terror besides, leastwise to those that don't know them. Once you do, why, they're really quite friendly beasts. Once you get to know them."

"You know them?"

"Aye, met them more than once."

"And you live in the Woods?"

"Aye, me and hundreds besides. There are villages scattered around the Black Cape in the Woods—villages of families—men, women, children. We are the Tircoilian people. I am bard," Gelanor said, nodding, "but it's the Wood Maid who's our heart."

"But I thought no one lived in the Woods—"

"A common mistake."

"And that the Woods are dangerous?"

"Aye, dangerous enough if you don't know what you're about. Or if you've got a pack of Black Scorpions on your back."

Kal chuckled. "To be sure, Gelanor, again, my thanks to you and your men for—"

"Bah, think nothing of it, nothing of it."

"And for my peevishness, my apologies."

"Aye, it's a hard day you've endured. But we'll have you rest soon enough."

"No, Gelanor, I have no time for rest. You see, my father—"

"You'd best be telling that to the Wood Maid, not her bard. I was just to mind you, not hear your story."

"Bard...But you are also captain of her force?"

"Aye, chief, but no better than any of these others in warrioring. Every man of them is a worthy warrior of the wolf hide." With that the big man threw back his head and gave forth a long, rising howl, the like of which Kal had not heard until just a few hours before. Soon the entire column of men had taken up the haunting, mournful cry. The howl swelled louder and louder, held sustained for several moments, then fell away. As the echoes faded in the Woods, the cry was taken up again from far off to the west and then joined by others to the south. Gelanor walked on, a broad grin spread across his face.

Kal stared at him, incredulous. The sound that returned to the men from far away in the Woods... "Waldscathes?"

"Aye." Gelanor still grinned.

"But... but what are they?"

"Woa-ho! But... we are they! We are they!" Gelanor howled again, but this time with ringing peals of laughter.

"So... you are the dread terror of the Woods of Tircoil?" Kal said when the bard had recovered himself somewhat. "You and your men? Ah..." The Holdsman nodded with dawning comprehension. "All clad in wolf pelts and howling out warning to all trespassers and fear to all hearers."

"Aye," Gelanor said, touching the side of his nose with a large finger. "That by popular superstition we are regarded as a fearsome and terrible scourge is really quite convenient. Aye, we are the waldscathes. We make our home in the Woods, venture out when needs be, usually to take what we might be in want of. Mostly, though, we keep to ourselves, provided others keep to themselves. And if a good tale serves, who are we to argue? To be sure, it's more often than not the happenings of the commonplace and the things familiar that are most like to be bent into fireside tales of legendary proportion by the strong draught of imagination spiced with fear."

Kal smiled. It was true. Why, that's what the oldlings of the Holding fed the young a steady diet of in the snug hearth glow of a winter's night, yarns spun from aged imagination for the sake of young imagination by the likes of Old Sarmel, a long-toothed spinner if ever there was one.

"So, waldscathes is it?"

"Aye, waldscathes it is."

"Then it was you I saw on the path to the Well earlier?"

"Aye, one of the men."

"Why were you there? How did you know to save us?"

"Again with coupling questions, little brother!" Gelanor grinned more broadly yet. "Well, it was the Wood Maid herself that sent us to follow you. We were to keep an eye—there are terrors in the Woods, you know."

"Aye, and worse ones than the waldscathes."

"To be sure, worse than the waldscathes to you, but not to the waldscathes. The Wood Maid knew that you were being tracked. Well, she sent us along to do some tracking, too. Sure enough, there were the Black Scorpions, a whole troop of them, Telessarian trackers besides, and their lymers—that's a nasty looking brute, is that dog. There were a couple dozen Southwoldsmen besides. They were none too happy to be trotting down Hoël's Dyke, let alone be driven into the Woods by their masters. Aye, but we've got them well trained." Gelanor winked and nodded his head sideways. "They balked. Wouldn't move more than a few paces into the Woods. Stopped dead. And dead is what a couple of them became, at the point of a Scorpion's sword sting, before the Scorpions gave up on them and the rest turned tail and ran away howling." The big bard laughed again. "It was sweetness to behold."

"But if you saw them, why didn't you come and warn us?"

"Aye, little brother, but do you think we were howling for our own sake?"

"You chased us back to the Well..."

"Aye, and the Well is the one sure safe place in the Woods, that and Mousehold. To be sure, Ruah's Well is hallowed ground, and no evil has ever broached the Wellvale. You see, little brother, it is sacred and protected, not just the Well but the whole valley, sacred and protected by Ruah herself. There was a time, a time long ago, that people might actually see the white hind there. The white hind, mind you, looking just like herself's stone image in the Well." Gelanor fell silent, lost in thought, taken by the thought of an ancient memory, one far beyond his remembering.

"I saw her."

"What?" Gelanor jerked his head up, looking at Kal.

"I saw her." Kal said softly, lifting his gaze from the ground in front of his feet and facing the bard. The big man had lost his grin, a look of stark disbelief now settling over his features.

"Aye, I saw her, when we first came to the Well, and then again as we returned in the afternoon, after you chased us back into the valley, like she was guiding us back to the Well."

"And still you left? After seeing her? Bolted in the middle of the night?" The bard shook his woolly head. "Aye, but you'd do well to better mind her bidding in the future, little brother. But that you saw her..."

"What of it, Gelanor? You make it sound as though it was—"

"Aye, and it is! Rare, uncommon rare. More than that. To be sure, no one's seen the white hind in years upon years, and even longer. That—well, that you did. It's a rare gift, something precious. Aye, more than precious... significant!" The bard spoke the word with triumph, then nodded slowly. "You'd best tell that to the Wood Maid right off when you see her. She'll know what it means, little brother. She'll know what it means."

Gelanor said nothing more, and neither did Kal. Both were lost amid their thoughts, pondering recent happenings and the strange meeting that was about to take place at Mousehold.

The column marched steadily on without stopping, steadily through the never-ending forest. Gradually, light grew among the trees, a faint light that unveiled trunks stretching upwards to the roof of leaf and branch. Now the first birds of day began a swirling trill of interlaced song, melodies weaving and overlaying one another. Before long, dawn broke. The sun having cleared the spires of the Radolans to the east, a virescent light filtered through the trees, forcing the forest shadows to retreat to the narrow ravines and hollows scattered through the Woods.

They had been walking for nearly three hours. No longer did Kal's head ache, nor did his knee, at least not badly. He felt tired and yet strangely alert. Perhaps it was his eagerness to meet the mysterious Katie Woodencloak again that imparted a lightness to his step and his spirit. Kal looked over his shoulder to where Gwyn plodded along. The mute Holdsman had withdrawn into himself once more, and Kal wondered if he had not been overwhelmed by the happenings of the night before. It must have been a horrible shock to the lad, and yet there was a depth of strength in Gwyn that Kal had only recently begun to notice—particularly so after the curious business at the Well. Something in Gwyn had changed, and for the good, of that Kal was sure.

Beside him, Gelanor strolled, silent but smiling, evidently enjoying the early morning jaunt that they were having.

"Kalaquinn Wright."

"Hmm?"

"Kalaquinn Wright," Kal said again. "My name is Kalaquinn Wright. It occurred to me that I hadn't yet introduced myself. My apologies. And this is Gwyn, Gwyn Fletcher." Gwyn blinked to life at the mention of his name and nodded at the bard, who looked back at him.

"Aye, good then," the bard said. "Kalaquinn Wright and Gwyn Fletcher. It is good to have known you these past few hours. I trust we shall know you for a few yet to come!" Gelanor laughed.

The column crested a small rise in the lay of the woodland, which fell into a narrow stretch of forest before climbing again up another small rise. A trail cut across their way, running along the depression, the rises on either side of it.

"Ah, look now. Here we are," said Gelanor. "Lads! Lads, we rest here a moment."

The column of men collapsed in on itself in the shallow depression that ran off to their left and right. Men sat on the ground or leaned against trees. It was the first time that Kal had got a chance to look at Gelanor's small army. There were, indeed, men of all ages, about seventy or eighty of them, and all seemed attentive to their chief as he looked cross-eyed through his beard at his chest, pulling at his pios.

"Methinks it be time for a tune!" the big bard cried as he managed to unfasten the tiny harp and hold it before himself, the thing barely visible in the man's huge hands. He looked over at Kal and winked. "Come, my lord bard. Let us play!"

With that, Gelanor plucked, or rather, Kal noticed with amusement, struck the tiny instrument. Nevertheless, from the small harp rose a sweet chord, followed but a moment later by a wordless song of such deep, booming resonance that it sounded not unlike the rolling voice of a cataract, not unlike the voice of Skell Force. Kal realized with wonder that, even though the notes were deep and earth-born, the tune was unmistakable—they had come to Carric-thona.

Kal saw the big bard wink at him even as he sang. In a flash, Kal plucked his own pios from his cloak and set his finger to its wires. Immediately, notes flew into the air, a chord blending with that of the other, even as Kal had heard the dawn-inspired birdsong do. Then, with the chiming harps echoing and re-echoing one another, Kal began to sing. To his astonishment, his voice had the mellow and pure tone of a flute, climbing and falling along the scales over the undercurrent of Gelanor's sonorous bass.

Kal looked at his fellow bard. The big man beamed broadly, his blue eyes dancing in the morning light, and, as he winked at Kal again, both men burst into lines of song.

> "Along the narrow woodland way well worn
> Amid a viridescence, morning born,
> Beneath the leafing roof of oak and beech,
> Take heart, the way is done, its end in reach,
> Safe haven from dark terror's thunder-stroke—
> 'Tis Mousehold! Home to Katie Woodencloak!"

Even as the two bards played and sang, the men quickly reformed into a loose and broader column and turned east along the floor of the hollow, which ran for but a furlong and then gave onto the falling and open glade in which was nestled Mousehold.

At the edge of the glade, Gelanor removed his hand from the pios and began pinning it back on to his wolfskin tunic. The men of his company had disappeared, disbanding unseen into the surrounding forest. Kal, too, stopped playing and held the pios in his clenched hand. Beside him stood Gwyn, a bemused expression on his face, looking around at the now empty woodland. In front them, in the centre of the dell, stood the grey-timbered cottage of Mousehold, and, between it and the men, flanked on one side by a stand of white birch, were the circular ruins and crumbling tower.

"Aye, there...," said the big bard, triumphing over the tiny brooch. "Such a fuss. Such a fuss, to be sure." He patted his chest and turned to Kal. "Right, then, you and Gwyn stay here while I go fetch the Wood Maid. She'll want to greet you right and welcome you to Mousehold herself. Peculiar, that way... So, I'll be right back, then."

With that the great red-haired, fur-clad man lumbered down the path to the cottage. On his back, a wolf's head, upside down and swaying back and forth, stared vacantly back at the two Holdsmen.

FIFTEEN

Gelanor disappeared from sight through the low greenwood hedge and around the corner of the cottage, but his booming voice rose to where he had left Kal standing. "Wood Maid? Ho, Mistress Katie!"

Kal smiled to himself and rocked his head slowly back and forth. Gwyn had drifted down the gentle slope and come to rest by the ruins of the glence. The young man sat on the grass, his weapons and codynnos beside him, his back against the crumbling stonework of the glence tower, which afforded him some shade from the sunlight that flooded the open glade. In a moment, the lad's head bobbed twice, then drooped heavily onto his chest.

Minutes stretched as Kal stood waiting, pondering the scene before him, overhung by a peaceful languor as by a haze. The silence was disturbed only by the lazy drone of insects and the summer song of birds.

Without even realizing it, Kal found himself descending the narrow path, following it as it skirted the tower beneath which Gwyn slept and bent around the tumbled walls of the broken glence itself. The path wound between stones that lay strewn in the grass about the ancient building, stones that had fallen from what was once the dome of the structure. The base of its circular wall remained, but for the most part it barely cleared waist height and rose higher only here and there, raggedly, overgrown with ivy and creepers. Only the glence tower, abutting the glence's wall, seemed to have more or less survived the ravages of time. It stood solid and intact, although roofless, crenellated by years of wind

169

and rain, and covered with choking tendrils that overtopped the empty lip of the tower.

Kal dropped his gaze again to the path as he rounded the walls and approached the front portal of the glence, now little more than a break in the low stone circle directly across from the tower not thirty paces away. The portal gaped open, a broken arch of smoothly cut fitted blocks flanked on either side by crumbling stonework. Its stout wooden doors had long since rotted away, leaving an incomplete set of heavy rusted hinges hanging loosely from pins still set in what remained of the arch.

Having never before traveled beyond the mountain-ringed bounds of the Stoneholding, Kal had not set foot in any glence other than the chiefest of them all, the Great Glence itself. Now he breathed the still air of these ruins and traced the fractured curve of the portal's stone with his hand. It was cold to touch, and he shivered involuntarily as a chill of wonderment swept over him. He crossed the threshold, measuring the remains of this glence against what Wilum had told him about these structures that dotted the landscape of Ahn Norvys, their beehive domes a reflection of the Great Glence.

This must have been one of the smaller glences, Kal mused as he surveyed the jagged rise and fall of the circular wall and the space within. At least the harpstone was still standing, just a few paces in from the doorway, a square pillar beneath which would be found the glence mark. Kal moved past the harpstone, across the broken and heaved flagstone floor towards the large round slab of the temen stone. It lay at the very middle of the structure, rising less than half the height of a man. Kal lifted his gaze. Directly across from him, on the other side of the temen stone, near the farther curve of the rear wall and overshadowed by the tower behind, stood the hindstone. These—the tower, the hindstone, the temen stone, along with the harpstone—would all stand on the songline. To his left and to his right, on opposite sides of the temen stone, were the dexter and sinister stones, the one still standing firmly planted, the other toppled and lying on its side amid grass-grown rubble.

Kal ran his hand over the smooth top of the temen stone and saw the telltale grooves worn into it. Here, for generation upon generation, the bard of this glence had placed his stool. Here he would sit and face the harpstone and, beyond that—far, far, beyond that—the Great Glence. Then, to the tune of his harp, the bard would chant the orrthon or recite passages and sing ballads from the *Criochoran.*

Kal turned around and hopped up to sit on the broad slab of the temen stone. He looked about himself slowly and let his gaze rest on the harpstone in front of him, the empty portal beyond that, and the grey cottage still farther beyond. Then he closed his eyes and let the morning sunlight bathe him.

To his mind flitted a picture of terrific desolation, eerily fleeting but overpowering. A wave of ashen sadness washed over him. As through a gossamer veil, he saw the Great Glence before him—its keeil a scorched shell, its tower fallen, the stone fragments of its vaulted dome strewn over Wuldor's Howe like a child's wooden blocks knocked over and abandoned. But—his heart leaped, his breath caught in his throat—there, stark in the midst of the desolation, rising bare and unshielded from the sky, remained the dark bulking mass of the Stone. The Glence Stone, standing where it had always stood, hallowing the spot even now.

Kal opened his eyes and blinked in the light, the vision of aged ruins replacing that of freshly wrought devastation. How long he had been lost in thought, he was unsure, but, over his shoulder to his right, he saw that Gwyn had awoken from his napping. The young Holdsman was now seated on a fallen block of masonry beyond the glence wall, hunched over an arrow, adjusting its fletchwork. The sun was growing warmer, and a tang of woodsmoke touched the air.

"Ah, there you are, little brother." Kal spun around. Gelanor filled the space beneath the broken arch of the doorway, grinning. In front of the big bard stood the lady who had sped them on their way the day before. She wore the same sad smile Kal had seen when last they met, and in her grey eyes lay the same depth of wisdom, still mostly veiled as by a shining mist. A friend, Kal remembered her saying, and known to Aelward.

"I'd wondered if we'd lost you," Gelanor continued, entering the ruins and coming to stand beside the woman. "Thought you might have wandered off into the Woods. Wandered off again, so that me and the lads would have to come and save your wayward hide!"

The woman placed a hand on the big bard's arm, looking up at him.

"I do not think that you realize in whose presence you have

been this past night, Gelanor." She let her hand drop. Then, turning to Kal, she bowed her head slightly, still smiling, and said, "Welcome. Welcome to Mousehold once again, my lord Myghternos Hordanu."

Gelanor reared to his full height, blinking with surprise.

The woman's smile broke into a gentle laugh that sounded as sweet as the warm spring rain pattering on a slate roof. Kal found that, while his shock at the woman's revelation of his true office was evidently not nearly as profound as was Gelanor's, he wondered nonetheless how the strange woman could have discerned that he was indeed the High Bard. She had called him by title before, just yesterday, when he and Gwyn had been taking their leave of her, but he had dismissed it at the time as something that she had not actually said, considering it rather something that he had only thought he heard—but now, here it was.

"For once, my good bard is caught speechless," the woman said. "Come, come, Gelanor, do bid welcome our master to Mousehold."

"And you ... you, Wise Mother. You must be Katie Wooden-cloak," Kal stammered as he scrambled off the temen stone and stepped across the narrow distance towards her.

"Why didn't you tell me, little bro— ah, rather ... my lord ... ? My lord Hordanu?" Gelanor bowed deeply, his face crimsoned. "My deepest apologies, my lord. To be sure, I did not know."

"But Mistress Katie ..." Kal, in his confusion, ignored the big man, who remained nearly doubled over before him. "How did you know me as anything more than a bard?"

"There is much, Master Kalaquinn, much that I know, and much more that I do not. But that you are High Bard of all of Ahn Norvys was clear to me the first time that I set my eyes upon you. It is etched in your being. And that you would come to visit me is not entirely unexpected. I have anticipated this moment, though you are more in the spring of life than I had imagined the Hordanu to be." She held Kal in a look coloured with just the slightest edge of suspicious scrutiny. This, however, faded quickly and vanished as she smiled warmly again. "But be that as it may, you are welcome, Master Kalaquinn, for now has Ruah, most gentle of the anagoroi, seen fit to guide your feet to my door. I do also apologize for my bard's overly familiar and less than respectful manner."

"My deepest thanks for your welcome, and for your assistance this past night and day, Mistress Katie. Rest assured that Master Gelanor has been most shrewd, attending to things more important than the petty courtesies owed the office of High Bard. I'd rather than not forego the courtesy and yet remain his 'little brother.' As long as I am 'little brother' to him, I remain in his good graces, and a safer place for the moment I cannot imagine."

Kal paused, then turned his attention to the bard still bent over beside him.

"Come now—stand, Gelanor. Is it not simple prudence that I conceal my identity? Given the nature of these days and the journey I undertake? Surely you, Master Waldscathe, understand that." Kal chuckled lightly as the great bard straightened himself. "Consider also, big brother, that doing so has afforded me the chance to turn table on you and render you payment in kind for your wolfish deceptions."

"Aye, payment in kind, my lord," Gelanor said, grinning sheepishly, his colour going down, "and payment in full."

"Well, now," Katie said, looking from the giant red-haired bard to Kal, "you'd think that, in his life of desperate outlawry, he'd have learned that appearances are deceiving." She turned towards the vacant doorway of the ruins, beckoning him follow. "Come, then, Master Kalaquinn."

Kal felt the awkward stiffness of the moment begin to thaw and soften.

"This glence...," he ventured, pointing around at the stones and overgrown rubble as he stepped behind the woman. "Why—?"

"Why is it fallen to wrack and ruin?" Katie said over her shoulder.

Kal nodded. "Yes, why?"

"It was found as it now stands. There is another glence that fills our need. It lies farther along Carric-thona. You shall see." Katie now led them out of the circle of stones towards the low hedge surrounding her cottage. Seeing the others making for the house, Gwyn left his stone and shambled in behind them.

"Me and my men, we've offered to repair it many a time, to be sure. We've offered to repair it and make it like it was built new," said Gelanor, looking ahead at Katie. He pressed beside Kal and seemed to the Hordanu to have wilted somewhat in his stature.

"But I've told them to hold off, to leave the ruins as they are." Katie stopped, turning back to the three men following her along the path to the cottage. "They are a reminder to me, these ruins, to us all, that we are but creatures of a day, that all we really accomplish, all we do, is as a puff of smoke before the wind. The crumbling masonry"—she looked past the men to the fallen glence—"and the weed-choked stones, they bid us be mindful of what happens to merely human strivings. They bid us be mindful of what is truly important...." Her gaze lifted to Kal's face, and she laid a hand on his breast. "Here... This is the heart of the matter. In truth, it is what you are that will bear out through the ages. The grand doings of head and hand—these may say something that lasts to speak to coming generations.... But the heart. Ah, the heart, it speaks things unseen and unheard, hidden, quiet. It speaks to eternity."

Katie lowered her hand to her side and in silence resumed her way along the smooth gravel path bordered by raised flower beds, past an ivy-clad trellis arched over a summer table, to the door of her cottage. Her words puzzled Kal and struck him as curiously out of step with the evident care and time she devoted to the gardens and grounds surrounding the small cottage. He shook his head at the paradox and, in the charming prettiness of Mousehold, remembered the beauty of the Well.

"But there are times, are there not, times when we catch even just a glimpse of what lies beyond the busy passing of our days? Surely we can see something that will remain, something that will never crumble or know decay," Kal said with more vehemence than he'd intended.

Katie paused, turning to face Kal at the threshold of the door, her face marred by a frown.

"How do you mean?" she asked pointedly.

"I... Well... I-I mean... Back at Ruah's Well—"

"He caught sight of herself, of the white hind. Not once, but twice," Gelanor said, stepping forward with thumb and forefinger raised to show the count. Behind him, Gwyn nodded his corroboration of Gelanor's report, his jaw set and expression grim.

Katie glanced first at her bard and the mute Holdsman, then back at Kal. Her grey eyes bore a look of urgency, of an intensity that demanded a response.

"I-I did...," Kal started. "I did. I saw the white hind, as real as you or me. I will never forget it."

A heavy silence fell over the group at the door to the cottage.

The woman bowed gravely and took Kal's hands in her own, as she had when they first met. "My lord Myghternos Hordanu..." She looked up into Kal's eyes, her own eyes growing wet. "My lord Myghternos Hordanu, in all the years we've lived here, there's not a one of us that has seen Ruah as you have. It is a privilege. It is a special privilege. No, more than that..." Katie's voice trailed off into silence for a moment. She broke her gaze from Kal, looking at his hands as she lifted them gently in her own, rocking them as if to add emphasis to her words. "But it is also as it should be. Yes, for she holds the Hordanu in her protection."

Kal nodded.

"Ah, me..." She sighed, let go Kal's hands, turned swiftly, and opened the door. "Come now, come in. Have a seat and break your fast. There's a pot of venison stew on the trivet."

"Courtesy of Baron Nuath's deer chase. A well-stocked larder, to be sure. Free of poachers, but not of wolf-men!" Laughing, Gelanor waggled the wolf's-head visor over his shoulder, then shepherded the two Holdsmen into the homely cottage.

Kal followed Gelanor's example as Gwyn followed Kal's, unslinging satchels, bows, and quivers, peeling off cloaks and boots, and unbuckling sword belts. All of these they hung on pegs behind the door or left neatly leaning by the wall.

The ceiling beams were hung with drying herbs above a floor flagged with well-worn slate. Katie had retreated to the hearth, where a small fire crackled happily beneath a heavy black pot suspended from the hook of a wrought-iron cooking stand. The woman lifted the lid and stirred its contents. A hearty thyme-spiced fragrance filled the air. Katie pointed to an oak trestle table lined with benches and covered with platters of cheese and bread, together with a moisture-beaded pitcher—ale, no doubt. Kal's appetite and thirst trebled in that instant. His mouth watered, and an ache clenched his gut.

Gelanor snatched up a handful of bowls from the table and marched to the fireplace. Standing over the stew pot, he inhaled, drawing a deep, savouring breath.

"Ah, Wood Maid!" He pronounced his approval and fumbled to produce a bowl, into which Katie ladled venison stew. "Here, for my lord Hordanu." He held out the bowl to Kal, who took it, nodding his thanks. "Now you, Gwyn. Come, lad," Gelanor said, beckoning the young man with another empty bowl, which he then held out to be filled with food. The two Holdsmen took their seats and sat waiting, looking hungrily at their bowls.

"Don't wait on us," Katie said. "You may eat. Please, eat."

The Holdsmen obediently fell to their meal without hesitation.

"Will you have some yourself, Wood Maid?" Gelanor asked.

"No, not for me." Katie shook her head. "Go, take your fill and show our guests that besides your talents with knife and cudgel, pios and voice, you're a passing fine trencherman. You've more than earned it, by the sound of things. It was a hard night's work, and I must make certain that my chief wolf's-head remains in good mirth."

"With victuals like this," Gelanor said around a mouthful of venison, "you're like to keep me in good girth as well." He patted his stomach and grinned broadly. Gwyn looked up at Katie and smiled, still chewing, his mouth full of freshly buttered bread.

For some minutes no words were spoken as the three men sated their hunger. Katie fussed in a small alcove that served as her pantry, leaving the men to the work of their food. Presently she returned to the table and asked if there was anything more they needed.

"Mistress Katie, I thank you for your kind hospitality," Kal said, rising from the bench and the empty bowl in front of him, his brow furrowing with concern. "I don't mean to be rude, but I must be returning to the Well. The two skins I filled with healing water were broken, the water lost in our flight."

"Indeed, Gelanor mentioned as much," she replied calmly.

"But I have to have the water, for my father's sake, and then make haste on to Kingshead Cove." Grim-faced, Kal shivered. A chill of foreboding crept over him. "There's no telling what state he's in, what with his wound and the poison. Already I'm afraid I've lingered overlong."

"Stay, Master Kalaquinn." Katie gestured with upturned hand, an unexpected firmness in her voice. "You may not go."

Kal froze, speechless with shock. Gwyn stopped chewing and looked up, spoon held in midair, while Gelanor peered over the rim of the bowl he had lifted to his lips. This the bard lowered slowly to the table, setting it down with a gentle thump, and wiped his mouth on his sleeve.

"There are things," Katie said, her tone softening, "things I would show you before you leave Mousehold. And there's little time, as you must resume a more pressing journey. There is not time for you to make the trip to Ruah's Well and back. There is not time."

Kal stared in disbelief. "But I—"

"Your folk await you, yes?"

"Aye, but my fath—"

"And the ship leaves at sunset tomorrow, yes?"

"Aye ..."

"And Aelward expects your arrival, yes?"

"Aye, yes, he ..." Kal knit his brow, bewildered. "But how do you—"

"There is much I would show you, Master Kalaquinn, and precious little time to do so. What's more, you need to take what rest you can, while you may. And there is no better rest to be had than that taken in the peace of Mousehold. There is simply no time to go to the Well, so do not worry yourself over the water." Katie flicked her hand dismissively.

"B-but y-you sent me off yesterday," Kal sputtered, his ire bubbling over. "Just yesterday, you sent me off on that journey—a journey, might I add, that about cost me my life—to fetch healing water, which was why I came here in the first place, to get the water, and now it's gone. And I need it. And you refuse to let me go for it? I-I ..."

Katie's grey eyes flashed as she fixed Kal with a penetrating gaze and said calmly, "The water is not what brought you here, and the water is not of first importance. You did not make a journey for the water—you made the journey for its own sake. Your heart knows this, Kalaquinn. Let reason be led. In all journeys of life, it is not in achieving the goal but in striving for it that one's purpose is found. Peace. All will be well."

Kal was nearly beside himself with consternation. He gave Gelanor an imploring look, begging the bard for some explanation for the woman's obtuse, rigid, riddling manner. The big man merely hunched his shoulders up to a face that wore an expression of bemused innocence, as if to say, "What do I know?"

Kal sagged, defeated, and heaved a sigh. He sank back to the bench.

"Wood Maid," Gelanor ventured timidly. "Perhaps I might go in his stead?"

Katie's smile returned and, like the summer sun, chased away the vagrant mists of frustration that wound about the Hordanu.

"Yes. Such was my hope, dear bard. And such is my desire, if you are willing."

"Aye, more than willing. More than willing, to be sure. I'll leave now," the bard said, then caught himself and turned to Kal. "If you would permit me to go for you?"

Kal nodded his assent, feeling somewhat giddy from the quick spin of events and emotion. "It would please me greatly if you would render me that service."

"Good, then, little brother! Um...ah...my humble apologies again, Master Kalaquinn." The bard blushed once more at his slip.

"Not at all," Kal said, laughing. "No, let it stand as 'little brother,' for I am honoured that you've been so ready, from the very first, to make me a member of your brotherhood."

"Aye, to be sure, I've thought of you as one of our own right from the start, from the start. As far as I'm concerned, you're one of our band. A waldscathe. And Gwyn, too." Gelanor raised his pot of ale in salute.

"Without benefit of ceremony, mind. And lacking naught but the wolf pelt," Katie said as she laughed and picked up the soiled bowls from the table.

"Which will be supplied in due course, in due course. And we'll not stand on ceremony, eh, little brother?" Gelanor winked and rose from the bench. "First things first, though. I'll go back to Ruah's Well, and, with all due respect, Master Kalaquinn, I'll make a shorter journey of it than you. Aye, to be sure, I could find my way there blindfolded if I needed to."

Gelanor took down a small wooden keg from where it hung by a leather strap from a beam in the pantry. He bounced the thing in a huge hand, studying it for a moment, then slung the cask to his back, looping its leather band over his shoulder, and started to the door. Gwyn had left the table and drifted to the bard's side as the bard pulled his boots on.

"What?" The huge chief of the forest straightened to face Gwyn, arms akimbo. "You want to tag along with me, eh? Is that it, little brother?" Gwyn bobbed his head once in agreement. His flame-red hair tousled, and a look of grim determination on his face, he planted his hands on his hips, matching the big man's attitude. Gelanor scratched at the tangle of red atop his own head and laughed. "Well, now, I'm not after telling you not to. Especially as you're a brother-in-arms, too. Aye, a brother-in-arms, a waldscathe like the rest of us. If it's all right with you, Master Kalaquinn? It's but a short jaunt. But long enough to work up a hunger. We'll be back in time for one of Mistress Katie's suppers. Something not to be missed."

"And that will be a second meal missed at your table," said Katie. "And sure, but you'll catch it from Ellyn on that."

"Bah! It should be safe enough. As will be the journey for the lad here—safe enough," continued Gelanor. "The men have scoured the woods clean of vermin."

"Right enough, Master Waldscathe. It's fine by me," Kal said. "If that's what he wants, and it seems it is, let him go along with you."

"Yes, by all means," Katie replied. "He'll be in good hands."

"But don't be fooled. Gwyn may be slight, but he's a man to be reckoned with. If there's danger to be met, I'd wager that there's not one of your band who's a better archer." Kal turned his gaze from Gelanor to Katie. "I'm puzzled though, Mistress Katie. Why did you not send Gelanor for the healing water when Gwyn and I first came to Mousehold?"

"Because he and his men were about their business elsewhere...."

Kal waited for Katie to continue. An uncomfortable silence ensued.

"And? And what else?" he asked.

"And..." The woman looked into Kal's eyes again. "Master Kala-quinn, does your heart not tell you what was the true purpose of the journey you made to the Well?"

"To fetch the healing water for myself?"

Katie lowered her gaze to the floor. "You do not yet seem to understand, so I shall make it clear to you. And may you soon learn to listen with ears other than those on your head...." Katie lifted her grey eyes to look at the young Hordanu. "I did not send Gelanor on that journey for the very reason that you were meant, as Hordanu, to visit Ruah's Well. You were meant, as Hordanu, to catch rare sight of the white hind. A foretoken of your mission. I did not know it at the time. Sometimes, a reason can only be known after the fact... if you have the eyes to see it." After a moment's pause, the woman smiled again at Kal. "But," she said, "it is enough. You shall learn this in time."

Kal fell silent. He remembered the fleeting visions he had experienced at the Well.

Katie rounded now on Gelanor, shooing him with her hands.

"No need for you to gawk here. Get on with you! And you, Gwyn! Go on!"

The big man snatched his silver wolf's pelt from its peg and fled out the door, followed closely by the young Holdsman, who stepped lightly in his wake.

Still lost in thought, Kal yawned, then realized that he was alone with Katie. "I'm sorry..." He yawned again. "Forgive me. I don't mean to be rude. Don't know why, but I'm so tired."

"Here, come. You need rest." Katie took him by the hand to a cot supporting a feather-filled tick in a snug room set off from the kitchen. A small window was hung with thick fabric that blocked much of the light from outside. "Lie down. Rest here. When you have slept a bit, I'll show you something that few folk outside of the Black Cape have ever seen. A wonder, though one less terrible than waldscathes."

Kal hardly heard the woman's words. A great weariness had overwhelmed him. His limbs felt leaden. Katie finished speaking and left the room, pulling the door closed behind her. Kal lay back on the simple bed and almost immediately slipped beneath the heavy blanket of exhausted sleep woven by the trials and labours of the last couple of days. It seemed like an age since he had left the peace and safety of Nua Cearta. It seemed an age.

SIXTEEN

Kal started awake. Sweat stood cold on his forehead, and his damp shirt clung to his neck, shoulders, and back. He looked up. Katie hovered over him.

"It is good now," she said softly.

"I saw him. . . . M-my father. He spoke to me, but he looked—"

"Hush. Be still. Whatever you beheld, it is good. Your face is smooth, no longer troubled. So, too, your eyes. Although, for a while, you had me worried, Kalaquinn. Your cries and groans, they filled my cottage like a storm."

Kal rose and sat on the edge of the bed. "But I think I'm too late, Mistress Katie. The healing water, it'll have come too late. I think he's . . ."

"It may be he is, yes. And if so, there is naught you can do about it but continue with your appointed task. You must not linger on what might have been. Take courage and be strong. There is much that lies before you that must yet be accomplished."

"Re'm ena, but that's near enough what he said to me himself."

Katie arched a brow questioningly.

"In my sleep, I mean. I dreamt . . . He said . . ." Kal shook his head. Then, looking up at the old woman, he began again. "I am encouraged by the words my father spoke to me in my dream." Kal saw his face gently reflected in her grey eyes for a moment. Then Katie hm-hmmed knowingly to herself and turned back to her kitchen.

"Come with me now. I've prepared a posset. It'll keep you until Gelanor and Gwyn return and we sit down to supper together."

"Supper smells delicious, whatever it is," Kal said as he pushed himself off the bed and followed Katie into the kitchen. The hearth fire had burned down to glowing coals, and the kitchen window had been thrown open to the sunlit warmth of the summer day. A breeze played in the sheer curtains.

"There you go. Help yourself." Katie pointed to a steaming mug on the table. Kal settled himself on a bench, lifted the cup, and sipped.

"Ah, good." The Holdsman sighed contentedly, warmed by the spiced sweetness of the drink.

"From the goats I keep out back. A hard lot to keep fenced in, but I've always held it's goat's milk makes the best posset."

"How long did I sleep?"

"Not nearly as long as you needed after your adventure with Gelanor's band. It's but midday. The good thing is that I'll have a chance to show you something you must see before leaving Mousehold."

Kal drained his mug and set it down in front of himself.

"You are done? Good, then. Let's be off," Katie said, snatching the empty mug from the table. Untying the apron from her waist, she bustled out of the kitchen. Beside the front door she lifted a hooded cloak from where it hung on a peg. A bright leaf-green in colour, it had a hem interlaced with elaborate patterns of gold thread. The garment seemed to be woven of heavy, coarse fibres. It had an awkward look. Nonetheless, when the woman threw it around her shoulders, it rippled and flowed like silk.

At the door, Kal lifted his sword belt from its peg. Katie turned to him and smiled, a twinkle in her grey eyes.

"Leave them. You won't need weapons. Not here, not on Carricthona in these waldscathe-infested woods."

Katie set a brisk pace from the cottage, striding past the ruins of the glence and up the flank of Mousehold's glade into the surrounding forest. The wide path ran for nearly a quarter of a mile along the bottom of a narrow depression lined on either side by the Woods of Tircoil. It was here only this morning that Kal, in the company of Gelanor's men, had joined the big bard himself in song.

Beads of sweat pricked Kal's forehead and trickled down his face. He found himself pressed to match Katie's quick stride. She began humming under her breath, a tremulous sound that blended in wonderful harmony with the twitter, rustle, and buzz of the forest. Kal recognized the tune at once and smiled. It was Carric-thona.

The woodland had the feel of an enormous hall, its floor clear of undergrowth and bramble, and its mighty trunks, branches, and deep canopy stretching up high overhead. He listened, enchanted by the tune Katie hummed, as they continued along the straight path between the ancient trees. For nearly two hours they walked unswerving into the depths of the Woods of Tircoil. Eventually, Kal marked a lightening ahead, a breach in the solid forest that grew steadily larger until the two came to a small stream, which they crossed by means of a quaint stepped bridge of sharply cut stone blocks. From the bridge, they came into the open. Kal blinked in the sunlight as Katie hurried on through a gateway in a low stone wall.

"Re'm ena, but that's a strange-looking glence! As shaggy as a sheepherder's dog, what with all the ivy clinging to it. And where's the glence tower?" Kal stood, puzzled, mopping his brow with a sleeve.

Before him, outlined against the sky, on a beautifully landscaped knoll that rose from the centre of a small lake, stood a domed shape covered with olive-green leaves. The ivy-covered glence seemed to glint and glimmer in the sunlight as the breeze stirred the leaves to life.

"Come along, Kalaquinn. Come," the woman said, bending her head and smiling.

Kal sprang forward after Katie through the opening in the wall and onto the cobbled path leading to the strange structure. A long expanse of low turf banked the lake to the left and to the right, dropping away in fragrant patches of thyme to its pebbled shores. The lawn was broken only by the footpath on which they stood and the ramparts of a stone well to their left overshadowed by a great old yew. Ahead of them, little rock gardens planted in terraced rows with stonecrop and saxifrage flanked the narrow tongue of grass that ran not a hundred paces into the lake, then widened and rose, footing the leafy glence.

Following Katie across the spit of land and onto the knoll, Kal looked up at the glence now looming over them. Its face was veiled by a dense mat of leaves attached to long branches as thin as tendrils. They mounted the rising ground, and Katie stepped towards a break in the foliage, a deep-set arch of intricately plaited withes. The braided and interwoven willowy twigs were still green, alive and in full leaf.

Kal entered the dome close behind the woman. It took a moment for his eyes to adjust to the murky half-light that seemed to seep into the windowless place.

"What kind of glence is this?" Kal stared at a grey column, the limbless trunk of a huge tree that rose from the centre of the glence where the temen stone should have been. "And the inside—the walls... Why, they are entirely hidden by ivy."

"Not hidden. Look closely, Kalaquinn."

Kal walked to the edge of the floor, head stooped, peering squint-eyed, then tentatively touched the densely knit mass. He plucked a heart-shaped leaf, its underside a muted silver-grey, like all the leaves concealing the inside walls of the glence. He turned the leaf over. Its glossy surface was a deep olive, and a filigree of veins chased the surface of the leaf to its toothed edges. He dropped the leaf and began to scrabble at the walls, trying to find something solid behind the silvery leaves with his probing hands.

"But what do you mean?" He turned back to Katie, frowning. "There are no walls here."

"Aye, there are no walls. Not leastwise walls of stone."

"Not walls of stone? You mean... you mean to say that this... this latticework of leaf and twig, that's the wall?" Kal moved back towards the centre of the chamber.

"Indeed, the wall. A living wall."

"Forgive me, Katie. I'm missing something in this. It must be my mind, still half bound by sleep." Kal rubbed his face and shook his head.

"I've been playing with you, Kalaquinn," Katie said and laughed. "There is no need for you to doubt your senses. What you see... No, what you're standing in is a—how shall I say it? What you're standing in is a glence tree."

"A glence tree? What's a glence tree?"

"Look around you," Katie said with a sweep of her arm. "All is living wood."

Kal stepped closer to examine the immense trunk at the centre of the chamber. Facing him was a large arching cleft, easily half again the height of a man, in the massive bole. As he approached it, he saw placed within the deep-set hollow, on a floor roughly knee-high from the ground, a simple wooden stool. Kal turned slowly away from the opening. There, between him and the bright entrance to the glence, rose a small pillar, a nubbled stump bark-covered and branchless. He had missed it when he first entered the glence, and now he moved towards it with fascination.

"Aye, the harpstone," Katie said. "Except that, like everything else, it's not stone."

Kal looked to his left. There, not thirty paces away, was another pillar, and directly across the domed space from that, to Kal's right, another. He knew a fourth pillarlike stump would be opposite him, hidden from his view by the tree trunk.

"Not stone," Kal said as if to himself.

"Root. They are roots pushed up by the tree."

"A glence tree." Kal looked up into the dark green reaches of the tree's crown far overhead. He could just make out the flit and dart of birds among the high branches.

"Aye, a glence tree, with living walls, living temen stone, living harpstone, living dexter, sinister, and hind stones. A living tree, aye. A glence tree," Katie chirped cheerily like one of the sparrows above.

"I've never seen a tree so...I've never seen anything of the like." Kal shook his head as he strode back to the tree trunk. He stretched out his hand and traced his fingers along the creased and furrowed pattern of dark runnels crisscrossing the smooth grey bark. "It even looks more like jointed masonry than bark. And it's so broad across the trunk."

"Big enough to make another chamber within itself," Katie said.

Kal lifted his gaze again to the branched roof high above him, his hand still resting on the trunk. "Re'm ena, but it is amazing." He breathed the words, then dropped his hand and turned back to look at Katie. "It must be nearly as big as the Great Glence itself."

"Bigger. Or so I understand. Go on, have a look inside," Katie said, pointing in the direction of the stool that had been placed in the heart of the tree.

Kal stepped up over the threshold and peered at the rounded walls of the small vaulted chamber only faintly illumined by the filtered light from the outside. The wooden walls felt rough to the touch, deeply pitted and scored, while, underfoot, the floor seemed unevenly hewn, although more or less level. On a stand in the back of the hollowed trunk, there was a harp.

Kal lowered himself onto the board stool at the centre. Facing Katie, he looked out past the harpstone root to the leaf-fringed entry of the glence tree and the falling path beyond. "Of course! It lies on Carric-thona!" He clapped to himself and chuckled, caught up in the excitement of discovery and feeling slightly giddy. "A glence tree!" He settled a little and looked around himself again. "But, Mistress Katie, how is it that the tree doesn't die with its heartwood hewn from it?"

"It's a glence tree. Nothing is hewn from it."

"You mean it grows this way?"

"Aye."

"With this great hole in it?"

"Aye, like all glence trees."

"Like all glence trees? There are more besides this one?"

"Yes, there are—or at least there were more. Many more. Alas, there is now but one, to my knowledge, in all of Ahn Norvys, and you're standing in it.... Well, rather, sitting in it."

"But why is it not talked about? Why is it that nobody knows about it? Wilum never mentioned it."

"Ah, there's a story. One that begins far away," Katie said wistfully with a sigh, seating herself sideways on the ledgelike lip of the oval opening. "One that begins far away on the other side of Ahn Norvys in a distant time." Her voice now changed in tone.

"Silence!" Her command rang from the hollow bole of the great tree. Kal was taken aback and looked at the woman, thinking that she was addressing him.

"Silence! Be still!" Katie said in a voice that belied her years with its strength. Kal realized that this was a part of the telling that she was giving. It seemed to him that the birds, the leaves, and even the wind had quieted themselves to lend their attention to the woman.

"Silence!" she said again, her voice trailing off. A moment passed, then she resumed in song, in a haunting melody that at once struck Kalaquinn with its stark beauty and its sadness.

"Harken, my hearth-kin, your hearts bestill,
   while great deeds dare I relate.
   May the doings deign to dwell in this tale-shaping
   of the ancients you are and shall become.

"You are the faithful fellowship, you friends of Jodris,
   whose blessed and brazen assays
   did foil the fiend's foundrous attempts
   to subvert the voice of goodliness.

"And you, whose blood still bears the boon-stain,
   you, progeny of the People, a chosen
   lineage, lost yet living still,
   you, exiled-ones, attend, I sing.

"Yet as bold and braw be my breasted heart-seat,
   Still I quail to quarter in song-frame
   the woeful words that welcome once more
   Joy's dour sister, sorrow.

"Though fingers will fumble upon frail strings,
   and tear-blind eyes will ache anew,
   brace yourself, my brave heart, brook thee not
   to let grief garner its victory.

"So hearken, my hearth-kin, and heed the rehearsal,
   for once blessed Beldegrayne did the anagoroi
   its mist-enshrouded mountain isles marvelously bedight
   with the Life-tree and its lyric life-melody.

"But by wile and wizardry, the wicked one stole
   into the hearts of the holiest
   and stole the song and so the seed
   of the People's promise and hope.

"Oh weep! Oh weep! The gleacewhinna are gone;
   lost are limb and leaf,
   every bough and bole are broken—but one!
   For in far-westerly woods, one grows,

"One graces a glade unguarded and wild;
   but its music is mute, and whispers
   in echoes of ages past, ancients long-dead,
   long-remembered, lost, lamented.

"Hearken, my hearth-kin, your hearts be unsettled,
by my telling of travail. Attend,
the Gleacewhinna woods a wasteland lie;
you, her People, deprived, lament! Lament!"

"Ah, me..." Katie fell silent, her head drooping. At length, she looked up into Kal's face. "That was the first bit of the 'Lament of Beldegrayne,'" she said, "but rendered into Arvonian by one of the last speakers of the mother tongue in the Black Cape."

"'Lament of Beldegrayne'? I don't recall ever hearing of it."

"No, I don't suppose you would have."

"But Beldegrayne... Ah, yes. I can only remember hearing of it once or twice. If I remember the myths correctly, it was supposed to have been a hidden island, some garden land. It was imagined to be somewhere deep in the Breathing Sea, was it not?"

"Myths, eh?" Katie eyed Kal with a brow raised in reproof. "Very few stories survive, but that's only because very few of the people survived. Beldegrayne has been forgotten in the histories of Ahn Norvys."

"It was a real place?"

"Aye, as real as you or me. But forgive me, Kalaquinn." Katie smiled. "I should start at the beginning. What do you know about the Ina Pik Whinna?"

"The Ina Pik Whinna? Very little. Only that they were an ancient people, a people of the Age of Echoes. Didn't they live in an area that is now a part of Kêl-Skrivar, in the shadowedland?" Kal leaned forward from the stool, his hands clasped. "But legend has it that they perished after the First Undoing, when their homeland fell under evil sway."

"So legend has it," Katie said, smiling. "So legend has it. But legend sometimes offers only a distorted reflection of the truth, especially when a legend has faded in a people's remembering. Ahn Norvys has forgotten the Ina Pik Whinna and their story. But the 'Lament' tells it true."

Katie fell silent, closing her eyes, and the muted tones of birdsong cascaded over them from above. At length, she looked up again at Kal.

"Beldegrayne was the home of the Ina Pik Whinna. Beldegrayne, not lands in what is now the shadowedland, as legend tells. The Ina Pik Whinna were the people of the tree." Katie paused and lifted her hand, sweeping it in an arc through the air above her. "You see? Ina Pik Whinna, People of the Tree. The People of the Gleacewhinna—this is a Gleacewhinna. The name means 'Tree that Is' or 'Tree of Being,' and the name is the most ancient word of my people."

"You are Ina Pik Whinna?"

"Ina Pik Whinnan, yes. A descendent of the People. The Gleace-whinna was a gift to the People—"

"Gleacewhinna," Kal blurted out in his dawning comprehension. "Gleacewhin . . . Glence! So that's why the tree looks like a glence. The trees—they were grown to resemble glences? But a gift from whom?"

"No, Kalaquinn, it is the other way around. It is not the trees that resemble glences, but glences that resemble the trees."

Kal looked at the old woman in confusion.

"Hush, Kalaquinn, stay your questions for the moment and listen. The tree, the Gleacewhinna, was a gift given at the very dawn of time, given as the symbol of life and blessing, of peace and prosperity. The Gleacewhinna is the peace of the heavens rooted in the soil of the world. It was given the People by the anagoroi. The People lived on Beldegrayne, an island, as you mentioned, hidden deep amid the mists of the Breathing Sea, among the islands of what you would now call the Wyvern Archipelago."

"But what—"

Katie raised a finger. "The Gleacewhinna," she continued, "grew in Beldegrayne, and multiplied until the whole land, the entire island, became a forest of these mighty trees. Ah, there were trees that would make this Gleacewhinna seem a dwarf. There our singers sang, and, in the woven melodies, even the Gleacewhinna themselves would give voice. That was life to the Ina Pik Whinna.

"But the peace of our hidden island was to be short-lived. Some of the anagoroi grew jealous of the gift. They coveted the Gleacewhinna for their own. This was the time of the First Undoing, and evil came to Beldegrayne, and evil perverted the hearts and minds of the Ina Pik Whinna. It was the vile creature Conna-gwyhn who set his mind on the Gleacewhinna and came with silken tongue to win the hearts of the People."

"Conna-gwyhn?" Kal could not contain himself. "The legends surrounding Ardiel make reference to Conna-gwyhn as the enchanter who subverted Vali, the forgeman, craftsman of the Talamadh."

"Aye, it may be so."

"But that would be hundreds—no, thousands of years after the First Undoing. And there are no accounts in the histories of Ahn Norvys of the First Undoing."

"Aye, yes, Kal, it was the dawn of time, but it was also the time of the People. It is all in the 'Lament,' as I said. And the evil of that time was the evil at the time of Ardiel and is the evil of this time, too. It is ancient and powerful, now as then. But listen, Kal, listen." Katie shifted where she sat.

"The singers changed song, and soon the forests themselves ceased their music, and the Gleacewhinna began to fail, becoming diseased—some, the young ones, even dying, leaving nothing but bole and branch, as cold, hard, and lifeless as stone. You see, the singers' song was to the Gleacewhinna as water and sunlight are to any other tree in Ahn Norvys. So with the death of the Ina Pik Whinnan song did the darkness of the world come seeping into Beldegrayne. This was part of the First Undoing, and with the First Undoing came the Age of Echoes.

"But some of the Ina Pik Whinna recognized what was happening. Among them was a woman named Jodris, herself daughter of the king singer of the People. Some say it was the anagoroi, some even say Ruah herself, that gave warning and so inspired a handful of the People to make ready to leave Beldegrayne. In secret were three ships built—ships in a manner of speaking, for the People were never a seafaring folk. The Ina Pik Whinna had never left their homeland isle, because there had never been need to leave it. But three ships were built, fewer than twenty people in each, and in each were smuggled a pair of Gleacewhinna saplings, pairs because a single Gleacewhinna cannot propagate on its own.... Ah, me, but the Ina Pik Whinna had to turn to stealing from the Ina Pik Whinna just to save all from being lost." Katie paused a moment, absorbed in her thoughts, and sighed.

"With no knowledge of the ways of the waters," she continued, "the three vessels and the people in them were at the mercies of wind and sea. By good fortune's favour, and with the aid of the anagoroi, no doubt, the three ships sailed out from the mists of the Breathing Sea, across the Dumoric Sea, through the Straits of Tindárman and into the Cerulean Ocean. But the Cape of Winds is aptly named. The three ships had made it safely that far together, only then to be caught in a gale. That storm blew for three days, sank two ships, and left the third wrecked on the rocks of the Black Cape. Jodris and most of the people with her in that third ship survived the wreck, but only one of the saplings did, the last surviving Gleacewhinna in all of Ahn Norvys."

"This one?" Kal said.

"Aye, yes, this one."

"But that would make it—"

"Ancient. Yes, very ancient, Kal."

Kal thought a moment, then said, "But, Mistress Katie, what of the Gleacewhinna in Beldegrayne?"

"You said that legend holds that the Ina Pik Whinna lived in an area that is now a part of Kêl-Skrivar, but it was not the People of the Tree that were taken to the valleys east of the Alnod River—it was the trees. Even before Jodris and those with her fled the island, Conna-gwyhn had begun to plunder the forests of Beldegrayne. He took hundreds of saplings to his own land. The Gleacewhinna will grow to mature size in but a matter of a few years, if tended carefully. Conna-gwyhn did take a few singers of the People to be guardians of the stolen Gleacewhinna. You see, the Ina Pik Whinna who remained in Beldegrayne all perished when the capricious favour of Conna-gwyhn turned against them. He had taken what he desired, the Gleacewhinna, so he killed the People. Without the People, the trees would not survive."

"What of the glence trees taken by Conna-gwyhn? Did they not survive?"

"Little is known, Kal. The People on Beldegrayne had been slaughtered, and those few who escaped with Jodris...Well, they planted the lone Gleacewhinna and settled in the forests of the Black Cape to protect it. The Woods of Tircoil were then not nearly as expansive as they are now, and the few surviving Ina Pik Whinna ventured from them occasionally at first to learn what they could of their new home and its peoples, but soon gave that up for the sheltered isolation of the young wilds of the Black Cape. They soon mingled with the folk that were already here, sharing their deep lore of the woods, adjusting to a new land, and teaching them love for the Gleacewhinna. In time they lost their language, but not their woodland ways nor their reluctance to take part in the wider world, preferring the hiddenness of life in the Woods of Tircoil."

"So they became waldscathes."

"Aye, Kal, over time. The legend became a convenient way to ward off unwelcome intruders."

"Just like the foggy mists around Beldegrayne," Kal said.

"Something like that, yes. It's been a protection, a welcome protection that none of us has ever abandoned, and very few from the outside, yourself and Gwyn included, have ever enjoyed."

"So, what happened to the trees taken by Conna-gwyhn?"

"As I said, little is known, other than rumours gleaned in the early years of the Ina Pik Whinna in the Black Cape. It was said that, in their exile, the singers taken to the valleys east of the Alnod River repented of the evil they had allowed to corrupt their hearts and their song. They did nurture their trees, but no sooner had the forests grown than Conna-gwyhn killed the singers, every last one, and sought to use the trees to his own purposes. But the Gleacewhinna, by their nature, become that for which they are desired and used, and, as evil begets death, the trees all perished.

"It is said that the very remains of Gleacewhinna in that place mourned the destruction of their singers, of the Ina Pik Whinna. It is said that the people native to that land, touched by the splendour of the Gleacewhinna even in death, heard their lament, and they themselves loved the dead trees and learned their whispered song. It is said that these were the first echobards, for the Age of Echoes had descended upon Ahn Norvys. Centuries upon centuries later, at the dawn of the Harmonic Age, glences would be built, glences built according to the ancient wisdom left by the great echobard kings, glences fashioned to resemble the Gleacewhinna." Katie paused again in her account and looked out into the shaded interior of the glence tree. She looked back at Kal and said, "Even your Great Glence, Master Kalaquinn. It was the first."

"You speak as if you were there. You're not..."

"Ageless? Immortal? As old as this Gleacewhinna?" Katie tossed her head back, laughing, the dim light beneath the limbs of the glence tree sparkling in her eyes. "Ah, me! No, Kal, no. I was not there. I am not that old. I have seen few more than seventy springs renew the life of these Woods. But I am of the People, and what has happened to the Ina Pik Whinna at any time in the past has happened to me and affects me as surely as if I had been there. The past of the People is my past. It is a part of me, and I am inseparable from it.

"It is like this cloak," Katie said, folding her arms to embrace the mantle she wore. "The woodencloak. It is nearly as much an emblem of the People as is the Gleacewhinna, for if the Gleacewhinna was a gift of the anagoroi to the People, then the woodencloak was a gift of the Gleacewhinna to the People. It was made from the first Gleacewhinna to grow in Beldegrayne and is the symbol of blessing upon the People. It has come down to me from Jodris."

"Jodris?"

"Yes, to preserve it also from the corruption that afflicted the People on Beldegrayne, she stole it from her father. She was the first Wood Maid of the Black Cape, and so the woodencloak has come one generation to the next, daughter to daughter, down to me. But it was Jodris's young son who became our first singer in the Woods of Tircoil. It is he who wrote the 'Lament of Beldegrayne' as an account of the Ina Pik Whinna and the events of the First Undoing. It was written in the tongue of the Ina Pik Whinna and later made over into the language adopted by the newcomers from those native to these parts."

"You mean it was rendered into Arvonian?"

"Old Arvonian first, yes, then later into the common tongue, and, in that way, has the history of our people been preserved, for, in the Woods of Tircoil, the original language of the Ina Pik Whinna has been lost from the earliest generations."

"How is it that you speak our common tongue and sing the orrthon—Gelanor is a bard—if you have been isolated from the rest of the world?"

"Yes, yes," Katie said, nodding, a smile on her lips. "We may be isolated from the world, but do not think that we are unaware of the happenings and ways of the world beyond these Woods. We are still the People of the Tree, guardians of the song. Our ways change in time and harmony with the ways of Ahn Norvys. Only Wuldor remains the same. We bowed our necks to the yoke of the Age of Echoes. We lifted our voices with Ardiel of the Long Arm. We have sung with Hordanus through the ages. And we wait, we wait." Katie held Kal in a long and steady gaze. "We are the People of the Gleacewhinna, and our fate is still bound to its fate. We must be, and are, ever ready to serve those who would serve it."

Kal shook his head and cast his eyes to the ground at his feet.

He found the woman's intense stare slightly discomfiting. "An actual account of the events of the First Undoing," he said at length.

"Yes, Kal, the events as I have just told you. Of course, they are far more beautiful as set in the verses of the 'Lament of Belde-grayne,' and even more so in the tongue of the Ina Pik Whinna." Katie paused. Kal rose to his feet and stepped towards her, his face alive again with wonder.

"May I make so bold as to request a copy of the 'Lament of Beldegrayne,'" he said. "As Hordanu, I must add it to the histories of Ahn Norvys."

"It is a fair and just request," Katie said, nodding slowly. "I will ask Gelanor to set about the task of copying the 'Lament' and all histories of the Tircolian people. It is right that you should have them. It will be an arduous task, but one that I'm sure Gelanor will be happy to perform. The texts will be here for you when next you visit us."

Kal shook his head again in wonder. "So, you mean to say that not even Wilum knew the secret of these Woods?"

"Not even Wilum. We're a close, secretive people. We've had to be, for our own sake, but even more so for the sake of guard-ing the Gleacewhinna. Most secretive—even Gelanor, for all his outgoing humours."

"Humours of which I've had experience," Kal said ruefully.

"Do not waste sympathy on your own behalf, Kalaquinn," Katie said in a light tone. Then suddenly she gained a serious aspect as she stood away from the opening to the small chamber and held his gaze, both her hands clutching her woodencloak close around her as if against the cold. "You do well to remember that you are the first Hordanu, indeed the first person save one other outside of the People, to have seen what you see, to learn what you have learned about the mysteries of the Black Cape and of the People. Over the centuries, others have come to join us in our solitude, but they must wait sometimes years before becoming one of the People and being shown the Gleacewhinna and learning what has been revealed to you in just this past hour. It is out of respect for you, my lord Myghternos Hordanu, and in the sure knowledge that times are ripe, that we have laid all our secrets bare."

"I am honoured, Mistress Katie. But..." Kal stumbled in his speech, struggling to collect his thoughts. "But who was the one other?"

"Ah, Kal, it is right that you should ask. In the early centuries of the People in these Woods of Tircoil, an echobard king came to the Black Cape. Undeterred by the rumours of waldscathes and wilds, and as if by some unspoken power, he slipped past all eyes and was discovered standing by the Gleacewhinna, the only one from outside the People to have ever done so. He bore a token of peace, an image embroidered on cloth. It was the image of a Gleacewhinna, and he said that he had come bearing a message. This prophecy he spoke to the Tircoilians, the guardians of the Gleacewhinna, beneath these very branches, within this very tree. 'One will come in time to restore peace,' he said. 'A singer will come to the Gleacewhinna. He will be the binder of what has been unbound, and the renewer of the order undone,' he said." Kal's mind swam as Katie's eyes rested on him, grey and serious.

"The echobard left as mysteriously as he had come," Katie continued, "but not before he requested a boon of us—a single slip, a twig in leaf, from the Gleacewhinna. A strange request it was, for a slip would never root and grow, leastwise not into a Gleacewhinna. But we gave it him. We gave it in gratitude for the hope he had engendered in our hearts by his word. Then he left. Some say he spoke of a hidden land, a dark realm beneath the heights of what are now the Burren Mountains. We never saw him again, nor heard of him." The old woman paused, her gaze drifting towards the entrance to the glence tree.

"That is when we built the Well," she said dreamily. "Ruah appeared to us then for the first time and led us to the place where we built the Well. We built it for her, and for the people, for the people of all Ahn Norvys."

"Within the Woods of Tircoil?"

Katie recollected herself. "No, it was just beyond the edge of the Woods at the time. The Woods of Tircoil have slowly but steadily marched, encroaching over the centuries on the lands that lie beyond its bounds. Mousehold and its glence are all that remain of a village that was once on the verge of the Wood. When the forest overgrew them, the village was abandoned and the glence fell to ruins. Since then, Mousehold has been the home of the Wood Maid."

"And the echobard's prophecy? What of it?" Kal asked.

"We thought it had come to fulfillment at the time of Ardiel. We waited for him to come, but he didn't." Katie's face softened, and she drew her arms from the folds of her cloak and stood.

"But come now, Master Kalaquinn, I have burdened you with the great weight of our stories. I can see it in your eyes. We should return to Mousehold. But before we do, you must grace this glence with your song." She pointed to the harp resting in the corner behind Kal.

The young Hordanu nodded, acquiescing to the Wood Maid's request, and stood to retrieve the harp from its stand.

"But first listen...," Katie said. "Listen to what song the Gleacewhinna would have you sing."

Kal sat again on the stool, cradling the instrument in his lap and closing his eyes. Far above him, a breeze stirred the leaves of the tree. Delicately he set his fingers to the strings, plucking the notes one at a time, letting them reverberate hauntingly through the hollow trunk and beyond. The Holdsman paused again.

"How's that?" he asked, opening his eyes.

"Wonderful," Katie said, recognizing the simple melody. "'The Summer Anthem.' The Gleacewhinna calls you to your most immediate task as Hordanu, for it is the orrthon for the Summer Loosening that you must soon sing. But don't stop."

Kal bent his head and continued playing the tune, its rise and fall a hypnotic backdrop to his chanting.

> "So bends the Year, with Spring's warm breath
> That once did herald Winter's fall,
> She sighs, in Summer's sufficiencies
> Content that what was once conceived
> Will fill field and fold, toft and croft
> In the care of Wuldor, the Husband.
>
> "What wonders are weaved in lengsome days,
> When warp of sun and weft of rain
> Plait golden pledge of swollen rick.
> The batten beats back Spring's woof
> and ties the twine for Summer's stuff,
> In the web of Wuldor, the Weaver.
>
> "The weanling Spring gambols game,
> Battens on the greenling mead,
> Crooks at brookside, then sated
> lies somnolent beneath fat sun.

All is promise, all is hope,
In the croft of Wuldor, the Shepherd.

"Now the waxing midyear days
will swell the hips of failed-flower Spring.
Between its stem and blossom end,
Fair flesh will blush, will cradle seed,
Will redden, ripen, hang plump, await
The hook of Wuldor, the Grower.

"In Wuldor's keeping, Summer comes,
Soft verdant days, a growing peace.
Ah! Naught is lost in Ahn Norvys,
For all falls under his watchful care—
The Foldsman, the Fruiter, the Farmer, is he,
Wuldor, the Father of all."

Soon his voice, and that of the harp in his hand, stilled and fell silent.

"Beautiful, my lord Myghternos Hordanu. Ah, 'The Summer Anthem.' But where will you sing the Loosening?" Katie asked.

"Wherever I happen to be at the solstice." Kal shrugged, placing the harp back on its stand. "Who knows where?"

"I would that you might stay with us the few days until then, but I must not deter nor detain you from your journey. It's strange, though, to hear someone other than Gelanor sing here," Katie said wistfully.

"How so?"

"Oh, no, no, it's not that there's anything wrong with your singing. It's just that Gelanor has been bard here in the Black Cape for so many years, time out of mind, it seems, and to see somebody else sit on that stool plucking at the harp..."

"Years?" Kal lifted a brow.

"Aye, many years. He's older than he looks. Ah, waldscathes." Katie sighed. "They age well in the Woods of Tircoil. It must be the freedom and the fresh air."

"And the wholesome fear they inspire. No vile human predators. Makes for a long life, I wouldn't doubt," Kal said lightly as Katie made way for him and he stepped back down onto the ground outside the trunk.

"Not only that, but Gelanor was made bard at an early age."

"Like Wilum."

"Like yourself, Kalaquinn, although in the case of Gelanor it so turns out that he inherited the role from his father, and his before him. Such is our way. It's Gelanor's father that I remember, too, from my youth, and Gelanor is his very image. It's uncanny at times how direct resemblances can be passed from generation to generation. But, speaking of Gelanor, we must get back. There's a good chance he and Gwyn will have returned to Mousehold by now."

Kal stepped quickly to the leafy wall, stooped and plucked up the leaf he had dropped to the ground. "May I...?"

"Yes, please do, Kalaquinn. As a token," Katie replied, then spun about on her heel and hurried past the harpstone out of the shelter of the glence tree back into the open air. Not a woman to waste time, Kal thought as he followed her blinking into the mellow afternoon light and broke into a jog to keep pace. Soon they crossed the thin spit of grass, climbed over the stone bridge, and were retracing the miles back to Mousehold through the deep shade of the Woods of Tircoil.

SEVENTEEN

"They're back," Katie said, sniffing the sharp tang of wood smoke. She resumed humming to herself as Mousehold hove into view through the trees.

It was a homely sight, Kal thought, after their long walk through the seemingly endless tract of forest. Smoke curled languidly from the chimney of the cottage in the still, early evening air that hung over the sheltered glen. The sinuous column twisted, dancing slowly in the shafts of golden light that slanted through the trees behind them.

"Aye, that they are, Mistress Katie," Kal said as the two stepped over the lip of the rise to where the path fell to the ruins below.

"That they are—mission accomplished, I hope, and no doubt as ravenous as a pair of wolves on the prowl."

Like an unexpected apparition, Gelanor rose to his feet from the far side of the crumbling glence wall, brushing leaves and dirt from the wolf's pelt that draped his back.

"Ho, Wood Maid! So, you're back!" the man bellowed across the clearing, lifting an enormous hand in greeting. "Not as quiet as you might have been! And my lord Hordanu treads more like the bear than the wolf. Aye, more bear than wolf!"

"We didn't want to catch you unawares and startle you, my good bard."

"What? Ho!" Gelanor let loose a great laugh. "Still, you did catch me taking a wee bit of a snooze," he said, stretching his arms as he stirred himself to wakefulness. "Figured we'd get the fire laid for supper, then have a rest 'til you returned."

"Well-earned, I'm sure," Katie said. "But where's your companion?"

"Here. Right here with me. And it's a sight, a sight to be sure!"

Already Kal and Katie were skirting the ruins, Kal pressing ahead of the old woman for once, weaving his way along the path around the fallen blocks of masonry. The great red-haired man now stood in full sight, unkinking his neck and limbs. Beside him, sitting leaned against the ragged stone of the wall, his knees pulled up to his chest, was Gwyn, hunched over a chunk of wood he was busily carving. A dun wolf's hide hung around his shoulders, all but covering his head and frame.

"You've no need to worry about him, believe me. I've never seen a fellow as brave, nor as good with a bow. The lad's a wonder. Wears his pelt with real pride, too, real pride," Gelanor said, fists planted on his hips, a twinkle in his eye. "And as apt with a knife as with a bow. But that's not the most of it, and if he were less taken in attacking that wood block of his, he'd be quicker off the mark to show you a rare thing! Come, now, Gwyn, show them your—" A look of astonishment spread across Gelanor's rough-hewn features as the young Holdsman scrambled to his feet. Flinging back his wolf's-head visor, he proffered his handiwork to Katie with outstretched hand. "By the hide! Would you look at that!" the big man said. "The lad's a wizard. Why, Mistress Katie, it's your very likeness. Can I see it, lad?" He snatched it from Gwyn's hand and held the carved block up before the Wood Maid in wonder and admiration, examining its subtle art. "Look, but he's captured you, to be sure, captured you to the very dimple of your cheek!" Gelanor laughed and handed the sculpted piece to Katie. Gwyn nodded and lifted his open palm to her.

"He means you to have it, Katie," Kal said. Gwyn nodded, then, fetching Kal a half-smile beneath a strange glance, turned heel and strode away, heading back along the edge of the ruins.

"Where's he off to now?" Kal said.

"Look more closely, little brother. As I said, it's a rare thing he's showing you."

Kal watched the young Holdsman retreat around the curve of the glence wall. "There's something—something's changed in the way he bears himself." It was Kal's turn to be astonished. "It's his gait. There's a trueness to his step. But how?"

"Ruah's doing. It was Ruah's water," Katie said calmly, looking up from the figurine that she held.

"Aye, to be sure, the water of the Well. Our Wood Maid, she knows. Seen it often enough, haven't you, Mistress Katie? In our band, many's the brother that's suffered a hurt from blade or bow."

"As you know well enough yourself," Katie said.

"That I do. That I do." Gelanor touched his side. "There's days when I still feel a twinge."

Gwyn had broken into an even-paced run past the cottage and around the edge of the glade. Kal followed him with his gaze, paying little attention to the banter of the woman and her bard.

"Last fall, just beyond the edge of the Woods, he had an encounter with Baron Nuath's master huntsman," the woman was saying. "We thought we'd lost him—"

"And would have, too, if it hadn't been for the water Ellyn kept handy. Aye, it was a deep wound." Gelanor jabbed a large finger to the left of his navel. "Like a needle through a ball of wool, his shaft caught me through here.... From behind, the craven wretch. He's lucky to have escaped. If he hadn't blown a summons—"

"Ah, Gelanor! I'd say that you had the better measure of luck," Katie said.

"She means, little brother, that it's foolhardy for a lone wald-scathe to venture beyond the Woods, for he endangers not only himself but the People."

"Hmm?" Kal looked at them distractedly.

"It was a trap," Katie said.

"Aye, that it was, that it was." Gelanor rocked his head gravely. "And a lesson to all our headstrong young men."

"And to their chief as well, I hope," Katie said.

"Gwyn! Your foot!" The young Holdsman had jogged back to the ruins, and Kal now rushed to him. "What news!" Kal gripped his companion by the shoulders and held him at arm's length. "What news! Re'm ena, but wait until the others see this. Fionna and Thurfar, especially." Kal clapped him on the back. "And your sisters!"

"Show him your foot, Gwyn. Let him see it," Gelanor said, approaching the two Holdsmen with Katie behind him.

Gwyn slipped off his soft leather boot. Kal stooped to have a closer look.

"I saw it myself," the big bard continued. "The misshapen twist to his foot. Then he waded into the pool. Then out he comes, as fine-footed as you see now. Fine-footed and able-bodied, too. It seems to me that even the rest of him is better formed after his dip. Solid and stout as a young oak."

"Aye, indeed. It seems the boy is become the man." Kal stood and thumped Gwyn on the back again, leaving him to bounce on one foot for balance as he pulled on his boot.

Gelanor chuckled at the young man. "Aye, to be sure, he had me hopping, too, just to keep up with him on the way back. And me weighed down by that cask." Gelanor winked.

"So, the water? You have the water?"

"Aye, rest easy, little brother. It's inside the cottage."

"So, we'd best think about leaving, Gwyn and I. Now, while there's still light. Already I'm afraid we've delayed too long. We have to reach my father, if it's not too late. He needs the water."

"As you need rest, Kalaquinn. I see exhaustion in your face and weariness in your burdened step," Katie said.

"There's a fine turn, eh, little brother? Next thing you know I'll be needing to carry you to Ruah's Well, carry you to ease you of your sore-footed lameness. That would be a task. Leave me lame, too. Lameness all around. In the end we'll all need healing water!"

Kal smiled thinly, his shoulders rounded.

"Already the sun sits low." Katie glanced up at the sky. "Stay here at Mousehold and sleep, Kalaquinn. Let your strength be restored. It would be foolish to set forth now with nightfall so close at hand."

"But my father," Kal protested again, weakly.

"Let him be as he is. At this moment, whatever course his illness has taken is not yours to sway."

Kal nodded in resignation. He was suddenly too tired to argue any further and knew better now than to press the point with this woman. A deep weariness crept over him.

"Come, now, let's have supper and then to sleep. Tomorrow, at first light, you can be on your way. Gelanor will provide you with a waldscathe escort to the northern margin of our woods."

"Aye, we'll make sure you come to no harm. From there it'll be but a short jaunt for you to your meeting place at Kingshead."

"Come, little brother." Gelanor's voice broke through the haze of Kal's sleep, his hand heavy on Kal's shoulder.

The Holdsman groaned and rolled over. He tried to free himself from the bard's grip, but Gelanor shook him again.

"Come, Master Kalaquinn, come. It's time to go."

"Time...? Already? Feels like..." Kal yawned and slowly opened his eyes. "It feels like I've just gone to bed." The small room was still dark except for the lantern held by Gelanor.

"I'm not surprised, not surprised at all. You were one tired body. It was all we could do to keep you from drowning in your soup. But it's time now. And I'm not after telling you what you're to do, but if you don't get to your feet, and get to your feet now, there'll be a graver danger to deal with, to be sure."

"What's that?" Kal asked, his head suddenly much clearer. He swung his legs over the side of the cot.

"Half a dozen surly waldscathes, dragged untimely from their dens only to be left twiddling their thumbs outside in the Wood Maid's garden. Twiddling their thumbs and waiting for the newest addition to their ranks." Gelanor's eyes and teeth flashed in the lantern light as he grinned broadly.

"What?" Kal skewed his head and squinted at the big man.

"That's you, little brother, that they'd be waiting for." The wald-scathe chief threw a black wolf's pelt onto Kal's lap. "That's for you, my lord Myghternos Hordanu. A fine piece of fur. No spot, no blemish. It belonged to the pack leader. An imposing animal, to be sure. Go on, then. Put it on."

Kal rose to his feet and swung the pelt over his back, then tied its neck fastenings and pulled up the hood to frame his head with the wolf's sinister muzzle.

"Now you're a fearsome sight, a fearsome sight to be sure. A true brother of the wolf pelt. A fit member of our band, I'd say." Gelanor inspected Kal with an approving eye. "Good. Come now. We've time for a quick bite of breakfast, and then we're off."

Kal slid the pelt off his back, and he and Gelanor left the small bedchamber and moved quietly towards the glow of the hearth fire.

"Ah, there you are, Kalaquinn," said Katie, turning from the fire. A lantern hung from the rafters over the dining table, where Gwyn sat eating. "Go on." With a big wooden spoon she pointed to a spot at the table beside the young Holdsman. "There's a bowl of porridge there for you, too. It'll sate you for the morning. And there's a pitcher of cream. Seeds and honey, too. You may help yourself."

"Thank you, Mistress Katie," Kal said, "but there's no time. The men wait outside."

Katie clucked. "Come, come. Not hungry? I can't imagine. Not after nodding off all through supper as you did last night."

"As fine a meal as you've ever laid on, Mistress Katie," Gelanor added.

"Sit down and eat," she commanded. "The men will wait."

Kal looked to Gelanor.

"If I were you, I'd do as the Wood Maid bids. There's some things more fearful than waldscathes." The big man winked, his face again spread wide in a grin.

Kal obeyed, lowering himself to the bench in front of a steaming bowl. He reached for the cream.

"You, too. I've set out a bowl for you as well."

"But Mistress Katie, I've been fed"—Gelanor patted his stomach—"and fed well, by Ellyn this morning, as you can see."

"Never mind. You must give our guests encouragement. Go on. Sit down and eat."

"There are some things more fearful than waldscathes," Kal said, eyebrows raised over the lifted pitcher.

"Well spoken, little brother, well spoken. You're quick to learn. No doubt it's a talent that will stand you in good stead," said Gelanor as he took his own seat across from the two Holdsmen.

In silence, they tucked into their breakfasts, and in but a few moments spoons rattled in empty bowls.

"Who'd have thought that even porridge could be made to taste so good?" said Gelanor as he rose from the table. "Let me tell you. As a cook, the Wood Maid, she takes second place to no one."

"You'll get no arguments from me, Gelanor. Nor from Gwyn, eh, Gwyn?" Kal said.

"Poor Ellyn, poor Ellyn...It's a good thing for you that she's not within earshot of such shameless flattery, else you'd be growing quickly thinner in the next while." Katie cocked an eye at the big man.

"Bah!" The big man feigned gruffness and cleaned his whiskers with the back of a hand.

"My thanks to you again, Mistress Katie, for your kind and gracious hospitality," Kal said, rising from the bench as Gelanor handed him the small wooden cask of Ruah's healing water.

Kal and Gwyn turned to the door to gather their weapons as Katie doled out provisions for the journey, listing the items as she tucked each away in their night pouches: honeyed seedcakes wrapped in cloth; nuts, soaked and roasted; and dried fruits, slices of apple and pear, plums, and berries that had been gathered in the woods. The filled satchels were slung over their shoulders beside the other tack of travel, and over all the wolf pelts were then donned. The men left the cottage, and Katie followed them through the door. Outside, a faint suggestion of light had begun to seep through the shadows.

"Ho there, Bildvek! Where have you gone to now? You and the rest of my skulking minions?" Gelanor called.

"Here, Gelanor. Marking time and more than ready to be off." From out of the shelter of Katie's bower stepped a tall, well-muscled man, his features dark and vague under the wolf's-head cowl. Five other waldscathes emerged from the verdure behind him, their likeness to wolf-men so uncanny in the early glimmer of dawn that Kal stiffened despite himself.

"Aye, Master Kalaquinn, they're a fretful sight but now your stout companions," said Katie. "Be assured that you'll come to no harm while your journey lies in these Woods of Tircoil." She looked to Gwyn and held out her hand in a gesture of farewell. "Dear Gwyn. May you prosper in Ruah's keeping." Gwyn bent to kiss her extended hand.

Turning to Kal, she looked up into his face and stood silently staring at him. Kal became aware of the waldscathes shuffling nearby in the grey dawn. Eventually, Katie placed a hand on Kal's chest and broke the quiet. "It has been an honour, an honour and a blessing, Myghternos Anadem. May Ruah guide your steps and Wuldor keep you ever in his smiling eye."

"My deepest thanks again to you, Wood Maid, friend and protector. I shall never forget your kindness." Kal took her hand in his own and kissed it as he bowed. "Briacoil. Until we meet again," he said.

In the ghostly light of dawn, they departed with their escort, who glided silent and sure-footed into the forest along paths that twisted and turned over hill and dale. For the most part, the group walked single file in a somber silence, with Gelanor and three waldscathes leading the way for Kal and Gwyn, the others following behind.

So much had happened in the space of two days. Kal was absorbed in thought. His mind wandered, flitting about from image to image—the grey-timbered cottage and its grey keeper, the glencelike tree surrounded by a lake, a white deer, blue flowers reflected in the still water of a well, Gwyn's sound foot, a long walk through mysterious woods, as well as the mysteries of the Woods themselves and the fearsome creatures living there. And here, those very creatures strode before and after him. He looked at the pelted figures in front of him, then at Gwyn beneath his own grey-brown wolf fur. He chuckled to himself as he reached up and adjusted the black muzzle on his own head and shifted the small wooden cask on its strap.

He should be fretting about his father. He should be, but he found himself unable to worry. The even, measured words spoken to him in the dream returned to him now, resounding in his heart, chasing away the spectres of anxious fear. Katie had said as much, too—that there was nothing to be done about past, or even future; one could do nothing but attend to the present, to the task at hand as best as one could. She had said many things to him. And Myghternos Anadem; she had called him Myghternos Anadem twice. Myghternos Anadem... It was a title, that much was clear, but it was one unfamiliar to him, and one he had only heard once before, in his own voice, sung in his Lay—

"There you go!" Gelanor stopped walking and leaned heavily on his bowstaff. He tipped his head. "Two landlocked Holdsmen that you are, I'd wager that you've neither of you seen the ocean before."

Kal, torn from his reverie, looked up at the big man ahead of him and then to the surrounding land. The morning had worn on. Its lingering dampness and shadows had been dispelled, replaced now by the sharp scent of salt-laden breezes. They had come to a rocky outcrop above a narrow bay. Its wind-tossed waves glistened bright in the sun on waters that stretched far into the distance, crowded by sloping forests on either side.

"The ocean?" Kal said.

"Aye, little brother. That it is. The Firth of Tircoil. You're not far from your meeting place, not far at all. Just up the Firth a few miles is Kingshead." Squinting, Gelanor pointed to the far horizon up the bay. "If you look hard, you can make it out, a headland that shelters your cove."

"And that would be the Black Cape," Kal said, gesturing to the vague mass of shoreline that loomed across from them in the near distance.

"To be sure. And a reassuring sight it is, isn't it? The heart of the Woods of Tircoil and home to the People."

"Aye, Gelanor. It's not often we're this far outside the Cape," one of the waldscathes said, a frown creasing his young face. "Are you certain it's still safe?"

"Come! Don't fret, man, don't fret," Bildvek chided, looking to his chief. "We may be off the Cape, but not out of the Woods yet."

"That stone building? Is that someone's home?" Kal had stepped away and was peering down a slope into the trees at their back.

"Was someone's home," Bildvek corrected. "It's abandoned now. It was abandoned by the march-dwellers."

"March-dwellers?"

"Them that lived on the edges of the forest. Couldn't abide its spread," explained the waldscathe.

"And we can't abide here, either. Time to move on," Gelanor commanded.

From here, the path broadened and continued within sight of the Firth for a time. After that, it branched east until it led them to within a stone's throw of Hoël's Dyke and then veered north within steady sight of the ancient trackway. The Woods of Tircoil pressed hard against the mouldering cobblestones, more fractured and decrepit here than they had been near Mousehold and the Black Cape. For all its disrepair, the Dyke managed to keep the thick trees of the forest at bay, fending it away from the open fields and a scattering of ploughland that lay on the other side.

It was still late morning under a cloudless sky when the path emerged from the Woods into a place of low scrub and bushes. Gelanor stopped and took a deep breath, then faced the two Holdsmen.

"Well, Brothers, here we are. The badlands. We've reached the badlands, as we call such places that lie outside the Cape and the Woods that serve as our lair—but only when we're of a dark and wolfish humour!" Gelanor laughed gently. "Mind you, the Wood Maid disapproves, for she says it sets up fellow highlanders like yourselves as the enemy somehow. 'Deeds follow words, even when spoken in jest,' she says." Gelanor paused and turned to face up the path. "Now, my lord Myghternos Hordanu, here's a parting of our ways. See, there's Kingshead, that ridge ahead. Beyond that is Kingshead Cove. Your way is clear. Just follow along this side of the Dyke for a couple more miles. You'll come to the Cove, sure enough. You'll see the old stone piers." Gelanor faced the Holdsmen again. "It was a fine place of anchorage in its day, fit for a king, to be sure, fit for a king. Aye, that is, until the nearness of the Black Cape and talk of waldscathes made it fall into disuse." He winked, then turned his face away, looking up the path. "So, you'll manage from here then, eh?" His tone had grown quiet and soft. "Aye, you'll manage from here."

"Briacoil, then, Gelanor." Kal looked up at the big man.

"Aye, briacoil, Master Kalaquinn, Lord High Bard." Gelanor pulled back his cowl and inclined his head before the Holdsman.

Kal raised his right hand and placed it on Gelanor's chest. He lowered his head. "May your song ever grace the Gleacewhinna," Kal said and withdrew his hand. The two men embraced. Then, clasping forearms one by one, Kal and Gwyn expressed their gratitude to Bildvek and the men who had guided them from Mousehold, and, in but a moment, Gelanor and the waldscathes of the Black Cape had melted back into the Woods of Tircoil.

Kal and Gwyn hurried northward, following Hoël's Dyke. Soon it rose gently higher through an open heath, climbing the steepening shoulder of Kingshead, affording them a view again of the Firth of Tircoil to their back. Kal felt the reassuring weight of the cask that dangled from its leather belt on his shoulder. He picked up his pace, matched by Gwyn striding beside him. The cove and his folk were not far off.

"Come on, Gwyn. No excuses, now. You're sound and strong." Kal broke into a slow, loping stride. "Come, let's go."

Now the roadway crested the ridge that thrust itself jaggedly into the Firth. To their left, the rugged headland stood high above the waters. This was Kingshead, pointing out to the shimmering ocean in the distance. Dense woods swept down from the spine of the ridge to a narrow inlet in the sheltered lee of the winds that kept the side which they had just passed grassy and treeless.

"Look, Gwyn, Kingshead Cove. We're there." Kal stopped and gazed down on the sheltered anchorage, its sides protected by the soaring headland on one side and a line of slightly lower cliffs on the other. From a shingle beach at the foot of the cove far below them, a stone pier jutted into the water. The inlet was empty.

Kal turned slowly to Gwyn, his own confusion mirrored on the face of his companion.

"Gwyn," Kal said, "where's the ship?"

EIGHTEEN

"They've got to be here," Kal said, squinting at the sparkling water on the horizon. Gwyn elbowed Kal and hooked his thumb back over his shoulder, gesturing down the path to the anchorage. "You're right, you're right. We'll get down for a closer look— Gwyn!" The younger man was already plodding ahead. "Wait for me!" Kal called after him and hastened along the roadway that branched from the Dyke and snaked down steeply towards the Cove in the shadow of Kingshead's high foreland.

Thick forest pressed in on the path again on either side, obscuring their view of the ocean. The stiffening breeze carried a brackish tang that Kal could almost taste. Overhead the air resounded with the screech of gulls riding the offshore winds, wheeling and falling out of sight down the steep wooded slopes to the water below. Torn tufts of cloud scudded across the deep blue of the sky, and a faint ring of light circled the morning sun, a bright spot on either side to the left and right. Sun dogs, Kal thought to himself. There'd be weather blowing in sooner than later.

The Cove reappeared ahead of them through a break in the trees, and the path gave onto a stretch of small grey stones and pebbles worn smooth by the sea. Kal and Gwyn trotted to the shoreline across the shingle, making for an old stone pier that extended into the Cove like a giant's gnarled finger pointing out to sea in defiance of the unceasing advance of white-capped waves.

"Halt! Stay yourselves!" A hard-edged voice stopped the two Holdsmen in their tracks. They spun around, reaching for their weapons.

"Hold, I say!" A figure emerged from the forest, bow raised and drawn taut. "Your hands where they may be—"

"Galli, it's me. Ease up. It's us—Kal and Gwyn." Kal had recognized the voice almost immediately, and the sudden surge of tension that had gripped him ebbed. Now, too, the well-muscled build of the figure that had stepped into the open and the twining tattoo that traced along his hairline left no doubt. The figure slowly relaxed his bow and frowned.

"Re'm ena, but it is you, isn't it?" Galli said, his guard easing. "It's a lucky thing for you that I've the huntsman's good sense not to take my quarry until I'm sure of what it is." He scratched his head and eyed the wolf pelts the two Holdsmen wore. He approached them and circled curiously.

"All the same, if I didn't know you already, I'd be hard-pressed to name you man or beast. From up there where I stood"—Galli tilted his head back over his shoulder to the heights of the landward end of Kingshead—"I had no idea it was you. The both of you looked strange creatures, not halfwise like men at all. Put me to thinking dire thoughts, let me tell you. And then I saw you making down towards the Cove, so I followed you. Trouble is that even up close you're like to turn a person's mind to dark fireside tales."

"Goes to show why they've managed to remain hidden for centuries," Kal said, lifting the small cask of healing water off his back and laying it on the shingle.

"They? What do you mean, Kal?" Galli said.

"Waldscathes. The waldscathes of the Black Cape. They're men, just men wearing wolf skins same as these." Kal unfastened the pelt from his neck and swung the cloak off his back. The stiffened face and muzzle lolled over Kal's arm, grinning sharp-toothed in a fixed snarl up at Galli. "They made Gwyn and me members of their brotherhood."

"Brotherhood? What do you mean?"

"We're waldscathes, sworn and vested." Kal lifted the pelt on his arm, meeting his friend's puzzled stare. "Believe me, we were as surprised at first as you are. It's a story . . . a strange story, indeed. But one that can wait. Come now, how is my father? His wound—is he all right? I've brought the healing water. It's here." Kal rapped his bowstaff against the cask that lay at his feet. "But where are they, the rest of the folk? Where's that ship of Broq's that is supposed to be waiting here?"

Galli averted his gaze, looking to his feet. "Frysan...He..."
He rubbed the back of his hand across his forehead.

"Go on, Galli, tell me straight."

The blond Holdsman raised his head. "He took a turn for the
worse, Kal, not long after you and Gwyn left for Ruah's Well. The
poison took hold. Broq tried...There was nothing we could do
but watch him fail. Your father...he's..." Galli sighed heavily.
"Kal, he's crossed the Birdless Lake."

Kal said nothing for a few minutes. Around them were only
the sounds of gull's cries, the wind, and the steady plash, wash,
and hiss of whitecaps as they broke against the stone wharf or ran
up the pebbled beach. At length, Kal combed his fingers through
the unruly strands of black hair that had blown across his face
and looked up at Gwyn. His mute companion's face betrayed
concern, but, beneath that, Kal saw a depth of serenity. Gwyn
nodded once, slowly.

"Yes." Kal shifted his gaze to Galli. "Yes, he's at peace. I know
it here." Still clutching his bowstaff, Kal placed a clenched fist
over his heart. "I had a dream. It was his time, Galli."

"Aye, it was his time. There was nothing we could do." Galli
laid a hand on his friend's shoulder. Kal was surprised by the
peace that he himself felt in the face of the news of his father's
passing. "Your mother and Bren were there with him at the end,
Kal. The women sewed his shroud the night before last. They
prepared his body."

"Who helped him in his passing? I was not there...." Kal's
voice faltered, a lump growing hard in his throat. "Oh, that I
could have been. But who served as *enefguthyas*?"

"Broq. He was Soul Warden to Frysan. He said the Prayer of
Passage, and eased your father's journey."

Kal turned to face the open water, breaking Galli's gentle
grip on his shoulder. He brushed away a brimming tear with
his sleeve. "*Gil nas sverender*," he whispered. "*Gil nas sverender,*
Frysan...Father."

Turning back to Galli, Kal saw his friend's head bent in concern.
The young Hordanu stiffened. "So, for the dead." He sniffed and
assumed a resolute face. "Now, to the living. What has happened
to everyone else? My people, are they safe?"

"I don't know."

"You don't know?"

"I mean the *Dancing Master* is not here. The ship is gone."

"Gone?"

"Aye, Kal, gone, with all on board, including Broq. Your father's body, too." Under his friend's scrutiny, the blond Holdsman paused and gathered himself to offer an explanation.

"Rhewgell, captain of the *Dancing Master*, was forced to weigh anchor in haste and leave or his ship would have been hemmed into this harbour. I saw two warships creeping down the far coast of the Firth from the north." Galli pointed again back up the slope behind him. "Artun and I were to watch for you from atop the ridge while everybody else remained aboard the ship, waiting for your coming. When I saw the ships, Artun and I went to warn the captain. It was a danger we had little expected. Rhewgell had encountered no sign of enemy ships in his journey here down the coast, but he wasn't a man to take the safety of his vessel for granted. As a sheltered harbour against ocean storms, this is near perfect. But it's a near-perfect trap, too."

"Gawmage?"

"Like as not. Any closer, I wager I'd have seen mastiff's heads painted on their mainsails."

"Did they escape, do you think?"

"The warships turned towards them, all right. But the *Dancing Master* is a trim ship, built for speed, and by all accounts the captain's a fine sailor, even though he struck me as an anxious sort. He surely didn't like the notion of waiting here for you and Gwyn. That man, you could tell he loves his ship and didn't want to stay a single moment longer than he had to. But chances are good they escaped."

"And Artun—where is he?"

"Left with the others. They pressed me to leave, too, especially Gammer, but I said I'd stay to watch for you." Galli lifted a hand to his friend's shoulder once again. "You're Hordanu, Kal, if we lose you—well..."

Kal's neck and ears burned as his face reddened at his companion's deference. "So they're gone," he said, regaining his composure. "And where does that leave us now?"

"Right about where we're standing, I'd say." Galli grinned, gesturing with an open hand to the beach where they stood.

"With a fair journey ahead of us," Kal said. "We can't stay here. The sack of writings, Galli, did it make it on the ship? The Hordanu's—"

"Yes, yes. As I said, everyone and everything was on board the ship waiting for you."

"Yes, of course." Kal drifted into thought for a moment, then said, "We've got to make Aelward's Cot some way."

"Aelward's Cot . . . That's a long piece away."

Both men fell silent, staring out to the Cerulean Ocean through the narrowed horizon afforded by the inlet's steep bounds. His back to them, Gwyn knelt on the stone pier, looking over its crumbling edge.

"Ah, look, he's found it."

"Found it?"

"The dory. It's what I used as a launch to get to and from the ship. The ship had to be anchored there in the deeper water." Galli pointed out into the empty inlet. "For a ship that big, the water's much too shallow this far into the Cove, especially at low tide."

"Let's have a look," said Kal, walking across the shingle to the wharf and stepping towards Gwyn. He paused to regard the small dory that bobbed against the stone side of the pier. "Not much of a boat, is it?"

"It's surely no seagoing vessel, if that's what you mean," Galli said.

"But if we could use a boat and hug the coast somehow, making our way north, it would be easier and safer than traveling overland through wildlands and strange clanholdings."

"Not in this thing, Kal. It's hardly more than a rowboat."

"No sail?"

"No, none." Galli paused, biting his lip in thought, then nodded. "Aye, but there are other boats."

"How do you mean?"

"Fishermen, I think. I saw them in the Firth from atop Kingshead. When the warships appeared, they scattered like minnows to the far side of the Firth and disappeared. Then, when the warships had left in pursuit of the *Dancing Master*, they crept out of hiding and spread their sails again."

"The far side of the Firth, you say?"

"Aye, Kal, over from the other side of Kingshead."

"That would be part of the Black Cape, then."

"I suppose."

"How far across from Kingshead would you say?"

"At a guess, I'd reckon a league and a half, two at the most, to the closest point."

"And it's, what, a league from here to the point of Kingshead?"

"Aye, Kal, or less.... What are you driving at?"

"Why, that's what we'll do. It's not that far. We'll take the dory out of the Cove, round the headland, and cross over to the Black Cape. There's sure to be dwellings there, a village maybe. They'll help us. I know they will."

"They who, Kal?"

"The Tircoilians. We've met them, Gwyn and me. I told you, we're members of their brotherhood."

"Are you sure, Kal? We can trust these folk?" Galli's eyes glanced at Kal's wolf pelt again with thinly veiled alarm.

"Sure, I'm sure. Trust me, Galli. I'll tell you more once we're on our way. Come on, we might as well be going." Kal threw his cloak over his shoulders and strode back to the beach to retrieve the cask of healing water. Galli and Gwyn had clambered down a rusted iron ladder into the bobbing boat by the time he had returned.

"Are we sure we want to lug this thing around with us?" Galli asked as Kal lowered the cask to him on its strap.

"If you had any idea what I've gone through for this, you wouldn't be asking." Kal swung himself over the edge of the pier and down the ladder.

When the three of them were settled, Galli untied the painter and swung the oars around on their tholes, wood creaking against wood. He handily maneuvered the dory away from the pier out into the small harbour. The small craft lifted and bobbed over the waves, and Galli grinned. The troubled surface was nothing worse than they had encountered regularly on Deepmere, and he was obviously enjoying it. While Galli rowed, Kal sat facing him in the stern and recounted his adventures at Ruah's Well and the Woods of Tircoil.

Taking advantage of the receding tide, they made the point of Kingshead in good time. As they rounded the towering headland, the open waters grew choppier and began to swell. Cresting waves lapped hungrily at the grim rocks of the cliffs behind them. They ventured out farther now into the Firth of Tircoil, struggling against the tidal current that ran abeam but urged on by the thin, dark shoreline of the Black Cape as a marker, closing with it gradually, spelling each other at the oars. In the offing here and there, too far to hail, small boats plied the water, their sails a smudge of white above the glistening waves. There was no sign of a warship though, Kal mused to himself gratefully. They'd have stood precious little chance against one in their little dory. There would have been no way to outrun the enemy without benefit of a sail. Yet they were small enough that they might pass unnoticed.

Before long, the features of the horizon grew more recognizable to Kal. The coast loomed larger. Thick forests came into view, immense trees crowding the ever more distinct contours of the shoreline.

"Look, there's a small boat," Kal said, pointing behind the oarsman. "It seems to be heading in to shore. Follow it in."

Galli rested his oars on the gunwale for a moment and looked back over his shoulder to gain his bearings.

"Here, I'll take over again," Kal said and gingerly traded places with his companion. Grunting with exertion, he laid his back into the rowing and propelled the boat forward towards the shoreline.

"I can't see it anymore," Galli shouted. "It's turned up inland. There must be a place of moorage there. Either that, or we've scared it into hiding."

"Because we might swoop down on them in our fearsome rowboat?" Kal said with forced humour between breaths. "No, they're a shy folk. But we'll follow them in. Gwyn, put on your pelt. Pull the visor over your head. With luck they'll recognize us as waldscathes."

"Waldscathes!" Galli shook his head in grim humour, grumbling to himself. "Lucky to be thought to be waldscathes? Hmm."

As they drew nearer the shoreline, they discovered a narrow channel that struck its way into the forest. Kal pulled at the oars, pushing the dory along the channel until the waterway elbowed sharply around a rock-faced bend. Cornering the bend, the Holdsmen saw that the dense forest on either side gave way to tilled field and pastureland.

"There, up ahead," said Galli in a low voice. "A village."

Resting his oars, Kal let the boat glide as he twisted to look behind him. Several small thatched dwellings lay clustered under a low hill that overlooked a wooden jetty at which some half-dozen fishing boats were tethered, empty masts swaying gently. Drying racks lined the shore. Kal turned around to face the stern again and dipped his oars into the water, pulling hard on the left, swinging the dory to shore. Slowly they slipped towards the boats, wary of the silence. Although smoke rose from two or three chimneys, all seemed deserted. There was not a soul to be seen or heard, except for a great shaggy dog that emerged from among the houses and bounded to the water's edge, barking at them.

"Hello! Hello, the shore! Is anybody home? Hello!" Galli hailed as they slid into an open spot along the quay. Standing on the bow, he took hold of the boat's painter and leaped onto the wooden planking. As he tied the painter to a post, Kal and Gwyn followed him onto the wharf. From shore, the dog had been following their movement with growing agitation. Now that they had landed, it charged along the narrow beach to accost them.

Galli glanced from the dog back down to the bottom of the dory where his gear lay. "Foolish, wasn't it, to leave our bows?" he said under his breath and drew his sword. The dog slowed to a stalking pace as it moved onto the quay, its hackles raised, teeth bared, and its barking now dropping to a throaty growl.

"Stay, Jig!" From behind the nearest dwelling emerged an old man, square-jawed, with a brown face creased and leathery, tanned like hide by the years of wind, sea, and sun. He held a rusty sword. The blade had clearly seen better days and little use in the meantime. Three younger men appeared behind him and came forward to flank the old man, two of them bearded, their bows held at the ready, each with an arrow nocked to its string.

"Jigger!" the weathered man barked.

The dog stopped in midstep and retreated. The old man drew closer, peering at them, squint-eyed and uncertain. From where it had withdrawn behind its master, the dog growled low and threateningly, hackles still raised, its body pressed to the ground.

"Who are you? What do you want?" demanded the old man gruffly. He eyed the three Holdsmen narrowly, his head slanted down and to the side. By now, he had reached the foot of the jetty.

"It's a trick, Noldran. Don't trust them. It's a trick," said one of the men behind him, drawing on his bowstring. "Mind not the pelts. We don't know their faces. They're not of the brotherhood."

"Aye, Nol. What if they've come from one of them warships?" said another.

"Briacoil! We come in peace." Kal took a step forward and held his hands wide in open greeting. "In the name of Gelanor, who made us members of your brotherhood and fitted us with this garb. And in the name of the Wood Maid, Katie Woodencloak, Protector of the Gleacewhinna."

"In the name of Gelanor, eh?" Noldran narrowed his eyes even more.

"Aye, in the name of Gelanor," Kal said expectantly.

"And in the name of the Wood Maid?"

"And of the Wood Maid."

"Well, then!" Noldran straightened as his face broadened into a smile. He took the sword firmly into his two hands and plunged the rusted blade into the soft sand and leaned on the pommel. "Briacoil, masters! Briacoil!" He turned his head to the left and right. "Put aside your bow, Hoff. You too, Peytar, and you, Safrus. They're friends. Friends and more than friends, I suspect," he continued, leaving the sword to stand leaning in the sand, knocked askew, as he strode forward to greet Kal. "My apologies for our suspicions. You might have come to us with evil in your heart."

"No harm done, Master Noldran." Kal couldn't help himself, but let a slight chuckle escape his throat at the mercurial change in the old fisherman's attitude. "We live in perilous times. The wise take stock of strangers," Kal said as he and Noldran met and clasped forearms, inclining their heads to one another. Noldran cast a closer look at Kal's pios.

"You are a bard, then." Noldran clasped Kal's arm more firmly still. "Now I know who you are. They said you were young. You saw Ruah. You've been staying with the Wood Maid."

"How did you know?"

"Word has long legs and swift feet in the Black Cape. And it's a rare day that we cross paths with any outsider." The weathered man released Kal's arm. "My name you know. They count me an elder here. Come, we'll talk."

Noldran led them into the village and seated himself at a table with benches set in a bower before one of the cottages. He dispatched one of the younger men to fetch food and drink and gestured for the Holdsmen to sit. Other men had begun to gather as women and children emerged from the cottages and milled shyly about the table, gawking at the newcomers. Noldran nodded his welcome to each as the assembly grew.

"Now," he said at last, turning his attention back to Kal, "tell us how you come to be in our village."

The fisherfolk stood by and listened as Kal began to explain how the forced departure of the *Dancing Master* at the appearance of Gawmage's warships had disrupted their plans and had left him and his companions stranded. Food arrived, and, dry-mouthed, Kal broke from his account to quaff a deep draught from the tankard set before him. He looked up at his growing audience. Noldran grinned.

"I told you, we ne'er entertain outsiders," he said. "Only our own woodfolk, and men of the brotherhood, like Gelanor. They come to fish and stock the larder." Noldran shook his head and laughed. "Ah, Gelanor. He grumbles that fishing's a chore forced on him by his wife. He's forever carping. But we know different, don't we, Hoff?"

"That we do, Nol. I'll tell you," the younger man said, then winked at Kal with a sideways nod, "Gelanor, he loves to hoist sail on the ocean waters."

"If he loved it any the better, he'd be a fish," another man said.

"Nay, a merman, terror of the ocean waves," Hoff said mirthfully around a piece of cheese that he had picked up from a platter on the table and shoved in his mouth.

"So you see, Noldran," Kal resumed the thread of his explanation, "we followed one of your boats here, hoping you might somehow help us secure passage up the coast. If you could just help us rig our boat with a mast and sail. We've sailed before—"

"Nay, nay, that'll not do." His mouth still half filled with cheese, Hoff shook his head so hard that the ale slopped from his mug. His hair, a mad black tangle peppered with sawdust, flew about, lending fierceness to the look of deep disapproval that blanketed his features. "It would be a job of work to make that tender of yours sea-sound. Nay, not worth the trouble. Better to start afresh, build a new boat." He planted his ale mug on the table with a thud.

"Hoff's our shipwright, none better," Noldran said, nodding pensively.

"What about the *Ellyn*?" another man piped up.

"Aye, I was thinking the same, Safrus, I was thinking the same," Noldran said.

"The *Ellyn*?"

"You recognize the name, no?" Noldran grinned at Kal.

"It's Gelanor's boat," the man who had made the suggestion said. "We hold it ready for him for whenever he comes to fish."

"In perfect sailing trim," Hoff said, a wide smile spreading across his face. "I've just overhauled and repaired her. Up the coast? She'd do fine by you. And I'd love to see the look on the big man's face, to be sure!" He winked again. "One on him, eh?"

A buzz of muted laughter and comment passed among the villagers. Noldran nodded and turned to Kal. "Well then, what do you say to the *Ellyn*? That's if you can sail her."

"We've sailed. We know a bit. Not near as much as you folk who live by the sea. But we can beat to windward or run before a wind," said Galli.

"She's a hard craft to handle, if we're to believe Gelanor. She gives too much leeway, he claims," Safrus said.

"Bah, you must take no mind of that." Hoff said, flicking his hand dismissively. "We all know Gelanor well enough. It's his boat and his wife that bear the brunt of his jestful complaint. When he's not grumbling about too much leeway on the water, he's nattering about too little of it on home ground. Take my word on it, the *Ellyn* is a fine craft. And named after a fine woman."

"It's settled then. You'll take the *Ellyn* upcoast," Noldran said.

"But Gelanor. It's his boat—"

"Peace, Kalaquinn," Noldran said. "Gelanor is a good man, a true brother of the pelt. As I know him, he would give his blessing. With full heart. He is our bard and our chief. That he should have made you members of our band and fitted you with the wolf pelt is something not to be taken lightly. No, not lightly." There was no doubting the respect he had for the man.

Galli looked up and caught the old fisherman's eye.

"Even you, Galli." He smiled, nodding. "To us the friend of a brother is a brother. You may count yourself a waldscathe, too. We'll fit you out with a pelt and hear your pledge. No doubt it's what Gelanor would wish."

"Then there's a further problem," Galli said.

"What's that?"

"How do we return the boat to you?"

"Don't you worry about bringing her back," Noldran said, shaking his head as his eyes narrowed and his lips pursed. "Just keep her safe and sound, for the sake of the boat. It's a small price, really, to be helping brothers."

"But I can't just—"

"Aye, you can and you will. Hospitality has been offered. You must accept. It's the waldscathe way," Noldran said, a glimmer escaping his old eyes. "Besides, we've lost more and finer craft in a shorter time in the teeth of a Calathros gale. You'll take the boat."

"Aye, it'll give me the chance to make a new boat for the big man," Hoff said, winking now at no one in particular. "And give the big man the chance to complain about something new!"

"How can I thank you?" Kal inclined his head to each of the fishermen around him. "I have nothing to give you by way of payment."

"Payment? That's foolish talk. Payment! Nay, downright insulting." Noldran rose from table and lifted his clay mug. "We're kindred, waldscathes, one and all. To the brotherhood!"

"To the brotherhood!" The refrain was taken up as men leapt to their feet. Lifted tankards were clanked one against another and drained. The women looked on with amusement, until everyone's attention was diverted by the howls of four or five young boys who had to be pulled off one another, their play at being waldscathes having gotten out of hand, turning into an all-out tussle under the feet of their elders. Mothers clucked at bloodied noses, scrapes, bruises, and torn clothing. Each turned for her cottage with a boy in tow, each boy yelping at the indignity of being led away by the ear.

"How soon can we weigh anchor?" Kal asked as the distracting mirth settled somewhat.

"Eager to leave us, are you, brother?" Hoff grinned then glanced up to the sky. "We can have you and your gear stowed aboard the *Ellyn* within the hour if you'd like. You can ride the tide out."

The folk of the fishing village remained gathered on shore, still waving their farewell. Even Jigger the dog had been there to send them off, ranging the beach and barking excitedly. Kal raised his arm in parting one last time as Galli and Gwyn each pulled at an oar. In but a moment, the boat slipped around the bend in the channel, and the village was lost to view. Coming out of the shelter of the inlet onto the Firth of Tircoil, Galli and Gwyn stowed their oars.

"Mind you keep a hand on that tiller now, Kal. You're my helmsman," said Galli, who stood to unfurl the sail and free the spars. The wolf pelt tied around Galli's neck flapped like bunting in the breeze.

"And mind you reef your sail," Kal called back to him over the freshening west wind, "or we'll have our first mishap—waldscathe overboard, a newly clothed one at that."

"Aye, Kal. It does catch a nasty bit of wind, doesn't it? I'd best take it off for the time being, like you and Gwyn. It may be a landsman's terror in the Woods of Tircoil, but doesn't make sense out here on the water. Gwyn!" Galli shrugged off the wolf pelt and attempted to attract the younger Holdsman's attention. "Gwyn! Hi, Gwyn!" The younger man looked over at Galli from where he had been sitting staring across the Firth. Galli tossed the pelt to him. "Here, stow this under the bow with the rest of the gear." Gwyn moved cautiously forward and shoved the wolf skin on top of a small pile of baggage and provisions. He remained there, leaning his elbows on the polished wood that covered the rounded bow, looking ahead, his red hair leaping like flames atop his head as it whipped in the sea wind.

Galli grasped the bundled sail and its spars and heaved them onto the lee side of a mast that stood in the open boat not far aft of the bow. He reached for a line and pulled at it hand over hand. Immediately, a long wooden spar shot up the short mast, lifting the lug-rigged sail behind it, its aft tip rising high above the masthead. With deft movement, Galli leaned to the weather side of the boat and tied the line off tight against the weight the straining sail would soon place on the mast. The boom wavered above Kal as he sat at the tiller, and the fluttering sail stiffened, pulling the boom to the port side of the boat against another line that Galli snugged and secured. Now the *Ellyn* drove through the waves by the power of wind on canvas, running under a fair breeze.

Galli moved beside Kal, leaning against the windward gunwale of the boat, a smile creasing his ruddy face. Kal wondered at his friend's easy competence with the small vessel. Had it been bee-keeping, or rather fishing, that Galli had been preparing himself for in the Holding? Either way, there was little doubt that he had spent more time on Deepmere than he'd cared to admit before—no doubt learning the lines of mast and sail under the tutelage of one of the Holding's weathered fishermen, while Kal himself learned the lines of *Hedric's Master Legendary* under Wilum's watchful eye.

"She's a fine little vessel, I think." Kal leaned to speak to his friend. "Handles well. Better than anything to be found on Deep-mere, I venture to say."

"Without a doubt." Galli nodded, pulling stray strands of straw-coloured hair from his face. "Aye, built tough, to be oceangoing. A good boat. Nice gift." His smile broadened. "Gelanor's a generous man."

It was a good boat, Kal mused. Sturdy and stable, broad in the beam with beautiful lines that ran from the stem of the rounded bow to a rounded stern. There was no doubt that it was a work-horse of a boat, perfect for the task intended of her, but Kal was surprised at the attention to detail and care that had been paid in her construction—that and the speed that she had! Kal gripped the worn wood of the tiller and felt the gentle vibration of the water slipping under the hull, along the keel, and across the rudder. His gaze traced the line of the mast up to the yard, then farther up the rising yardarm to the sail's peak. From the topmost point of the spar, a yellow pennant danced in the wind, its tip snapping out to sea. On the banner rippled the image of a small harp. It was a bard's boat. Kal smiled to himself. Fitting.

Gwyn distracted his attention, pointing to a scattering of fishing boats similar to the *Ellyn* that dotted the waters of the Firth, most of them on the windward side and too far to hail. Casting his eyes the other way, Kal saw that they had come up even to the point of Kingshead, which they soon passed. At Galli's instruction, Kal pulled the tiller gently towards himself, and the little vessel nosed to the west. They set a course that followed the eastern coast of the Firth, which lay to starboard, its features marked by massive cliffs and jagged outcroppings of rock surrounded by a heavy mantle of green that bore little sign of human habitation.

As the day's light grew weaker and fell low across the water, they emerged from the protection of the Firth into the open ocean. The cries of the seafowl seemed more shrill and wild. The air turned more chill and the wind more brisk, shifting astern of the small craft, rising from the southwest under high wispy clouds in a purpling sky.

Galli quickly unfastened the mainsheet, allowing the line to run out as he dropped sail. Again he lifted sail and spars around the mast with an economy of movement that betrayed the practice he had gained on Deepmere. Kal shifted, ducking to the windward side of the boat, and gripped the tiller in his other hand. Hoisting the sail once more, Galli grinned with satisfaction and tied off the sheet to the opposite side of the boat, then snugged the lines to the boom that hung far out over the starboard side. They bore off, so that the wind came at their port quarter, driving the *Ellyn*, trimmed and balanced, speedily up the mainland coast. Dusk fell with silent stealth, obscuring the detail and contrasts of the landmass that lay to the east, rendering it a long dark slab of formless shadow.

"Keep your helm down, Kal. You heard Noldran. Mustn't steer too close to shore," Galli said. "Wouldn't think it, eh? More dangerous than the open sea. Shoals and sandbars and tidal rips."

"Aye, aye, Captain Clout. Helm to starboard."

"You may jest, but it's good that there's at least one serious sailor on this bucket."

"And here I was thinking that a Telessarian's only element was the forest."

"Don't forget, I'm only half-Telessarian. And lucky for us I spent more time than you haunting the waterfront and learning the difference between a tiller and a turnbuckle—"

"Look, there's the first star," Kal said, and the two fell silent, watching for long moments as pinpricks of light pierced the deepening darkness and grew in strength and number. The wind was steady and whistled gently in the simple rigging of the *Ellyn*, a sound overlaid by the wash of the waves against the boat's bow and sides. Beneath that, the two men heard the hushed rhythm of Gwyn asleep and snoring in the bow. Galli yawned.

"The breeze is holding fair," he said, "and we will hold this course 'til dawn. How long until the moon rises, do you reckon?"

"Two, two and a half hours."

"We could take turns getting some rest."

"How about you rest first, now that sail and helm are fixed on course? After all, you said you're the one serious sailor—ouch!"

Galli kicked Kal in the shin. "Ah, go on with you."

"But it was you that said it," Kal said in a voice that feigned injury.

"Right enough, I did...." Galli yawned again. "And seeing as that's the case, I will grab a wink first. You're all right to hold this course, Kal?"

"Sure. Look, there's the North Crown, and the Pole Star stands"— he stretched his thumb and little finger out at arm's length against the deep, luminous mist of the starfield—"one...two...exactly two hand spans from the top of the mast."

"Good, then. But make sure you wake me if the wind changes or shifts, or when you're ready to be spelled off, or if anything happens."

"Aye, aye, Captain Clout, sir," Kal said, thrusting his jaw out.

Galli made to lay a playful kick at Kal's shins again and laughed, then stretched himself along the bottom of the boat under an old canvas tarp. Almost as soon as the man laid his head down on his arm, he fell into a slow, steady snoring.

"Ah, the sounds of the sea," Kal said aloud to himself. "Wind in the rigging, the splash of the bow, the gull's cry, and Galli's nose music."

For a while, Kal concentrated on the stars and the dark water beneath them, his hand gripping the tiller loosely. The boat drove its way through the starlit waves, riding the crests, making good speed. If these conditions held, thought Kal, it would not be long before they made landfall farther up the coast at the Asgarth Forest. Not long after dawn, perhaps. And by this time tomorrow evening they might be in the company of the Holdsfolk again— theirs and that of the mysterious Aelward fellow.

Kal's attention was drawn to the disjointed rhythm of his friends' snoring. He was surprised that he had remained so alert, not feeling the least tinge of tiredness, and was happy to let his companions sleep on. His mind began to wander the avenues of memory. Events of the past, both distant and recent, came to his thoughts in a chain of loose association. Beneath the blanket of the ocean's night sky, time slipped away.

Kal became aware that the breeze had let up slightly, almost imperceptibly, and that the *Ellyn* had slowed somewhat. Looking up at the star patterns, he recognized from their new places in the sky that nearly two hours had passed since Galli had gone to sleep. He smiled to himself—perhaps it would be midmorning before they made landfall. The moon should be rising soon, he thought, and he craned his neck to look around the dark sail. No light yet showed on the eastern horizon. In fact, there was no light at all to the east or to the north. The *Ellyn* slowed further still, the breeze dropping steadily. Kal was puzzled—no stars shone ahead, nor to port, nor to starboard, and, off the mast, half the North Crown had disappeared. The star-littered dome of the sky simply slipped into nothingness, into a thick velvet blackness that engulfed a full third of the night's face.

The breeze faltered, then came in gasping fits that teased the

Ellyn's sail until it dropped off altogether, leaving the sailcloth hanging limply from the top spar. The boom tugged listlessly at slack lines as the boat rolled gently on the oily sea.

A purple flash cut the darkness. Kal leaned forward and peered into the pitch black of night off the starboard bow. The air had grown still. Kal found it oppressive and hard to breathe, and his skin prickled at some unseen, unknown tension that seemed to charge the dead air. Then he heard the first low rumblings, as of a deep drum rolling on and on, growing in intensity, then subsiding with a restless grumble. In the wake of the thunder, he heard another sound, hushed at first, then higher pitched and becoming more insistent. It was a whisper that grew steadily louder and became a whining howl, threatening to become a roar.

Again, the darkness was torn. Long purple-white fingers flickered in the distance, chasing across the horizon, probing violet mountains of towering cloud that filled the northern sky. In that moment of sustained light, Kal saw a long, broken line of white spray, rank upon rank of wind-whipped waves charging across the still sea, driven by the storm and bearing down upon the *Ellyn*.

"Galli!" he cried, and leapt to his feet. "Galli! Galli, wake—"

The storm winds hit first. The sail snapped tight, and the boom swung with fury over the boat, hammering Kal in the side of the head before tearing itself from the mast. Kal slumped onto the deck planking as the *Ellyn* heeled and yawed.

"...cut it loose, Gwyn. Cut the rigging..."

Someone was shouting. His head pounded.

"...clear the sail from the..."

He struggled to regain consciousness, like a man grasping for a rope that bounces from the fingertips but remains painfully out of reach. Someone stumbled over him. He heard panicked breathing.

"...give her lee helm—the tiller, Gwyn, to the left..."

The storm howled overhead.

"...keep the wind astern...must let her run before the..."

He was wet. And warm between his legs. It was raining hard. He tasted salt—salt and the metallic bitterness of blood.

"...Kal? Kal!" Someone was calling him....

He wanted to respond....

He wanted to call back....

Stars swam before his eyes. And darkness washed over him.

NINETEEN

Kal lay facedown. He felt heat on his back and on his head. His whole body ached. Something pulled gently at his legs, then stopped. They were wet, but his head and back felt dry. He lay still, struggling to clear his mind. Something pulled at his legs again. He thought he heard the distant rush of wind....No...no, it was the sucking ebb of surf. And the cry of gulls. The storm had passed, that much was sure, but he was no longer sprawled on the hard deck of the *Ellyn*. There was grit in his mouth, and his cracked lips stung. Slowly, he opened his eyes, but he could not summon the strength to move.

His consciousness drifted again....

The sound of a horse's whinny drew him back to his senses. There was a jangle of harness and tack. He sensed the soft pad of feet on sand nearby. He struggled to raise his head, but it remained heavy, resistant to his bidding. A sharp jab of pain jolted his side, and he felt himself being rolled over, limply, like a rag doll, so that he lay face to the sky, spread-eagled and blinking in the severe light of the sun. A leather riding boot lay planted on his chest. Shadow fell across his face as someone leaned over him, an arm extended straight. Kal looked from the stiff arm down the gleaming length of a sword blade poised over his throat.

"Stand!"

It was a sharp command, given with authority, although the voice was that of a youth, high-pitched, not yet broken and made husky by manhood. The boot was withdrawn. Dazed, shaking his head, Kal slowly pushed himself over and on to all fours.

Seawater swirled around his knees and hands then washed back down across the sand.

"Up!"

The Holdsman rose shakily to his feet and grimaced at the pain. The sword stayed trained on him, its point inches from his stomach, as he stood. Kal looked down on a fresh, unshaven face framed by shining black hair cut straight in an even line below the ears and around the base of the skull. *But a stripling,* Kal thought groggily. *Not but a lad.* Kal looked the fellow slowly up and down. Before him stood a slight figure, his sword arm unwavering, clad in hose and a coarse, loosely fitted military tunic, its hood flung back. But for all his youth he was fierce-eyed and unflinching and seemed ready to thrust the shipwrecked Holdsman through at the slightest provocation. The boy reached forward and stripped Kal's hunting knife from its sheath at his side, glanced at the highland blade, and tossed it to the sand behind him before returning his hard gaze to Kal's face.

"Perhaps this one will speak," he said, flicking the sword tip to Kal's throat again. The point brushed the delicate shape of the pios. "Ah, a bard is it, then? Well, that's imaginative."

"Tell us, man, if you know what's good for you," said a gruffer voice that rang out from behind the boy. "Are you one of Lysak's hirelings? Tell us the truth now. Was it he that sent you?"

For the first time, Kal became aware of something beyond the swordsman in front of him. A dozen grim men in battered leather jerkins had dismounted from their horses and stood ready but a few paces away with swords unsheathed. In their midst, behind the harsh-voiced questioner, sat Gwyn astride a horse, his hair and clothes bedraggled, his bound hands clutching the saddlebow.

"Gwyn...," Kal croaked, his throat parched and tight. "Gwyn, are you...?"

The bound Holdsman nodded to Kal.

"Ah, so you have a tongue. Not like your friend here," said the young swordsman, stiffening, drawing Kal's attention back to him.

"Who...who are you?" Kal managed to ask. His tongue felt thick and swollen.

"No, rather, who are you? And why have you come to our land?"

Kal tried to swallow. "Water...Water, please...."

The boy shot a glance back over his shoulder to the man nearest him and jerked his head. The soldier slid his sword into its sheath and stepped forward, loosening a flask from his belt, which he handed to Kal. Seeing that the boy made no attempt to stop him, Kal slowly reached for the flask, took it, and lifted it to his lips. Kal closed his eyes and let the water slake some of his discomfort.

"I am a bard," he said at length. "Here...my pios." Kal brought his hand up to the brooch.

"Yes, a bard—so it would appear. But I doubt it. Tell me your name then, bard. Where are you from?" The boy's lips curled in something between a smile and a sneer, revealing a row of even white teeth. Light played in his green eyes. "Though I think you be from Lysak's land, and you be Lysak's man."

"Lysak? I don't know who that is." Kal felt a twist of fear in his stomach, and his hands grew damp with sweat. His mind began to race through possible explanations for his presence on these unknown shores. The truth, he knew, must be guarded and portioned out with care. The boy's eyes narrowed at the pause, and Kal thought he felt the sword point press closer in impatience. He settled on a story that he felt least betrayed the truth and steadied himself.

"I-I am Kalaquinn Wright," he said. A pang of fear clenched his gut. He shouldn't have given his real name. Nothing to do now but continue. He swallowed hard. "I don't know who Lysak is, but I am, in truth, a bard. My people are from the Keverang of Pelogran, the Asgarth Forest. My friend Gwyn and I were in a fishing boat when a storm arose and blew us out to sea. I can't remember what happened, as I was knocked unconscious in the boat. Next thing I know, I'm washed up here on your shores."

The young man eased the grip on his sword and lowered it a touch.

"Careful, milady." The gruff voice warned. "Don't trust him. We all know that Lysak's a snake. With all the many ruses he's tried, this may be yet a new trick."

Kal's eyes widened as he looked from the speaker to the boy in front of him. "My lady?" Kal echoed. "Wh-who are you?"

"Bind him! You're right, Durro. We must take care." The swordsman glanced back at a tall dark-browed man, the one with the gruff voice, then turned again to look at Kal.

"I am Bethsefra," the swordsman said curtly, "daughter and sole heir to my father Uferian, King of the Oakapple Isles. You are in my custody." Bethsefra thrust her sword into its scabbard, turned heel, and strode towards the horses. "Take them back to town and secure them in the donjon. We'll question them further." There was a hint of delicacy to her movements not disguised by her boyish appearance or attire.

So, Kal thought to himself as he watched the woman walk away, the Oakapple Isles... they had been driven by the storm as far south as that! It was a wonder that they hadn't been swept right out into the middle of the Cerulean Ocean. And here he was, found by the king's own daughter—and a wary and distrustful thing she was.

"But Bethsefra," Kal protested, trying to suppress his rising ire, "I speak the honest truth! My friend and I, we are not your enemy. We bear you no ill will." Two burly soldiers stepped up with rope. "Wait! You must not do this! You've mistaken us!"

"I hope so—for your sakes," she said, looking back at him. "For the time being, you'll be our guests."

"But you must believe me..."

Bethsefra returned to her horse and swung herself lightly into the saddle, leaving Kal to the rough attentions of the two heavy set soldiers assigned to secure him.

"You mustn't do this! I demand that you release—"

"And another thing, Durro."

"Milady?"

The woman wheeled her horse around until she sat looking down at her lieutenant. "Gag him. I think I prefer his companion's company. He's quieter. We'll break from our training for the day. Have the rest of the men search the shores. See what can be found. There may be others, so have them stay alert."

"Yes, milady."

Kal was manhandled onto the horse behind Gwyn, his wrists bound and a soldier's sweat-stained neckcloth placed between his teeth and firmly tied behind his head. Durro barked sharp orders, and his men broke into two groups, each riding off in an opposite direction along the beach. Durro got astride his own horse and snatched up the reins of the horse on which the two Holdsmen sat. He and four other men followed Bethsefra, whose mount trotted along the beach then turned away from the sea and scrambled up an embankment. With only Gwyn's tunic to grab hold of, and with two hands bound tight, Kal found it increasingly awkward to keep his seat on the horse. Still, he ventured to look back over his shoulder at the water, now calm save for a gentle swell, and hoped that Galli had escaped the storm's wrath, that he was safe, that he might find and rescue them.

They crested the steep rise and crossed a windswept stretch of moor that had been set up as a makeshift grounds for martial exercises with quintains and straw-stuffed dummies, some of which sprouted arrow shafts left from an interrupted practice. The open heath broke against a forest of stately oaks, into which they plodded. The familiar musk of moist earth, leaf mould, and undergrowth was underlaid by the strange tang of sea air. The rope bit into Kal's wrists, and he hurt worse than ever, each jostle on the horse's back sending shooting pain through some part of his aching body. It seemed that the well-trodden track stretched interminably on and on, rising, then dipping, then rising again, but eventually they stopped in a clearing by a bridge that spanned a gorge loud with the sound of running water. A dour-faced man pulled the two Holdsmen ungently down from their mount one at a time. Bethsefra conferred with Durro, who kept an eye cocked on the two captives. At a nod from the woman, the lieutenant strode over to the Holdsmen, thrust a waterskin at Gwyn and cut away the gag from Kal's face. Kal gratefully took the waterskin from Gwyn's hand and rinsed the sour taste of the soiled cloth from his mouth. He handed the skin back to his companion and stepped towards the woman, only to be barred by a soldier and brusquely pushed back.

"May I ask a boon, Bethsefra?" Kal cried out. "My lady?"

Bethsefra turned to him. "You may ask," she said flatly. Durro's brow creased with suspicion.

"A small boon," Kal ventured again, dropping his voice and holding up his bound hands. "My lady, have you tried sitting a horse with wrists lashed together like so, and naught but a scrap of tunic for a handhold?"

"Yet another trick, milady," Durro said. "Don't trust him. No doubt he's as sly as Lysak, his master."

"I tell you, I know no Lysak," Kal said wearily.

"Bah, he lies. He lies through his teeth. Let me muzzle him again, milady."

The woman lifted her hand to stay the soldier.

"Look. Your men are fine archers." Kal tried hard to sound

reasonable. "I'm a highlander—I have an eye for these things. How far would I get before they shot me down, bound or unbound?"

"Our seaholding stands in the balance, and we'll not take any chance," said Bethsefra. "You will remain bound."

Kal sighed heavily.

"Be thankful I don't let Durro gag you again. Lomric," she continued, addressing the soldier nearest the Holdsmen, "get them mounted again. They've rested long enough."

"But I won't try to escape. I can promise you as solemnly as you wish," Kal said, twisting away from the grip of his guard.

"And I can promise you," Bethsefra said slowly, enunciating each syllable, "as solemnly as you wish, Master Kalaquinn Wright, if that is who you are, that if you do not do as you are bidden, I will have you lashed to that horse's rump like a sack of flour. Now, silence." Her eyes bored into Kal's for a long moment before she spun away and leapt to her saddle. With a shrug of resignation, Kal stopped struggling and let himself be helped onto the horse where Gwyn already was seated.

"It seems we're in a tight fix again, Gwyn," Kal whispered to his friend's back. The mute Holdsman merely lifted his shoulders in a shrug, and Kal fell into a despondent silence at the realization that there was no escape from their predicament.

When the party emerged at last from the forest, they entered a patchwork of rolling pastureland, fields in crop, meadows, and garden plots. A scattering of steadings dotted the countryside. The slow, rhythmic clang of hammer on steel ringing from a not-too-distant smithy met them, and here and there smoke rose lazily from stone chimney stacks.

"It's Lady Bethsefra!" a small boy cried out, pointing with great excitement from the front door of a dwelling that pressed near the road. "And she's got two prisoners! Mean-looking fellows." Curiosity drew people from house, garden, and shop to gape at their lady, her soldiers, and the captives as they passed.

Dominating the landscape in the near distance ahead loomed a gleaming white citadel, high on a hill. For a brief moment, Kal caught his breath. He forgot the chafing pain of the ropes that bound him and the dire thoughts that harried him. Swanskeld—he knew it must be Swanskeld, the town seat of the Oakapple Isles, a city of ancient renown. History accounted the town as spectacular not only for its location high on the chalk cliffs above the innermost end of the deep ocean inlet, Swanskeld Sound, but even more for the semblance that the white stone town, set upon the white cliffs, with its fortress walls and tower, had to the gentle creature that its name suggested.

Bethsefra lead the party up the steeply climbing cobbled surface of the road, and the gently rolling farmland gave way to scrub and rocks and stunted trees. As the road climbed higher still, the ocean appeared far below to their left, its breakers crashing along the base of bold cliffs that curved to the foundation of the town's curtain wall. Indeed, the sweeping chalk cliff on the opposite side of the sound looked like the wing of an impossibly immense bird stretching forward to the open ocean from a white breast of stone ramparts overtopped by a citadel tower that was thrust upward, like the neck of a swan crying to the sky.

As they drew nearer the town, Bethsefra and the horsemen did not slow but rather picked up their pace, turning from the road onto a less traveled path, spurring their mounts to an easy canter. Kal had slackened his grip on Gwyn's tunic and lurched to regain his balance for fear of tumbling off the horse as it, too, broke from a walk. Soon they had ridden into the shadow of the walls footing the base of the citadel. They reached a small iron-studded oak door, and all dismounted. The two Holdsmen stretched, stiff and sore. Kal looked up and along the curtain wall. Farther down the ramparts stood two larger towers. Men loafed atop them, leaning against their crenellated parapets. That would be the main gate, he thought, opening to the road they had traveled—this, then, would be the postern gate.

Durro pounded at the door with his fist and gruffly hailed those within. The door creaked on its hinges and swung open. Beyond the door, a raised portcullis hung suspended, like wolf's teeth ready to snap shut. Kal and Gwyn were bundled inside and prodded through a guardroom that was milling with armed men, who snapped to attention at the sight of the woman. They came to another heavy door set into the opposite side of the ramparts, the inner side. It stood open. The two were pushed through it and found themselves staring up at a huge bastion, far taller and larger than the towers set into the curtain wall. To the left and the right, Kal saw protected within the walls a town bustling with market stalls and shops.

The imposing structure before them was circled by a moat,

over which a drawbridge had been lowered, leading to yet another gateway, one even more imposing and well-protected than the postern gate. They crossed the drawbridge into the citadel itself, to an open chamber lit by torches that gave onto flights of stairs leading both up and down.

"They're yours now," Bethsefra said to Durro. "You know what to do." Without a further word, she departed, bounding up stone steps two at a time towards the upper reaches of the citadel. Kal wanted to shout after her but knew it was pointless. She was gone.

"Time to show you where we entertain spies," said Durro mirthlessly. He plucked up an unlit torch from a pile in a box on the floor and reached up to touch it to one burning in a sconce fastened to bleak, smoke-stained walls. His torch kindled to life in a bright gush of flame. The lieutenant and one of his men turned towards the stairs and began to descend the steps. Lomric lifted a torch to light it as well, then turned to Kal and Gwyn.

"This way, guests. This way to your new quarters," he said with a sweeping gesture, then pushed the Holdsmen stumbling after Durro.

The stairs uncoiled into the rock beneath the citadel. Here and there, branching passages broke the monotony of their descent, and from some of these there blew fresh salt-laden breezes, fluttering the flames of the torches. Kal thought he saw a new glimmer of light filtering through to them from below, beyond Durro and his torch. The light grew steadily stronger, until the stairs gave onto a landing. Beyond the level break in their descent, the steps continued down into darkness. Durro led the group from the landing along a broad passageway, the light growing steadily stronger. They entered a large chamber, a brazier in its centre, where an armed guard warmed himself against the coolness of the stone room. The flames in the brazier wavered and danced in the steady draught of a sea breeze that blew into the chamber from a row of bright and generous openings. Kal blinked at the light. Along the far end of the chamber ran a wall of heavy iron bars partitioned by further grillwork into small cells. In each cell, an opening set chest-high in the thick outer wall was fixed with iron bars. At one end of the cell block, the lone occupant of the prison, an old man, cackled and made a rude noise.

The gaoler stood from the fire and shouted at the prisoner, "Shut up, you old fool!"

"Naughty! Naughty!" The old man waggled his finger at Kal and Gwyn, and began to cackle loudly again, leaning through the bars of his cell.

"I said shut up!" the gaoler yelled, then approached Durro, the old prisoner still clucking and mumbling. "Sorry, sir."

"He's in again?"

"Yessir."

"Stealing again?"

"Aye, picking pockets. Didn't fare well at it, mind. Naught but a few coins. Can't say as he's much of a thief—"

"Needed to buy meat for my children, Cap'n, hmm-hmm, meat for my children," the old man piped up. A broad grin revealed a few half-decayed teeth and a tongue moving wormlike behind pink gums.

The gaoler spun around. "Shut up, you old rotter!"

"Gabaro, hold your tongue," the lieutenant said in a level voice, "or you'll find yourself moved down."

The old prisoner retreated to the back of the cell at the threat and continued to mutter to himself while he eyed the soldier warily. The lieutenant ignored the old man and indicated the two Holdsmen.

"These are captives of her ladyship," he said. "They're to be held here for questioning. I leave them in your charge. Mind them carefully, or it will be your hide to pay."

"Y-yessir," the gaoler stammered. "Right in here, sir." The gaoler fumbled with a large ring of iron keys that jangled loudly in the hollow chamber until he found the one he sought. He stepped to a cell in the middle of the row, fit the key into a heavy lock, and swung the door open. The two Holdsmen were jostled into the cage. There was dry, though musty, straw on the floor, but, other than that, the cell was empty. The door clanged shut behind them. The lieutenant grunted his approval and strode out of the chamber, followed by his men.

At his departure, the old prisoner muttered a stream of half-audible imprecations and began to cackle again. He was silenced by a long glance from the gaoler as he crossed the chamber and returned with a badly dented basin. He pressed the pan through the bars of the Holdsmen's cell and let it fall clattering to the stone floor.

"Mind you don't foul the cell. I like it clean. Use the pan.

Dump it out the window." The gaoler turned back to his brazier, sat on a stool, and took up a small block of wood that he had been whittling. Gwyn looked at him with curiosity, but the gaoler ignored both the Holdsmen and the old man, who had taken up a muted conversation with himself.

Any thought of escape that Kal had entertained vanished as he stepped to the window and leaned over its deep ledge, soiled from the activity of the cell's previous occupants. Pressing his head between iron bars set in crumbling masonry, Kal discovered that the window was cut into the sheer walls of the cliff face, falling hundreds of feet to where the surf broke against a jumble of rocks. Above him, the cliff stretched up until it met the curtain wall of the town. He could not see the citadel itself, as it was set back inside the walls.

He looked out into Swanskeld Sound, framed by the long white cliffs that swept away from the window like outstretched arms to welcome and embrace the Cerulean Ocean and the horizon beyond, blue on blue. The sky was clear. Kal filled his lungs with the sea breeze and savoured its freshness. His mind, however, laboured under the burden of their situation—they were held captive in a strange country, with little prospect of attaining their liberty, judging from the disposition of her ladyship and her men; Galli was lost and possibly drowned; his people were abandoned to the fickle mercies of fate and fortune; and hope of fulfilling his greater purpose was, at the very best, faint.

Kal sighed heavily and closed his eyes against the beauty of the scene before him. Unbidden, words drifted to his mind—soft, measured phrases. He began to speak to himself, quietly, in the rhythm of his breathing: "Though these works of thine wax old, thou art ever the same, and thy years shall not fail, from generation unto generation. . . ." As quickly as a summer zephyr falls still, the words ended, drifting into silence. Though the words had brought with them a calm that blunted the edge of his distress, he still felt unsettled and anxious. Kal sighed again and turned away from the window.

Across the cell from him, his back to the iron grille of the door, Gwyn sat on his haunches plaiting straws into an intricate pattern. His face was clear and open and his eyes focused on his task. As if sensing Kal watching him, the mute Holdsman looked up over his handiwork and met Kal's gaze.

"We're in a tight spot now, Gwyn. A very tight spot, indeed."

His companion shrugged almost dismissively and returned his attention to his work, fingers flicking and bending the yellow stalks.

"What? You don't believe we're through? Come now, Gwyn. Check the lock. We're in a prison. Held here for—"

Again Gwyn shrugged his shoulders, then gently shook his head and looked up at his friend. His eyes were intense and sad. It was as if he was chiding his companion. Yet beneath the chastening gaze was a peace, a serenity, that shook Kal.

"You know something, don't you, lad? Though how you know it...Well." Kal chuckled to himself. "Ah, Gwyn, I should pay better attention to your humours. You're like a weathercock—you know how the winds blow. If I could just learn to read you better. But for now, it seems, the wind blows fair and in our favour!" Gwyn glanced at Kal and half-smiled. Then his hands began to work again at the straw.

Kal chuckled aloud, which attracted the attention of the older inmate and precipitated another round of staccato laughter from the far cell that abated quickly.

"Spies! Spies! Lysak's spies!" hissed the old man. "Seen 'em before. See 'em again. Hmm-hmm, spies." He glared at the two Holdsmen through rheumy eyes, then retreated to the shadows in the far corner of his cell.

Kal glanced at the gaoler. The man had stirred up the fire in the brazier and now sat on the stool, legs spread wide apart, elbows on his knees, with his head lolling on his chest. The man had assumed what was obviously a well-practiced posture of sleep.

"Gabaro...," Kal whispered hoarsely, looking back at the bent figure huddled against the far wall of the chamber.

"Spies, spies, spies...," came the voice thinly from the shadows.

Kal glanced again at the sleeping gaoler. "Gabaro!" He dared to raise his voice. "I know you can hear me. I would talk with you."

The slight form of the man pressed itself again into the light. Knobbled hands, knuckles swollen and deformed by age, clutched loosely at the iron bars. Thin white hair stood out wild in all directions, the stubble on his cheeks and chin bristled, and he glared at Kal through red-rimmed eyes. He began to shake. It looked to Kal as though he would explode in anger and begin yelling at the top of his lungs. Kal glanced again at the guard, who remained in a stupor, oblivious. But then the old prisoner whispered in a voice barely audible, "Spies, spies, spies. Won't talk to spies. No, won't talk." He fell still and silent for a moment, before he made a rude noise again and burst into his hysterical cackling.

Kal turned away from him and sighed. "It's of no use, Gwyn. He's mad. Completely out of his mind."

The mute Holdsman looked up at his companion, then slowly stood and faced the old prisoner, fixing him with a level stare. As he met the young man's gaze, Gabaro's eyes widened and he froze. Kal, too, stared wide-eyed from the young Holdsman to the old prisoner, marveling at the effect the one had had on the other. Then, recovering himself, he cleared his throat.

"Gabaro." The old man blinked at the sound of his name and seemed to relax somewhat. Kal continued, "I am Kalaquinn, and this is Gwyn, and we are not spies—"

"Gwyn, Gwyn, Kalaquinn!" the old man sang quietly.

"Yes, Gabaro. Kalaquinn and Gwyn." Kal pointed from himself to his companion. "Who is Lysak? We are accused of being his spies, but who is he?"

"Spies, not spies . . . Aye," Gabaro fluted, then fixed his rheumy eyes on Kal. "Lysak. Bad man, a bad man. Son of Torras. Of Melderenys . . . Father and son, father and son, father and son . . ."

"Melderenys . . . It's the seaholding north of the Oakapple Isles, where we are," Kal said in response to Gwyn's questioning look. "They're the two Arvonian seaholdings, in the Arvonian Sea. What does Lysak want?" Kal addressed the old man again.

"Father and son, father and son . . ." Gabaro grinned. "The father wants the father, the son wants the daughter!" He cackled. "Hmm-hmm, son wants the daughter!"

"The father?"

"Torras, hmm." Gabaro nodded as if his head were too loosely fixed to his neck.

"Wants the father?"

"Hmm, wants Uferian's house . . . Hmm, his house . . ." The old man continued to nod.

"And Torras's son, Lysak—"

"Wants to house the daughter, hmm, yes, to house the daughter!" He laughed shrilly.

"Bethsefra . . . Are you saying—" Kal tried to gain Gabaro's attention again. "Are you saying that the king of Melderenys has designs upon the rule of the Oakapple Isles, upon Uferian's throne?"

"The Isles, the Isles...Spies, Gwyn, Gwyn, Kalaquinn, always spies, spies..."

Kal sighed wearily. He felt as though he were swimming against a strong current and decided to take a different tack.

"Gabaro, you've seen spies?"

"Hmm-hmm, spies."

"From Melderenys? From Torras? Lysak?"

"Hmm-hmm, spies."

"You've seen them here? In the prison?"

"They come. Cap'n brings 'em. Hmm, spies come. Then he takes 'em down..." Fear had coloured the old man's tone.

"Down? The soldier said you'd be moved down—"

"Hmm, down." Gabaro's eyes darted here and there, and the man seemed to look paler. "Down, down, Gwyn, Gwyn, Kalaquinn. Listen and you can hear 'em...the cries, hmm, the cries... Spies, spies, spies—but, shhh!" He held a crooked finger to his thin lips, then whispered hoarsely, "He wakes! Shhh!" With that, he retreated again to the back of his cell, muttering to himself.

The gaoler stirred on the stool, stretched and stood, then stirred the coals in the brazier with a poker and went to fetch fuel from a box by the inner wall of the chamber. Kal nodded to Gwyn and silently returned to the window. He stared blankly out to where the wind lifted the surface of the Sound into whitecaps, pondering the fragmented information he had gleaned from the crazed man.

The day slipped away as the patch of sunlight from the barred opening slid across the stone floor. The gaoler left once for several minutes and returned with a flagon of weak, sour wine and a small loaf of heavy black bread, which Gwyn tore in half and Kal picked at with disinterest.

As the horizon purpled into evening and the light from the brazier grew more noticeable, Kal heard the sound of footsteps from the passage leading to the prison. A flickering light grew, until he could see a group of men led by the thick figure of the lieutenant.

"Guard!" the lieutenant barked even as the gaoler leapt to his feet at the party's approach. "Here's another. Mind him, he's a scrapper."

In the lieutenant's wake strode Galli. His hands were bound behind his back, but he held his blond head high, in obvious defiance. His left eye was swollen shut and shadowed by a bruise, and blood trickled from a split and bloated lip.

"Galli!" Kal yelped. Gwyn jumped up and stood beside him at the door to the cell.

"So, you know him," the lieutenant said, glaring at Kal. "I thought you might—not with them!" he yelled at the gaoler, who had made shift to open the door to the Holdsmen's cell. "Over there. That one." He pointed to a cell one removed from Kal and Gwyn's, to which the gaoler scurried. Fumblingly, the gaoler found the key and swung the door open then closed behind Galli.

The lieutenant stepped in front of Kal's cell and fixed him with a steely stare. The torch's flames licked the air above his head. Something flashed in his hand, and his mouth spread in an unkind grin. He flicked his thumb. A silver coin spun through the bars and rang on the stone floor.

"No one carries one of these in their pocket, unless they are in the pocket of Ferabek. As Torras and Lysak are. As Lysak's men are. As all Melderenysian spies are...." He left the implication hanging in the air as he turned on his heel, snapped his fingers for his men to follow, and strode out.

Kal bent, picked up the coin, and ran his thumb over it. Ferabek's face scowled from its stamped surface.

"It's a Gharssûlian groat," he said. "Is it the one we found outside Owlpen Castle? The one Wilum took—?"

"Aye. And the one I took from Wilum's pocket after he had died," Galli said, looking over at Kal, his head hung in shame. "I took it. It was a token, a reminder to me of why I had to keep on fighting. And why I could not give in to despair. Now it seems to have betrayed us, as all things having to do with the Boar will—betray." Galli pushed himself away from the iron bars and slumped against the stone wall. "I'm sorry, Kal."

Kal fingered the coin. He nodded his head slowly, as if in understanding, and fell into a brooding silence.

TWENTY

Moonlight had silvered the seascape outside and pooled on the floor of the cell when Kal left the window and looked at the gaoler by the brazier. He slept again, sitting astride his stool in profile to Kal, his chin on his chest. Gwyn slept as well, as did the old prisoner, noisily snoring and mumbling in his sleep. Two cells away, however, Galli stood at his window, peering out into the soft night.

"Galli," Kal whispered softly. The broad silhouette of his friend lifted its head and turned to look in his direction. Galli left his window and leaned through the bars of his cell, his face shrouded in shadows.

"I'm really glad to see you alive," Kal whispered again, then tapped an iron bar with his palm. "Even if it's under these circumstances. How did you survive?"

"I'm sorry about the coin, Kal. I should have realized it was stupid to carry it."

"How would you know? Don't worry yourself, Galli. I don't think it makes a great difference anyhow. Even without the coin, they reckon us spies. They all seem to be decided on that point." Kal cast a glance at the gaoler again. The man hadn't moved. "But it's not over yet. There's always hope, eh? That's what's kept us going so far. But how did you manage to survive the storm?"

"It was terrible, Kal. I've never seen anything like it. The wind came up out of nowhere, the *Ellyn*'s bucking, and you're unconscious, lying in the bottom of the boat..." Galli shook his head slowly. "Gwyn and I did what we could—cut the rigging, lost the sail, and tried to keep the wind to stern. The storm drove us hard, hard and fast all night. I thought I heard the roar of surf at one point, and that's when you and Gwyn were swept over, when the *Ellyn* broke apart. I managed to grab a loose line and cling to the wreckage. Most of the bow was still holding together. I got washed up on shore just as dawn broke, and ran into the forest until I was sure it was clear. I was salvaging what I could of our gear, but they found me and caught me. Must have been watching me for a while. They took me by surprise. But not without a fight." Galli's hand instinctively touched his swollen eye, and he winced despite himself.

"I wish we were in the same cell, Galli. Even without my codynnos I could probably do something for that eye."

"Bah, it'll be all right." Galli grinned a lopsided grin. "But they paid to get that one in."

"I'd imagine so."

"Aye, I think I broke one fellow's arm. A couple of noses, anyhow—but what do we do now?"

Kal sighed and stared absently at the starry sky beyond the window for a moment. "I can't say that I know, Galli. I can't say that I know."

"But Aelward and Broq," Galli said. "They'll be looking for us. Broq said so before they left on the *Dancing Master*. And when we don't arrive...? Aelward won't know where we are."

"I can't say, Galli—"

"He won't know where to find us, and it doesn't look like we'll be getting there soon....Or anywhere, for that matter, except to the gallows, perhaps."

"Easy, Galli, easy." Kal returned his attention to his friend. "I know it looks grim, but something tells me it's going to be all right. Look, do you remember how Gwyn behaved at the Seven Springs when Diggory about got carried off by the gathgours? Or when Relzor killed Wilum? Or on the wolf hunt in Nua Cearta, or when Kenulf shot my father? It was like he sensed danger before it even happened."

"Aye, he's a strange lad, that one," Galli said. He bent his head forward and fixed Kal with a penetrating stare. "What of it, though?"

"Well, he's changed, Galli. Remarkably so over the past several days. Something to do with Ruah's Well. It's like he was a rough blade, now honed true." Kal looked over at the sleeping Holdsman and continued, "You saw how his body was made sound by the water, even though he's still mute. But there's something else..."

"What, Kal?"

"Re'm ena, I know it sounds strange, but it's as though he knows how something is going to turn out in the end, for good or ill. And there's peace in him now. He seems completely without worry about our current predicament."

Galli shook his head, and his blond hair fell over his face, veiling his expression in deeper shadow. "I don't know, Kal, but if he's got some gift from Ruah, this will surely be the test of it."

"Aye, to be sure, to be sure," Kal said as if to himself, and grinned. "Anyway, there's naught we can do about it but wait and see."

"Well, I don't mind the wait," Galli said with dark humour. "It's what comes after the wait that concerns me."

"Don't worry. I trust the folk are safe, at least. Broq will get them to Aelward's Cot, don't you think? That is one less worry. Then Aelward may—"

Something moved, Kal was certain of it. Out of the corner of his eye, he had seen the slightest hint of a movement. Without shifting his head, he looked towards the sleeping gaoler. The man was still and quiet, elbows leaning heavily on his knees, his head bent forward, looking sound asleep. Then there was a glint, a tiny reflection of the brazier's subdued light. The gaoler's eye flickered, barely opening, gleaming dully with the orange glow of the coals, then shut again. Kal turned his head away from the gaoler and lifted a finger to his lips, then pointed with his thumb over his shoulder at the guard. Galli nodded in understanding and, following Kal's lead, withdrew to his own window.

For several minutes the silence was disturbed by only the restless slumber of the old man in the far cell. Then Kal heard the gaoler rise from his stool, stir up the coals in the brazier, and add more fuel, making no effort to be discreet. He coughed loudly and spat in the fire, then snatched up a torch from near the brazier, kindled it, briefly surveyed the cell block, and left the chamber.

"I'm afraid there are no secrets here, Galli," Kal whispered long after he had heard the gaoler's footsteps grow faint and disappear down the passage. "I hope we didn't say anything that might be used against us. I don't know how much he heard."

"I don't think so." Galli didn't sound certain.

"No, I'm sure not. But I think we should remain quiet now."

"Yes, that would be best. But what are we going to do?"

"Nothing, Galli. Nothing but wait and hope and trust. Maybe Gwyn's right."

"I truly hope he is."

Galli's words lingered, ringing in Kal's ear, until he heard approaching footfalls echoing down the stairs and along the passage to the prison.

The gaoler returned, carrying a heavy cast-iron pot and a dirty canvas sack. He touched his torch to another in a bracket on the wall and doused the first upside down in a bucket of water. From near the entrance to the cavern, he grabbed an iron trivet and set down both trivet and pot clattering over the brazier, then sat on his stool, poking desultorily at the coals and occasionally lifting the lid of the pot to stir its contents with the same iron rod he used to stir the fire. Soon a weak vinegary odour filled the cavern that made Kal's mouth water despite the acrid edge to the smell. He was hungry, and his stomach growled its complaint. As if in response, the gaoler pulled three deep tin plates from the cloth sack and ladled food from the pot into each. Reaching again into the bag, he produced a loaf of the black bread, which he tore into three pieces, dropping one unceremoniously into each of the dishes. These he carried to the Holdsmen.

"With 'er ladyship's regards," he said as he pushed Galli's plate to him under his door. "A late supper ... Early breakf'st, if you prefer. Enjoy it while you can. May be your last."

"Thank you," Galli ventured to say, picking up the plate.

The gaoler checked himself, turning back to look at Galli. His face broke into a sneer of contempt. "You'll have less to thank me for soon enough, I should think."

Kal stirred Gwyn awake, and the two fell to their meal, leaning against the iron-grille door of the cell. It was a thin stew, comprised mostly of turnip and onion, with a few bits of unidentifiable meat that were almost too tough to be worth the chewing. But still, it was hot and filled his stomach, and for that Kal was grateful. They were soon wiping their plates clean with the remaining black crusts.

"Small blessings, eh, Gwyn?" He smiled at the red-haired Holdsman and placed his tin plate on the floor.

"Small blessings, indeed." The voice startled Kal, and he leapt to his feet, spinning around. It was the woman. She stood just two paces away, staring at him, her green eyes cold and hard. Half a dozen men, her lieutenant among them, stood behind her. "And you should be exceedingly grateful for small blessings at this point. In truth, you should be more than thankful for any blessing bestowed upon you—light!" The woman snapped her fingers, and, immediately, men began to ignite torches around the chamber, until ten of them blazed, flooding the space in firelight.

At the disturbance Gabaro awoke, muttering loudly until he saw the men; then he began to cackle.

"They've come for you! They've come for you! Down, down, down you go, Gwyn, Gwyn, Kalaquinn! Spies, spies, not spies! They've come for you! Down you go, down you go, Gwyn, Gw—" His ranting was cut short by a fit of coughing that left him doubled over and heaving for breath.

"Release him. Take him to his son's house," Bethsefra ordered, looking across the chamber to the old man's cell. Then, casting a glance over her shoulder at the soldier nearest to her, she said, "And, Lomric, tell his son that if this old fool tries his tricks again, it will be his son who pays for it."

"Yes, milady." The response was spoken, even as Gabaro's cell door swung open. The old man gamboled out, stooped but spry enough for his age.

"Thankee, thankee, lady," he piped as he made to approach Bethsefra. Thinking better of it, however, he stopped, turned heel, and sauntered off behind the two soldiers that led the way out of the prison chamber. His mad giggling faded into the rock beneath the citadel.

In the light, Kal noticed that the young woman had changed from the rough garb of the field of martial exercise into garments that, though masculine, fit her form more agreeably. He followed the delicate line of her neck with his gaze and discerned the shapely curve of her torso, waist, and thigh beneath the belted leather tunic and leggings that she wore.

"What is it that you admire, Master Kalaquinn?" she said, rounding to fix him with an icy gaze. He felt his neck, ears, and face prickle.

"I-I was ... I ... my lady, I—"

"Well, as you seem to be indisposed, I will tell you what I

admire." She reached behind herself and, with a flourish, unsheathed a sword. The long blade rang from the scabbard and spun through the air, glinting and flashing in the torchlight. The blade whirled at her side, wheeled over her head, and its tip came to rest between the iron bars but a hand's breadth from Kal's chest. "I admire a fine sword," she said, "and this is among the finest I've ever seen."

Kal's eyes traced the razor-edged length of steel. The bronze hilt looked heavy in the woman's hand, yet, despite the size of the sword, she held her hand steady, her arm fully extended, stiff and unwavering, her balanced sideways stance that of a trained swordsman. She slowly twisted the weapon in the space between them, revealing first one face of the blade then the other, both etched and chased in a filigree of Old Arvonian characters. Light flashed red and faded as the torchlight caught the two small gems set in the hawk's head quillion block over the shoulder of the steel blade.

"Perhaps the finest," she stated.

"Rhodangalas...," Kal whispered, barely more than mouthing the word. He looked up at the woman. She arched an eyebrow. In the light that filled the prison, Kal saw that Bethsefra's green eyes were fringed by a ring of violet, each like dark emerald set in the deepest amethyst. The woman lifted a corner of her mouth in a half-smile that Kal recognized as anything but friendly.

"Ah," she said, "you know the blade."

"M-my sword. Yes, Rhodangalas."

"Indeed?" Bethsefra withdrew the sword point from the Holdsman's chest and laid the blade flat in her palm. "'I am Rhodangalas, truest offspring of the craft of New Forge,'" she read aloud, then turned the blade over in her hands. "'Who would wield me must be swift of limb and keen of eye and true of heart.' True of heart...." She repeated the phrase and looked up at Kal. "A curious weapon to be carried by a fisherman, wouldn't you say?"

"I did not say we were fishing, simply in a fishing boat."

"Ah. But you are a bard?"

"Yes."

"And this..." She lifted the blade. "Rhodangalas... This is your sword?"

"Aye. Yes, a gift from a friend."

"Indeed? It is no ordinary gift."

"It was no ordinary friend."

"Hmm...And you, you are 'true of heart'?" she asked as if reading the words again, but did not wait for a reply before she continued. "We shall see. There may be truth in what you say. Your friend's story corroborates yours. Three men, highlanders all, one a bard, one a mute, caught at sea in a small fishing boat. It was a vicious Calathros gale that blew last night. Such storms are wont to happen. It is seasonable...But then so are spies seasonable." Her eyes narrowed, and Kal grew wary. The woman bent her head in Galli's direction. "Your friend here, he is no ordinary friend—tattooed after the fashion of the Telessarians. He swears he's a true highlander, but we all know that Ferabek engages the assistance of trackers from Telessar. Did you know that Ferabek uses Telessarians?" Again she awaited no response but began to pace slowly back and forth in front of Kal's cell. "Torras and Lysak are the sycophantic pets of Ferabek. Fawning leeches. He is their liege lord." She paused and lifted the sword blade in front of herself, as if reflecting on its keen edge. "Truly, a magnificent weapon....Tell me, who is your liege lord, Kalaquinn Wright?" She lifted her gaze and held Kal in a stony stare, then quickly turned away and handed the sword to the soldier behind her, who held its scabbard.

He fought to keep his temper under control. He found that this woman's questions and tone nettled him, and yet in her presence he felt unhinged by a strange allure. Indeed, the more he watched her, the more he realized that she had an inexplicable power over him, not entirely unlike the thrall that the Boar himself was able to impose upon those in his presence. But this woman's charm bore none of the elemental malevolence that Ferabek's did. Rather, hers was born of grace, a strength of beauty that Kal felt more than saw. She was beautiful—not simply pretty but profoundly handsome. Given the current circumstances, the fact only vexed Kal. He heard her repeat her question, and her insistent tone further fueled his ire.

"I serve the rightful heir to the throne of Arvon," Kal said, an edge of defiance in his voice.

"Ah, the rightful heir to the throne of Arvon..." She resumed pacing. "An ambiguous answer to a simple question. Do you know—ah, perhaps you do, but I shall tell you anyway. Torras, king of Melderenys, styles himself the rightful heir to the throne of Arvon by virtue of his claim to the Seaheld Throne at one time established in these isles of the Arvonian Sea"—she swept an arm in gesture toward something that lay beyond the walls of the prison—"what was once the realm of Ogasny-enesou. To assert his claim, he seeks to unite the two seaholdings by stealing authority from my ailing father and marrying me off to his own pustular blister of a son."

Kal had been unable to hide his expression of bewilderment. That the throne of Arvon had at one point been established in Tarkhuna, the capital of what was now Melderenys, was a fact commonly known, but that anyone would seek to press a claim to the high kingship of Arvon by reestablishing the Seaheld Throne...?

"Ah, this comes as a surprise to you?" Bethsefra was watching him. "Perhaps my father is correct. Perhaps you and your companions are not spies. Perhaps you were simply hapless enough to have blundered into the middle of our quarrel and be mistaken for them. But then again..."

Silence fell over the prison, and Kal could hear only the hiss of the burning torches, a sound that seemed grossly amplified by the night stillness, coupled with the weight of tension that burdened the chamber's atmosphere.

"Tell me how you have come to know Aelward and his servant Broq." Kal was as surprised by the nature of the question as by its suddenness. "It has come to our attention that you know Aelward. What is your association with him?"

Kal's eyes flicked to the gaoler hovering near the brazier. The man winked at him, touched his finger to the side of his nose, and then grinned viciously.

"Tell me how you have come to know Aelward," Bethsefra repeated. "And what is your association with Wilum, High Bard and Keeper of the Talamadh?"

Kal found his mind reeling again, set off-kilter by the tough woman interrogating him. Next to him in the cell, Gwyn stood smiling serenely to himself. He looked at him with sparkling eyes beneath the shock of red hair that shone in the torchlight. He nodded at Kal, and Kal felt a peace settle over his own heart with a sensation not unlike the warmth of a hearth fire that first eases and then drives away the damp chill of a winter's day. He turned to see the woman still looking at him hard. To his surprise, a response sprang easily to his mind and his lips.

"Master Wilum, the Hordanu, I count as mentor and friend, and I have had many occasions, even from my years of earliest memory, to visit him at Wuldor's Howe in the Clanholding of Lammermorn. Indeed, it was at his hand that I was made a bard." Kal instinctively touched the pios at his throat, and he saw Bethsefra's eyes widen slightly at the revelation. He had caught her off guard, and he could not help but feel a smug sense of satisfaction. "Broq I have met, Aelward I have not. But it was at Aelward's invitation and Master Wilum's insistence that I led a band of my own people, some thirty in total, to meet Aelward himself. To achieve that end did I first meet Broq. But circumstances have separated me and my closest companions from the rest of my party."

Kal was pleased with his account. He had spoken the truth and yet had not been indiscreet with any detail that would have betrayed his full identity or purpose. Though Bethsefra remained stonily silent, her astonishment was obvious, and Kal could tell from her reaction to his words that, as yet, news of the fall of the Great Glence and Wilum's death had not yet reached the remote seaholdings. That was a good thing, Kal realized, or it might have complicated matters and begged further explanation.

"I must consult with my father."

"May we be brought before the king? May we plead our case and offer evidence of our goodwill?"

"No, it is not possible," the woman stated flatly.

"Is there no way that we may we see him?" Kal pressed.

"No, it is not possible!" Bethsefra snapped. She turned away from Kal and paced across the room, paused, then strode out of the prison chamber, her men-at-arms following close at her heels. Their footsteps faded and disappeared.

Kal glanced at Gwyn beside him. The mute Holdsman smiled broadly, nodded, and retreated to the back of the cell to stare out over the water of Swanskeld Sound. Galli, in his own cell, merely shrugged at Kal, but spoke no word. It was nearly a quarter of an hour later that the clattering sound of boots on stone steps grew louder, and Bethsefra reappeared with her soldiers.

"While it fails to impress me," Bethsefra said, coming to stand before Kal with her fists firmly planted on her hips, "what you have said impresses my father, the king, and the king is of a mind to set you free. I, however, am reluctant to do so. Too many times have Torras and Lysak played us the fool. Sadly for you, trust has been the first and most costly casualty in this our subtle war of intrigue, connivance, and deceit."

"But, the king—" Kal started to speak but was silenced as Bethsefra lifted her hand to stop him.

"My father is impressed that you claim to know Master Wilum so closely, and that you also claim knowledge of Aelward."

"As I said, I have not met Aelward yet, but was on my way to do so."

"Yes, but you speak of Aelward with ease, and his is a name that does not rest easily on the tongues of the wicked...." Bethsefra's words drifted into thought. It was several moments before she spoke again. "We have come to know Aelward from his travels over the years. More than once has Aelward the Wise journeyed to our isles, and he is friend to the House of Swanskeld, though his last sojourn was many years ago, when I was but a little girl upon the knee of a healthy man. My father avers that anyone who can lay claim to Aelward's friendship may lay claim to his own and that of his house."

"Your father is unwell, you said?" Kal asked.

The woman cast her gaze to the floor.

"Is it serious? Is his affliction grave?"

The woman nodded. She suddenly looked smaller to Kal, and fragile. When she spoke, her voice sounded distant.

"His infirmity prevents him from receiving guests, be they welcomed or no. He remains confined to his chambers, his heart as blighted as his flesh, both diseases precipitated by the wound of my mother's death in my birth....But why do I tell such things to you, who are foreign to my heart?" Bethsefra raised her eyes to look at Kal. For a fleeting moment, Kal recognized that something had melted and softened in the woman, that she had dropped her guard, but the moment passed in a breath, and she grew steely again. "This is nothing to you and none of your concern."

"But I would offer a token—"

"A token? A token of what?"

"Of my goodwill and pure intent—of my friendship to the king and his house. Durro—" Kal addressed the lieutenant—"when you discovered my companion, Galligaskin, you discovered some of our possessions, my sword among them, and for that I offer you my thanks. Did you happen to also find a small cask?"

The lieutenant made no answer, but looked to Bethsefra.

"Answer him," she commanded.

"When we took your companion, we found in his possession the sword you saw, with its scabbard and belt, another blade in its sheath, a bow and a quiver full of arrows, and a small sack of provisions all wrapped in a sodden wolf's pelt. There was no cask."

A soldier stepped forward and said, "Sir . . . Excuse me, milady." Durro turned to look at him as the man nodded first to Bethsefra and then to him. "Beg pardon, sir, but what he said—we found in the wreck. We looked after you'd took him." The soldier fetched a glance at Galli. "I suppose he didn't get to taking it before we found him."

"Was it broken? Or broached? Was it intact?" Kal's questions tripped one over the other.

"N-no, sir" the same soldier replied, looking at Durro as though the lieutenant had asked the question. "It was sound."

"Bring it to me," Kal demanded.

"Sir?" The soldier still looked at Durro.

The lieutenant looked to Bethsefra, then back at the soldier. "Go."

As the soldier disappeared into the dark passageway, Bethsefra looked again at Kal.

"The cask—what does it contain?"

"Water."

"Water?"

"Yes, but it's water from the Well of Ruah, healing water. Have it taken to the king."

Bethsefra's eyes hardened again. "Ruah, I know. Healing water, I know nothing about. How do I know that you do not deceive? And in so deceiving do intend the murder of the king's person by poisoning?" Again the prison fell into an uneasy silence until the approach of the soldier bearing the vessel attracted the attention of all in the chamber.

"Remove the bung and bring the cask to me," Kal said. Bethsefra nodded, and the soldier drew a knife and pried the stopper from the small wooden barrel. Kal slid the tin plate he had used under the cell door. "Fill it."

The soldier obeyed, and Kal withdrew the plate, gently lifted it to his lips, and drank. He then handed the plate to Gwyn, who gulped the water, emptying the plate.

"How is this a ruse?" Kal asked, locking eyes with Bethsefra.

"Upon my word, it is healing water from the Well of Ruah and will bring healing to the king. You must trust me."

The woman stepped to the cell. "The plate," she demanded, picking it up from the floor when it was shoved under the bars of the door. She turned to the soldier, took the cask from him, and poured water into the tin plate. This she held out to the soldier. "Drink!"

The soldier blinked in confusion, looking first at the tin plate, then at Bethsefra, then at the lieutenant, finally returning his gaze to the proffered water.

"I said drink!"

Tentatively, the soldier took the plate and lifted it to his lips, slowly tipping it.

"Drink it all," the woman commanded.

The soldier lifted his eyebrows in acknowledgment of the order and tilted the plate back farther, until he had drained it of its water. He lowered the plate, his eyes filled with fear and apprehension.

"Well?"

"Water, milady. It tastes like water."

"And how do you feel?"

"Uh, fine, milady." The soldier grinned sheepishly and nodded his head, then grinned wider still. "Aye, fine. I feel fine. Better than fine, milady. It's only water."

"It's more than only water," Kal said, "It's the means of your father's restoration, if you will it."

Bethsefra looked about the room distractedly, caught on the horns of a dilemma. She finally fixed her gaze on her lieutenant, but said nothing for a long moment. Then she stiffened, as if resolving something in her mind, and said, "Take the water to my lord, the king. Prepare some to be given him. I will attend you directly. He shall receive it from my hand, none other."

The woman turned slowly to face Kal and stepped close to the iron bars, looking up at the Holdsman. "Know you this, Kalaquinn Wright," she said in a whisper. "My father is my greatest strength. And my greatest weakness. Despite myself, and perhaps despite my better judgment, I will place trust in your word. But know you this also. Should anything—and I mean anything—happen to my father, you shall die . . . slowly and unpleasantly."

TWENTY-ONE

Kal was disappointed when the quick flurry of hurried steps approaching the prison turned out to belong not to Bethsefra but to a young page. The boy looked apprehensively around the chamber as he handed a folded note to the gaoler. The man read the message and grunted his acknowledgment to its bearer.

"Wait here," he growled at the boy. Then, with paper in hand, he scowled at the Holdsmen in their cells. He was clearly disapproving of the missive's content.

"Was it up to me...," he said, leaving the empty threat dangle in the air, then shook his head and shrugged. "Well, it'd seem you'll live to die another day. Her ladyship's heart seems to have softened. You're to be released."

The gaoler jangled his keys as he approached the long wall of iron bars. "You'll follow this here boy," he said, pointing with the key he held to the page, who stood torch in hand near the dark entrance, looking nervous and ready to bolt down the passage and up the stairs. "He'll show you to where you're to go."

The boy greeted each of the Holdsmen with a deferential nod of his head. "Sirs, my lady, the princess Bethsefra, offers you each her gracious goodwill and bids you follow me. Your immediate comforts are to be attended to, so if you would please..." The boy dipped his head again, ushering the three Holdsmen out of the chamber.

Before leaving the prison, Kal turned to the gaoler and sent the Gharssûlian groat spinning through the air with a flick of his thumb. "For your efforts at hospitality during our stay here," he said as the man caught the coin. "To my mind, it's payment fitting the service rendered." The gaoler glared at him as Kal chuckled to himself and fell in behind his two companions.

The page led the three Holdsmen far up into the citadel, eventually directing them down a hallway and into a spacious room. Three windows opened onto the town of Swanskeld, recumbent below, quiet and grey in the muted predawn light. In the room, three baths had been drawn, and each stood steaming beside a dressing table on which sat towels, oils, and a neat pile of fresh clothes. Against one wall was a table laden with food—meats, fruits, bread and cheeses, and a large flagon of wine. On another, Kal saw Rhodangalas in its scabbard, the other weapons Durro had mentioned, Galli's codynnos and one of the waldscathe wolf-pelt cloaks. There was no sign of the cask of water from Ruah's Well. It was fair to assume, Kal thought, that the gift given would never be returned.

"Sirs, my lady, the princess Bethsefra, bids you attend to your needs, as you so desire, in this room." The page indicated the baths and the tables. "Bathe, dress, and eat, but please remain here. Your soiled clothes may be left beneath the dressing tables. They will be dealt with. My lady, the princess Bethsefra, will call upon you in an hour. Please see that you are ready to receive her." With that, the boy walked to the doorway, turned, bowed, and, exiting backwards, closed the door to the room.

Kal slowly stripped himself of his torn, salt-stained garments and gingerly lowered his naked body into the hot water, his aching muscles relaxing with the heat. He leaned back in the high metal tub and sighed deeply as a shiver of contentment ran through his body. To his left, Galli sat in his own bath, examining the extent of the damage to his face in a small hand-held looking glass he had found on his dressing table. Gwyn, for his part, had opted to eat prior to bathing and stood by the food happily gorging himself on a fat leg of chicken.

"Pour us a cup of that wine, would you, Gwyn?" Kal bade his companion, who immediately put down the half-consumed leg, filled three goblets, and carried two of them across the room. Kal accepted the cup offered him gratefully, drank long, and sighed again, closing his eyes.

The three Holdsmen passed the time in quiet snippets of conversation, each savouring the comforts of clean body, clean clothes, and full belly. Outside the windows, dawn broke, gilding the white-stoned town in soft sunlight starkly punctuated by the blue shadows that filled narrow alleyways and clung to the westward faces of building or wall.

When the knock came on the door, the three men were dressed and ready. Kal wore Rhodangalas at his side, the pios clasped to his tunic, below his throat. The door swung open, and Bethsefra stepped into the room, followed closely by Durro and three other men-at-arms. The Holdsmen bowed as one to the woman, and, as he straightened, Kal hazarded a glance at the green eyes and delicate features of her oval face, framed by her neatly clipped black hair.

"My lady Bethsefra."

"Master Kalaquinn." She locked eyes with Kal and smiled demurely. "It would seem that I find myself in your debt." Kal bowed his head in obeisance. "My father has regained a decade of his life in these past two hours and steadily improves, becoming stronger by the minute."

"I am pleased to have been able to assist King Uferian in his plight. Would that I might be able to remedy the troubles that plague his court and his daughter as easily."

"Yes, and to that..." Bethsefra's expression grew hard again, and she looked away. "While I stand in your debt in the matter of the king's well-being, it is in the other that I still have reservations. Uferian hails you all as friends to his court and bids you all welcome in his domain. I will not countermand the express desire of my father; however, I must act in obedience to the dictates of conscience and good sense, especially in these days of increasing uncertainty and danger. So, it is to you, friends of Uferian, friends of the Oakapple Isles, that I offer passage to the destination of your choice. A ship and crew stands provisioned and ready to sail. Durro will see you to the harbour. You will depart within the hour."

Kal was speechless as Bethsefra looked at him again, bowed her head almost imperceptibly, then turned and left the room.

Durro stepped forward. "This way, my lords, if you please." He waited for the three Holdsmen to gather their few belongings before he led them out of the room and down the hallway, his men following close behind.

✧   ✧   ✧

The small boat scraped the bottom of the beach.

"There you go, lads. Looks all clear. Safe home, now," said the sailor, swinging his oars to rest and remaining seated. He had rowed Kal, Gwyn, and Galli from the ketch that lay at anchor in the offing, its lines and rigging set, ready to depart back to Swanskeld with the return of the ship's boat. The three men thanked the sailor and scrambled overboard into the lapping waves. Knee-deep in seawater, Galli turned and gripped the bow of the small boat, giving it a shove back off the beach, allowing the boatman to strike back out towards his ship.

It had been a good journey and uneventful, their first time on a larger seafaring vessel. They had left Swanskeld and beat up along the isolated western shores of the seaholdings. Rounding the northern tip of Melderenys, a following wind rose and drove them across the Arvonian Sea towards the lonely coastland of the Keverang of Pelogran, where they searched for a decent landing spot, ever on the watch for Gawmage's warships. The journey had taken but the space of a day and a night.

Now they hurried along the open expanse of sand and mounted a small rise on the very edge of the Asgarth Forest, its shadowy depths slowly filling with the soft glow of dawn. They stopped beneath the spreading tree limbs for a moment and turned to look out to sea. On the waves, the bobbing rowboat crabbed its way back to the *Tern*. The boatman lifted his arm briefly in a gesture of parting. They waved in reply and turned north along the edge of the forest until they passed out of view of the ship behind a grassy dune.

"We'll wait here for a while, 'til they're farther offshore," said Kal, lowering himself to sit on the ground, picking up a stick, and making patterns in the sand at his feet. "We must be careful not to chance being seen by them. Otherwise they'll wonder why we head south rather than north, towards Cor'gwella. We'll follow the coastline south"—he pointed with the stick—"until we come within shadow of the Sheerness Spur. It's simplest that way, I think—lessens the chance of getting lost—and then we'll push east."

"Heading where?" asked Galli.

"To what may be left of Hoël's Dyke in these reaches. It'll take us into the marshlands and, with some luck, allow us to meet up with Broq and our folk."

"And Aelward," Galli added.

"Aye, and Aelward."

Well-rested and well-provisioned, the three made good progress through the margin of the Asgarth Forest along the coast, always aware of the sea to their right, skirting beaches and headlands and even the odd fishing village that broke the stark emptiness of the coastline. Late in the morning their path had mounted a stretch of crags and soaring cliffs, wave-washed and desolate. At the highest point, they stopped. Before them stretched the vastness of the blue-grey Cerulean Ocean, flecked with whitecaps and broken by the snaking line of rock and sand running off to their left and to their right. Along the shoreline, the sea met the forest, itself spreading like a dense green ocean, rolling away far behind them until it came to lap against the immovable flanks of the Radolan Mountains to the east.

"Look. Mountains there, too." Galli had turned to the south and pointed to a hazy line of jagged peaks that obscured the horizon.

"Aye, the Sheerness Spur. Look, Gwyn," Kal said, his arm outstretched, sweeping along the line of mountains that cut inland from the coast. "See how the mountains of the Spur run from the Radolans all the way to the sea? That's why it's called the Sheerness Spur. It's a spur off the Radolan range." Glancing up at the sky, Kal quickly gauged the angle of the sun. "We've walked a fair piece. It's time to make our way inland, I think. We don't want to get too near the foothills of the Spur. The terrain there is like to be steep and rough. The Spur is not called Sheerness without reason. And getting too close will make cutting east across land all the more difficult."

The three Holdsmen climbed down from their vantage point and plunged into Asgarth Forest, picking their way through the undergrowth over ground that rose and fell gently. They followed game trails wherever they could, often marking their bearings by the sun to make certain they had not strayed. They sweated from the exertion. It was hotter work than it had been along the coast, for there were no cool sea breezes to refresh them. In the forest, however, they found streams and springs with clear, ground-chilled water flowing pristine from unsullied rocks and mosses.

"Ah, but I needed that," Galli said and sighed, his mouth and chin still dribbling water. He eased himself from the lip of a broad, flat, moss-covered stone on the edge of a small stream. "A nice spot, this."

"Aye, it is beautiful." Kal pushed himself to a crouch by the stream's edge and cast an eye upstream to where the brook gathered itself into a still pool against a low hillside. He followed its course with his eye as the crystal water tumbled sparkling down a rocky outcrop then reformed itself as a stream near where he and his companions rested. Beside him, Gwyn poked and prodded at the moss covering the stone and brushed away leaf mould and forest litter with a stick. Kal saw Galli's eyes widen as he snatched the stick from Gwyn and began hurriedly scraping at the rock on which they stood. He raised his head and took two steps to another broad, flat stone that lay slightly higher that the first. Beyond it another stone lay, as wide and smooth and as high again.

"Re'm ena..." Galli turned around. "Kal, these are steps, hand-hewn steps, well-worn and overgrown, but still intact, each about two paces deep. Look here—"

"In the middle of the forest?"

"Aye, come here. I'll show you." Galli cleared away leaves and moss with his foot, then stepped onto the next stone and stooped to pick up a fallen branch,which he tossed aside. More than a dozen of the broad stones lay evenly tiered, forming a long, gentle flight of steps, and Kal and Gwyn followed Galli, who bounded up them to a level area thick with bushes. Suddenly, Galli stopped, his hand raised and his body stiffening.

"Quiet!" he hissed as he cocked an ear to listen. "Do you hear that?"

Gwyn nodded. Kal could make out a voice, too, low and indistinct.

"Someone's there," Galli whispered. "Other side of the bushes. Wait here." He crept forward to a gap in the undergrowth, then motioned to his companions again. Silently, they slipped to his side. Galli pointed with a nod of his head. In a clearing, now visible from where they crouched, hidden, not even a stone's throw away, stood a thin rail of a man, white-bearded and wizened, with rounded shoulders and a noticeable stoop, carrying a staff in one hand and a wicker basket in the other. The old man scanned the ground at his feet, muttering to himself, seemingly not heedful of the three Holdsmen, although he was shambling his way closer and closer.

"Ah, Slippery Jacks for Old Jock's table." The undertones of the old man's voice came to them more clearly. He chortled and bent to gather a clump of yellow-brown mushrooms, which he placed in his basket. Then he put his basket down and straightened his frame. Leaning on his staff, he spoke again more meaningfully, gazing in their direction, but vacantly, as if looking past them, or through them.

"But what shall we do with these slippery jacks, Old Jock? It's not often we see strays in these woods. What shall we do with them, then? Shall we bring them to Jock's table?" The old man's words rose in tone. He no longer muttered under his breath. The three Holdsmen regarded one another with uncertainty. Kal crept forward for a better look. The strange old man seemed to start.

"What should we do, then? Perhaps they'll follow us home?" The old man gathered up his basket, turned his back on the Holdsmen, and began to walk away. Briefly, he stopped and scratched his head and then continued on his way.

"Old father!" Kal stepped out from the bushes and called out. "Old father, who are you?" It was as if the old man had not heard him. He did not break his slow shuffling stride.

"Stay, old man, stay!" Kal called again.

"Stay, Old Jock, stay!" The old man said, his voice lilting in mimicry. He checked his pace and turned, casting a feeble gaze in Kal's direction from eyes moist and milky with age. Galli and Gwyn had advanced and now stood by their companion's side, staring at the stranger.

"What shall we do then, Jock? Three young clansmen traipsing about in our forest. From southern parts. Shall we take them home with us? Three jacks for Jock's table?" The old codger knit his brow in thought. "No. What do we do with strays, then? Word's gone out. Aye, we take strays to them what are looking for these ones. That's what we do, then." With low chuckling noises he nodded, his long white beard brushing along the front of his threadbare jerkin.

"Master Jock, sir—?"

But before Kal could question him further, the aged woodsman turned on his heel.

"Aye, Old Jock it is. This way. Come, come, fall in behind Old Jock," he said, treading along a path that wound through the clearing and into the trees again. The three Holdsmen stood rooted to the spot. "Come, come, there's naught to fear, not in

Asgarth, not from Old Jock, nor the others," said the strange old man of the woods, glancing back over his shoulder and grinning broadly, his face lit up with mirth. "No telling but that we'll find more mushrooms—shaggy manes or pig's ears."

Was he to be plagued by curious oldlings, Kal thought to himself? Jock put him in mind of Gabaro; however, Jock's madness seemed not to be without purpose, as Gabaro's most certainly had been. Kal shook his head and chuckled, but it was only after Gwyn stepped forward that the other Holdsmen abandoned their hesitation and fell in behind the old man, who began mumbling to himself unintelligibly once again.

Through the forest, they wended their way. Old Jock set a brisk pace, matched by Gwyn, who kept to the old man's heels. Sometimes, when Kal and Galli lagged behind, their old guide would chivvy them along in a spirit of crotchety good humour. Other times he would stop to harvest plant life for his basket, not just mushrooms and woodland edibles, but weeds and flowers, strips of bark and odd roots, often burrowing and scrabbling for the object of his desire, laughing toothlessly over some choice discovery, over which Gwyn would show great interest.

"Strange old bird, a rag and bone collector," Kal whispered to Galli as they scrambled towards the crest of a hill along a stepwork of tree roots.

"But should we trust him? Could this be a trap?" Galli replied under his breath.

Suddenly, the old man halted again and swung around, glowering down on Kal and Galli. "Old Jock's no old bird. Nor's Old Jock hard of hearing, neither. Mayhaps Old Jock's a fool, though! Aye, a fool to play waywarden to foot-draggers and mocking young jacks!"

The rebuke was so keen-edged, so direct and unexpected, that it brought the two Holdsmen up short. They fumbled with an apology, but Old Jock had already resumed his progress, only to stop again just short of the brow of the hill to dig in the leaf litter.

"Except for the mute lad," the old man muttered aloud. "Wisest of the lot, he is. All for Jock, he is. Old Jock'll bring him to those that seek him, him and them other two strays." The old man stopped scrabbling and stood rooted to the spot as if lost deep in thought, then started to walk again. "Aye, stray sheep to the Flockmaster. Come then, lambs."

Lapsing into silence, he continued to a clearing that crowned the hill. From the clearing, the ground fell away in long, gentle slopes to an expanse of marshland that stretched off, footing the mountains of the Sheerness Spur. A path, much wider than the one they had been treading, ran into the distance over the rolling ground and down into the marsh, a line straight as an arrow, though broken and indistinct in many places, until it vanished into the trackless bogs.

Kal smiled at Galli. They had come to the Marshes of Atramar. Somewhere ahead of them, deep in the vast expanse of marshland, stood Aelward's Cot. Kal followed with his eyes the line of the Sheerness Spur along the horizon from the coast in the southwest to where it met the Radolans in the southeast. The range of the Spur broke midway, its mountains' flanks falling into the Marsh of Atramar, and, in the narrow gap, just visible to him, stood a black finger of rock, the Llanigon Mark Stone.

With Galli and Gwyn to his left and his right, Kal couldn't help but wonder if Ardiel himself and the Seven Champions of Ruah had at one time, long ago, stood on this very spot and looked ahead to the place where they would seek shelter and find safety from the dire predations of Tardroch. Had Ardiel himself, Kal wondered, experienced the same emotion that he now felt—the sharp sense of relief and elation at a journey nearly completed, muted and blunted by the realization that it was in fact only the first leg in a much longer, more arduous and far more dangerous journey? Perhaps his remnant folk were there already—

The strong blast of a hunting horn rent the air over the clearing in which they stood.

"What? What's he doing?" Galli shouted as Kal looked about the clearing. "If he's betrayed us, I'll…" Galli, his face fierce and full of fury, his mouth open, yelling, rushed at the old man. As Galli charged, Old Jock pulled the white horn from his lips and, pivoting sharply, struck him backhanded across the face with it. Galli reeled away from Old Jock, off balance, and fell sprawling on the ground. A fresh line of crimson creased Galli's cheek beneath the purpled eye. Calmly, the old man drew the horn back and held it before his mouth in readiness while he spoke in low chanting tones. With the back of his hand, Galli wiped his cheek where the hard edge of the horn had caught him and looked at the blood that stained his hand. His eyes narrowed, and he glared up at the old man. Kal stepped forward and laid a hand on his companion's shoulder.

"Wait, Galli. Stay back. Listen. He's no enemy," Kal said.

"Old Jock summons Broq. Old Jock summons Broq. Old Jock summons..." The strange old woodsman kept repeating the same words in rising tempo, staring down the broader trackway. Then he winded the horn again in a longer, louder burst, a burst so long and hard that his face reddened and his cheeks swelled. Once more, he took it from his mouth.

"Old Jock summons Broq...," he said, but with longer intervals of silence between the words, wherein he cocked his head to one side and seemed to be straining his senses, waiting. Gwyn put a hand on Kal's arm and cupped a hand to his own ear.

"Aye, Gwyn. Do you hear that, Galli? From way down there." Kal pointed down the incline towards the widening path. "It's another horn, isn't it? An answering horn."

His face softening into a gap-toothed smile, Old Jock advanced a few steps and brought the horn to his lips again. This time he winded it still longer and louder than before, then stopped to listen. The answering blasts drifted to them more clearly, the sound, once distant, coming closer and closer.

"Follow the straightway," Old Jock said as he let down his hunting horn, still staring into the air. "Heed the horn. Follow the Lyndway."

Turning silently, without so much as a glance in the direction of the Holdsmen, the old man retraced his steps, seeking his basket. Gwyn raced ahead and retrieved it for him, leaving Kal and Galli frozen in their places, stunned for a moment at the unexpected turn things had taken.

"Time for Old Jock to trundle homeward with his dainties," said the aged woodsman as he took the basket held out to him by Gwyn. "Old Jock's had his fill of wayward clansmen from the south. Present company excepted, of course. Go on, lad, strays with strays." He flicked his hand in a gesture of dismissal, but, grinning, caught Gwyn's eye with a broad wink. "Your friends will need someone with a head on his shoulders, else they'll miss the straightway. Scarce seems possible, though, for any but a fool to misfollow it." He chortled to himself. "Briacoil, lad," he said and turned his steps away. Gwyn raised a hand in silent farewell to the lone figure as he marched towards the far side of the woodland clearing.

"Many thanks, Old Jock, old friend. Peace, and may the woodland ever be your home," called Kal, who now stood beside Gwyn and lifted his hand as well. The old man strode away, disappearing into the woods.

Galli glared at Kal from where he remained seated on the ground.

"What?" Kal said, turning to him and shrugging.

"It's what you just said."

"What did I say?"

"Those are words from the Pledge of Peace," Galli said in a low voice that sounded almost a growl.

"It seemed appropriate—"

"But you're not Telessarian."

Just then, the blare of a hunting horn lifted through the air again.

"I'm sorry, Galli. I didn't mean to cause offence." Kal stepped over to his friend and, extending a hand, pulled him to his feet. "I didn't realize...Anyway, we should 'heed the horn,' eh? 'Follow the straightway'? 'Follow the Lyndway'?"

"Aye, if the mumbling dotard is to be trusted."

Gwyn stepped forward and clapped Galli on the back, grinning, then turned onto the path that led down into marshland.

"Right you are, Gwyn!" Kal called cheerily. "Nothing for it but to carry on. Straight ahead then. Broq awaits us, as do the folk. Come on, Galli."

TWENTY-TWO

ENTRY OF KALAQUINN, NINETY-SEVENTH HORDANU IN SUCCESSION FROM HEDRIC, DATED THIS THE 10TH DAY OF FORESUMMER'S MONTH IN THE 3019TH YEAR OF THE GREAT HARMONIC AGE, THE YEAR OF THE FALL OF THE GREAT GLENCE.

It has been a full three days now since my arrival at Aelward's Cot in the Marshes of Atramar with Galligaskin Clout and Gwyn Fletcher, boon companions both, and fellow Holdsmen who have journeyed here with me from the Black Cape.

In the Woods of Tircoil, which cover most of the Black Cape, Gwyn and I visited Ruah's Well, a place ancient and legendary, and enshrouded by mystery. At the Well, I was favoured with a vision of Ruah herself and obtained her healing water—too late, alas, to help my father, Frysan Wright, for little did I know then that his prayer of passage had already been sung, and he had already crossed the Birdless Lake. I pray that Kenulf's spirit may find some measure of peace in Wuldor's mercies on those nether shores; although how the traitorous wretch may, I know not. The mortal remains of his last victim are laid to wakeless sleep in this place, beneath a cairn which stands not far from Aelward's Cot. Frysan Wright is deeply mourned, not only by his wife, my mother, and his son, my brother, as well as the surviving folk of the Stoneholding, but by all who live in these Marshes, who knew him by hearsay from Aelward as having been a man of honour and courage. I am proud to be called his son.

It was in the wooded depths of the Black Cape that Gwyn—

263

himself strengthened in limb, if not voice, by Ruah's favour and the healing waters of her Well—and I found safety and shelter with Katie Woodencloak, the Wood Maid, as she is called by her folk and the much-fabled waldscathes. The waldscathes that populate dark lore and night-time tales and fire the horrors conceived by a fanciful mind are, it would appear, little more than bogles, creatures that have no substance beyond myth and imagination. The waldscathes, in truth, are but men of the Woods, a fellowship garbed in wolfskin that play upon the terror of outsiders. By this ruse, by this trickery perpetuated by generation upon generation of Tircolian Wood dwellers, do they secure their solitude and ensure their peace. I hope that, by herein making this revelation, I have not shattered the surety of their life of peace; they are a people of the goodest will, a people whom I hold in great respect. It was in the wisdom of Wuldor and by Ruah's hand that I was guided to them, haplessly blazing a trail into their sequestered society, and I trust the final purpose, even if I do not see the immediate end.

But, a marvel greater than the waldscathes' true nature was to me revealed by Katie Woodencloak in the Black Cape's depths. There I was shown the wondrous Gleacewhinna—the glence tree—a living semblance in root, trunk, limb, and leaf of a stone-built glence. According to Mistress Katie, the Gleacewhinna is, in truth, and to my utter amazement, the very origin of the glence, the dead stone structure being but a poor imitation of the living thing.

Under the spreading canopy of the Gleacewhinna of Tircoil, Mistress Katie sang to me a part of the "Lament of Beldegrayne." It is an ancient ballad of her people that renders an account of the Gleacewhinna and the flight of her ancestors, the Ina Pik Whinna, from their homeland of Beldegrayne, even at the time of the First Undoing. This history is a rare discovery, indeed, for it may well provide one of the few accurate descriptions of the happenings of that time, which form a common foundation to the histories of all peoples in Ahn Norvys. Mistress Katie has promised that her bard, a fellow of the most blithesome disposition named Gelanor, shall make a copy of the "Lament" and also all of the writings of her folk. These I shall include in the Hordanu's collection. Needless to say, I shall dwell at further length on this in a later entry, when I have received and studied these writings.

From the Woods of Tircoil, Gwyn and I hastened to Kingshead Cove, where a ship waited ready to carry us up the coast and to safety. We hoped to meet Broq the Bard at the Cove, and those of our folk who had escaped the ravages of Ferabek the Boar. Instead, we were met by Galligaskin, who had insisted upon remaining behind to watch for our coming. He informed us that the remnant folk of the Stoneholding had been forced by threat of an enemy warship to weigh anchor and sail without us up the coast to Aelward's Cot.

The three of us—Galligaskin, Gwyn, and I—borrowed a small boat in order to follow and join them at the Cot. Caught in a storm, a Calathros gale, we were blown off course and shipwrecked near Swanskeld in the seaholding of the Oakapple Isles. Here the King's own daughter, the Lady Bethsefra, mistook us for spies and held us captive. However, we were once again in the keeping of Wuldor's gracious gaze. The healing of Bethsefra's ailing father was effected by Ruah's Water, some of which we had brought with us, and this became the warrant of our friendship, prompting King Uferian to grant us passage to the Keverang of Pelogran on one of his ships.

Without incident, we made landfall and began the journey on foot to the Marshes of Atramar. Thanks to the good offices of an aged woodsman named Old Jock, whom we happened upon, we were led safely through the Asgarth Forest to an outlying picket of Aelward's men. They had been posted to watch for us, though they did not expect us to approach the Cot from the north but rather on foot from the south. Taken in hand by Aelward's men, we set upon the mouldering trackway that follows the Horn of Lynd. This songline runs through the Marshes of Atramar and skirts Aelward's Cot, to which we were guided to meet the remarkable man himself.

The word "Cot" is a quaint misnomer. The place bears closer resemblance to a stronghold, ancient and well-fortified, than to the shepherd's humble dwelling conjured to the imagination by the word. The castle lies nestled among the rugged peaks of the Sheerness Spur in a fastness just below the Black Rock Gap. The Cot is of a construction dating back, they say, even to the time of Ardiel and the Seven Champions of Ruah. Its halls are filled with a colourful array of shepherd's implements and oddments.

Though wondrous and ancient-seeming be the Cot, still

more so is its master, Aelward. My predecessor Wilum was correct—words cannot describe the ageless peace and wisdom of his demeanour, of his bearing.

Flockmaster of the West, Wilum called him. Never a title more just, for he has shown a care and concern for my people that is overwhelming. He has lodged them in long-abandoned dwellings that are situated near the Cot—the remains of a village. Although fallen into disuse, these stone houses are still remarkably sound, for they were sturdily built. Aelward's folk have come forward from every corner of the marshlands and have helped to make them snug and habitable. Even Old Jock, I am told, has lent a hand in the work of restoration, although they say that he is far more expert at scavenging the marsh and woodland for all manner of root, herb, mushroom, and natural medicament than he is at repointing old stone walls.

Now, once more, smoke lifts from the chimneys of these homes and warmth glows from their windows. Gardens long bound by weeds have been turned and seeded. My mother, Marina, says that the rich dark soil promises a bountiful harvest. Flocks of sheep have returned and throng the pastures that are nestled in this boggy waste, which no stranger dares to broach. The pathways that are sound to travel upon lie hidden in a vast expanse of sedge and reeds, so subtle in feature that only those native to this area know where they may be found. Other pathways, however, seem to offer firm ground for a person to tread on, but are, in reality, deadly traps to the unwary. Even the ruined remains of Hoël's Dyke, upon which we were led, have, in many places, disappeared into the boggy mire of the Marshes of Atramar. Clearly, it is a natural haven protected from outsiders by the fatal treachery of the marsh, the secret approaches to which are the privy knowledge of the local folk. These people compose a fellowship no less close-knit than the waldscathes, fiercely loyal to Aelward, just as surely as it is a point of ancestral pride to them that they once harboured Ardiel and the Seven Champions of Ruah.

The sound of laughter and light banter livens the air, but it leaves me strangely forlorn and cheerless. Yesterday, unknown to her, I caught sight of Marya Clout, Galligaskin's winsome cousin. She was training an apple sapling across a trellis and was aided in her delicate task by a young fellow of Aelward's.

A demure smile lit her face at words spoken by the young man. It caused me no small pang, for at one time, before the Great Glence fell, she and I had an understanding. Alas, it is sundered, for now, more clearly than ever, I know that I cannot linger here. Duty calls me, with ever-increasing urgency, to a long and arduous journey—a journey fraught with danger, a journey from which I may well never return. Nonetheless, I am glad that the Holdsfolk are settled and can start to rebuild their shattered lives—especially my mother and brother.

It is all on account of Aelward, whom I met on the very day of my arrival here. To his keenness of mind and wisdom I owe the first glimmers of understanding about all that has befallen me and my people. The discussions that my companions and I have had with him are like sharp shafts of sunlight cutting through dark stormcloud. So much has become clearer to me.

As to Ferabek—himself rising like a black and boiling stormcloud that covers the sun's face and turns the natural light of day into an unnatural perversion of night—Aelward has told me that recent report has reached his ear telling of the quick and successive rout of the last few quarters of resistance in Arvon immediately following the fall of Lammermorn. The Boar now holds sway, ruling by law of martial might through that puppet pretender to the throne of Arvon, Gawmage, over every lowland and marchland county, over every keverang of the Calathros Peninsula, and over every highland clanholding. Arvon has been pressed into the Gharssûlian League, which has spread like a dark blight, almost entirely obscuring the face of Ahn Norvys, consuming before it both life and hope. Aelward says that, as recently as five days ago, news arrived telling that Ferabek trumpets Gawmage's triumph and the assertion of his right to the throne. The Boar himself makes for Dinas Antrum, there to hold council and to parade through the streets of the capital his prize and trophy, the Talamadh.

My heart misgives me at this news. Hope seems like an ethereal and elusive thing, flitting amid the twilight shadows of evil that enshroud Ahn Norvys. But Aelward offers sage counsel, ever drawing my heart and my mind away from the terrors that lie to the left and to the right of the path that stretches before my feet, ever drawing my attention back to what first and foremost needs be done—to find the rightful king.

Of principal importance to this task is what Aelward has discovered in his travels, namely, the origin of the puzzling heraldic device, that of the sun in eclipse, worn by those who abducted Prince Starigan as a babe in the arms of Queen Asturia. This emblem, he has found, belongs to the Order of Sarfeks, a cohort in the hidden service of the Lord of Kêl-Skrivar far to the east. According to Aelward, the Sarfeks style themselves Knights of the Five Towers or the Order of the Black Sun, but beyond that, little is known of them other than that they are very dangerous, men of great martial skill. Nor is much known about the Lord of Kêl-Skrivar himself. Even his name is elusive. Aelward, however, ventures to suppose—and that with a spirit most grave—that he is a formidable figure. It is Aelward's impression that Kêl-Skrivar is far more to be feared than Ferabek and may well wield arcane powers in secret—with a pernicious cunning that would make the Boar himself seem of little threat to the peace of Ahn Norvys. Although he remains a vague figure, his influence seeps out of Kêl-Skrivar, pervading the Shadowedland and the eastern parts of Ahn Norvys like an icy winter mist. Aelward believes it likely that Starigan will be found somewhere in Kêl-Skrivar, the heart of this mysterious power's dominion. I am chilled to the quick by this unknown and unplumbed menace that threatens to break upon an already fragile world, and into whose domain it seems I must venture.

During the days that preceded my arrival here, Aelward puzzled over the reason behind Ferabek's keen desire to lay his hands on me before ever Wilum made me Hordanu by Right of Appointment. In what way, Aelward asked himself, did I, as a Wright, figure into the motives underlying Ferabek's invasion of the Stoneholding? He realized that, on the surface, the Boar was spurred by reports of my strange resemblance to the portrait hidden away in Owlpen Castle, that of King Colurian as a young man. He also became convinced that the real key to unlocking this secret lay hidden in the manor rolls of the Stoneholding, these having only recently received their seven-year amendment. Why else had the Boar felt a dire compulsion to obtain this record of those who have resided in our clanholding through the ages? By a stroke of good fortune, the rolls were saved from his depredations and conveyed to Aelward's Cot, along with The Chronicles of the Harmonic Age. *Aelward, aided by Broq, whom Aelward evidently treasures as he does his right arm, pored over the rolls, paying particular attention to the several generations of my ancestors.*

Here they discovered something very much out of the ordinary. They found that, in the year 2705 H.R., more than three centuries ago, an outsider, a fellow named Reonyk, settled in the Stoneholding—an unusual occurrence made all the more odd in that no place of origin was inscribed into the rolls for him, although Reonyk is a common-enough name in the highlands, indeed, fondly overused in the Stoneholding. Reonyk was a wheelwright by trade and went by the surname Wright. Four years after his arrival, he married a local woman, and from this union was directly descended Frysan Wright, my father. Aelward's interest was stirred by this listing. Reonyk's arrival in the Clanholding of Lammermorn came at a time of momentous reversal in the history of Arvon and its high kingship, for it was the previous year, 2704 H.R., that had witnessed the end of the Seaheld Throne with the shattering Battle of Flitterholt.

Garso was the High Bard during this time. It was near the outset of the many years that he was to fill the office of Hordanu. He was a man of great hardihood and is still remembered for his wisdom. With just reason. In his foresight, taking to heart the uncertainty of the times, he caused a copy to be made of all the manuscripts in his care in order to ensure that this vital record of Arvon might survive the prevailing unrest and upheaval. By way of precaution, he had these copies sent to this very place, what would become Aelward's Cot, where they remain to this day. In this set of copies, it was one of Garso's last entries in the Chronicles *that caught Aelward's eye, causing him to delve further. It is dated the 15th day of wane-autumn's month, 2706 H.R., and because of its importance in the account that follows, I give it here in full:*

"It has been more than two years since the blood-riddled Battle of Flitterholt. While it marked the final tragic demise of the Seaheld Throne, its ill effects still linger in Arvon, potent and festering, like a poison that the body has not purged. Because the times remain perilous and unsure, I have made bold to do what, to my knowledge, no other Hordanu before me has done. I have had single copies made of the ancient store of manuscripts in my keeil and will send them away for

safekeeping. This arduous task is near completion, and, within the year, the chronicles and cultic texts of Ahn Norvys will be safely preserved outside of Wuldor's Howe. That times should become so perilous, so minacious to that which is good and true and right, as to make this contingency necessary, is almost beyond thinking. It puts one in mind of ancient and prophetic passages of the holy Criochoran, *of Hedric's bodeful soothspeak of the end of things. Is this, then, the time of the Howe's harrowing? Is it the time the Hordanu's exile? Does death march long-shadowed across the face of the world, and Ahn Norvys become the unquiet grave?*

"How much woe and unravelling can arise from one man's blind pursuit of passion, even though he be a good man and evil be not his intent! So much more so when that man is High King, as Corinnis was, when in his heart were sown the seeds of love for the Princess Tyhlana, seeds watered by the tears of her shrewish discontent, the bitter fruit of which became the Seaheld Throne. Let my short account stand as a cautionary tale for those who may come to read this in future years.

"The reign of Corinnis began auspiciously enough in the year 2599 H.R., when, at the age of twenty-one, upon the untimely death of his father, he was crowned High King of Arvon, as tradition demands, at Templevney Edge. Even as a young man, he had always been fond of ships and sailing, an only child who savoured the solitary freedom of wind and wave. Thus inclined, he made it his praiseworthy task to refurbish and expand Arvon's small fleet. Soon he was given to long absences from his royal capital at Dinas Antrum, plying the waters off the coasts of Arvon as he oversaw the building of his navy.

"One fateful day, three summers after his coronation, he put into the harbour of Tarkhuna with the flagship of his fleet. [At that time, the seaholdings of Melderenys and the Oakapple Isles were a single kingdom held in fealty to the High King of Arvon. Only in later years, as a result of civil war after the fall of the Seaheld Throne, did the Isles divide into two realms. Tarkhuna was the seat of this kingdom of Ogasny-enesou, as it was then called. ~ K.W.] The vassal king of Ogasny was Stonostyr, doting father to the Princess Tyhlana, a young woman whose surpassing beauty was matched only by her willful self-absorption. Falling thrall to her comeliness, Corinnis found himself deeply

*in love and pressed his suit. They were soon married in Dinas
Antrum in a ceremony so grand that it became the stuff of
legend. There they lived but a few months after the wedding,
until, lonely and homesick, the Queen grew more and more
disaffected with life in the capital. With woeful pleading and
dreadful shows of temper, she overbore her husband, until, at
length, the royal pair made their way back to Tarkhuna, for
a season it was agreed at first. Season, however, soon gave
way to season, and seasons stretched slowly into years, until,
at last, it was clear that Queen Tyhlana would never return
to Dinas Antrum.*

*"And so was established the era of the Seaheld Throne in
Tarkhuna, for neither did High King Corinnis ever return to
the royal seat of Arvon. Nor did his descendants return, for
over a hundred years holding court in Tarkhuna and conduct-
ing affairs of state at a distance by emissary. With the passage
of time, the merchants and guildmasters in Dinas Antrum
grew more and more powerful, and insolent in their power,
until their sway rivalled that of the High King himself. At long
last, it was Beotwyn, of recent memory, the great-grandson of
Corinnis and Tyhlana, who came to the realization that his
very kingship was in peril. Thus, having sought and been given
my counsel, he summoned his resolve and decided to return
to Dinas Antrum with his queen, Caleta, and their three sons,
the princes Rathad, Dystann, and Imdan, who were unwed but
of age to be warriors.*

*"At the same time, their taste for power whetted, and fearing
its curtailment, the merchants and guildmasters fell into open
rebellion. Having mustered an army, they sent it west to meet
and depose Beotwyn, arguing that, by removing to Tarkhuna,
Corinnis and his descendants had abdicated the throne of Arvon
and no longer merited the High Kingship.*

*"In turn, aware of the force that had been raised against him,
and with a small host of loyal troops, Beotwyn and his family
made landfall in the highlands and hastened east through the
Radolan Mountains towards the capital. In the great forest of
Flitterholt that covers the southern reaches of the marchland
clanholding of Derowek, the two forces met. Although the
army ranged against them was far larger, the royalist forces,
augmented by a band of highland archers, carried the day.*

The cost of victory, however, proved very high. Not only was High King Beotwyn slain—may he walk ever with his fathers, kings all, on the peaceful shores of Lake Nydhyn—but so, too, apparently, were his oldest and youngest sons slain, although amid the terrible carnage their bodies were never found. Gossip persists that one or both survived, taken hostage by the guild-masters to provide themselves with a tool of leverage in their traitorous negotiations against the Throne. Though there has been no evidence to prove the veracity of this politick rumour-mongering, the merchant class remains a scarcely dampened force in Dinas Antrum.

"Nonetheless, the Ardielid dynasty survived in the person of Beotwyn's middle son, Dystann, who proved his valour five times over, and again, on the field of battle. With his father lying in death, Dystann led the charge and, in his battle-rage, routed his enemies. He scoured Flitterholt for sign of his miss-ing brothers, until, at length, he could in all justice do nothing other than presume them dead. He sent for me then, bidding me join him at Flitterholt. From the dire scene of royal victory in that blood-drenched woodland, he hastened with his retinue, and that of the High Bard of Ahn Norvys, to the Corona-tion Stone at Templevney Edge. There, for the sake of peace in Arvon, he let himself be crowned High King. I witnessed the Coronation; and I invoked Wuldor's benediction upon his kingship. When I returned to Wuldor's Howe, Dystann, now vested with his father's authority and that of every High King of Arvon since Ardiel himself, marched into Dinas Antrum and assumed the throne, finding it gravely weakened by a century of self-wrought exile amid the isles of Ogasny-enesou.

"High King Dystann remains locked in an uncertain struggle with the merchants and guildmasters. They stand as an enduring threat to the line of Ardiel and to me as Hordanu, inasmuch as I am perceived to be of the royal party, the guarantor of his kingship. Because of this, I have taken the precautions that I see fit in the hope that, come what may, something of Arvon's glory and destiny may be salvaged from the growing shadows that fill me with deep foreboding."

Thus ends Garso's short account of the Seaheld Throne and its immediate aftermath, written some two years after the Battle of Flitterholt.

Aelward read and re-read the foregoing account with care and with no small puzzlement. He considered it now in the light of his discovery about my mysterious ancestor Reonyk, gleaned as it was from the manor rolls of the Stoneholding that he held ready to hand, their importance emphasized for the first time. Aelward told me later that he knew there was something more to the account than first met the eye. He grew certain that Garso was privy to some secret, that he was hiding some knowledge that bore on my ancestor, new come to the Stoneholding from parts unknown.

Surely, Aelward reasoned, it could not be a coincidence that Reonyk had come to the Stoneholding so soon after the Battle of Flitterholt. So he combed the rest of Garso's writings, those that had not been a part of the body of copied texts with which Aelward was familiar, but which had been brought to the Cot along with the manor rolls, a part of the hoard of manuscripts that had accumulated in the Hordanu's keeil for the three hundred years following the end of the Seaheld Throne. These later writings of Garso's were many, since he went on to hold the office of Hordanu for more than a half-century after the Battle of Flitterholt, living to see the deep winter of his life settle its hoary shroud upon his head.

Aelward felt Garso's writings might hold the key to the mystery that preyed on his mind, and his suspicions proved correct. It was on the evening of my arrival at the Cot that he finally found what he sought, a passage easy to overlook, since it was buried inconspicuously in one of Garso's lesser chronicle entries, a disjointed, rambling account of the seaholdings and their lore that Garso had made towards the very end of his years. It was clear that Garso meant for its wistful longwindedness to put off all but the seeking mind, alert to the words on the page. Aelward's grey eyes gleamed like smouldering coals when he read it to me as follows:

"As is well-known by all folk of the kingdom of Arvon, after High King Beotwyn forsook his court in Tarkhuna to reestablish his throne in Dinas Antrum, the vassal kingdom of Ogasny-enesou was torn asunder, its fabric rent even more direly than that of Arvon, of which it was once the beating heart, so that the isles of Ogasny-enesou became two kingdoms in place of one on account of the war that broke out between Melderenys to the north and the southern isles. This great upheaval, this divorce of life from peace, happened when Valistor of Tarkhuna, one of Beotwyn's uncles, argued that, by leaving, Beotwyn had abdicated the Seaheld Throne and thus the throne of Arvon. Valistor himself laid claim, by violence of temper and steel, to the throne, turning the blade on all who opposed him, styling himself High King instead of Beotwyn. His opponents included Comatas, the vassal king of Ogasny, who was forced, for the safety of his person and his house, to take flight with his family to Swanskeld in the southern isles, the white pearl of the Arvonian Sea, and there take up arms against the usurping and villainous Valistor, warding off the latter's attempts to gather north and south into his power.

"Now, alas, the sundering of Ogasny seems fixed, set unalterably by the longstanding years, the contesting realms acknowledging an uneasy truce that, by time and custom, has been woven into the fabric of a life braided by mistrust, suspicion, and enmity. Similarly, in Dinas Antrum, the power of the High King is hemmed and hedged beyond precedent, as if from time immemorial, by the merchants and guildmasters, who have pressed for the creation of the Mindal, which is to be a body of royal advisors who will, beyond any reasonable doubt, do little more than advance their own interests at every turn, to their profit and to the detriment of both Crown and Throne, and the peace, order, and harmony which these betoken.

"Still, as my life draws towards its tattered end, I am heartened by the hope that the dire plight of Ardiel's heir and his dominion shall not be ever thus. I cling with a ferocious hope to the slender thread of the ageless promise that there will be a mending. It is my boon companion, a fellow of this lakeland redoubt that is my home and home to Wuldor's Howe, now, alas, standing on the far side of the Birdless Lake—gil nas sverender, my friend of friends—who claimed, with a fey certainty, that all things shall be remade in years to come, that the warp and weft of peace and harmony shall, by Wuldor's hand at the loom of destiny, holding the shuttle of Ardiel's Scion, be rewoven long after both us have crossed the cold waters of Nydhyn. From personal experience, I trust him, for he has a mystic gift of foresight, a true gift that I have witnessed in the past in other matters which we have discussed together; even so, he is chary in its use, and, of the Holdsfolk, none but I have knowledge of it. Perhaps this gift may be attributed to his origins, for from the root does the flower draw that which sustains its colour, and it is the root which warrants the grace-filled gift of the flower's beauty.

"Of the gentlest ancestry, a simple man possessed of an unassuming nature and with modest ambition who craved a peace far from the hurly-burly of the great cities and the connivances of their rulers, he fled to Lammermorn's mountain-ringed sanctuary as a young man to seek out the equally young Hordanu. He came, a broken man, not long after the great and fell clash of arms that rang amid the trees of Flitterholt, a battle in which, he said, an elder brother had fallen and his own peace lay cloven. He quickly shed his outlander's name and all traces of his accent, which ebbed, even as his joy was renewed, flowing afresh into his heart and limbs. It was his accent, long-lost, which marked him to me from the very first as one born and raised among the Isles and as one of station, for in blood is the second sight not infrequently to be found, especially on the part of youngest sons. To all eyes but mine, he was no more than a highlander, a Holdsman bred to the bone, solid of carriage, even to his name, a name which I gave him when he first bound me to silence."

Tallying the arguments, Aelward laid out the meaning of this subtly phrased passage, although I saw it clearly enough myself and felt a shiver prickle down my spine even as he read it aloud to me. It is obvious that by wordplay and by hints, both subtle and not so subtle, Garso refers to my ancestor Reonyk and to Imdan, youngest son of High King Beotwyn, as being one and the same person. At the same time, however, he is clever and mentions neither by name.

According to the manor rolls, Reonyk was the only outlander who had come to the Stoneholding as a young man not too long after the Battle of Flitterholt, Aelward explained. Garso could only be speaking of the recently departed Reonyk in this account of his old age. There is no doubt. And Reonyk, Aelward avers, was Imdan, a prince of Ardiel's line, younger brother to Dystann, heir to the throne of Arvon.

To say that I was taken aback would be sheerest understatement. My head was reeling as Aelward put into words *his reasoning, telling why Reonyk must be Imdan. Reonyk would have been of roughly the same age as Garso, and so, too, Imdan. Also, in Garso's more personal chronicle entries as Hordanu, Reonyk is mentioned with some frequency as a friend. A "boon companion," in Garso's own words. He clearly points to this Reonyk, the newcomer, as having been Imdan. Who else but Imdan could be a youngest son, of gentle birth, from the Isles, and a survivor of the Battle of Flitterholt, where an older brother perished? And who else but Reonyk Wright could be described as "solid in carriage, even as to name"?*

What settled the matter to Aelward's mind was the passing, though pointed, reference to ancient lore associated with Ardiel, namely that those of his blood would be graced with a gift of prophecy. Never, though, in all the lore of Ardiel was this gift attributed especially to a youngest son, and it is the reference to the youngest son that Aelward recognized as pointing to his friend's place in the Ardielid family. How cleverly Garso interweaves his description of the two, Imdan and Reonyk, who are in truth one and the same. It would seem that in his own slow approach to life's end, Garso needed to free himself, to unburden his heart of the load of secrecy from which he must have felt released by the passing of his friend Reonyk, in truth the prince Imdan.

Thus it appears that I am of the House of Ardiel, an Ardielid, descended from a prince of Ardiel's line. This, at least, offers some explanation for my resemblance to the young High King Colurian, as depicted in his portrait. As cruelest fate would twist it, Ferabek was right to hunt for me, and yet I am not the heir to the throne of Arvon. I am not Starigan, as he may have hoped.

How this new knowledge impinges upon my immediate task of finding my kinsman, the Crown Prince—and that, deep within the Shadowedland—and then journeying with him to the Balk Pit of Uäm to secure the Sacred Spark, I cannot see, and my royal blood is a cold comfort. There is much that I cannot see, and dark despair gnaws at the fragile threads that yet bind me to hope.

But now comes a knocking at the door to my chamber. I am summoned. Aelward would speak to me, and my foremost hope is that he may offer me guidance, counsel, and direction on the task that presses ever more heavily upon my heart and mind. I must go.

TWENTY-THREE

Aelward stood leaning on his knuckles, his tall frame bent over a table bathed in candlelight and littered with sheets of ancient parchment and paper, a few scrolls, and several large leather-bound volumes, one of which lay open and held his attention. Kal stepped from the corridor into the dark chamber and closed the door gently behind him. The sun had already sunk behind the jagged peaks when Kal climbed the rising land to the Cot, leaving the black mountains silhouetted by a purpling sky stained in a wash of pastel pinks, oranges, and reds. Darkness was not long in falling in this sheltered refuge, and Kal was certain that by now little more than the faint glimmer of starlight would be visible through the windows of the room, had they not been barred by stout shutters.

As it was, the gloom of the chamber was broken only by the glow of four tapers that burned in a holder on the table and one stout candle set on the mantel above a small and sulky peat fire. The candle's fat, guttering flame eerily illumined several items ranged along the stone shelf. From the shadow-clad walls of the room, other oddments winked, reflecting the flame's wavering light. Kal knew from his previous visits to the otherwise sparsely furnished chamber that it contained an aggregation of tools, mostly pastoral in nature, implements of the flock and fold covering all four walls. Kal had long since shrugged the strange collection off as little more than another of the quaint peculiarities of the Cot and its keeper, the Flockmaster of the West—or so Broq had heralded the tall, trim, muscular man, who now stood before him, stooping over some obscure text.

Kal shivered at the unseasonable chill that touched the night air over the marshes and had found its way into the Cot. The fire was too small to be felt across the room, although the pungent musk of the smoldering peat filled his nostrils. Yet for all its stark austerity, this chamber, and indeed the whole Cot, had proven to be an ideal place of privacy in which to hold conference and marshal what scraps of knowledge could be garnered from the writings in the Hordanu's hoard, or from reports Aelward had collected of the happenings in Ahn Norvys during his travels. Perhaps, Kal mused, just perhaps, they would be able to cobble together some sort of strategy that might accommodate a tolerable compromise, if not a comfortable union, between his duty-bound ambitions as Hordanu and even the remotest chance of success.

"It's a curious thing," Aelward said at length, interrupting Kal's brooding reverie, though still apparently absorbed in the manuscript. The play of candlelight and shadow on his angular features made him look fierce. "Aye, it's a curious thing, indeed. Had the blade of fate not been parried, had it bitten more deeply into Corinnis's house, you, not Starigan, might have stood heir to the Ardielid throne." He lifted his gaze from the page and set his steely grey eyes on the Holdsman from across the room. "But it wasn't to be, Kalaquinn, and so, here you are—by fate's cruel wit—royal, but not quite royal enough to relieve you of the journey you needs make to find the one who can broach the Balk Pit and secure the Sacred Spark, the one who is legitimate heir to the Throne of Arvon. But, enough of that." Aelward straightened and walked around the table to greet Kal, a thin smile on his face creasing the iron-grey stubble of his close-cropped beard. "I trust that you have rested well?"

"Aye," Kal said. "I have rested, and written, and pondered."

"Good, good. You are hungry?"

"No, thank you, Master Aelward." Kal shook his head, looking at the cheese and heavy bread that sat on a round wooden platter amid the clutter of papers on the table.

"A drop of something, then."

Kal accepted the simple clay cup offered him without demur and nodded his thanks as he lifted it to his lips. The liquid burned its way down his gullet, the fumes filling his nose. Kal coughed and sputtered.

"It's vile," Kal said, holding the cup at arm's length with a look of suspicion.

"Uisgé beatha, an acquired taste." Aelward grinned at the young Hordanu.

"A unique taste—I'll grant you that. What is it? It tastes as noisome as the fire smells, like damp earth, or an old boot set afire."

Aelward's eyes sparkled with amusement, narrowing above high cheekbones. He ran his hand across his scalp, and the short grizzled hairs bristled between his fingers. "Aye, an apt description, I'd say, Kalaquinn. Uisgé beatha is a spirit made by the marshmen hereabout. They use peat smoke in making it, and they smoke the casks they use to store it in as well. Tastes odd at first, but give it a couple sips and you'll warm up to it soon enough"—Aelward lifted his own cup in salute of Kal—"even as it chases the chill from your bones."

Kal took another small sip of the harsh liquor and set his cup down on the table, hoping it would be forgotten. "What were you studying?" he asked.

"Ah, I was reviewing that last entry penned by Garso." The tall man strode around the table and set the long fingers of his unburdened hand lightly on the open page. "It is a truly remarkable thing. It's as if he wanted the secret to be discovered and yet could not bring himself to reveal it openly. Perhaps it was meant to be a matter of time, and now, it would seem, is the propitious moment for this discovery—but that you should be of the House of Ardiel. Of the House of Ardiel and Hordanu as well." He fell into silent wonderment at the yet unplumbed significance of the discovery.

"Aye, the propitious moment..." Kal broke the still quiet that had settled over the chamber, then pressed his lips together, drawing them into a firm line as he wrestled to put a thought into words. "Ah, Aelward," he said, slowly shaking his head. Hair fell around his down-turned face, curtaining it from the candlelight until he combed the loose black mane back with both hands and looked up into the grey eyes that had once again fixed themselves on him. "So many things that have lain hidden for so long seem to be coming to light in these hours that now engulf us. Still, it all remains so confused, meaning and purpose frustratingly veiled. The happenings foretold in prophecy seem like dark shapes looming out of the mist of ages past, as the fog thins before the chill breath of these days. But for all that they remain indistinct, lacking clarity, colour, true form.... I'm sorry, I sound like Wilum." Kal forced a wan smile. "You know, earlier in my chamber, I was thinking of something Wilum told me, something from the *Criochoran*, something he had mentioned a couple times in light of the events that befell us in the Stoneholding."

Aelward raised an eyebrow in mute question.

"It was lines he quoted, something rather obscure, he said." Kal paused and then began to intone ancient words in a quiet voice that filled the shadow-shrouded chamber with a susurrus like the rustling of dry leaves.

> "When Wuldor's Howe is worsted by the brazen foe
> And the Great Glence in utter ashbound ruin lies razed,
> When the dark host of dreosan doth stain the Vale
> And the Hordanu leaves the harrow of the Howe—"

" 'Shall rise a second foe upon whom few have gazed.' " The grey figure took up the prophetic lines as Kal's eyes widened in surprise. " 'From half-lit shadowedland of ancient dormant tale. The royal one shall then rebel against the gloom, his rank new-marked by crown and arms...' Yes, 'The Unquiet Grave'—I am familiar with it."

It took Kal a moment to recover himself. "Do you think," he said at last, "do you think the Lord of Kêl-Skrivar might be that second foe?"

"I cannot say," the tall man said, his face expressionless, his gaze steely. For all his moments of charm and companionable intimacy, Aelward was proving to be a most inscrutable character. Often as not, he retreated into an implacably stolid silence, aloof yet watchful, his grey eyes sharp, almost hawklike, as if observing Kal and the others around him, present to the moment but somehow not fully a participant in it. Wilum was right. It was very hard to say just who Aelward was.

"You miss him." The grey eyes flashed.

"Miss him? Who?"

"Your mentor."

"Wilum? Aye, yes, I do miss him. There is so very much that he would be able to explain. And so much counsel that I would seek from him."

"Hmm, he was a good man, and wise. His loss will be felt, for it is a great loss, indeed. But it is you who are the Hordanu that left the harrow of the Howe. It is you who are the Hordanu of prophecy, and of royal blood, destined for this hour. This you must believe."

"I don't know, I don't know," Kal said, shaking his head, balking at the thought as he had so many times before. "How can it be?"

"It matters not how it can be. It is so. That alone you must accept." Aelward leaned towards Kal, his eyes cold and piercing. "You hang upon the hooks of the past and the future, on one hand ashamed of your humble beginnings, feeling the guilt of inadequacy in the face of your high calling. On the other, you are wracked by fear and apprehension at what that calling may hold in store for you, where it may lead you. But these things—the past, the future—these are beyond your power to do anything about. Such is the way of life. And yet you toss your head from side to side, looking from the future to the past, then to the future again, all the while distracted from that which is truly and solely within your power—the moment. This moment, now. The path lies before you. You have but to place one foot upon it to make a start. Will you?"

The question hung in the charged air of the chamber. Kal's ears rang, and his heart, crashing in his chest, felt as though it would burst up into his parched throat.

The tall man straightened and seemed to tower over Kal, his voice thundering. "Enough! Enough 'Shall I? Shall I not?'! Hedge no more! The fate of this world hangs in the balance, and it can countenance no more of your irresolute tepidity. I know who you are. And I know what you shall become, if you will only learn to be forgetful of yourself and mindful of Ahn Norvys in these grave days that afflict her."

Aelward's expression softened, and he smiled as he passed a hand over the coarse stubble on his head. "Kalaquinn, you may not see it now, but I can, and I do. As Wilum was a great man, so shall you be even greater. Of Wilum's spirit you have received a double share. It is stamped upon your inmost being and empowers you to walk the path along which you are called, a path that has been charted, made plain in your Lay of Investiture. I beg you, for the sake of Ahn Norvys—for your fate determines hers—stiffen your resolve. Become what you are. Be bound to your destiny. Set your heart to it with no resistance. So you swore in your

Debrad, when you first set your hand to the Talamadh. Do not withdraw your hand now."

The Holdsman broke his eyes away from Aelward's, his gaze falling to the table where lay the contents of the oiled canvas sack that Galli had carried for Wilum from their home country. Here and there a page showed the elegant flowing script of his master's hand. He traced one or two of these with his outstretched finger. A dull brown sheen caught his eye from among the pages, and his hand settled on the strap that had been cut from the Talamadh by Relzor in his perfidy. Beside it lay a small pebbled leather case. This he picked up and opened. The translucent green half-round chrysoprase vessel slid into his palm, its fine gold chain slipping to dangle between his fingers. He contemplated the object, turning it over in his hand.

"So much there is that yet remains hidden from my mind," Kal whispered, closing his eyes against the Pyx of Roncador's simple beauty.

"But not from your heart," Aelward said. "You knew to lay your hand upon that which is of first importance."

Kal slid the Pyx back into its wallet, carefully coiled the chain in beside it, and closed the case. He placed it back on the table and exhaled a deep sigh that betrayed itself as a groan.

"What? Would you despair?" Aelward asked. "You who sang of the very hope of hope itself? Would you so easily rescind your pledge?" He began to recite lines:

"Now know wherein this hope lies fay—
Not in the Harp, but hands that play;
The one who sings, and not the Lay;
Mark, it is he who sings today,
For I Hordanu am.

"Hordanu born of Hedric's line,
Hordanu born midst eglantine.
Hordanu destined from all time
To be Hordanu peregrine—
To quest both king and flame."

Kal's eyes glistened, tears welling, when he lifted his head. Aelward's face had lost all hint of severity. "Yes, I have studied your

Lay of Investiture. Now, come, my lord Mygthernos Hordanu, born midst the sweetbriar-covered slopes of Lammermorn, born to venture from the Stoneholding with the authority of Hedric himself—"

"Born 'to quest both king and flame'... 'for I Hordanu am'... 'for I Hordanu am.' Yes, Aelward, you are correct. My thanks." Kal managed a strained smile. "Forgive me my weakness. I know that nothing happens for nothing. Everything serves a purpose, though it be veiled from feeble eyes and feeble mind. I have been ordained for this fate, and it is obvious that destiny has ordered it that I, Hordanu in this time of the failing Harmony, make for the Shadowland to retrieve my kinsman, Starigan. And if, or rather, when I find him, together we will venture the Balk Pit."

"Good, good," Aelward said, relieved, and bowed his head in deference. He recovered himself and trained his clear eyes on the young Hordanu. "Naturally, I am supremely relieved that, under Wuldor's watchful eye, the office of High Bard has been preserved in your person. I am well pleased that this fact yet remains hidden from Gawmage and Ferabek, and from perhaps more sinister forces still. I think that you would do well to follow Broq's advice, for it is mine also, to keep your true identity concealed. Your connection to the House of Ardiel as well, I think. This may well prove to be of profound importance and help in the days ahead, even with the loss of the Talamadh itself."

"Well, after all it's 'not in the Harp, but hands that play; the one who sings, and not the Lay.'" Kal grinned sheepishly.

"Quite right," the tall man said and smiled. "Quite right, indeed."

"But what of Starigan? Shall he be crowned, then?"

"Well, that is rather for you to decide. It is your right by office to name the date of coronation and effect it by your own hand. But here's something I would show you, something I have been guarding for that very occasion. Look you here." Aelward stepped away into a shadowed corner of the chamber. Kal heard a bolt slide in its slot and the complaint of seldom used hinges as a door opened. In a moment, the tall man returned, drawing a sword from its scabbard. The blade glistened in the candlelight. With a fluid movement, he flipped the sword in the air and, deftly catching the flat of the blade, offered the hilt to Kal.

"My lord the king's sword," he said.

Kal looked at the exquisitely crafted weapon, then gingerly placed his fingers around the grip and lifted the blade from Aelward's open hands. It was perfectly balanced, a delicate weapon and breathtakingly beautiful.

"It-it's magnificent. The king's sword? It's not really..."

"Lightenhaft?" Aelward finished the question. "Yes, it is. Lightenhaft, sword of the high king of Arvon."

"Impossible!" Kal said, his eyes moving from the weapon to the man.

"Very little is, in truth, impossible, only highly unlikely."

"Re'm ena, but how did you...?"

"I'm surprised that your father never told you about the sword."

"No, never."

"Aye, but he told you about Dinas Antrum, his service as a Life Guardsman? About the death of Colurian and the rescue of his queen and the infant prince, Starigan?"

"No, nothing, really. And certainly nothing about Lightenhaft, although Wilum mentioned, in his last days, that my father had discovered the sword. But he said no more than that."

"Ah, well, then, perhaps it has fallen to me to tell you."

Aelward rendered an account of the death of the last high king of Arvon, the rescue and subsequent loss of Queen Asturia and Starigan, the death of Frysan's men, Frysan and Wilum's flight to the highlands, and the secrecy to which they had sworn each other upon returning to the Clanholding of Lammermorn.

"Ardiel's sword," Kal said when the grey-eyed man had finished recounting his story and fallen silent. "But I thought it lost."

"And so it was, until Colurian happened upon it while stagging in Thrysvarshold. It seems that in pursuit of his wounded quarry, the late king discovered a cave that gave onto an underground keep. There he found Lightenhaft."

"Was it in chase that Colurian happened upon the place, or was he rather led by the stag to discover the sword?"

"There is wisdom in your words, Kalaquinn, and truth. It was in fact no stag. Queen Asturia told your father that the king, in his passion for the hunt, had shot a hind, a hind that stood fearless before him as if inviting his arrow. A white hind."

Kal glanced up. "Ruah."

"It would follow, yes. Such is the nature of these times. Wonder heaps upon wonder."

"After three thousand years, Ardiel's sword found." Kal rested two fingers on the blade and drew them away sharply, a bead of blood growing on the pad of each. "After three thousand years, and with still a razor's edge!" he exclaimed.

"That is the least of the wonders attached to the weapon."

"Then the rumours and legends, they are true?" Kal looked up at Aelward, his eyes wide.

"What? The glow?"

"Aye."

"Indeed, yes, in the hand of a crowned king of Arvon, but none other. Your father saw it when Colurian wielded the blade just before his own death."

"Remarkable."

"Well, no more remarkable than that the Talamadh should make windsong in the Aeolian Aperture."

"Which it hasn't in generations."

"No, you're correct. It hasn't. But it's in its nature to make wind-song, and were it not for the weakening of the Great Harmony and the wane of the Harmonic Age..." Aelward's eyes flashed, the iron-grey bristle of his head, cheek, and chin golden in the mellow light of the candles. "So it is with Lightenhaft. It is said that in Ardiel's hand the blade not only glowed, but well-nigh sang."

"Sang?" Kal glanced up again.

"Aye, sang, ringing with the same strain as the Talamadh itself. And so it should be, for the fate of both harp and sword are bound one to the other. Both were born in the fires of the same forge, beaten on the same anvil by the same hammer, crafted by the same hand."

"By Vali the Betrayer?"

"Aye, though I question so naming him."

Kal's brows knit in question. "But that Vali gave himself over to evil after making the Talamadh is common knowledge."

"True, that is commonly understood. But I cannot reconcile to my own mind and heart how the hand that could fashion both the Binder of Peace and the Defender of Peace might be possessed by a false heart. It is beyond my reckoning."

"Binder of Peace? Defender of Peace?"

"So may be called the Talamadh and Lightenhaft, one the binder of the Great Harmony, the other its defender, and so also of peace, a peace dearly paid for. Which reminds me, Kalaquinn"—Aelward looked to the table and began riffling through papers—"in your Lay of Investiture, there is a passage that I find most perplexing, a puzzle to which I thought you might offer a solution, or at least upon which you might shed some light. Ah, here..." He found the sheet he wanted and held it in the light of the candle and read aloud:

> "As Ardiel sage Hedric sought
>   To forge and temper what was wrought
>   With Vali's Harp, the peace dear-bought
>   He broke asunder; rendered naught
>   The strength of bard royal..."

Aelward paused and looked to Kal, but when no answer was forthcoming, he continued. "Or the part that follows next, clearly referring to you as the new Bard."

> "Now as the Age nears to an end,
>   Must fresh-blessed Bard now make amend,
>   By dire sacrifice unrend...

"No doubt you are the 'fresh-blessed Bard,' but what must you unrend? The broken peace? And by whom was the peace broken? Surely not Ardiel." Aelward's thoughts tumbled out one upon the other, and he began to pace behind the table, page in hand, musing as much to himself as questioning Kal directly. "Could it refer to the maker of the harp, Vali? But it doesn't read that way. Then did Hedric break the peace? Is the peace the Great Harmony? But, no, how could the Harmony have been transgressed? And what is meant by 'the strength of bard royal'?" Again, Aelward's words were met with silence. "What say you, Kalaquinn? Can you offer any explanation to the puzzle posed by your own Lay of Investiture?"

Kal knit his brow and shook his head. "No, Aelward, I can offer no explanation." He sighed. "The same lines have perplexed me. I've no doubt that the lines are bound by prophecy, and by the revelation of something in the future may something of the past be seen in a new and clearer light. I remember Wilum often saying that the past and the future are but notes of the same chord, and it is only because we do not hear them sounded at the same time that we fail to hear their resonant harmony."

"Again, there is wisdom in what you say. But would you offer no suggestion as to how these lines might be understood?"

"It is prophecy, Master Aelward, and unless prophetic words offer their own explanation, then I'm afraid it is impossible to know and idle to speculate at meaning. But such is the way with prophecy."

The tall man nodded, the corners of his thin lips lifted in a slight smile. "Aye, such is the way with prophecy, the accurate and true interpretation of any only clearly known in its fulfilment," he said and returned the page he held to the table. His hand lingered on the table for a moment before he lifted it to point at the weapon in Kal's hand. "And the blade, what say you of it?"

Kal started and looked down at the sword he was clutching, as if he had forgotten it was in his hand. "Lightenhaft..." He half-breathed the word. "I still can't believe that this is truly Ardiel's sword." He lifted the blade closer to the tapers burning on the table. The chased steel glistened. Strange characters ran along the length of both sides of the blade. "These runes," he said, looking at Aelward. "They're the same..."

"What?" The tall man stepped beside the Hordanu and leaned over the sword.

"I recognize these runes," Kal said, lifting Lightenhaft closer to the tapers, twisting the blade in the candlelight. "I mean, I cannot read them. I don't know what they say, but I recognize them." He examined the blade more closely still, slowly scanning its length then turning it over and studying the opposite side. "Yes," he said with finality, "yes, indeed." He straightened and handed Lightenhaft to Aelward. "They are the same runes as are etched on the Talamadh."

Aelward's already sharp features seemed to sharpen further still, and his eyes fell to the sword in his hand. "The same runes as are on the Talamadh?" he asked.

"Beyond a doubt. Exactly the same."

"And you have no knowledge of their meaning?" He glanced up at Kal.

"No, they have remained a mystery to every Hordanu since Hedric. As you are undoubtedly aware, runes are a mystery left us from the echobards, and no key to their deciphering has ever been discovered."

"Yes, yes, of course, of course. A most intriguing mystery." Aelward studied the blade of Lightenhaft with an intensity that made it seem as if he had never set eyes on the weapon before. Kal

was surprised by the discomfiture that the otherwise dispassion-
ate man exhibited. The revelation had obviously astounded him.

As if searching for some explanation to the strange coincidence,
Kal cast his gaze about the chamber where the shepherd's implements glimmered feebly from the walls. On the table, candlelight
pooled over the bound volumes, scrolls, and loose sheets of parchment and paper. There lay the Pyx of Roncador in its case and
next to it the worn leather of the strap cut from the Talamadh.
Something fell into place among Kal's disparate and disjointed
thoughts, and his hand shot out, seized the strap and lifted it
from the table, spilling pages to the floor.

"No, it couldn't be...." Kal held the strap taut in both hands
for a moment before dropping it from his right hand to dangle
from his left. "The scabbard. Lightenhaft, it has a scabbard? Give
it to me!" Kal snapped, holding his empty hand out to Aelward,
who, even in the wan candlelight, visibly blanched at the suddenness and immediacy of the demand. The tall man had held
the sword's sheath all the while, and now handed it to Kal. On
the table, on top of the papers and books, Kal laid the broad
leather strap and, beside it, the empty scabbard. It was a simple
sheath of hardened leather, finely tooled and richly embossed but
otherwise unadorned, a fact which struck Kal as curious given
that it belonged to the single most important blade in the history
of Ahn Norvys. It was the words embossed in the leather of the
sheath's one side that held Kal's attention, words in Old Arvonian.

He pondered the text, then began to laugh. "Now do riddles
couple and so beget meaning!" he said.

"The words on the scabbard?" Aelward asked.

"Aye."

"I've pondered them often, but their meaning has always eluded
me."

"No doubt it has. Look here." Kal moved aside, affording the tall
man a clear view of both objects lying on the table, and pointed
to the Talamadh's strap. "This strap is, in fact, the fifth made in
copy of the one dating to Hedric's time. The first, which Hedric
received from Ardiel, moulders but remains preserved in the
Hordanu's keeil—" Kal felt the cold grip of remembrance seize his
throat, and he glanced up at Aelward. "No, that's not true," he said.
"Alas, it, too, is now gone. Lost with the Great Glence." The young
Hordanu paused for a moment to recollect himself. "I'm sorry."

Aelward nodded in understanding, then gestured to the leather belt. "You were saying?"

"Yes, well, over these many centuries, no one has ever made sense of the words on the strap, which seem nonsensical and incoherent."

"Just as does the line on the scabbard."

"Aye, and as you can see, though one be a counterfeit, the craftsmanship admits that both were originally formed by the same hand."

"Yes, indeed. So it would appear."

"What is the history of Lightenhaft and its scabbard?"

"I know no more about it than would you, Kalaquinn," Aelward said, lifting the blade into the candlelight. "In the *Master Legendary*, Hedric mentions that, before Ardiel left on his final journey, the sword was sent to Thrysvar."

"Ardiel's general and close companion, yes. But does that not strike you as an odd thing for the high king to do—to leave his sword behind when embarking on a journey?"

"Yes, indeed..."

"And no doubt it was Thrysvar who secreted Ardiel's sword away in the underground keep where Colurian found it."

"No doubt. And it was only Thrysvar's untimely death that kept Lightenhaft's hiding place a mystery for those three thousand years."

"What of the scabbard, then?"

"The scabbard? No mention is made of it, to my knowledge, and I am aware of no other history pertaining to it."

"And Ardiel—he never returned from that last journey, did he?"

"No, never," Aelward said, lifting the scabbard from the table. Lightenhaft gave a low, sibilant whisper as its steel slid against the hardened leather. "Never was he seen again. Nor ever heard from, either. He simply disappeared from the histories of Ahn Norvys. In accord with his bequest, his son became high king in his stead." He placed the sheathed sword on the table.

"Never heard from again..." Kal let his gaze fall to the weapon, lost in his thoughts. The charged atmosphere of the room grew palpable in the silence as the hair stood on his neck and arms. "Or was he?" Kal looked again at Aelward, and the tall man lifted an eyebrow.

"It has long been understood that Ardiel himself fashioned the strap for the Talamadh," Kal said. "It would seem now that

Ardiel also fashioned the scabbard, for it is plain that strap and scabbard were both the work of the same hand. And the lines in Old Arvonian on both—the one complements and so, perhaps, explains the other. If no mention is ever made of the scabbard, as you say, could it have been sent to Thrysvar after he'd received the sword? Even after Ardiel had already departed on his final travels?"

The tall man nodded his grey head once, slowly. "Aye, it's possible."

"And no history accounts for the scabbard, because none was recorded. All knowledge of the scabbard passed with its keeper's untimely death."

"Again, possible. But it's no more than a scabbard. Why should anyone bother accounting for the sheath when it's the sword—"

Kal raised a hand, forestalling the question. "No," he said, "it is much more than a scabbard if it was, in fact, fashioned by Ardiel's own hand. We know from the Hordanic lore of the Talamadh that the strap sent Hedric was made by Ardiel, but no one mentions when Hedric received it. Is it possible that these, scabbard and strap, are, in fact, Ardiel's final missive?"

The tall man's eyes widened and fell to look at the sword and scabbard. He passed a hand over his scalp. It stopped, resting atop his head, the iron-grey hairs standing between his fingers. "The bard without harp in his tower will seek the forgelord." He translated the embossed words on the scabbard aloud to himself. Then, dropping his hand to rest on the broad leather strap, he read, "Without a throne the king in his tower will find the lay's meaning." He shook his head.

"Look, do you not see it?" Kal said. "Ardiel did give a final message to his closest and most trusted companions after he left for his final journey, a puzzle that they alone could decipher. Only now do we come to see it."

"You are full of surprises for one so fresh upon the path of life, Kalaquinn." Aelward lifted his gaze to the young Hordanu. "How do you come to know these things?"

"One does not study under the High Bard Wilum and walk away empty-headed."

"Nor, it would seem from your passion, empty-hearted."

"No, indeed. And Wilum's great passion was versecraft. Well, that and his doves."

"A necessary passion, the doves," Aelward said. "He relied upon them, as do I."

"But his particular love," Kal continued, "was the word work of the ancients. He tutored me at length in the poetics of the early centuries of the Harmonic Age. This is no scrap of doggerel etched in the leather. There is purpose here, and with it meaning. Only now do we begin to discern Ardiel's intent, as the two pieces are brought together."

Aelward read the lines again to himself, then said, "But even one with the other, the meaning is obscure—"

"Yes, yes, of course, but look—" Kal clapped his hands. "These two pieces fit together not as hands clasped, but rather as hands with fingers intertwined." He laced his fingers and held his hands up in the space between himself and Aelward. "But this...this is the key." He tapped his thumbs together. "The common verse on both the scabbard and the strap—'in his tower.' It's a hinge verse. The other verses fit around it."

The tall man stared at Kal. "A hinge verse?"

Surely he understood the significance, Kal thought. Was Aelward being deliberately obtuse in his apparent inability to grasp what he himself had now recognized? Kal heaved a sigh, then shuffled through the papers on the desk until he found a blank page.

"A quill and ink?" he asked.

Aelward stepped to the wall inset with drawers and returned with a fresh quill and a small clay pot. These he set before Kal on the table.

"Look," Kal said, pulling the stopper from the inkwell. "'In his tower' is the hinge verse around which Ardiel built his message. It's a piece of Old Arvonian kingsverse, so named because Ardiel himself was a master of the style, as well as its deviser—he and Hedric. It later became a convention of Old Arvonian versecraft, but I would suspect that, when this was written, only Ardiel and Hedric would have been aware of the style and so of how to solve this riddle." Kal paused to look at Aelward again. "I'm surprised that this is not known to you."

The tall man's grey eyes were keen, and the candlelight glinted in their surface. "Please, continue. I am intrigued."

The man was proving to be almost as much an enigma as the lines themselves had been. Kal dipped the tip of the quill into the ink, then tapped it against the inner edge of the bottle's mouth.

"So, if you were to translate the lines from Old Arvonian, they might run something like this. On the scabbard..." Kal scratched words on the sheet of coarse paper, pausing once to refresh the ink on the quill.

> *The bard without harp in his tower will seek the forgelord.*

"And from the strap..." Kal dipped the quill again and wrote:

> *Without a throne the king in his tower will find the lay's meaning.*

He withdrew the quill point from the paper. "So the lines might run in loose translation, rendered into the speech of our own day. But in the original, three of the characters in each line are emphasized in appearance." Kal flipped the quill over and used the feather's vaned tip to three times touch first the Talamadh's strap and then the scabbard, where letters were more deeply impressed in the tooled leather surfaces. "Three characters, one at the start of each phrase."

"These are significant?"

"Indeed, they are," Kal said. "They provide the key." Aelward stared fixedly at him, but said nothing, and he continued. "The key by means of which one can know how to order the verses around the hinge verse. Look here." He refreshed his quill in the ink. "If I was to render these lines in a more literal translation—though the language may seem a bit stilted—so as to preserve the stressed characters, the lines might run..."

> *Deprived of harp the bard **m**idst his tower **l**ooks for the forgelord.*
> *Throneless the king **m**idst his tower **h**appens upon the lay's meaning.*

" 'D'... 'm'... 'l'... 't'... 'm'... 'h'...," Kal said as he retraced the stressed letters in each line. "These letters would mean something significant to Ardiel, and to Hedric, too, for Ardiel would expect him to recognize and so solve the riddling kingsverse using the key."

"Do you have a sense of the solution?"

Kal's lips lifted in a half smile as he glanced up at the grey-haired man beside him. "As a matter of fact, I do. Let me show you. 'Midst his tower' is the hinge verse, so it stands in the middle and is written only once in kingsverse—though its meaning is determined in delicate balance, like a swinging door, by the two verses before it and then by the two verses that follow. So, in effect, though the hinge verse appears but once, it is rightly read twice. Because it appears on both the strap and scabbard was the sign to me that it was indeed the hinge verse." Kal wrote the hinge verse on the page. "The other four verses fit around it according to the key. A key with the four letters 'd,' 'l,' 't,' and 'h' around the one 'm.' A key with meaning to Ardiel and Hedric..."

"Yes, ingenious."

"Do you see it?"

"Yes. It is that which is of meaning to both Ardiel and Hedric."

"And that which, I suspect, was of key importance to Ardiel's last journey—"

"And what set him on the path at the first—the Talamadh."

"And so," Kal said and bent over the page once more, "arranging the verses according to their first letters, our piece of kingsverse would read so...." The quill scratched again over the surface of the rough paper. Kal's hand paused occasionally to revisit the ink vessel.

Throneless the king
Looks for the forgelord
Midst his tower
Deprived of harp the bard
Happens upon the lay's meaning.

"But what meaning does this new riddle, begot from the two, render to your mind?" Aelward said, turning to study Kal's face in the candlelight. The young Hordanu could feel the older man's scrutiny. "If it is, as you suggest, a message from Ardiel to his closest companions, then what is its meaning? What was Ardiel trying to tell them?"

"I-I would...I'd suggest," Kal said hesitantly, "that the hinge verse indicates the place to which Ardiel journeyed." He paused and cleared his throat, coughing gently into his hand. "And it is not the tower of king nor that of bard, as we might have—"

"And who is the forgelord? And what the lay that he speaks of?"

"I would suggest that it is—"

"And who is the throneless king? And who the bard deprived of harp?"

Kal was beginning to feel badgered by the tall man, whose hawkish eyes remained fixed on him. He knelt to the stone floor and reached out to collect the pages that had fallen scattered there in the pooled light and shadow. He would not be nettled by the man's insistent questions, he told himself; Aelward could wait for an answer. The stillness of the chamber felt strangely oppressive, despite the homely glow of the candles and the earthy scent of peat smouldering in the hearth.

"Ardiel himself," Kal said at length as he picked up the last sheet from under the table. He straightened and placed the neat sheaf of pages on the table, then turned to face Aelward again. "Clearly, Ardiel speaks of himself as the harpless bard and the throneless king. He abandoned both harp and throne, one at the beginning of his reign, and the other upon his departure on his final journey." Aelward remained silent and attentive, and Kal spoke on. "That he fashioned the strap for the Talamadh and the scabbard for the sword—harp and sword each emblematic of the respective offices of Hordanu and king—shows that he had distanced himself from both, entrusting them to those whom he knew would be the only ones able together to decipher the meaning of his cryptic message. And so doing, follow him."

"To...?" Aelward asked, his eyes gleaming in the candlelight.

Kal met the tall man's gaze with a level stare. "To the forgelord's tower, to Irminsûl."

"Irminsûl," Aelward said and nodded, his face expressionless.

"I suspect that Ardiel discovered something of great import about the Talamadh at Irminsûl," Kal said, dropping a finger to the page on which he had written the verses. "No doubt, that's why he used the word 'talamadh' as the key to discerning his kingsverse riddle. Perhaps he was summoning his companions, Hedric and Thrysvar, to conjure meaning from the puzzle and so journey to join him. Only Thrysvar's sudden demise prevented that from ever happening. Indeed, Thrysvar's death left the message unknown to any since Ardiel first framed it."

Aelward nodded again. "And the lay? The lay in the kingsverse?"

"His own Lay of Investiture, I would assume. 'The Lay of the Velinthian Bridge.'"

The tall man raised an eyebrow.

"Much of Ardiel's Lay has remained obscured from understanding, even from its first singing. But that Ardiel should venture to Irminsûl and make some significant discovery stands within reason. Whÿlas, his mentor, chided Ardiel repeatedly throughout his twenty-some years of high kingship that he had not fulfilled that which had been laid before him to accomplish, that which had been foreordained in his own Lay of Investiture. 'King and bard together shall quest the master's hidden tower forge'—so run the lines in 'The Lay of the Velinthian Bridge.' What, according to Whÿlas, ought to have been one of Ardiel's first quests as high king was in fact his last—to venture to Vali's ancient home, the Tower Forge, birthplace of both the Talamadh and Lightenhaft. It all stands to reason. But, what did he discover there?" Kal fell silent for a moment, rereading the kingsverse in the candlelight before lifting his gaze to the tall man. "I suspect, as is the nature of these things, that there is a prophetic bent to the riddle's meaning. Only now does the prophecy come to bear the fruit of meaning. I wonder if my fate and Starigan's are not also bound in these ancient lines. Perhaps it is within Wuldor's watchfulness that we should happen upon the message now, in these days. Perhaps it is Starigan, the throneless king, and I, the harpless bard, that were meant to venture to Irminsûl."

Aelward nodded yet again, the faintest hint of a smile tugging at the corners of his mouth. "So, you hit the mark with your reasoning, Kalaquinn, and arrive at the same conclusion as I," he said.

Kal looked from the man back to the words written on the page, his brow knit, until, in dawning comprehension, it smoothed, and his eyes first widened, then narrowed. Blood rushed to his head, and the back of his neck prickled and burned. "Have you played me the jack, Master Aelward?" He rounded on the tall man. "You have known all along of the kingsverse and its significance, haven't you? Tell me! You have known all along of it, haven't you? Am I not correct?"

The silence crackled between the two men as the elder regarded the younger. Aelward's aloof smugness irked Kal, and he struggled to contain his anger. At length, the man lifted his open hands in gesture of entreaty.

"Peace, Master Kalaquinn," he said. "Be at peace. Yes, I guessed at the puzzle when first I studied the Talamadh's strap. But I needed to test my conclusion against your own. Forgive me for leading you on. But know this—what took me nearly two days to discover, you solved in but the span of an hour."

Kal felt the tide of his anger begin to ebb. Of course, he told himself, Aelward had been astute to let Kal come to his own solution to the riddle and so confirm what the man himself had already discovered. Kal sighed, then said, "My apologies for my outburst, I—"

The tall man raised a hand as he dipped his head, eyes closed. "No. No apology is necessary, my lord Myghternos Hordanu." He set his grey eyes on Kal again and continued, "We have arrived at the same conclusion, and now we must speak of what action needs be taken."

"My heart misgives me at the thought...." Kal stared absently at the page in his hand, then placed it on the table atop the sheathed sword and leather strap. "Yet another dire leg in an already impossible journey."

"Kalaquinn, do not listen to the voice of fear, for fear is a very bad counselor," Aelward said, then placed a hand on Kal's shoulder, stooping slightly to look him in the eye. "And do not be afraid to hazard the impossible, for, in doing so, you will learn by necessity to depend on a strength that is not your own, but on one that is far, far mightier. In Wuldor's keeping, you will not be asked to do that in which he will not himself sustain you." He slapped the young Hordanu on the back. "Come, we have a journey to plan—two, in fact. You to find the lost prince, Starigan, and with him to acquire a spark from the Balk Pit of Uäm. Broq and I to the hyperboreal lands to find the hidden Tower Forge of Irminsûl and so scout it for you and Starigan."

A smile creased the tall man's face, and he squared his shoulders. "Ah, Kalaquinn, do you see it? These are indeed days of wonder. The Hordanu and the heir to the throne of Arvon—you and Starigan will venture forth like a new Hedric and a new Ardiel! I have waited a long time for this hour. But, come," he said, turning his attention to the paper-strewn table, "we will leave at dawn the day after tomorrow, and, if we are to leave so soon, then we have much preparation to make and little time to make it in. But first, who shall accompany you to Kêl-Skrivar?"

TWENTY-FOUR

Night was gently seeping away with the rising dawn. Atop the low stone wall that girded the hilltop upon which stood Aelward's Cot, Kal sat huddled in his cloak, chilled by the damp marshland air. He regarded the heavy sea of mist that covered the dwellings below. He had not been able to sleep, so at first hint of light he had stolen from his bed and climbed the slope to sit alone with his churning thoughts. For nearly an hour, as the darkness leached from the sky, he cherished the peace and stillness of the mist-shrouded landscape. His heart was filled with joy that his folk had found a safe haven. As for himself and his chosen comrades, this brief respite, he feared, would prove to be little more than the calm before the storm.

A marsh pony nickered distantly from stables on the far side of the Cot. The verge of the mist gave way to the steady influx of morning light, allowing Kal a glimpse of a few ghostly dwellings set along the edges of the rising hillside, now out of reach of the ebbing tide of fog. A rooster crowed from somewhere below him, and the village stirred with the signs of slowly wakening life, men and women rising to their chores.

From the door of the nearest dwelling emerged a large stout-limbed figure, unmistakably that of Devved, night pouch slung over his shoulder, short sword at his hip, and bowstaff in hand, ready, as they had agreed, for departure at break of day. Close behind him followed a slighter body, hobbled by a leg wound that would never fully mend—Devved's son, Chandaris. Outside the stone cottage, Devved turned to face the boy and leaned his bowstaff against the wall of the dwelling. He placed his hands on the lad's shoulders, then spoke to him, his head bent over the slender figure. Chandaris looked up, nodding now and again to his father. After a time, the burly blacksmith gathered his son to his chest. He held him for a long moment. Then, finally, after stooping to kiss his son's forehead, he stepped away and slid a sleeve across his eyes.

Chandaris stiffened. His chest swelling and his chin held raised, the boy played the part of the resolute young man. Father and son faced one another, the one a small caricature of the other, and Kal felt an unnerving qualm of guilt and doubt. Had he been too selfish in choosing Devved as a companion for the journey? Had he pressed him into service out of his own need for the Holdsman's iron-wrought strength, as solid and reassuring as a storm-weathered oak?

Devved again spoke a word to his son, then retrieved his bowstaff and, placing his arm across the boy's shoulders, led him towards a snug cottage that loomed visible through the thinning mist not a stone's throw away from them. It stood on the other side of a track that led through the marshland village up to Aelward's Cot. A plume of wood smoke rose from the cottage chimney to merge with ragged tendrils of mist. A taller boy careered from the door, a sword held aloft in each hand. Kal smiled. Bren and his makeshift weapons. He was forever sparring, his mind ablaze with the heroic feats of arms and the warrior. Bren rushed to Chandaris and thrust one of the wooden swords into his hand. The two young friends fell to playful blows, as they had many times over the past few days, in a reckless exchange of thrust and parry. At the same time, Kal's mother stepped from the door, lifting an arm in greeting to Devved. While Marina and the blacksmith talked, they regarded the lads with amusement. More than once, Marina nodded in emphasis of something she said to the man, placing a hand on his forearm. Kal knew the gesture well. No doubt Devved was feeling reassured, content in the knowledge that his son would surely be left in the best of care. So, too, Kal began to shed his own sense of misgiving. Marina would be to Chandaris like his own birth mother. Similarly, to the boy, Bren would ever be the watchful older brother. Even now in the swordplay Bren was showing it, for clearly he held back, not pressing his advantage in age and soundness, granting leeway to the younger boy. Soon enough would manhood come to both the lads, and each would have his own path to tread—and in manhood there were no easy roads, no sure way to escape hardship and toil. Kal sighed. It had been a hard decision, choosing Devved, but it was the right decision.

Devved glanced over his shoulder, his attention attracted by the approach of two men. Gwyn and Galli strode up the road. Like Devved, each carried a bowstaff, each wore a sword, grim reminders of the perilous journey ahead. They had come on foot from the lower dwellings, which remained wreathed in a deeper mist. The blacksmith and Marina turned to greet them. For a short while, they conversed; then Galli stepped towards the boys, who paused in their sparring. Borrowing Chandaris's weapon, he illustrated a finer point of swordsmanship, advancing on Bren, who was forced to scuttle backwards on the defensive. The onlookers' laughter rose to where Kal sat as Galli handed the wooden sword back to Chandaris and thumped him on the back. The three men took their leave of Marina and the two lads and turned to climb the hill to Aelward's Cot. Devved lagged behind a step and swung his body around to give a final nod of the head to his son, who stood gazing up the slope, wooden sword held slackly in his hand, until Marina beckoned her charges indoors for breakfast.

As the three trudged farther up the gentle rise, Gwyn spotted Kal on the stone wall and pointed him out for his companions. Kal waved to them, then slipped from where he sat to join them at the crest of the hill.

"Ah, Devved. Briacoil. All is well?" Kal said.

"Aye, the lad's settled in nicely with your folk," the blacksmith said, patting his night pouch with a big pawlike hand. "And I'm ready to leave when you are."

Kal turned to Gwyn and Galli and, after a further exchange of morning greetings, the four men advanced along a path that led to the iron-bound oak door of the Cot. Drawing nearer, they met grooms leading saddled marsh ponies to hitching posts before the stone walls of the keep.

"Our trusty steeds," Galli said with a wide grin.

Devved stopped with the others and turned to look back at the stocky ponies. "Don't laugh, lad. I tell you, in all my years as a smith, I've never encountered horseflesh quite like this. I've helped with the farriery and seen them at close hand. There's sinew enough lying beneath that shaggy coat."

"Devved's correct. They have a strength that is out of all keeping with their size," a voice behind them said. The heavy door to the Cot stood open, and there, in the dark portal, stood Broq. "Amazing creatures—sturdy, sure-footed in these treacherous boglands. They have the uncanny and unerring ability to find ground that's safe to tread, where you and I would see none. And these," he said, holding an upturned hand towards the ponies, "they are a gift to you, and a most generous gift, from Aelward, who awaits you within. Come." Broq stepped to the flagstone doorstep and stood aside, bowing his head and touching two fingers to the browmark that wound high across his forehead. Galli returned the gesture as he bowed to the older Telessarian.

Followed by his companions, Kal stepped past Broq and entered a windowless antechamber, torchlit but still gloomy, with a flight of stairs directly ahead. The stairs led to a narrow hallway from which they entered a chamber already familiar to Kal—the room where he and Aelward had unravelled so many tangled threads of meaning. Now its shutters were flung open to a morning light, which, though feeble, was strong enough to chase away the shadows from the crooks, staves, shears, ewe's and ram's bells, pipes, horns, horn vessels, wolf traps, and other oddments that adorned the walls. All the manuscripts and parchments that had littered the table and the floor were now stored away in their cabinets and pigeonholes. Except for the large map still laid out on the table in the centre of the chamber, there was no evidence of the disarray they had left two nights before.

"Briacoil, Kalaquinn. Briacoil, my boon companions. Welcome. It's good to see you," Aelward said as he turned from a window. "You've probably already eaten. Or perhaps you haven't yet. Either way, help yourselves. We've a long ride before us today— an uneventful one, I hope—but still, food may become a scarce thing in the days ahead. Come, do eat." Aelward held out his arm, inviting them across the room to a sideboard filled with loaves of warm bread and platters of cheeses and dressed meats side by side with brimming flagons of ale.

"Don't mind if I do, Master Aelward. Speaking for myself, I'm famished." Galli lifted the codynnos from his shoulder and left it with his bowstaff leaning against the wall of the chamber. Devved and Gwyn did likewise and followed him to the food-laden side-board. Broq and Aelward joined their guests in breaking fast and, as they ate, made animated conversation with the Holdsmen.

"Be at ease, Devved. There's not a safer spot in all of Ahn Nor-vys," Broq said between bites of cheese. "The Marshes of Atramar are an impregnable haven. Indeed, there is truly no safer place for your folk to remain. It was with good reason that Ardiel and the Seven Champions chose to hide here, in order to regroup their meagre forces." The Telessarian bard went on to explain how the Cot dated back to the very time of Ardiel and possibly even before. "So, truth be told," he said, the hint of a grin teasing his lips, "this Cot was, in the early days of its construction, someone else's Cot, not Aelward's."

Aelward himself soon left the others to talk among themselves and fell into subtle conversation with Gwyn, drawing the mute Holdsman out and communicating with him by means of word, gesture and expression.

For his part, Kal felt a curious want of hunger. Perhaps it was the anxious excitement of this day, or that Aelward had thrown a sumptuous feast the day before, at which he had eaten his fill. He picked desultorily at a plate of food, but soon abandoned it and drifted to the map in the centre of the chamber.

He traced their route again with his finger. From the Cot, all six of them—he, Aelward, Broq, Gwyn, Galli, and Devved—would strike out along Hoël's Dyke, which lay mouldering and marsh-bound, in most places not discernible as even the faintest footpath, impassable to all except the marshfolk and their rugged ponies. From Hoël's Dyke, they would veer east to where the marshes merged with the Asgarth Forest, making for the vicinity of the town of Melgrun in the Keverang of Pelogran along the foothills of the Bowstaff Mountains, which were in effect a northern exten-sion of the Radolan Mountains. At this spot, later today, if all went well, they would part ways to pursue their separate ventures.

Aelward and Broq would proceed by their own devices to the tower at Irminsûl, while Kal and his three companions crossed the Bowstaff Mountains as stealthily as possible, trying to avoid detection along the Westland Road. Once they gained the leeward side of the Bowstaff Mountains in the marchlands of lowland Arvon, they would make their way through the sparsely popu-lated county of Glastanen, bypassing the town of Woodglence and striking north into the cover of the thick forest of Rootfall Frith. From this great forest, they were to head across open country to the protection of Stonderwood, yet another ancient woodland, and thence onward to the coast to the isolated port of Seabank.

Kal's finger hovered over the map at Seabank as he considered the strategy that Aelward had proposed during their deliberations. At Seabank, he had suggested, they would find any number of mercenary seamen, from whom, if the price pleased them, they could secure passage to wherever they wished with no questions asked. But as an added measure of prudence, to avoid drawing suspicion on themselves, Aelward had counselled that they break their sea voyage in two. It would be best, he argued, for them to secure passage to Gorfalster first. There was an old acquaintance of his in Gorfalster, Aelward had said, a resourceful merchant named Telin, who would be able to provide for them both ship and crew to sail them on to Kêl-Skrivar.

Kal's finger followed the coast of the Dumoric Sea from Seabank south and east past the boundaries of Arvon to the Hoffgar River and then upriver to the bustling port town of Gorfalster. The advantage of Gorfalster, according to Aelward, was that it enabled them to lose themselves in the coming and going of trade traffic from all parts of Ahn Norvys that made use of the busy river port. But at what cost? Frowning, Kal tapped the map at Gorfalster and considered its distance from the sea. It added needless miles to the total length of their already long journey.

"Not hungry, my lord Hordanu?" Broq looked over to where Kal stood leaning over the map. Kal shook his head and made reply absently, still lost in thought.

"Come," Broq said and gestured to the depleted sideboard. "By midmorning, after a few hours in the saddle, you will wish you'd eaten even a little."

"He's too preoccupied in brooding over something," Aelward said, turning his attention from Gwyn. "Look at the knitted brow."

Kal glanced up from the map, his frown deepening. "I've been studying our course again. Do you truly think it wise that we split the journey in two, Aelward? Making the side journey to Gorfalster? It's a fair stretch out of the way."

The grey man's sharp features tightened with mirth, and his eyes sparkled. He moved from the sideboard, taking a couple of slow paces closer to Kal, his hands clasped behind his back.

"What you mean, my lord Hordanu, is, 'There we'd be up the river'—so to speak—'in a garrison town crawling with spies and informers. Can this Telin fellow be trusted?'"

Kal fixed his gaze, wide-eyed, on Aelward. "How did you ... ?"

"I sensed your misgiving, even when we first discussed our possible courses of action. You gave way to my counsel against the inner protest of your own doubts—" Aelward raised his hand to forestall further comment from Kal. "But I tell you, Kalaquinn, calm your fears. Telin is indeed to be trusted. Although he's an artful merchant, he is also a man of honour, and he will provide for my friends, even as he would his own—even as I do mine." Aelward returned to the sideboard, where he pushed breadcrumbs into a line with his finger, then took up his ale mug and lifted his cool gaze to Kal. "As for the bustle and intrigue of Gorfalster, its teeming dangers—they're all as meat and drink to a man like Telin. He thrives on them, but manages all the while to remain totally trustworthy, utterly above reproach. I cannot say the same for whomever you may hire to take you from Seabank. I'd not trust them past Gorfalster, if even you can trust them that far. But, that, for now, is in Wuldor's keeping."

Kal's eyes fell again to the map, and he leaned on the table, his head hanging. "So, he's our fellow," he said, then looked sideways at Aelward. "Forgive me. I stand humbled by my doubts."

"No, no, Kal. It's not your doubts that have humbled you. Rather, what led to your discomfiture, shall we say, was your reluctance to give utterance to your doubts at the fitting moment, when we first discussed the options before us. Your failing was that you were too ready to defer to Aelward Lamkin. That's never a good thing, my lord Myghternos Hordanu—to attend not the promptings of your heart." Aelward's face held the thin hint of a smile, and he shook his grey head, turning his attention once more to the victuals on the sideboard.

"Aye, Aelward, that may be so." Kal straightened, combing stray locks of black hair from his eyes, a crooked half-smile on his face. He left the map table and clapped a hand on Galli's shoulder. "The trouble is that you're too easy a man to trust. It would help if you were a simple shifty-eyed Telessarian like Galli here, with perfidy stamped all over your features. I think I will eat." He stepped to the platters and laid a thick slab of cheese on a piece of honeyed bread.

"If I may, my lord Hordanu," Galli said, turning to his friend with the slightest bow of his head. "There is a small matter that this troublesome Telessarian would bring to your attention. Something that you may not have considered."

"And what might that be?" Kal asked.

"Our folk are safe and provided for. And we are well planned and provisioned for as we embark on this journey that needs be made. But there are still other duties that you must attend to. What of the Summer Loosening, Kal? It's less than a fortnight away. You know the orrthon must be performed, but where and how?"

"He's right, Kalaquinn. We've not discussed it yet. Perhaps we should now, though I doubt not that you have already considered the event." Aelward's grey eyes had resumed a serious cast. Broq nodded in agreement.

Kal shook his head and washed down a bite of the bread and cheese with a long pull from his mug, then shook his head again, placing the empty cup on the sideboard. "No, there's no need," he said, wiping a sleeve across his mouth. "Come, the morning sun is gaining on us. We've lingered over breakfast long enough. We'll worry about the Loosening when we must, closer to the time, for so my heart prompts me."

"Well-spoken, my lord Hordanu. Well-spoken, indeed," Aelward said and nodded to Kal.

Kal wolfed down the last of his food and strode across the room to retrieve his codynnos, his bowstaff and quiver, along with his sword belt and Rhodangalas at the entrance of the meeting chamber. Close on his heels followed the rest of the group, as if infected with Kal's sudden air of urgency, and they left the room and turned down the stairs.

Outside the Cot, the marsh ponies waited, their saddlebags well stuffed. The grooms helped each of the companions adjust their stirrups and settle on their ponies. Kal grinned with amusement at Devved, whose legs dangled almost to the ground. He looked almost as big as his mount. An expression of helpless uncertainty passed across the blacksmith's broad face.

"Don't look so worried, Devved," said Broq. "This pony has carried marshmen bigger even than you."

"Aye, Devved. You should know," Galli said, a mischievous glint in his eye as he sidled his pony beside the blacksmith's. "You said yourself you've not seen horseflesh better." With that, the blond

Telessarian slapped the pony's rump, sending the big man reeling to keep his seat as the small creature lurched forward to join its fellows along the path.

The marsh ponies, with their riders, plodded down the hillside from the keep, now bathed in light from the rising sun. Below them, the roofs and chimneys of the sprawling settlement could be seen through the thinning fog. Bren and Chandaris emerged from Marina's cottage to wave a last farewell. So, too, did Marina, brushing hair from her eyes, a kitchen ladle in her hand. Kal bowed his head to his mother. The rest of the village was stirring, and the vaporous morning mist was lifting, even as the smoke of cooking fires filled the air. Kal nodded to Thurfar, who stood with his arm around Fionna, clutching a handful of arrows. Thurfar left his wife's side and stepped to the roadside to meet his son. The mounted company stopped.

"Here, more arrows for you, made last night," he said.

Gwyn took the shafts from Thurfar's hand, appraised them for a moment with an admiring eye, then nodded his thanks and slid them into the quiver slung by his saddle.

"Mind you keep your bowstring dry, Gwyn, and they'll shoot true. And don't you waste them. Make every one count." Thurfar turned his attention to Kal. "You'll keep an eye on my son, Master Kalaquinn? Make sure he takes no fool risks."

"The past has proven that he keeps better care of me than I of him," Kal said, breaking into a thin smile. "But rest assured that I will mind him, Goodman Thurfar. I will mind him as surely as I count on you to look after these folk of the Holding here in the marshes. Briacoil to you." The two men locked eyes. They understood one another. Then, in silence, Kal nudged his pony, and the company continued plodding slowly along the path, each man acknowledging last words of encouragement from Holdsfolk and from the handful of marsh dwellers there among them.

Aelward pulled up alongside Kal as the riders left the settlement, the way still open and solid underfoot, running straight through a broad meadow of lush grass that merged in the middle distance with a wilderness of reedy marshes between the rugged walls of the Sheerness Spur. Far off ahead, through the break in the mountains, a towering pillar of black granite rose hundreds of feet into the air from the seemingly endless bogs. Kal squinted, looking at it—the Llanigon Mark Stone, the Black Rock—standing like a lone dark sentinel, solid and immovable, over the vast treacherous reaches of the swamp.

"Thurfar's a good man, Kalaquinn. You've left your people in good hands," Aelward said, staring ahead at the broken remains of Hoël's Dyke.

"Aye," Kal replied without looking at him. "With able help from your own folk."

The two rode together, leading the party for a time, until the way grew spongy and uncertain, and Kal fell behind. Broq moved forward to join Aelward. From soft, moist ground, still covered by grass, they entered the perilous beds of the marsh in single file, the ponies boldly picking their way across half-submerged tussocks. Once their path led through ooze and muck, and Kal felt the raw power of his sturdy mount as it pulled its hoofs from the sucking mire step upon step. Leaning back, Broq spoke to Kal over his shoulder.

"It's far easier with the ponies. We'd have a far longer way through the marshes without them. They follow trails that would be death to a man."

"Even a Telessarian?" Kal said.

"Aye, even a Telessarian."

By midmorning they had passed between the dark walls of the Sheerness Spur that loomed over the marshes and passed the bulking mass of the Llanigon Mark Stone, against which their path pressed, climbing for a short time out of the muck of the marsh only to plunge once again, disappearing into the slurry of mud and peat-stained water. Soon, however, the dull sameness of reeds and sedge began to yield to marshland broken by bushes and stunted trees that grew on hillocks ringed around and separated by brackish water. After half an hour's more plodding, they entered a sodden woodland laid open to the sky now and again by stagnant ponds where silver-grey trunks, stripped of life and bark, stood like guarding sentinels over the murky swamp water that had choked them. They skirted the spaces of open water, clinging to treed verges, their way often blocked by tangles of rotting windfalls. But then their path rose across a gentle swell of low rolling hills that grew from and fell into shallow valleys, until, at length, they reached a long clearing on a rise of land. Here they stopped and let their ponies graze. Before them stretched the faintest seam in the swaying grasses of the open field, a line running straight into trees that broke the sea of meadow more than half a mile away.

"I recognize this place," said Galli, twisting in the saddle to look around. "This is Hoël's Dyke, what Old Jock called the Lyndway."

"That it is," said Aelward. "We've been following it all along, though the Marsh has claimed much of it. Old Jock's haunt goes right through the Black Rock Gap."

"Miserable countryside to be prowling around in," Devved said as he dismounted to wipe his swamp-stained feet and shins clean of mud in a clump of tall grass.

"Provides a road for the enemy," Kal said softly.

"Hardly," Aelward said, snorting a chuckle, as he reached for his waterskin. "No doubt we'll encounter patrols, Gawmage's or even Ferabek's, but not yet and not here. In these parts, Hoël's Dyke is a path fit only for marshmen and their ponies." He lifted his skin and drank.

"The best of the Lyndway's like this," Broq said, "and a welcome enough respite it is for the next couple of miles, so thickly covered with sod that you can scarce make out the cobbles, save in spots where they have been heaved by tree root or winter frosts to the light. Even within short years of its construction, many long centuries ago, the Dyke was already tumbledown and derelict, disappearing into the swamp. But here, at least, it remains sound."

"Suits me fine after that wretched bog," said Devved, wiping the last of the loose mud from his boots.

"For now."

"For now?"

"Wait 'til you see the rest of the Lyndway," Broq continued. "Where it hasn't been overgrown by forest, its embankments have been rutted and gouged by the rain of centuries upon centuries. Or else washed away entirely into the surrounding marsh."

"Well, let's have done with it, then," said Devved as he remounted his pony.

They continued north along the decrepit remains of the ancient trackway and soon entered woods. Wherever their way was not obscured by trees on either side of the Hoël's Dyke, they overlooked a wasteland of marsh stretching as far as the eye could see and were grateful that for the most part they were able to remain atop the raised bed of the ancient roadway, no matter its state of disrepair.

By late morning, the wide views of marshland had disappeared, replaced by a pressing, dense phalanx of trees that stretched into the distance wherever they were afforded a point of vantage on a ridge or a height. They had entered the Asgarth Forest, Aelward explained. As the path led them through the forest, Kal had recognized landmarks from their first meeting with Old Jock, but soon enough the woods grew unfamiliar to him as he peered into their shadowy depths.

"He's watching us, I wouldn't be surprised," said Aelward.

"Who?" Kal asked, startled from his thoughts.

"Old Jock. It wasn't far from here that he found you. But he won't show himself without good reason."

"Or what he considers good reason," corrected Broq from behind. "Strange old bird, he."

"Aye, but he'd not thank you for describing him so," Aelward said over his shoulder, then scanned the surrounding woods. "All the same, if he hasn't shown himself by now, he won't, for we're passing out of his range."

Slowly, the roadway began to improve. In many places, the bare cobbles were now visible, and there were recently made ruts from the traffic of wagons. Soon they arrived at a well-tended track that forked away from Hoël's Dyke, running northeast to their right. Aelward called the party to a halt.

Kal sniffed the air. "I smell smoke. Can you?"

"Charcoal burners. They ply their trade in these woods, supplying the forges of Melgrun and thereabout," said Aelward. "At one time they supplied forges even in the marchlands, as far afield as Woodglence. But those days are now passed." He shrugged and shook his head, then nodded forward. "From here Hoël's Dyke goes on to meet the Westland Road. That's too far out of our way. We'll leave it now and take this sidetrack. It meets up with the Westland Road, but farther east, near Melgrun. We'll avoid the town, skirt around it, and then take our leave and embark upon our separate journeys."

"It looks well-travelled. Is it safe?" Devved asked.

"You'd rather be following the swampland trails, Devved?" Galli said, grinning at the blacksmith's ill ease. Devved waved his hand in a gesture of dismissal.

Aelward ignored the banter. "It's used by the charcoal burners. They look after it, as they do the Lyndway hereabouts. They use these roads to cart their wares from their hearth heaps in the forest. Broq and I are known to them. They are friends to the marshfolk. All the same, we must be on our guard, especially as we get nearer Melgrun. It'll be an important marshalling point— the town seat of the Keverang of Pelogran and the first place Gawmage's soldiers encounter when they're crossing the Bowstaff Mountains from lowland Arvon." Aelward pressed his pony forward along the new trackway. "Come now, mind you keep your voices low and your eyes and ears sharp."

It was midday as the party followed Aelward and Broq onto the cart path. The sun shone bright, and the soft trill of birdsong cheered the air, which remained tinged with the acrid smell of smoke. Despite the apparent peace of the woods, they kept a watchful silence, letting their ponies tramp the miles in an even, monotonous gait.

Broq stopped abruptly, holding up his arm to bid them hold. "Up ahead. Just over the rise. Something's wrong." The sound of voices drifted on the breeze.

"This way," Aelward said, leaping from his pony. "Get off the road into cover. Quickly now!"

TWENTY-FIVE

The men hurried behind Aelward, each leading his pony by the bridle into the dense stand of trees to the left of the road. Creeping through the undergrowth, they kept well away from the road.

"I'd swear that was a woman's scream," whispered Devved.

Aelward raised a hand, his finger extended in warning. He turned his head to look back over a shoulder at his companions.

"Let's see what's happening, but watch your step," he said. "Very slowly, now. Be careful."

They angled their way back towards the road. The forest cover thinned as the ground gently rose, and the men emerged onto a sloped clearing, still out of sight of the road. Aelward gestured for them to quickly hobble their ponies and follow him. Again, a woman's cry rose to them on the breeze, and with it now another noise, what sounded to Kal like the gabbling of geese. Now it grew clear—the voices of children clamouring in distress. Kal pressed behind Aelward, as the company waded forward through waist-high grasses until they crested the rise and so regained a view of the thoroughfare that curved through a long swale and was lined on the far side by great overspreading trees.

Kal stared down the grade to the road, not forty yards away, to where a horse and cart were stopped. On the road beside the cart were a man, lying doubled over on his side in the dust, holding his head, and a woman clad in highland homespun, two or three children clutching at her skirts. The woman and children shrank back from a small company of armed men that hemmed them in at pike-point. Another child, evidently the eldest, a stout lad of nine or ten, was being pulled, kicking and scratching, from the wagon. Set to the ground, he caught one of the soldiers in the shin, sending him hopping, and dashed to where his father lay. There he stood his ground, jaw set and fists clenched. This seemed to amuse the soldiers standing by, for they shuffled a little, and the sound of coarse laughter now underlay the continued wailing of the frightened children.

"Gawmage's lowland dogs!" Devved spat the words through clenched teeth. Indeed, Kal could clearly make out the snarling mastiff's-head device on the front and back of the dun-coloured military tunics that the men wore.

A new commotion of voices drifted to the ears of the hidden onlookers. One of the armed men, tall and heavy framed, had climbed up onto the bed of the wagon and was bent over, rooting through it. As he stood up again, he threw a wooden crate onto the road. It burst open, and chickens scattered wildly in all directions. Laughing raucously, a couple of the soldiers kicked at the escaping birds, which disappeared into the trees and long grass on either side of the cart track. With a wide malicious grin, the man on the wagon bed lifted and emptied a large basket of eggs onto the road. They splattered amid angry curses as the soldiers were forced to leap back. The man on the wagon laughed uproariously and bent over again. When he rose, in his arms was a small cask, hoisted high and held above him like a prize. He lowered it to pry out the bung with his dagger; then, having managed to free the plug, he raised the cask aloft again and tilted his head back, his maw open wide. The amber liquid overflowed his mouth and slopped onto his unshaven face. Jeering, his mates demanded their share. The man pulled the cask away and grimaced, then, coughing and sputtering uncontrollably, tossed the cask down, letting its contents shower from the open bunghole. One of the men made to break its fall and cursed when it slipped through his hands and fell onto his foot. The others jostled and fought one another for a handhold on the swiftly draining cask. Recovered from his bout of coughing, the man aboard the cart rose again with laden arms and flung down a side of meat. At this, the carter pushed himself off the ground and lunged forward to retrieve the meat from the dirt of the road. The soldiers quickly lost interest in the empty cask and stopped the man. They circled him and taunted and shoved him, driving him staggering from one tormentor to the next.

"Filthy bullies. Time to teach them a lesson they'll not soon forget!" Devved said, his face florid. Head thrust forward, he drew his sword and took a step. Aelward reached out his arm to restrain the blacksmith.

"No, not yet."

Devved bristled. "What do you mean?" he snapped at Aelward. "They're highlanders, and in need of our help. Are you blind, man?"

"I see." Aelward's grizzled features tightened, and he rounded on Devved. "I see that we have a mission to accomplish," he hissed, "a dire mission. By guile and stealth, if we may. By main force, if we must, and only if we must."

"Aelward's right, Devved. Stay yourself," Kal said, fixing the blacksmith with a level stare.

Devved flexed his jaw, his cheeks undulating as he held himself back and lowered himself once more to a crouch in the long grass. All eyes returned to the scene unfolding below them on the road, where the man knelt on a single knee, dishevelled, beset by his tormentors, blood running freely over half his face. Still his eldest son stood by him, glowering over his father at the soldiers.

The boy struck fast, like an arrow let loose, rushing the nearest pikeman, but the soldier was faster still and spun his pike staff around, catching the boy in the side of the head. A sickening thud reached Kal's ears as the boy came sprawling to a rest on the packed dirt. There he lay, unmoving.

The carter rose to his feet and charged forward. Caught off balance, the soldier who had cracked the boy's head stumbled backwards and fell on his back, the carter atop him, to the clear amusement of his companions. The carter was seized and dragged from the pikeman. When the soldier regained his feet, he threw down his pike staff and unsheathed his sword. He drew his arm back and stepped to where the highlander was held, arms and legs fixed by the soldier's mates as surely as a fly in a spider's web.

"No! No! No! No..." The woman screamed and sobbed. Devved glanced fiercely at Aelward, who inclined his head.

"Make ready your bows," the grey man whispered.

"No...Wait," Kal said. "He's sheathing his sword."

On the road, something had happened. At a word from his fellows, the soldier had allowed himself be pulled back from his intended victim and had returned his weapon to its scabbard. The woman's eyes darted around the ring of soldiers, then up at the wagon bed. She screamed again. One of the men laid the back of his hand hard across the woman's mouth, and she was silent. The children were in a fit of howling by now, still clinging to the woman, as her husband was jostled back roughly against a cart wheel, arms flailing, by three of the pikemen.

"There's why he's housed his blade," said Aelward, nodding towards the soldier who had been so busily ransacking the cart. "Not from any sudden outpouring of mercy."

The man on the cart stood with a coil of thick hempen rope that he had found amidst all the other booty. He yelled out and threw it down. One of his comrades caught it and walked towards a great-limbed oak by the far side of the road. The rest of the armed men had closed on the solitary highlander, blocking off his escape, cornering him and wrestling him to the ground. In a swarm, they bound his hands behind his back and dragged him to the tree. One end of the rope had been quickly fashioned into a noose and hung over a branch several feet above his head. The men slipped the loop around the highlander's neck, and one stout soldier began to pull on the free end of the rope, drawing its slack taut.

"No...No...Th-they're going to hang him," said Galli. "Aelward, for mercy's sake, we must act now!"

Below them on the road, the woman's pleading grew more frantic and anguished, rising in tone to an hysterical pitch.

Still Aelward waited, his hand raised and finger poised, holding them back. His jaw was set, and his eyes glinted with a fierce light. "Ready your bows...," he breathed to the men beside him without looking away from the road. "Ready your bows...All of you..."

Devved remained motionless beside Kal. Eyes narrowed and blazing, he clenched the grip of his sword in a white-knuckled fist.

Now the carter was being hoisted up, in small jerks, from the road, his neck straining against the tension of the rope, his back arched and toes pointed in an attempt to stay supported by the ground. The woman's screams filled the air as she struggled to free herself of her captors' hold.

Without warning, Devved broke from the tall grass and charged down the field towards the trackway, sword raised high, roaring the highland battle cry.

"The fool!" Aelward growled. "Now are we committed to the path of blood!"

"Gwyn," Kal cried, his own bow at full bend. "The hangman!"

The young red-haired Holdsman raised himself to a knee and let loose. Not a split second behind Gwyn's shaft, a flight of arrows sped across the gap. The soldier hauling on the rope collapsed, an arrow fixed in the middle of his back and another in his side. The carter fell to his knees, gasping and coughing, struggling to remove the rope from his neck. Three other soldiers fell, each grabbing at the shaft of a highland arrow where he had been pierced.

Galli led the company headlong down the slope behind Devved. For a stunned moment, the lowland soldiers had sought cover from the rain of arrows. Three of their own lay dead. One had been wounded and lay writhing in a spreading pool of muddy blood on the roadway. Now, they emerged to meet the onslaught, chivvied forward by their leader, who remained standing in the cart.

"Have at 'em, boys," he howled. "You two there, get up! Pike and sword. Steady yourselves. Their arrows are spent, and there's more of us than them." He leapt down from the wagon, drawing his own sword ringing from its scabbard. "They're but highland whelps, and we'll bring them to heel!"

Devved charged him, and the two men clashed like a crushing wave breaking against stone. In a fit of rage, the blacksmith parried the soldier's first overhand blow, then regained himself and spun around to cut the man down, cleaving his chest nearly in two with the powerful stroke of his blade. Only the man's leather cuirass dampened the might of the blow.

On either side of Devved, Kal and Galli had joined the milling fray. With ease, Kal dispatched his adversary, who proved himself a clumsy swordsman. A second lowlander fared no better, for, no sooner had he stepped in front of Kal in the wake of his fallen comrade, than the Holdsman ran him through and drew back a bloodstained sword. The hours he had spent in practice with Alcesidas were bringing their reward.

Catching a breath, he flexed his sword wrist, savouring the coiled readiness of Rhodangalas in his hand. From the corner of his eye, Kal saw a flicker of movement. By the edge of the cart, a soldier skulked, sidling away from Kal towards Galli. He was going to blindside the Holdsman. Kal felt a cold rush of alarm. Galli had engaged a young lowlander, whose movements seemed clumsy and inexpert—another poor swordsman. That one should be easy for Galli to dispatch, Kal thought. Rhodangalas lifted, he dashed to take care of the third man, who turned with a start. The man had a pale, cadaverous face, heavily stubbled and lined with scars, and an arrow-torn ear. The soldier checked himself and raised his sword, inviting Kal to combat, helmet askew, his pallid face beaded with sweat.

Kal smiled grimly and darted his sword forward, feinting to the head then thrusting towards the midsection. With an unexpected swiftness and strength, the man parried the blow, knocking Rhodangalas flying from Kal's hand. Kal reeled back in shock. The man stepped forward nimbly.

"You've a way with the blade," he said, grinning. "And a pretty one it was, too." The man pressed forward, feinting jabs. He had the light feet of a swordsman—a good swordsman. "Time to pay the tallyman," he said, his forced smile dissolving into a scowl as he swung his blade roundly to hack through Kal's gut. Kal backstepped desperately and flinched as the sword tip caught the weave of his tunic. While he struggled to regain his balance, the soldier followed through with a quick powerful thrust to the throat. In that instant, Galli whirled round, as lithe as a cat, and slashed down on the man's arm, severing it from his body, sending the sword with a dull thud to the ground, its hilt in the grip of lifeless fingers. Galli dispatched the stricken soldier, who stared with a look of unbelief at his bleeding stump, as Kal scrambled to retrieve Rhodangalas.

Rising with his sword in hand again, Kal realized that the sounds of fighting had subsided and given way to the moans of wounded men and the frightened sobbing of children.

"Routed, every last one of them! Paid back in kind," said Devved, his face sweat-stained and grimy from exertion. He stood close by and wiped his gory blade clean on a patch of cloth he had torn from the cloak of a fallen lowland soldier.

"Aye, all dead . . . or dying, though I take no pleasure in carnage," said Aelward as he bent over a man still clinging to life and moistened his mouth and lips with water.

"And Gwyn?" asked Kal.

"None the worse for wear, as you can see. Nor are any of the rest of us," said Broq, busily untying the cords that had bound the hands of the carter. The woman and her children rushed to embrace him. "Nor this fellow, although it was a close-run thing,

I'd say, with him more than just starting to feel the bite of the rope around his throat."

"He wasn't the only one who came near to paying the tally-man," Galli said, casting an eye towards Kal.

"Tallyman?" Aelward asked. Devved, Gwyn and Broq, too, looked up.

"Aye, the tallyman," Kal said, grinning ruefully. "I came too close to being tallied among the dead. But for Galli—"

"It was overconfidence on your part. Overconfidence, plain and simple, else you'd have taken him without any help from me."

"Aye, too much sparring with Alcesidas. Not enough hard practice to make me battle wary. Ah, well, a lesson learned—"

"At what cost, Kal? We nearly lost you. And we can't afford to lose you."

"Galli is right, Kalaquinn," Aelward said slowly, glancing up again at the Hordanu from where he stooped over the dying man. "We cannot afford to lose you." The quietness of his voice gave weight to his words.

Kal looked from one man to the other, then chuckled. "Peace," he said, and lifted a hand, as if to dismiss their concern. "I am unharmed. Do not fret."

"You would do well," Aelward said softly, fixing his grey eyes on Kal, "to avoid battle in the future. If at all possible, avoid any danger to your person." The grey man rose to his feet and stop-pered his water flask. He glanced to the lowlander he had been tending, now still and lifeless, then turned to the carter, who hugged the woman and children close. "And now, introductions are in order. What is your name? Tell us your story."

"Aye, how did you come to be attacked by this lot?" Devved said.

"And do you think there are more of them about?" Galli asked.

"Hold. Hold with the questions." Aelward lifted a hand, palm out. "Give the man leave to speak."

"Thank you for saving him," blurted the woman. Two girls and a small boy still pressed about her legs.

"Aye, br-briacoil," the man by her side said hoarsely and inclined his head, a hand at his neck. "I-I owe you a debt of th-thanks that can never be paid. You . . . you have saved me—saved us, for they would . . . they would surely have killed us all." The man placed a hand on the shoulder of his eldest. The stout lad, standing once again by his father's side, sported a large, purpling goose egg on the left side of his brow. The man straightened. "I am Latryk. I am—" He coughed; then, after swallowing hard, said, "I am a charcoal burner in these parts. We were on our way home from Melgrun with supplies, having sold a load and visited my sister and her new bairn. We were beset by these men. They came from the other direction, from deeper in the forest."

"They must have been just ahead of us on the road," Broq said, looking in the direction the charcoal burner pointed. "They had a rough look about them."

"They all do," Latryk continued, his words coming more easily, though he still rubbed at the livid welt around his throat, where the rope had bit him. "They said they needed to search our cart for weapons. Said they were going to put an end to the troubles they'd had with the folk hereabout. And troubles they've had, for sure. I can attest to the truth of that. Mostly from the burners hereabout. It's not with open arms that we've welcomed the lowland rabble to these parts. No, but it's been with arms borne!" The man plucked up an arrow from the ground, smiled and squinched one side of his face in a wink. "Aye, and they were in an angry frame of mind, too, since our folk had made themselves scarce."

"Indeed, there's no finding a charcoal burner in the Asgarth Forest, if he doesn't want to be found," Broq said.

The man looked at Broq sideways, scrutinizing his face with a narrowed eye, and lifted the arrow to point at him. "You've a browmark like that young fellow there, but you're a marshman, aren't you? Aye, I've seen you before."

"No doubt, you have. I am Broq, and this is Aelward." The bard held out an open hand to the grey man.

"Well, there's a thing! Saved by Broq. And by Aelward himself!" The man grinned lopsidedly and looked to his wife. "Aye, there's a thing."

"And so they ransacked your cart and aimed to hang you simply to indulge their malice?" Kal said.

"Aye, that, and to make an example of me. So they claimed."

"There are more of them about?" Galli asked.

"Aye, there's always more of them. It was just poor luck that we came on them. Thought we'd miss them on the road today," the charcoal burner said and looked again at Broq and Aelward.

Kal let his gaze wander over the cart and the dead men on

the road. "Well, here's trouble," he said. "They'll be keen to pay us for this, once they discover their patrol has been slaughtered."

The charcoal burner chuckled. "Aye, I'd think so. But this won't be the first of their patrols to go missing. They've already got their hackles up anyway for the trouble we've been giving them. There's not a highlander in these parts that doesn't have his heart set against them, if not his steel, especially those of us that live here in the forest."

"Still, there is no point in baiting Gawmage's mastiffs," said Aelward. "It would be better if these bodies were hidden away beyond discovery, or at least taken off this roadway. That way, the disappearance of one of their patrols might remain a mystery."

"A missing patrol? They're learning fast that there's little mystery in that," Latryk said with a crooked smirk.

"Still...," said Aelward.

"Aye, well enough, then. Me and my fellows, we'll take care of it." Latryk nodded, then glanced up sharply at Aelward as a thought struck him. "Aye, we can fix it right, we can. Not but half a mile from here is a fresh-laid heap about ready for burning."

"Good," said Aelward, his gaze cast to the ground, "that would work."

"Aye, it would, it would. Let them fuel the fires that will fuel their forges. Aye, I like that." The carter's wife raised a disapproving brow and shooed her children back up into the wagon.

"Now, ourselves," Kal said, "we're bound for Glastanen over the mountains by way of the Westland Road. If we avoid Melgrun, is it possible? Are we likely to meet with problems?"

Latryk cocked an eyebrow. "Problems aplenty, I can tell you. Aye, you'd be courting real danger that way, you would."

"Even outside Melgrun?"

"Aye, even outside Melgrun. No, you'd best keep right clear of Melgrun. But the Westland Road isn't much better. It's crawling with dog's-head troops—all of them pouring into the highlands. Once they pass the mountains, they make for the barracks at Melgrun. From there, some march west to the other keverangs, but most turn south along the Old High Road into the clanholdings."

"So these roads are heavily travelled?" Kal asked.

"Most times, aye, clogged with soldiers. Mind, too, these soldiers are well aware of the fight that remains in the highlands. We cause them some sore trouble. They're bound to be wary—"

"And not gentle, either, I should think, as we have seen," Broq said.

"Aye, and it'll not help," Latryk continued, "if they see you all armed to the teeth with sword and bow." With the hem of his tunic, he cleaned the dust and grime from the arrow he held.

"But if we wait for nightfall and travel in stealth?" Kal suggested.

"Nay, not possible." The man shook his head and handed the arrow to Gwyn. "There's always movement. Night marches, besides. And the pass through the Bowstaff is narrow, scarce more than a bottleneck in places. If you was stopped, aye, you'd be caught for sure, trapped like flies... Well, like flies in a bottle."

"Re'm ena, but you're just the fellow we needed to lift our hopes high for this journey ahead!" exclaimed Devved, clapping a thickly muscled arm on Latryk's slender shoulder. He turned to the woman seated in the cart. "Is he always this encouraging?"

She smiled demurely and said, "My husband's a good man. He'll not leave you to the dangers of the road, not after what you've done for us."

"Now, how are you going to manage that, Master Burner?" Smiling, Devved planted himself, his arms akimbo, before Latryk.

"The Traders' Trail," the woman said, looking at her husband. The charcoal burner smiled at his wife and winked at Devved.

"The Traders' Trail?" The blacksmith knitted his brows.

"Aye. There's another road over the Bowstaff Mountains, fallen out of use for many years now. In the old days, our folk used it to carry charcoal into the marchlands. It was a way to sidestep the levies imposed by the Mindal. Then, when the king died, those men on the royal council grew more cruel. They harassed and often killed any of the traders they caught on the leeward side of the mountains—"

"The Mindal called it the Traitors' Trail," the woman interjected. "His own father was slain in one of the raids made by their soldiers."

"Aye, and that's why I've not stepped foot on it since I was a lad. No one's used it for many a year. But it's a sure enough way to cross over into the lowlands, and secretly. I can take you to the highside post. It's the way station this side of the mountains. Once you're there, you follow the track to the lowside post. It's not too far from Woodglence."

"Is it not watched?" Kal asked.

"Nay. There is no need for them to watch it. Folks learned to fear using it. Aye, and to fear the path itself. It's thought to be haunted by them that were killed for using it. It's got a black name now. Has for years. I'll take you there, but I'll not set foot on it. Never again."

"We'd be much obliged to you for your help."

Latryk made a dismissive gesture. "Nay, Master Aelward. It's me who's obliged."

"So long as you can direct us to this Traders' Trail of yours without delay," Kal said.

Latryk bowed his head. "As you wish. But I'll first see my wife and our children home safely. It's not far from our way."

The highland men removed the bodies of the slain troops from the road, concealing them in the underbrush that footed the nearby trees as the carter salvaged what he could of his pillaged load from the roadway. At Kal's bidding, Galli and Gwyn ran up the slope to gather the marsh ponies, then rejoined the company on the path. Following Latryk and his family in the cart, the companions went back up the road the way they had come, returning to the fork in the road that they had passed earlier. They turned to continue following Hoël's Dyke and, little more than a bowshot's distance farther along, left the path. A faint cart track veered off into the trees, its opening well disguised by foliage. A man hid there, who stepped out to challenge the group of strangers, but, recognizing Latryk, he let the company pass. A short while later, they crossed a rickety wooden bridge and reached a small settlement of scattered cottages nestled in the forest by a stream. Latryk led them to his home, where he left the care of the cart to his son as he unhitched the carthorse, replacing its harness for a badly worn saddle and bridle and bit. All the while, he explained what had happened to a pair of village men who had come to investigate the situation.

"Don't worry, Latryk," said one of them, a hardy fellow with a firm-set jaw and an open face. "We'll make sure the bodies are never found."

"Aye, that's good, but the sooner the better. I should be back by nightfall." Latryk turned to kiss his wife and children and then mounted the horse, an animal that dwarfed the marsh ponies.

Led by the charcoal burner, the company headed back to Hoël's Dyke. In short order, they left the road and entered the trees again, following a series of narrow trails, pressed and scratched on either side by the dense undergrowth. Eventually, the forest thinned and surrendered to a tamer countryside, one of open fields checkered by tended woodlots. These they skirted, clinging to the shadows until, at length, they reached the Westland Road, which they discovered to be in excellent repair, laid evenly with paving stones. They crossed it, alert for the least sign of traffic, and continued through open country marked by pastureland and here and there a copse. Slowly the gentle dip and swell of the land gave way to rising hills and thicker forest. Before them, the Bowstaff Mountains rose, dominating the eastern horizon. As the afternoon wore on, they climbed steeper terrain, following the spine of a series of ridges, the roots of the mountains thrusting up the slopes ahead of them.

The company came upon a narrow green valley, its verdure bounded on one side by the crag upon which they stood and on the other by a mountain's sheer side. The air above the rift in the mountainside resounded with the thunder of falling water. Above them, a cataract slipped down the rock face. On the valley floor, the waters formed a raging stream that boiled and pooled, then rushed through a tight gap in the walls that penned it in before tumbling recklessly down the flank of the mountain.

Latryk reined his horse down a trail that wound back and forth across the precipitous wall of the valley. Reaching the valley floor, he led the men along the purling stream towards the base of the waterfall. Kal and the others hung back for a moment, remaining a few paces behind. It was a dead end, or so it appeared, until, suddenly, Latryk was swallowed by the uneven wall of rock.

"Skell Force...," Kal muttered, then turned to Galli and yelled above the deafening roar of the waterfall, "It's like Skell Force at Tarn Cromar!" Galli nodded, and Kal urged his pony forward, drawing near the wall, at the verge of the shining cloud of mist and fine spray that footed the waterfall. He edged towards the spot where he had last seen Latryk, running his eyes over the rough face of rock, puzzled that he could discern no break in the stone. For an instant, fear seized his gut, as the thought of a trap about to be sprung leapt to his mind—here they were, caught in a narrow valley with no chance of escape. The pony shifted, as if sensing its rider's anxiety, and shuffled nervously to the side. It was then that Kal saw it, a subtle cleft in the wall where the stone split in two and doubled on itself, overlapping to create a gap. He swung down from his saddle and caught his pony by the bridle, then led the shy creature into a passage that opened wide enough to admit a packhorse. It was some five or six paces long and closed overhead like an arcade; the sight of sunlit grass ahead, however, prompted both man and beast forward.

When Kal emerged into the light, there lay spread out before him yet another small valley, as lush as the one he had just left. Here, however, the valley floor was scattered with a clutch of decrepit stone huts engulfed by weeds and thickets of scrub brush, their slate roofs crumbling and exposed in places to the rafters. Latryk sat atop his horse, staring at the scene before him, a distant, pensive look spread across his features.

"It's been a long time...Aye, a long time. I was a lad of fourteen when I was last here. Came with my father." The charcoal burner turned to face Kal, who was now joined by the others. One by one the men dismounted from their ponies and stood stretching their limbs. Latryk made a sweeping gesture with his arm. "The highside post, or what's left of it. Burners used to lay up here for the night, their pack animals laden with charcoal for the marchland smithies and forges. Often my father'd bring me and my younger brother with him. We'd water the horses and rub them down, and next day we'd stay here to do other jobs and keep the post while the men went over the pass to trade.

"Only once, before the death of Colurian, when times were less dangerous, did Father take us with him to the lowside post. Normally, though, we'd stay here. One day, he and the four others who had gone down with him never returned...." Latryk slipped into thought, staring at the hovels. Kal stroked the neck of his pony as he watched the charcoal burner.

"My brother and I waited five full days," the man continued. "When food ran low, we two made our way back home to the forest. It was a dark journey. Though we neither of us spoke it, we knew it in our hearts. And our mother knew of it before we'd even got home, for the Mindal made a habit of posting lists in Melgrun, lists of the men arrested by their tollmen for illegal trade. My father's name was on that list, posted four days after he'd crossed the mountains, and his companions' as well. They'd been taken in ambush just outside of Woodglence. Aye, we all knew well that to be arrested was as good as death. He never returned. Nor have I to this place, since that day. This is the highside post, and I'll go no farther, not a step."

Though his eyes had not left the man, Kal's hand paused on the neck of his marsh pony. "No farther?"

"It haunts me here, this place does. I feel my father's spirit here. Aye, and he's restless. . . . Taken in violence with none to sing him peace." Latryk lifted his eyes and scanned the air around him, distracted by somber thoughts laden with the pain of reawakened memories.

"What was his name?"

"Eh?"

"Your father, what was his name?"

"Ammath. His name was Ammath."

Kal nodded and dropped his hand from the pony to his codynnos and drew forth the small harp-shaped brooch. Beside him, Aelward took a step and leaned close, saying, "Kalaquinn . . ." in a hushed tone that bespoke caution.

Kal pinned the pios to his tunic and, as Latryk watched wide-eyed, drew a finger across the delicate wires and slowly intoned the syllables of the dead man's name. Though the pios made little more than a tinkling sound, Kal's voice rose resonant amid the cliff faces encircling the highside post. Three times he plucked the strings slowly, and three times he called the name, before he fell into measured lines in the ancient tongue. The mournful syllables hovered over the men as the bard sang the prayers of remembrance. In a few moments, Kal fell silent, and his song faded, leaving only the dull echo of the waterfall behind them.

Tears welled in the charcoal burner's eyes, and, while he made no attempt to speak, he cleared his throat and bowed his head. Aelward withdrew to where he had stood before.

"Come, now, Latryk. You must tell us where we are to go from here," Kal said, breaking the silence.

The charcoal burner looked at him, his eyes still damp, and said, "My thanks to you, bard."

Kal smiled and nodded. "Come, tell us where we must go now."

"Aye, aye, that I will," Latryk said, collecting himself. He turned to point across the valley. "The pass over the mountains to the lowside post runs through that gully, straight ahead there, beyond the last hut." He turned back to face Kal. "That's the Trader's Trail. Keep on the path. You'll find it impossible to stray from."

"Even now after many years of disuse?" said Kal.

"Aye, even now. Don't worry. It was well worn into the stone of the Bowstaffs. It'll take you to a cave that overlooks the Westland Road, not but three or four miles from Woodglence. That's the lowside post. It's half a day's journey from here. I suggest you lay out your beds and leave at first light."

"What about you, Master Burner?" said Broq.

"Well, if I leave now, I should reach the forest by nightfall. And that with a heart ever grateful to you that my children are not without a father, like me. And I think my own father's found some peace today." A crooked smile spread across Latryk's face, and he bowed to them. "Briacoil."

"Indeed, he has," Kal said. "Briacoil, Latryk, friend. May Wuldor guide your steps safely homeward."

The man bowed once more, then turned and walked his horse to the oblique opening in the cliff face and disappeared, swallowed again by the circling rock.

"Do you think that was wise?" Aelward said to Kal as the other men went about scouting the stone buildings of the highside post.

"What?"

"To have given away your identity as—"

"As simply a bard and no more," Kal said, fixing Aelward in a calm stare.

Aelward sighed and slowly shook his head, his lips drawn in a tight line across his grizzled face. "As simply a bard... That may be all a person needs to know these days to condemn you. Then all is lost."

"In these days, yes," Kal said. "But is not a man to be afforded some peace? Some consolation? Especially in these days? I mean, look at the man, Aelward. He is no danger to us."

"I hope not—"

"It was my duty. I am not worried by it."

Aelward ran a hand over the short hairs of his head and shrugged, arching an eyebrow. "That may be so," he said, "but still I would counsel you to be more cautious in the future. Far more cautious. But perhaps you have a better sense of these things than do I." The grey man laid a hand on Kal's shoulder. "Just be careful, Kalaquinn. You are the Hordanu, and, as Galli said, we cannot afford to lose you, especially through simple foolishness." Aelward nodded and turned away to join the others in their exploration of the structures.

They found two of the four stone huts in passably good repair, their floors and walls solid, still well-sealed against the elements. The remaining two structures, it seemed, had been stables, more roughly constructed and so more prone to the ravages of time. Once they had unsaddled the marsh ponies and watered them, they let the animals graze while they ate a cold supper from their supplies, too tired to bother lighting a fire. After that, although it was only dusk, and dark had not yet descended on the upland meadow, they settled the ponies in the old stables and spread their bedrolls in the two good huts. Braced by the cool, clear air of the mountains, they were quickly overcome with the sleep of exhaustion.

It was still dark, when Kal half woke and sensed with alarm that he was alone in the stone shelter. Aelward and Broq were gone. He sprang to his feet and rushed outside. Dawn was just beginning to uncover the long, deep shadows of night, slowly seeping its grey light into the mountain heights. Aelward and Broq were lifting saddles onto their marsh ponies.

"Ah, briacoil, Kal," Aelward said, looking over his shoulder. "I was just about to wake you. It's time for us to part ways and so go our separate journeys"

Kal rubbed his eyes and gaped dumbly. "W-What?" he stammered.

"You know that Broq and I must be off."

"So soon?" blurted Kal. "But I thought—"

"Indeed, so soon. Daybreak, I said last night, now that the charcoal burner has left us to return home—"

"With a tale about the six men he led over the mountain on marsh ponies," Broq said wryly. "An honest tale from an honest man, but not a true accounting of our numbers, once we part company. The misdirection makes both your journey and ours all the safer."

"Come, Broq, we must go. It's a long way to shipboard on the coast, and it's a way rendered that much longer by every step the two of us have trodden farther along this mountain trail."

"And from there across the sea to the wilds of Kevnÿek?" Kal asked.

"Aye, yes. And you to your own wildlands far to the east, my lord Hordanu," Aelward said, pulling hard on the saddle to test the tightness of the cinch.

"Until we meet next spring in Seabank."

"Until—" Aelward paused, his chiselled face strained, as he pulled his cinch tighter. "Until, if fate be kind, and Wuldor smiles on us, we meet next spring in Seabank." The tall man swung his leg over the marsh pony, looking slightly ridiculous astride the small animal. He looked at Kal and smiled, bowing his head. "And so, my lord Myghternos Hordanu, briacoil. Watch yourself with care. I pray Wuldor hold you ever in his eye."

"And I you. And you, Broq. Briacoil."

When Aelward and Broq had gone, Kal went to rouse the others, although he found Gwyn already stirring. Soon they were mounted on their marsh ponies and leaving the valley, heading east into the heart of the Bowstaff Mountains through the grassy straightway gap that lay beyond the last stone hut. In the growing light, they picked their way along the trail, following its serpentine twists and turns as it passed between the peaks to the marchlands. Sometimes it curled around sharp-edged mountain flanks over rocky ledges that fell away into dizzying drops. Sometimes they found themselves balanced on razor-backed ridges, panoramic vistas unfolding on either side. Other times they followed narrow defiles in gorges cut deep into the stone of the mountains. Soon their way began to fall, descending the leeward side of the Bowstaff range, often opening onto alpine meadows thickly carpeted with hardy flowers.

The charcoal burner had been correct. The trail was easy to follow. Short pillars, stones piled atop one another, marked the way at regular intervals. By midafternoon, after a brief rest beside a small stream, they entered a more wooded terrain with gentler slopes. Still they kept descending, until at length they reached an area where the trail continued level in an easterly direction, but winding southward all the while, through a great hardwood forest free of undergrowth. After they had gone the distance of a league, the trail came abruptly to an end, turning aside through dense woods, doglegging into a huge cavern. To the right ran a low ridge of rock with nothing but empty sky beyond, its edge a precipitous drop. They had reached the lowside post. As soon as they stepped inside it, they saw numerous signs of human habitation: slack-gated wooden animal stalls strewn with musty hay, leather-bound gourds and horse harness, now brittle with age, eating utensils and frayed, crumbling bed pallets, as well as other oddments.

"This place is as deserted as deserted can be," said Devved, looking about the cavern. He climbed from the back of his pony, picked up a broken-hilted sword and ran his hand along the nicked edges, dislodging a thick layer of dust. "Poor workmanship, too," he added.

"Now what, Kal? Shall we spend the night here?" Galli asked, standing beside Devved.

"Puts one in mind of the Cave of the Hourglass," said Kal. "Let's have a look outside."

Flanked by his companions he walked to the opening of the cavern and mounted the gradual rise of rock that girded one side of it like a breastwork, shielding it from prying eyes.

"Look at this! What a view!" cried Galli who was first to scramble up to the limit of the rock.

"Careful, Galli! You too, Gwyn. One wrong step and there'd be nothing left of you but hapless bits of carrion for the vultures and fellhawks," said Kal, who stood on the edge of a sheer cliff looking hundreds of feet down onto a road that snaked its way through a gorge.

"The Westland Road," Galli said.

"This way, lads. You're too easy to spot like that. Better to look from here," called Devved. His head bobbed up from a sunken crevice in the rocky surface that sloped at their feet.

Kal moved towards him and found a rounded portal hewn from the rock, with a short flight of stairs leading to a chamber just below the top of the escarpment, its one side open so that it afforded a clear view of the valley below.

"An observation post," Kal said.

"They must have used it to keep from being skylined to onlookers from below," Galli said.

"As you all just were, yes," said the blacksmith. "It's a perfect spot for smugglers who needed to keep an eye on the road without drawing attention to themselves."

Gwyn sidled up beside Kal and nudged him, pointing down to the road.

"Aye, it seems fairly well travelled, doesn't it?"

"That's not all, Kal," said Galli. "He means that you should mark the travellers themselves."

"Soldiers...," said Kal, squinting into the distance below. "Aye, soldiers marching up towards the mountains, to the Pass and Melgrun, I suppose. And wagons carrying timber."

Gwyn nudged Kal again, looked at him with meaning, and pointed to the section of the road nearer Woodglence, which lay to the east, faint wreathes of smoke marking its place on the Winfarthing River.

"Now I see.... Galli, see those two clusters of horsemen? You can see their livery and the pennons...." Kal grew silent and fell to musing as he peered down the valley, his mind drifting back to his school days in the Holding. He could still hear the tone and inflection of Landros's voice.

Bengonnar's red eagle glides
Above the Sheerness blue-grey sides.

The white seabird of Calathros' shores
O'er a sky-blue ocean soars.

Cor'gwella's deep, dark woodgreen cloak
Holds the mighty ashen oak.

Dowren, clad in purple gay,
Boasts the mythic Wyvern, fey.

Ewynek's sea-green capes embrace
Silver fish in swirling chase.

Melderenysian russet shores
Shall host a blue crown nevermore.

Oakapple Isles' soft sable-stoles,
Each a silver swan enfolds.

The Velinthian Bridge, in victory's stain,
Stretches on Orm's ochre plain.

Pelogran's sun-goldened heart
Bears black tools of forgeman's art.

South Wold wreathed in Radolan mist
Wears its grey with a sable fist.

Shining mountain, Tanobar's head,
Rises silver o'er fields deep red.

Thrysvar's sons in snow-white mantle
Bear his swords yet stained from battle.

And though the least, fair Lammermorn,
Holy Keep, Arvon's first-born,
Will ever in his arms enfold,
In deepest blue, the Harp of Gold.

"They're clan colours," Galli said at length. "The riders are dressed in colours."

"Clan colours, yes," said Kal, stirred from his reverie. "The highland clanholdings and keverangs—"

"Two parties of them, each with a pennon bearer. Yellow surcoats for Orm, or is it Pelogran, and dark red—must be Tanobar, although I can't make out the actual devices. But they're clan colours. I'm sure of it."

"Orm's is a darker yellow. And if it's Pelogran, it'll be a black hammer and anvil—"

"Of course! And a shining mountain, Myst-Hakel, silver on the dark red tunics of Tanobar."

"Your boyhood lessons remembered, too, eh, Galli?" Kal said, looking down upon the road again. "It must be a formal embassy or a state occasion of some kind, something that requires the personal attendance of the thanes and their retainers. It's the only reason they'd be in colours." Kal fell silent. "I wonder...," he continued after a moment and turned away from the opening. "Something's afoot." He turned back to face his companions. "Listen, we've easily a few hours before dark. That's time and enough to slip into Woodglence, gain some sense of what is occurring, and slip out again."

"Are you mad? The place will be crawling with Gawmage's troops. Besides, we've a long enough journey ahead of us as it is, without making sidetrips to Woodglence."

"No, it must be done. Who knows but that the success of our mission hangs on the knowledge we gain about the enemy and his designs? It won't take us but an hour there and an hour back on foot. According to Latryk, we're not three or four miles from Woodglence."

"Listen to Galli, Kal," Devved said. "The place is like to be thick with Dog's Heads. If not Ferabek's Scorpions besides."

"That much the more danger. Devved's right," Galli said.

"I didn't say I mind the danger, lad." Devved grinned, crossing his thick arms.

"Still, there is danger," Kal said, "and we will mind it, Devved. We'll stay on the edge of town, test the waters, and gather what information we may without running any risks."

Leaving the edge of the precipice, they hurried back to the cavern. There they unsaddled the ponies and watered them at a spring near the entrance, which bubbled up into a pool walled in by four square sides of fitted stone. After taking their own fill of the water and wolfing down a hasty meal, they put the animals to pasture in a paddock behind a tumbledown fence that adjoined the traders' haven and set off on foot, carrying only their weapons and night pouches.

Beyond the paddock, the ground folded into a ravine, where they discovered a bleached horse's skull that marked the remains of a trail. The track's broad stony bottom still held back the weeds and brush, even now after many years, making travel easy. They descended the sloping ravine for a couple of miles until it levelled to a flat stretch of woods, which opened in turn onto fields and fencerows. The sounds of lowing cattle could now be heard and the occasional cries of children at play. Ahead of them, the trail dipped down a long hill through a copse to a wide dirt roadway, a scattering of dwellings on either side. These gave way to a dense tangle of streets and buildings crowded around the coiling flow of the Winfarthing River, its glistening waters thick with water traffic.

Kal's pulse quickened. The Holdsmen stopped in hesitation. They had reached the outskirts of Woodglence. Somewhere a dog barked and a door slammed shut. Then a louder sound rang out in the summer evening air. Devved's face erupted into a smile. It was the familiar clang of hammer on anvil, and it came from one of the buildings nearby, to their left.

"There, that's a smithy," Devved said, nodding his head in the direction of a low stone building. "There's as good a place as any to get a notion of the happenings hereabouts."

"Let's have a look, but be careful," Kal said as they moved out onto the road, the hammer blows sounding louder. Suddenly, he stopped in his tracks and turned to his companions.

"That sign—what do you make of it?"

"It's just a shop sign, Kal. I had one myself," Devved said. "In the case of a blacksmith, it's usually the mark he stamps on his work as well."

"But this one? What does it signify?" Kal said.

"It looks to me like a bridge," Galli said.

"Look at the piers of the bridge. What do they look like, if you were to turn them over?" Kal said.

"What are you driving at, lad?" Devved said.

Galli considered for a moment, and then his face lit up. "The piers, yes, they look like the points of a crown, a crown laid upside down," he said.

"I think so," said Kal. "Put the two together and you get—"

"Crownsbridge! You mean—"

"Indeed, just that! Crownsbridge!"

"What are you two on about?" growled Devved.

"I remember your father telling us about it, Kal," Galli said, ignoring the blacksmith.

"Devved, Crownsbridge was where the main barracks of the Life Guardsmen were located. Just outside of Dinas Antrum," Kal said. "And the crown like that, wrong side up. A crown overthrown perhaps? The fall of King Colurian? I'd wager this fellow was a Life Guardsman."

"Either you're a fey dreamer, Kalaquinn Wright, or as Hordanu you see what others don't see," the blacksmith said.

"Not Kalaquinn. And not Hordanu," Kal said.

"What are you on about?" Devved asked.

"Call me Kalestor, or Kal," he replied. "Kalaquinn may be a name that is being hunted. Should anyone ask, my name is Kalestor. And of course you can still call me Kal. I am not Kalaquinn, and I am certainly not the Hordanu. Mind that, Devved, Galli."

Kal quickened his pace towards the open doors of the shop. The clanging stopped. A man in his late forties, of middling height, slight in build and wiry, looked up from his anvil, his face glistening with sweat. The long fingers of his right hand were clasped around a hammer, while his left hand gripped the tang of a hiltless sword in a pair of heavy tongs, the fire-stained blade smouldering with heat.

"A fine-looking blade you have there," Kal said.

The smith considered the men at the door for a moment with

wide, coal-black eyes that shone beneath a shock of unruly grey hair. There was a distinct mousiness about the man, Kal decided, that made him seem somewhat ill-suited to his place by the anvil; yet, Kal could see from the forgework that filled the corners of the shop that there was little question as to the man's ability in the trade. The smith closed one eye and, with the other, peered down the length of the blade, examining the trueness of his handiwork.

"A man needs a good weapon these days," he said.

"Why so?" said Kal.

"These are dangerous times. You're strangers here," said the smith more by way of statement than question, a squint of suspicion in his eye as he looked at the visitors to his forge again. "One of you a Telessarian, and the rest of you highlanders by the look of things." He returned his attention to the blade in his hand. "An odd company these days."

"No odder than a blacksmith in Woodglence who makes Crownsbridge his mark," Kal said.

The man looked up at Kal and slowly lowered the unfinished sword to the anvil. "What of it, lad?"

"I'd venture a guess, if I knew no better, that you were once a' Royal Life Guardsman," Kal hazarded, holding the man in a steady gaze.

"And what if I was?" The smith's tone was cold and dismissive, and he lifted the blade's edge to his eye again.

"Then there would be a bond of sorts between us," Kal replied.

The smith snorted brusquely. "You've a right strange sense of humour, lad. Why, you weren't even born when I—" His manner grew suddenly more wary, and he placed the blade into the forge's belly and snatched out another, glowing yellow, which he placed on the anvil and fell to shaping with solid hammer strokes amid showers of sparks.

"When you served? No, but my father was. It was he that served as a Royal Life Guardsman. Frysan was his name...from Pelogran."

The blacksmith laid down sword and tool on the anvil and scratched at his tangled grey mop of hair. His manner had changed, as quickly as fire-angered steel is tempered when plunged in the smith's brine. He glanced up at Kal.

"I remember a Frysan fellow vaguely. He was probably of the other camp."

"The other camp?"

"The king's camp. The true king's camp," the smith said, lowering his voice and looking about him with the air of a conspirator. "In defiance of the Mindal."

"In defiance of the Mindal?"

"They were good men, and honourable. Though I'm careful to whom I'd say that. But I've a good sense about you all." He picked up the hammer and pointed it at the men standing in his smithy's doorway. "Aye, I've a good sense about you all. You saw the Crownsbridge and knew it for what it was." He lifted his hammer to strike the steel again, but thought better of it and returned the cooled blade to his forge.

"Good men, and honourable? That would have been my father. Of the other camp, as you say. He left the service rather than bend to the Mindal."

A look of pained sadness passed over the blacksmith's face. "I stained my honour. I sided with Baldrick and his lot." He shook his head. "The times were uncertain. I was young and easily swayed. I've spent years now seeking to make amends, siding with those who resist Gawmage and the Mindal."

"And your name, Master Blacksmith?" Devved asked.

"Tromwyn Tressilias, born and raised in Woodglence here." The blacksmith smiled, lifting his head. "We're fellow tradesmen, I see. I can tell by your arm, and the eye you have for the forge."

"A well-placed guess, Tromwyn Tressilias. True and on the mark," Kal said.

"As was yours, Master...?"

"Kalestor," Kal said, "And these are my companions, Galligaskin, Gwyn, and Devved, a fellow forgeman to you."

"I bid you welcome, all." Tromwyn grinned and bobbed his head, setting the disheveled grey thatch atop it to flight. Kal could not help but grin himself, for it was obvious that the expressions of jocundity better sorted with the face and manner of this marchland blacksmith than did those of wariness and suspicion.

"But what brings you to the door of my forge this fine evening, friends?" the blacksmith asked.

"We travel through these parts from Pelogran. It was Devved that heard the ringing of your hammer and anvil, and Devved that encouraged us to stop in. We have been travelling by little-trod ways these past few weeks and have had little occasion to learn of the recent happenings in Arvon, though we've seen strange traffic on the roads. Devved suggested that a forge is as good a place as any to gain knowledge of events."

As Kal spoke, he turned to nod to the big man standing beside him, and, as he did, the edge of his cloak pulled back, exposing the hilt of Rhodangalas. Tromwyn stared at the ornate grip and forward quillion that poked out from cover. Then, blinking, he looked up at Kal.

"Ah, a fine-looking blade you have there," he said.

Kal lifted the edge of his cloak over the sword again. "A man needs a good weapon these days."

"Aye, indeed, he does," Tromwyn said, his brow furrowing slightly. "Indeed, he does." Then, as if coming to some decision, he nodded and met Kal's look, his black eyes wide and glinting in the low light of the forge. "So, travellers from Pelogran in need of a reckoning of the recent happenings in the world at large," he said and smiled. "That's all you need tell me. And if it's a reckoning you want, then there's only one place in Woodglence to be—the Mourning Crown. Aye, that's where I'll take you lot."

Kal glanced nervously at his companions. The blacksmith caught the look and chuckled. "You've naught to worry you, Kalestor, friend," he said. "The Crown's an inn on the riverside, and its keeper is a good man, loyal, a Life Guardsman, too, or was. Paerryn's his name. Come"—the blacksmith turned back to the brands in his fire—"give me a moment to close my forge, and I'll take you there."

"Allow me to lend you a hand, Tromwyn," Devved said, stepping to the forge. The marchlander smiled, and the two blacksmiths fell into banter as Galli and Gwyn waited outside, looking at the town lying below them, and Kal paced restlessly, his hand set on the hidden hilt of Rhodangalas and his on mind on leaving Woodglence as soon as possible.

Less than half an hour later, led by the marchland blacksmith, they left the forge and started down the road into the town.

TWENTY-SIX

Woodglence lay sprawled along both banks of the upper Winfarthing River, its buildings, in varied states of decrepitude, leaning against one another as if wearied by the fret of trade and industry that absorbed the town. The group of men passed without drawing undue notice through the rabbit warren of filthy rutted streets and narrow alleys. Occasionally, they were caught in a swirl of children at play that would burst around one corner only to disappear noisily around the next. Old men and old women sometimes looked as the group passed and either scowled at them or smiled toothlessly. Once a cur leapt from a shadowed doorway and stood to challenge the men, its hackles bristling as it growled and barked. Its mistress emerged from the same door, broom in hand, and berated the creature, calling it to heel and begging the pardon of the startled men. For the most part, however, the men were simply ignored as they made their way through the town. The whole time, Kal noted, Tromwyn kept a hand not far from the hilt of his sword.

There were beggars there, too, many of them, both young and old, and all wore the same drawn expression that openly advertised their plight. To each beggar they passed Tromwyn gave a small copper piece, with a nod and a smile or a brief word of solace.

"It usen't to be like this," he said to Kal as he walked on after giving one old crone her coin. "I grieve to see what has happened to the folk here."

"What do you mean?" Kal asked.

"I'm sorry. I shouldn't worry you with my own concerns."

335

"No, please, I would know. What has befallen your people?"

Tromwyn cast a quick glance to either side. "I'd not say this openly, else my neck might get stretched," he said. "But to a high-lander such as yourself... Well, it angers me. Thirty-so years past, this was a thriving and wholesome town. Pride of the marchlands, without doubt. But in the last years of the king, with the rise of the Mindal's power, and since then... Well, few here rose with the Mindal, you might say, only the few that control the flow of trade by road or river. Or the handful of mill owners, millwrights, and leading timbermen. They did right by themselves, I'd say. But the rest fell. Aye, and fell hard, too. Many took to smuggling simply to survive, though that proved to have an even higher cost in the end. But a man does what he can, or sometimes what he must.

"Me, I went for the Guardsmen as a youngling—honour, glory, prestige, and the like. A young man's dreams, eh? But when the Mindal disbanded us, I saw what was coming, so I came back here to do what I could. I do well enough for myself. The shop is busy, a steady bit of mill work. Something's always broken at one of the mills and in need of mending at my forge. Aye, but there's not much left for most folk now, naught but work in the forest, if a body's able, or in the mills. Most of the wealth leaves the town. Aye, and so does most of the hope of life, it seems."

The marchland smith continued to speak to Kal, but the Holdsman's mind wandered. Indeed, the townsfolk had the air of a people broken by the vagaries of life under the iron fist of the Mindal. But there was more to it, Kal knew. Life was resilient. It could be seen in the flash of a coin given by a blacksmith in solidarity with a beggar, and in the nod and smile in recognition of the gift and the message it conveyed. No, hope was a hard thing to kill. These folk would survive, even as his own had, though it might be an even harder road ahead.

Glancing down a broad side street, Kal caught a glimpse of the grey stone dome of the glence from which the town had gained its name. The noble structure had at one time stood just outside of the village in an ancient wood along the river. The forest, however, had long since been pushed back, its trees felled and turned into a clutter of buildings that surrounded the glence and crawled away in all directions from it along fetid and muddy lanes. These structures in turn fell down to be overgrown by yet another generation of narrow houses, shops, and hovels. All around him, it all looked the same—the great sagging piles of the latest growth mounded over the remains of the past.

They turned another corner, and it occurred to Kal that he had lost all sense of direction in the maze of lanes beneath the overhanging dwellings. A young man stopped as the group passed him by and fixed Kal with a hard-edged stare of, or so it seemed to the Holdsman, defiant malice. Kal shot a glance back over his shoulder. The young man remained still, watching the group's progress, a cruel-looking dirk thrust in his belt, his hand restive upon its grip.

He had been a fool! Here he had entrusted himself, his life, the lives of his companions, and, for that matter, the lives of every free man, woman, and child in all of Ahn Norvys to this black-smith, this stranger, who was, for all Kal knew, a rank impostor leading them to their very ruin. His heart skipped in his chest, and, in his agitation, he lifted Rhodangalas in its sheath beneath his cloak. Tromwyn caught the movement beside him and looked at the Holdsman quizzically, but before Kal could say or do any-thing, they moved around another corner and out into the bright early evening sunshine of the riverside.

"Ah, here we are, then," the marchlander said. "It's up this way a piece." He set off to the left, along the broad cobbled street that edged the river.

The air was washed clean of the town's stench by a breeze blowing downriver from the mountains that bore the strong scent of freshly sawn lumber. Even this close to its source, the Winfarthing River was broad, fed by both the Radolan and the Bowstaff mountains, and deep enough to harbour river craft. Colourful banners snapped in the wind from the mastheads and lines of river sloops docked nearby. Kal looked to his right. Just upriver, on the opposite bank, a massive structure overshadowed the water, a huge waterwheel slowly turning beside it and a jumble of sluices, spillways, and slips running this way and that around its sides. Farther upstream, there was another mill on the near bank, just visible as the river bent away beneath a long bridge set on high, arching stone pillars. Kal knew that there must be other sawmills along the river out of view, for moored across the green water was a vast fleet of barges, their loads of squarely stacked lumber gleaming golden white in the evening sunlight, ready, no doubt, to be floated downstream through lowland Arvon to Dinas Antrum.

Kal strode quickly to catch up with the others. People pressed about him on the crowded riverside road as they moved about their business—pedlars, tradesmen, boatmen, merchants, townsfolk, and small knots of travellers, some of whom wore the distinctive livery of their homeland keverang or clanholding. Horses and carts rattled along the cobbles in either direction, and men shouted orders, insults, and curses at one another as they tramped up and down gangplanks or swung bulging nets from makeshift derricks, lading small ships for the downriver run.

"How much farther is it?" Kal asked as he caught up with Tromwyn.

"Not much. But a minute or two's walk."

"The Mourning Crown?"

"Aye, not the best inn in Woodglence, mind, but the safest. The keeper's a good man, one of a mind with me—and with you, I'd wager," Tromwyn said and grinned. "Come, you needn't be crabbed. There's naught to worry—"

"Master smith, a moment of your time, if we may." A soldier stepped in front of the group of men, blocking their path. Three others stepped smartly in behind him, pikemen, all in the dark green tunics of Glastanen, though the leader's voice had no hint of the marchland accent in it. Kal exchanged anxious glances with his fellow Holdsmen as Tromwyn lifted his hand away from the hilt of his sword and addressed the soldier.

"What do you want, then, Kyven?"

"Only that you state your business, and that of your friends here." The soldier looked slowly from one Holdsman to the next.

"What? Are strangers to Woodglence no longer welcome here? If it be so, Kyven, then you'd best look to yourself and your men—"

"And you'd do well to look to your tongue, smith. There are many strangers here, and all must give an accounting. The thanes travel through Woodglence, and we must ensure their safety. So, please, state your business."

Tromwyn raised a hand in gesture of peace and bowed his tousled grey head to the side, then discreetly winked to Kal. His black eyes sparkled, and he looked to Devved.

"This is Devved, a fellow blacksmith and a guildmaster from the Clanholding of Pelogran. He has come with his apprentices"—the marchland smith sidestepped with a sweep of his arm—"one even from as far as Telessar, as you can see, to lodge at my forge—an honour by which I am more than humbled—on his way to Dinas Antrum. He has been summoned by the Mindal's smithmaster to present himself and receive honour for the excellence of his craft, even at this most significant moment in our history." Out of the corner of his eye, Kal could see Devved pull himself to his full height and swell his chest. The soldier looked discomfited at the news but was committed to his course and had to play it out as best he could. He hastily surveyed the group of men again.

"You are armed," he ventured in a tone of authority that lacked conviction.

"Aye, what of it? These are dangerous times."

"But ... bows—"

"Aye, bows. And any highlander worthy of the name wouldn't be caught without one, not in these days. Particularly highlanders who enjoy the favour of the Mindal."

"Yes, the, ah, Mindal ..." The sergeant's eyes drifted to the cobbles at his feet as his men fidgeted behind him.

Tromwyn coughed delicately. "I'm sure my friend would gladly provide you with papers in evidence of his ... ah, business, if you desired to see them, Sergeant. Of course, obstruction of the Mindal's business ..." The blacksmith paused a moment as the soldier's mouth worked silently at expressing some unformed thought. Then he nodded and said, "I was about showing my guests the town. We were just on our way to slake our thirst at the Boatman's Gaff. Perhaps you and your men would care to join us?"

The soldier came to himself quickly. "Ah ... No, Tromwyn, thank you, thank you kindly. We must be about our duties—"

"And we ours. So, then, I will bid you a good evening, Kyven."

"Ah, yes, yes. Briacoil to you," the soldier blurted and shuffled out of the way to let the blacksmith and his companions pass.

When they had walked out of earshot, the blacksmith began to laugh. Kal glowered at him. "What were you thinking?" he demanded.

"What? Ah, be not alarmed, Kalestor, I simply bluffed a bluffer—"

"Aye, Kal," Devved said. The big man grinned broadly. "What's the matter? That was a fine jest. Just fine. To think, me the master smith, you three my 'prentices!"

"And you, called to Dinas Antrum by the Mindal itself, too!" Kal fairly growled the words and rounded on the two smiths, stopping them in the middle of the road. "And what if he had pressed for some proof of those fine words so easily spoken? What would you have to show, Devved? Tromwyn?" He looked one to the other. "I don't think you—either of you—fully appreciate our situation. I think..." Kal faltered in his anger. Gwyn moved to his side, his expression stolid.

"It was a brazen lie, and foolhardy," Kal said at last.

"Peace, Kalestor, peace," Tromwyn said and raised his hands in a placating gesture, looking from Kal to Gwyn to Galli, then back to Kal. "Come, friends!" he said and laughed again. "Aye, it was a brazen lie, but the brazen got the beat of the lie! Kyven is a swaggerer, a braggart and a boaster. The one thing he is not is brave. And fear can be made a ready ally, if one but knows how to woo her." The marchlander winked suggestively. "Aye, at the first mention of the Mindal, he quakes like a leaf in a gathering storm. The sergeant wants nothing to do with that band of thieves—not any more than the rest of us here do. He'll not press you any further. Come, the Mourning Crown is just at this corner. We'll slip around back of the Crown and go in by way of the kitchens. We can see and not be seen that way."

The blacksmith had a winning way about him, and Kal found that he was quickly mollified and reassured by the man's confidence. He had managed them out of a tight situation, that much was certain. Perhaps he was to be trusted. Either way, there was nothing for it now but to follow and watch and listen.

Tromwyn led the four men farther along the row of shops that fronted the riverside road until they came to a narrow alley that flanked a building from which hung a heavy wooden signboard on an iron bracket. On the board was painted an ornate black crown, nothing else. The marchlander shot a glance up and down the road and, content that they were being ignored in the bustle of foot traffic, slipped into the alley, its shadows deepening in the gentle light of day's end. The Holdsmen followed him closely between high walls until the passage ended at a gate that gave onto a small courtyard in which a clutch of scraggy chickens and a pair of ill-tempered hogs scrounged through a scattering of kitchen scraps.

The blacksmith lifted the latch of the gate and stepped gingerly across the yard to a rough lean-to structure, fenced off from the animals by another rickety gate. The blacksmith bade the Holdsmen leave off their weapons—swords, bowstaves, and quivers—and stow them out of sight in the shed to avoid attracting unwanted attention in the tavern. Kal felt vulnerable without the weight of Rhodangalas at his hip as he watched Tromwyn pick his way across the courtyard to a door, upon which he rapped loudly. The blacksmith did not await a response, but, grinning at his companions, allowed himself into the back of the inn. The sound of voices raised in laughter, the clang of pots and pans, and the sizzle of cooking, mixed with the savoury odour of roasted meats and frying onions, spilled out into the dirty courtyard. The Holdsmen piled into the bustling kitchen behind the blacksmith.

"Tromwyn!" Half a dozen voices lifted in greeting.

"To see and be unseen, indeed," Kal whispered to Galli, who nodded and arched an eyebrow beneath his winding browmark.

"Aye, Trom! Come to see me again, have you, my love?" said a short woman of enormous girth, holding a large wooden spoon. "Missed me, then, did you?"

"Well, missed your cooking!"

"You'll not be stealing anything from my platter," she scolded, patting him on the backside with her spoon.

"Naught but this tasty morsel," the blacksmith said, plucking a bit of roasted chicken from a board, where it was being carved by a laughing man, and tossing it into his mouth. "But I will pay you for it," he said and leaned over to give her a peck on the cheek.

The fat woman's flushed face glowed a deeper crimson and folded in upon itself, her immense bosom jostling as she chuckled. "Ah, Trom, you old sausage!"

"Aye, sausage it is, Mearie. So, you'll fix me up something nice to eat? Something for me and my friends?"

"And who have we here, then, Trom?" The fat woman turned to look at the four Holdsmen as if noticing them for the first time.

"Just old friends passing through Woodglence—"

"A bit young, most of them, to be old friends, eh, Trom?" she said, and smiled. "Come to see Paerryn, then, have you?"

"That, and sample the best cookery in Woodglence."

"Ah, go on with you!"

"Is he about?"

"Aye, Trom, you'll find him in the front. I'll send word for him to look for you—aye, Sahn...Sahn!" She called to a young boy who stood stirring a cauldron of stew at the hearth. "Leave off that and go tell your master that Tromwyn would like a word with him. And be smart about it." She turned back to the men. "You lot can go in and take your place. I'll send you along something shortly."

"You're a dear, Mearie, a dear."

"That may be so, Trom, but mind, my love, I've got my eye on you—"

"And I'd not have it any other way!" The blacksmith stooped to kiss the jocund woman again. She received the kiss, giggling, then turned back to direct the order of her kitchen, issuing a series of good-natured commands to her staff as if making up for lost time.

Smiling, the marchlander led the Holdsmen through an open door, along a short hallway and into a hall filled with voices, smoke, and mirth.

Kal surveyed the room and its occupants. Most seemed to be townsfolk cheerfully engaged in talk, but here and there were groups of men in the habit and gear of various local courts—courts local, however, not to Woodglence, or even Glastanen, but to the scattered clanholdings and keverangs of northwestern Arvon. Among these groups, some men carried themselves with an air of dignity, even haughtiness, and seemed, by their very presence, to command from those around them a respect and deference—thanes, no doubt, Kal thought to himself, or their appointed emissaries. There must have been four or five such figures, and Kal, by the livery surrounding them, identified Calathros, Tanobar, and Bengonnar, at least. And there was Pelogran, also. They would have to avoid that company if they were to maintain the soundness of their story.

Kal followed his companions to where Tromwyn had taken a seat at a table, one of the few left unoccupied in the inn, in the back corner of the hall next to the cold hearth. An empty table stood between them and the nearest group of patrons.

Tromwyn leaned forward, resting his elbows on the table. "Well, lads," he said in a low voice, "if it's news you'd be after, then there's naught better a place to be than in the Mourning Crown. And naught a better soul to get it from than Paerryn. A king's man he was, through and through, though that's a bit of knowledge he'd not want made too public. Mind you, most folk know it's so, and there's few who'd want to help the Mindal in any way at all. And those who might know full well that most folk in Woodglence would not suffer them to do so. Aye, Paerryn's a good sort. I'd trust him as I would myself—" Tromwyn glanced up. "Ah, and here he comes."

Moving slowly through the crowded room came a tall, thin man, an apron tied around his waist and five clay pots of ale clutched in his two hands. He nodded to patrons as he approached the corner table, exchanging words of greeting or the occasional rejoinder and quick laugh to a proffered quip, until, at last, he laid the five pots on the table in front of Tromwyn and stood wiping his hands on his apron. The man had a narrow face, hooded eyes under bristling wiry brows, a long raptorial nose, and a mouth that, though ready to smile, did not find a smile its natural form.

"Briacoil, Trom. A good evening to you."

"And to you, Master Paerryn. Will you join us?"

The innkeeper took a quick look around the room, gestured to another man in an apron, then said, "Aye, I can, for a wee bit, at least." He pulled up a chair from the empty table behind him, and sat, legs splayed, backwards on the seat, leaning on the chair's back. He eyed the four Holdsmen questioningly as the blacksmith set in place the ales, one before each of his companions. "Friends of yours, Trom?"

"Aye, of mine...and of the crown."

"Indeed?" The thin innkeeper looked at him, then again at the Holdsmen. "Friends of the crown? Well, sirs, you are welcome here. Any friend of the crown is a friend in the Crown." He glanced over his shoulder, then returned his attention to the men. "How might I be of service to you this evening?"

Kal grew wary. To his mind drifted the image of Old Golls, Persamus Meade, with his open face and broad smile between hanging jowls, looking so welcoming, so avuncular, just the sort of man to confide in—to one's peril! Kal left his ale untouched and fixed the innkeeper with a level gaze.

"We are but travellers through these parts that have had the good fortune of making the acquaintance of Tromwyn, a fellow smith to Devved here." Kal laid a hand on his companion's thick shoulder. "I am Kalestor, and this is Galli. And this, Gwyn." Kal nodded to his friends in turn. "We have been travelling the byways these past few weeks and have not had occasion to learn the recent happenings in Arvon, though by the look of things on the roads and in Woodglence here, there is much to learn. Tromwyn brought us here, saying that you were a man to know."

"And from whence do you hail? Ah," the innkeeper said and raised a hand, "forgive me. It is you that seek information, not I. I should not have asked."

"No, Master Paerryn, it is a just question. We are from Pelogran, recently. But our business, you understand, we will keep to ourselves. So, what news is there?"

Paerryn nodded, though his eyes narrowed slightly. Tromwyn seemed to sense the innkeeper's suspicion.

"Peace, good innkeep, all is well." Tromwyn smiled and slapped Kal's back gently. "Our young friend here is too modest. In truth, he is son to a Life Guardsman, so he has told me. Son to one Frysan, who quit the Guard rather than turn Mindal, to his credit."

Kal lowered his head. Fear clawed his gut. Beside him, Devved scowled and Galli and Gwyn exchanged quick glances. Instinctively, Kal reached for the grip of Rhodangalas beneath the table, but realized, in the instant, that, even had he his weapon, there would be no fighting his way out of this.

"Indeed? The son of a Life Guardsman?" the thin innkeeper said, raising a bristling eyebrow.

"Aye," Kal said, looking up at the man. "But I think our new friend oversteps his bounds. Come, will you share what news there is to be had, or will you not?"

"Come, come, Kalestor. There is no call to be nettlesome. Tromwyn is trustworthy, as am I. Both of us have seen action in the service of the king, though it be years ago now, eh, Trom?" The blacksmith looked somewhat crestfallen at having been chastened, but nodded his agreement. Paerryn leaned away from the table. "Well, now...The news of happenings in Arvon. Its telling may take longer than I have time to afford you."

"We will be grateful for whatever you can spare us," Kal said, forcing a smile and bowing his head in an attempt to humour the innkeeper.

"Very well. As you can see, there are many travellers abroad. Most notable ones, at that. Lord Ferabek has called a council—"

"You would call him 'lord'?" Devved interrupted.

"Aye, it's prudent to do so, given the nature of the times in which we live."

Kal placed a hand on Devved's arm. "My apologies, Master Paerryn. Please, do go on."

"Aye, well, he has called a council—a Convocation he calls

it—of all the lords of the counties, clanholdings, and keverangs of Arvon. Many have already passed through Woodglence in the past two days. Many more still may. The council is set to begin in little more than a week's time. It is supposed that he intends to assert his authority. No doubt he'll play the puppet Gawmage until Gawmage is no longer useful. Then he'll dispense of him. And I'd not be surprised if he, with every manor seat in Arvon vacant during the gathering, moves Scorpions to fill them all. Aye, but that's no more than idle chatter, that." The innkeeper paused and again looked behind him over the noise-filled hall.

"And Lammermorn's fallen," he said as he turned back to the table. "No doubt that news, at least, has reached your ears."

"Aye, sadly, it has. And the Talamadh taken as trophy to Dinas Antrum, I've heard also," Kal said.

"Indeed. So not all is news to you, then."

"No, not all is news. But what else of the Boar of Gharssûl?"

"Well, Lord Ferabek has indeed taken the Talamadh to Dinas Antrum. He intends to have Messaan sing the Summer Loosening on it, to begin ten days of pomp, before the council begins in earnest."

"What of the true Hordanu? Any news of Master Wilum?"

"No, none. Only rumours. It is said that the Stoneholding was completely destroyed by Black Scorpion Dragoons, with all who were in it as well. It is said that the High Bard perished there, and that the Great Glence itself is fallen. If that be so, then these are dark days, aye, dark days indeed." The innkeeper fell silent. For a while, no one spoke.

At length Kal broke the lull in conversation. "Aye, these are dark days, darker than any in a long, long while," he said. "But what of the thanes? You said many had travelled this way."

"Aye, thanes and their retainers, their liegemen, their emissaries, and some of them, their henchmen. Look you there . . . ," Paerryn said, pointing with his thumb to a group of revelers dressed in bright blue surcoats, each affixed with the image of a white seabird with wings outstretched. "Calathros. And there," he continued, indicating now a party clad in deep red, each man with a silver mountain embroidered on his chest, "that's the thane of Tanobar and his retinue. Aye, the thanes travel, you see. Here one, there another. Never has Woodglence seen such a fuss and bother.

"Melderenys arrived today. . . ." The thin innkeeper bent his frame over the chair again, settling into a story. "Aye, and there's news there to be told. It seems that tragedy has visited that house. It was the young lord, Lysak his name, that arrived this morning with his men. And a surly lot they are, too." Kal looked up first at Paerryn then at Galli. "Aye, you've heard?" the innkeeper said. Kal shook his head and encouraged him to continue with a gesture of his open hand.

"Well, the young lord has taken his father's place after the old thane was most brutally slain. Word has it that it was their neighbouring seaholding, the Oakapple Isles, that killed him. Uferian, the lord of the Isles, was next to dead himself and only recently restored to health. And a wonder that, too. He, saved from gravest illness. It is he that's been accused of rebelling against Torras—that'd be the thane of Melderenys, or the dead thane, leastwise. Torras claimed all the isles of both seaholdings as his own by right. Uferian murdered him, or so reports seem to claim. Mind you, Kalestor, as the most vocal condemnations come from the new lord of Melderenys, the arrogant strut-cock, Lysak, I have my doubts about its truth. Lysak's too friendly with Gawmage and Ferabek to be trusted.

"Anyway, we've had strangers aplenty in Woodglence these days, so you should be able to pass through here without being noticed, if that's your intention. Just follow the stream of livery down the Westland Road. Or down the Winfarthing, if you prefer. There's more than one pretty boat being decked out for the journey east."

"My thanks, Paerryn, for your intelligence," Kal said, bowing his head to the thin man. "You'll forgive us, however, if we keep our intentions to ourselves. Be content to know that our allegiance lies with the king and the old order of things, and that we are about the king's business, you might say, finishing something that my father began many years ago."

"Aye, that I will, Kalestor," the innkeeper said, then leaned even farther over the chair. "But perhaps you might better share with me than I with you how things fell out in Lammermorn?"

Kal gripped the edge of the table. Beside him, his fellow Holdsmen stirred.

"Master Paerryn," Kal said with slow precision, "I am not sure that I follow your meaning."

The innkeeper pushed himself away from the table and smiled. "Come, Kalestor, I served long in the Life Guardsmen. Perhaps too long. But in my time, I knew but a handful of men named Frysan in the service of the Crown, and only two were highlanders. By the cast of your face, the sound of your voice, I know you for your father's son. And he was no more from Pelogran than I am from Arvisium. If I guess aright, and I'd wager I do, you are of Lammermorn, and have escaped the Boar's rage, if only for the time being."

"Aye, Master Paerryn, you do guess aright, and I'll not play at denying it. I, and a few others, have escaped the destruction of the Stoneholding and the Boar's rage, and we'd like to keep it that way. The Great Glence is fallen and the Hordanu dead. More than that I will not say—"

"Other than that you are about the king's business and finishing the work of a highland Life Guardsman?" The thin man raised an eyebrow.

"I will say no more."

"There is really little more to say. There is little that could be done for a deposed and dead king.... But there is one thing you might attempt?"

"I will say no more, Master Paerryn. I ask that you press me no further," Kal said. A strained quiet settled over the table, and the Holdsmen sat, staring at Kal, who was ashen and shaking. Not one day out of Aelward's keeping, he castigated himself bitterly, not one day, and already he had broken the man's sage counsel.

"Whatever it is, whatever you venture, let me join you." Tromwyn broke the stillness, speaking in a hoarse whisper, his black eyes wide and flashing with eagerness.

"No," Kal said, not looking up from the table. "Will you let us depart, Paerryn? Will you permit us to leave now, or will you raise the alarm? Call the guard? Turn us over?" Kal lifted his eyes from the coarse-grained boards to the thin man across from him. "I've no doubt that there is a rich purse offered for our capture."

The innkeeper nodded his head, pushed himself from the chair, returning it to the table behind him, then stood looking down at Kal.

"Aye, mayhap there is," he said, "mayhap there is. But I'll take no gold, not in any amount, from the likes of the Boar. Not for him to do with the rest of Arvon what he's done to your clanholding. Rest you easy on that, Kalestor, rest you easy on that."

"Let me join you, please." The marchland blacksmith leaned towards Kal.

Paerryn's face broke into a smile as he wiped his hands again, wringing them in his apron. "Don't fret, lad, your secret is safe with me. They'd have to stretch this old frame of mine to get a noise out of me—and then it would only be the sound of my bones snapping."

"You'll let me join you? I've nothing here. Kalestor, please... To make right an old wrong, let me join you now."

"Tromwyn," Kal said, looking now to the marchland blacksmith beside him. "You do not know what you ask of me."

At that moment, Paerryn straightened. "Ah, I see that Mearie is tending to your more immediate needs." He held out an arm as the boy, Sahn, approached the table with two large platters. These the boy set on the table, one laden with fat sausages, the other brimming with boiled vegetables—potatoes, turnips, carrots, and onions. The boy nodded, excused himself, and scurried off to fetch plates and knives.

"And, so, I leave you to your meal," the innkeeper said with a bow of his head. "Rest assured—I will do what I can to aid you. Do not worry." He looked again at the men around the table, then said to his fellow marchlander, "Tromwyn, would you join me for a moment?"

Kal watched the two marchlanders stand aside to speak with one another as Sahn quietly came and left again.

"What did Paerryn say to you?" Kal asked the blacksmith when he had returned and the men had fallen to their meat.

"Only that I should no longer press my suit with you. He said that yours is a venture that I should not be a part of—but I would go with you. I would help you, however I may."

Kal smiled at the man's earnest enthusiasm. "And I would that you could join us, Tromwyn, but I do not think that Wuldor destines it to be—" A look of surprise sprang to the blacksmith's face. "What is it?" Kal asked.

"Nothing. Only that few now invoke that name."

"Indeed? Would that more folk did."

"Not in these days, Kal. And you might do well to be wary of it, for you'll draw notice to yourself, too," Tromwyn said and turned to the plate in front of him.

The men ate in the silence of their thoughts amid the clamour of the Mourning Crown's patrons. More than once, Kal caught Paerryn casting a glance in their direction while he bustled about the business of the inn. Kal paid it little mind, though. He had garnered from the innkeeper what news he could and had shared with the man more than he wanted. But there was nothing he could do about that now. And nothing he could do but trust that the man would be faithful to his word, although trust, he remembered, had cost him dearly in the past. He looked at his fellow Holdsmen. They would have to be on their mettle now, and they knew it, too, for anxious caution marked the faces of each of them. Gwyn glanced up at him and smiled thinly, then fell back to his food. They would finish their meal, Kal decided, and then he and his companions would leave Woodglence as quickly and as quietly as possible, make for the lowside post, collect the animals, and head northward immediately, tonight, under cover of dark.

They had not but half finished eating when a disturbance at the riverside door to the Mourning Crown attracted their attention. Above the din of the crowded hall, voices were raised, though indistinct. Four men had entered the inn and now stood bullying a group of boatmen that sat at a table near the entrance. One of the newcomers, clearly the leader of the lot, stood by and watched, laughing and egging on his fellows, but before things got out of hand, Paerryn intervened. The leader engaged him, and Kal could tell by the man's gestures that he was making demands of the innkeeper. Paerryn was evidently not intimidated by the abuse, but just when it seemed to Kal that the innkeeper was about to throw them out into the street, he turned and pointed across the room to where the Holdsmen and their companion were seated.

Kal felt the sinking dizziness of panic as the leader called his men to heel and started pushing his way across the room. Closer they came and closer, until, coming to the empty table beside the Holdsmen, they dragged out the chairs and sat down, talking loudly among themselves. The leader ran fingers through his fair hair and pushed his chair back, rocking on its back legs. He placed his booted feet on the table, then commenced to twist the two points of a forked red beard. One of the men, noticing that the Holdsmen had been watching them, leered at the group.

"Eh! What you looking at?" he barked and slammed a fist on the table. His fellows, laughing, turned to look at the Holdsmen and Tromwyn.

Devved began to rise in his seat, but Gwyn laid a hand on his arm, stopping him.

"We've no quarrel with you," Kal said in a level tone.

"Not yet!" the man snapped to continued laughter.

"Aye, not yet. And let us keep it so. You let us eat our meal in peace, and we'll let you eat yours in peace." Kal gave his attention to the remains of his sausage.

The newcomers cursed at Kal, who ignored them. Soon enough, they tired of deriding the Holdsman, turned back to their own table, and began calling loudly for ale to be brought.

"They mean trouble, Kal," Devved leaned over and said.

"Aye, well, they'll find it soon enough, if they're not careful. Do you know these men, Tromwyn?"

"No, I've never set eyes on them before. No doubt they're with some thane. First time in a big town. They'll swag around 'til someone gets fed up with them and knocks them about, clears their thinking for them." The blacksmith grinned.

"Aye, you may be right. All the same, I'd like to be moving on soon. We've got what we came for, and a good meal besides—"

At the table next to them, the conversation had increased in volume.

"Will he be looking for you there?" one man said to the leader.

"No, but he'll surely find me. I've as much a right as ever my father had."

"But he had little success in his embassies—"

"Aye, he did have little success," the leader said, removing his feet from the table and leaning forward in his seat. "Little success happens when little action is taken, and he was a man of little action." He sat back in his chair again. "But not me!"

"Nay, not you!"

At that moment, pots of ale were placed before them. These were snatched up and lifted.

"To action, and men of action!" the leader crowed, then drained his mug to the loud approbation of his fellows.

"You see," he said, wiping foam from his whiskers, "one should not waste time in artful negotiation, politicking with the mincing subtleties of court. No, rather, one should—no, one must—take what is his to take. Seize it. Own it. Power is in the will to do.... And now he is dead, and I will have what is mine!" A boot heel struck hardwood as he crossed his ankles on the table and rocked back in his chair again.

Kal listened, not looking up, pretending to be engaged in conversation by Tromwyn. Without a doubt, here was a ruthless man. His cruelty was etched upon his face and gestures, and rang from his words like battle-struck sword steel.

Another man pressed his way across the room towards the Holdsmen, but stopped short, breathless, before the other table. He nodded his head.

"Well?" the leader snapped.

"My lord—my lord Lysak...," he blurted and paused to catch his breath. Kal sat bolt upright and shot a glance at Galli and Gwyn.

"What is it, Kal?" Devved asked.

"Shh, later," Kal said, his eyes fixed on the men at the other table.

The leader put his heels against the table's edge and shoved the table skidding away from him. It slammed into the midriff of the man across from him, doubling the man over with a yelp. As the others sniggered, the leader stood and faced the new arrival.

"What news, Hogur, you louse? Out with it now, as you value your hide," he said slowly through clenched teeth, spittle flecking the air, his eyes narrow and his face furrowed in lines of anger. The messenger glanced to the others at table. There was no help for him.

"M-my lord Lysak—"

"Yes, you said that already!" Lysak snarled in the man's face.

"He has come. He is here, in Woodglence. She is with him."

"What?"

"She is with him—she is here with him," the man said, pointing blindly behind himself in the direction of the door through which he had entered only a moment before. "They only just arrived, but now make ready to sail. They will leave, even at this late hour. Their ships lie ready, and they leave within the half hour."

A thin smile spread across Lysak's face, and his eyes flashed. He pulled at the points of his beard and turned to those at table with him.

"And so, now is the time for action. Now is the time for me to take what is mine." The smile disappeared. "Come!" he barked and started across the room as men scrambled to their feet.

"Bethsefra...," Kal breathed with dawning comprehension. "Now we have a quarrel."

"Who?" Devved said.

"Later, Devved, later. Gwyn," Kal said, looking to the mute Holdsman, "follow them out. Watch where they go. We'll meet you at the alley to the side, with the weapons. Wait... wait a moment so they don't see you following.... Good, go now."

Gwyn slipped through the crowded room. When he had left the Mourning Crown after Lysak and his men, Kal led the others out through the hallway by which they had entered.

"What, leaving already, my loves?"

Mearie's short bulk blocked the way through the kitchen. The woman stood with her turned wrists planted upon her hips, the same wooden spoon firmly in the grip of one hand, and eyed the group with disapproval. Tromwyn pushed past Kal.

"Mearie, dear, were it not for more urgent matters that demand the attentions of my companions here, we would, without a doubt, be still at table making demands upon your kitchen craft—oh, but if they could taste your tarts! But sadly..." The tousle-haired blacksmith fumbled with his purse and managed to extract three coins, which he pressed into the fat woman's hand as he bent to kiss her round cheek. "With our compliments," he said. "Please pass these along to your goodman."

The woman broke into a smile as Tromwyn released her hands and led the other men out into the rear courtyard to the parting salutations of cooks and scullions.

Galli and Devved retrieved the weapons stashed in the shed, and Galli handed Kal Rhodangalas on its sword belt, which Kal strapped around his waist as they darted up the alley to the riverside road. There Gwyn stood, and, as they met him, he strode off, leading them farther downriver, pointing to the hurrying figures of Lysak and his men jostling their way through the press of traffic on the cobbled street.

"Uferian!"

A voice drifted to the group above the din of the crowded street. People turned to look for its source.

"Uferian!"

Ahead of them, Lysak had come to a stop in front of two river sloops. From the masthead of each ship, a long black pennant furled and unfurled languidly in the evening breeze. On each pennant was applied the figure of a silver swan. On the quayside, Lysak and his men from the Mourning Crown were joined now by three others in the reddish-brown tunics of the seaholding of Melderenys, a blue crown on the chest and back of each.

"Uferian!" the young Melderenysian lord yelled again.

A crowd was gathering around Lysak and his men in hopes of a spectacle. Kal lifted a hand to stop his companions as they neared the back edge of the growing ring of people. Through the throng, Kal saw a cart and several pack animals being unburdened of their loads. The cart and animals were hurriedly led to the rearward ship, away from the Melderenysians, by a handful of men who cast anxious glances to one another.

"Uferian! Show yourself!" Lysak bellowed, his tone insistent and increasingly impatient. "Uferian!"

From the cabin on the first of the two ships, a silvery head appeared, and a man, long-haired and bearded, dressed in black leggings, tunic, and cloak, the silver swan of the Oakapple Isles upon his chest, stepped onto the deck and came to stand amidships at the rail. There was a palpable strength in the man's carriage, and his face was expressionless as he looked down upon Lysak and his men. From the cabin behind him, a young woman emerged, her fair skin white against the black of her short-cropped hair and the dark green dress that she wore. At sight of the woman, breath caught in Kal's throat. She walked to the rail beside King Uferian.

"Bethsefra." It was Lysak who spoke, and though Kal could not see his face, he knew from the tone that the blond man leered at the princess.

"Lysak, you toad," she said. "What do you—" Her father placed his hand upon hers where it rested on the ship's rail, bidding her to silence. He turned, pulling the edge of his long cloak behind him, and descended the gangplank to the quay, coming to a standstill in front of Lysak. In his wake, on the river sloop, two retainers in black livery appeared on deck. These took a quick survey of the situation, then strode down from the ship and drew up on the cobbles, flanking their lord, their hands poised on their sword hilts. Snatching up a sword from somewhere on deck, Bethsefra also hastened from the ship and pushed past one of the men to stand at her father's right side. Lysak had not moved, nor had his men. Kal could sense the tension thickening over the crowded quayside.

"Uferian, you'll not hold out against me any longer. I've come to take what's mine." The malice and hatred in Lysak's voice were unmistakable, and it was some moments before the silver-maned lord addressed him. When he did, it was with a voice of calm authority, low, though still loud enough for the entire assembly of onlookers to hear.

"I regret your father's death, Lysak. He was a man of some nobility, though greatly misguided by his ambition. Sadly, not a shred of what little greatness he may have had can be found in his son."

"You dare speak of greatness? What would you know of it? I will show you greatness, for it is not measured by the man, but by his actions. I will accomplish what my father never had the courage to do."

"You insult his memory."

"And you insult me. I will have what's mine!"

"And by what right do you make claim to the throne of the Oakapple Isles?"

"I will have what is mine!"

"What claim can you make to my throne, Lysak? Speak!"

"Your throne? Your throne? You and your throne are but a nuisance. There ever was only one throne for all the isles of the seaholdings—mine. The true seat of all of Arvon. The Isles are but a start. My father never saw beyond that, but I do. I will make suit with my lord Ferabek for my rightful place as the high king of Arvon, for I occupy the true throne, not the Mindal's dog, Gawmage. I hold the true throne of Arvon. I do. I sit upon the Seaheld Throne, king in unbroken succession from Ardiel himself, and I will wear his crown!" Lysak's voice had reached a fevered pitch, and, as he fell silent before the implacable sternness of Uferian, the air seemed to crackle with the strain of enmity between the two men.

All work had stopped on the ships, and two more men in black livery now stood at the opening of the ship's rail atop the gang-way, even as three men from Uferian's other ship edged through the encircling throng. Beside Kal, Gwyn had discreetly readied his bow. At a nod from Kal, Galli and Devved did likewise. Then Kal pressed closer into the crowd behind Lysak, his companions following his lead.

"You are mad," Uferian stated flatly, his cold blue eyes locked on Lysak, "mad if you think Ferabek will grant you anything other than the sharp edge of his—"

"Ah, but I have assurances, guarantees that whoever serves Ferabek faithfully—"

"Faithful? You?" Uferian laughed mirthlessly. "Boy, the Boar makes no promise that he intends to honour, of this you can be sure. And you—"

"I will take what is mine," Lysak said. "And to start, I will take a queen." In a flash, Lysak shot a step forward and seized Bethsefra by the arm, shaking loose the sword she held, which fell to the street with a clang, and pulled her back to his side. The young woman struggled against the Melderenysian's grip.

"Let go of me!" she cried. "Take your hands off of me at once!"

"I will do as I please," Lysak said, pulling her closer still and, with his unencumbered hand, slapping her hard across the face. "And I will have you."

The sound of steel drawn from hardened leather filled the crowded quayside as Uferian and his men unsheathed their weapons. In immediate response, the russet-clad men beside Lysak drew their weapons.

"Release her," Uferian said, raising his sword. "Release her at once."

Lysak laughed. "What? Will you stain your sword with my blood as well?" he said, dropping his voice. "Is it not enough that you should fell the tree, but that you would strike at the sapling as well? Press your point now, and, so doing, you confess your guilt and condemn yourself. It would be a deed in proof of what you stand accused."

"Of what I stand accused? You whelp! I may stand accused of your father's death—accused by you—but I am faultless of the deed. Your father's blood drips from your sword, not mine."

"My sword, your sword, what is the difference? Torras died because of your stiff-necked refusal to submit to the court of Tarkhuna."

"What is this madness?" Uferian said, his brow furrowing in exasperated anger.

"But submit to my will, you shall. I will denounce you, old man, before Ferabek. This Convocation in Dinas Antrum will be your end. But act now, do, try to kill me, and justice will be served. You won't live to see the stars tonight—or perhaps she won't." Lysak seized the woman and swung her around, her back to his chest, and drew a knife to her throat. He began to retreat slowly with Bethsefra backwards into the crowd.

"Madness, this is madness...." Uferian broke his gaze from Lysak and began to look around himself, his face growing pale. "This is madness...," he said again, his tone betraying his sense of desperation. He lowered his sword and, with a gesture of his hand, bade his men to lower theirs.

"Father?" Bethsefra whispered. "Father? No, no, no!" she began to scream in dawning realization of what had happened, struggling anew against her captor's grip.

Still, Lysak and his men backed away from Uferian, the crowd giving way to them step by step.

"Let her go," Kal said. The point of his hunting knife dug into Lysak's back between his shoulders. The man stopped in his tracks and gripped Bethsefra's arms more tightly. "I said, 'Let her go,'" Kal whispered into his ear through clenched teeth. He pressed the knife, and the blade's point bit through the man's tunic. Lysak flinched at the knife's prick. To his left and right, pushing past his own men, Holdsmen stepped forward, each with a bow drawn to full bend.

"All right," Lysak said, releasing his grip on the woman, who immediately fled to her father's side.

"Your men...," Kal whispered in his ear.

"Drop your weapons," Lysak said. At first the Melderenysians were hesitant to obey. "Do it! Now!" Lysak barked, and one by one his men let their swords fall, clattering, to the cobbles.

Kal slowly circled the Melderenysian lord, keeping his knife at the man's neck, until he and the other Holdsmen stood facing Lysak's men, their backs to Uferian and his.

"So, it seems that we do have a quarrel after all," said Lysak, staring at Kal through narrowed eyes.

"Galli," Kal said without taking his own eyes from Lysak's.

"Aye, Kal."

"If he moves..." Kal let the implied threat hang in the air as he lowered his knife, replaced it in the sheath at his belt and, stepping back, drew Rhodangalas from beneath his cloak and levelled the sword at Lysak's throat. From the corner of his eye, Kal saw Tromwyn, his own sword drawn, step through the line of Lysak's men. The marchlander, his grey thatch wild, his black eyes wide and darting around the crowd, sidled up to Kal.

"Go, Tromwyn," Kal said in a low voice, not looking at the man. "Leave now, while you may. Before the town guard comes, go."

Lysak's pale face split in a grin, his eyes on Rhodangalas. "There's a pretty blade for a pretty boy," he said.

"My lord Uferian," Kal said, raising his voice to address the man standing behind him, "do your ships stand ready to make sail?"

"Ready enough," came the response.

"Then I would invite your lordship, the princess Bethsefra, and your lordship's party to board," continued Kal, still holding Lysak in an unflinching stare. "And, by your leave, my lord, you'll have a clutch of new passengers."

"And how shall I address the rescuer of my daughter?"

"We would call ourselves friends of Uferian and friends of the Oakapple Isles, we and our companions."

"It is Kalaquinn, Father," Bethsefra said. "He upon whom you bestowed the title 'Friend' as the one to whom you owe your life—now twice, and I myself once."

"You highland ditch rat," Lysak hissed, his grin vanished from a face now twisted in rage. "I'll not be stopped by the likes of you, nor my designs foiled. You'll not escape me this easily. Uferian's throne will not last long enough for you to hide behind."

Uferian issued a series of quick commands to his men to prepare the ships for sail without delay, then said, "You and your companions are right welcome, Kalaquinn."

Kal shot a look over his shoulder. Men hurried over the river sloops, stowing the last of the baggage, hauling on lines and sheets and readying the sails to be set. Several of Uferian's men now stood on deck along the rails, their bows trained on the Melderenysians. Kal nodded and said, "Gwyn, Devved, let us go."

Galli glanced at Kal. "But, Kal, our plan—"

"Has changed. Onto the ship, carefully now."

Tromwyn remained nearby and once again pressed beside Kal and whispered hoarsely, "Let me come with you, please. Please... Kalaquinn"

"Tromwyn, this is not your fight."

"But I would join you."

"No. Leave now, while you still may." Kal looked at the blacksmith. "If you follow me, it may well cost you your life."

"Then I would die," said Tromwyn, leaning even closer. "But at least I would die in service of the king."

Kal saw the earnestness in the man's expression and heard it in his voice, and in the man's shining black eyes he saw the reflection of his own face. Kal turned away from him.

"No. You must leave at once," the Holdsman said. "There is still time. Go now, Tromwyn, and may Wuldor ever hold you in his eye."

The marchlander hesitated, half turned away and hesitated again as if caught in the throes of a dilemma. Finally, he slid his sword into its scabbard and melted into the press of people on the quayside, still gripped by curiosity.

Kal glanced around him. All of Uferian's men, as well as the three other Holdsmen, were aboard the ships now, the first of which, at Uferian's command, was already nosing out into the river. At last Kal lowered his weapon from Lysak's throat, turned, and ran aboard the remaining ship, where archers lined the rail. No sooner had he set foot on deck than was the gangplank pushed overboard into the water and the mainsail hoisted.

Following her sister ship, the river sloop slipped slowly away from the quay. On the quayside, Lysak remained standing, unmoved, though Kal saw him turn to give a sharp command to his men, two of whom disappeared into the crowd. In the failing light of evening, Kal could still see the man's expression as he turned back to look at the retreating ships across the growing span of water. He wore a smug, knowing grin as he twisted the points of his red beard with one hand and stepped to the edge of the quay. In but a few seconds, Lysak's men had returned to his side dragging between them the struggling marchland blacksmith. Lysak's grin spread into a gash of a smile as his harsh laughter drifted across the water. The blacksmith's head jerked back as Lysak grabbed his hair, and Kal saw the flash and glint of a blade, reddened by the evening sky. Blood washed down the blacksmith's breast. His limp body began to crumple, until Lysak pushed it forward and it fell with a splash into the green water of the Winfarthing.

A stunned silence gripped those standing with Kal along the rail of the ship, a silence broken only by Lysak's continued laughter, now grown shrill and maniacal. The lifeless body bobbed to the surface and slowly turned, facedown, amid a red-black cloud of blood that blossomed and billowed around it in the river. Devved, standing to Kal's left, drew a deep sobbing draught of air. Like a great bellows venting, he screamed, "No, Tromwyn, no!" In that instant, before Kal had time to act or even speak, the big man drew back his bowstring and let loose an arrow with a twang that sounded as thunder.

Not two dozen yards away across the water, Lysak's laughter suddenly died and his eyes grew wide. His hands grasped the fletched end of the highland shaft that protruded from his throat. His mouth opened and closed noiselessly as he staggered back a step, overcompensated, and fell face-first into the river, knocking into the blacksmith's corpse and sending it sluggishly spinning out after the river sloops into the upper Winfarthing River.

TWENTY-SEVEN

"That's twice now, Devved. Twice, you've committed us to a path of blood." The young Hordanu did not look at the broadly built Holdsman leaning beside him at the rail but continued to contemplate the play of morning sun on the gently stirred surface of the water between the two river sloops. Beyond their sister sloop, along the north shore of the Winfarthing, the forest was thinning, replaced now by an irregular pattern of field and copse, with here and there a stretch of ploughland. On the riverbank, a farmer, watering his oxen, looked up at the passing ships. Devved remained silent, his face lowering and sullen, seemingly oblivious to both Kal's words and his presence.

Kal had lain awake in his cot most of the night, wrestling with the most recent turn of events and how they might further complicate an already impossibly complicated plan.

"So, do you feel that your hunger for revenge has been sated?" Kal spoke again.

"He was a highlander in need," Devved said in little more than a low growl, still staring fixedly across the water to the other ship. "A highlander...A highlander about to be ruthlessly slaughtered." His thick fingers toyed with a bit of frayed yarn that he had plucked from his sleeve.

"The act would have fallen on the conscience of the doers—"

"And on us as idle onlookers, for pity's sake!"

"Wrong on two counts, Devved," Kal said as he turned to his companion. "It was not for pity's sake that you broke cover and committed us to battle on the road. And say not 'us,' for it was not your tender conscience that bore the terrible weight of that moment." Kal raised himself to full height from the rail of the sloop, his demeanour grown stern. "Do you really think that Aelward stood there idle and unfeeling? That he wasn't racked by the choice laid balanced before him? And do you really think your pity overmatches his? Or mine?"

"No . . . I-I don't. Of course not. That's not what I meant."

"Still less can you claim that pity moved you when you slew Lysak. Tromwyn was already dead. He was beyond human help when you let fly."

Devved tossed the bit of yarn into the waters churned by the ship's hull, following its swirling progress with his eyes until it was lost from sight. He sighed heavily and lowered his eyes, rocking his head slowly from side to side like a bull preparing to charge.

"I needed to act, Kal. You don't understand. It was overpowering. I wanted to make them pay, and pay dearly."

"I understand, Devved. I feel the sting of Tromwyn's death. If only he would have listened to me and fled right away. Or I could've brought him along and then we could have put him ashore once we'd reached safety. But once he was dead, you didn't reckon on the evil you might bring upon the House of Uferian, did you? What price might he now have to pay for your rashness, sharing in the taint of Lysak's slaying?"

Devved started from the rail, hammering it with his fists, as though it were his anvil, and turned on Kal. "The whoreson slit his throat laughing, Kal! Slaughtered him right before our eyes—"

"I know. And the image haunted my dreams last night. But who gave you warrant to be both judge and executioner?" Kal met the blacksmith's defiant stare. "No, Devved. You were bent solely on revenge. Revenge, pure and simple. Your very anger in this moment betrays you. And blinds you."

Devved clenched his teeth, his neck and face crimson and corded with barely contained rage. "You have no idea, Kal. No idea. The blood lust—how it comes over me. It's like a craving, as strong as aught else I've known in life."

"As strong as your honour? As strong as the good faith you bear to the memory of your loved ones—wife and children?"

A cry caught in Devved's throat. He gripped the crown of his head with two hands and seized fistfuls of hair. He seemed about to tear the dark thatch from his scalp, but his fingers relaxed and slid down his face until they caged his eyes. His hands trembled.

"I'm sorry, Kal," the blacksmith said at length, peering at the younger Holdsman through his fingers. "What's happened to me, I don't know. The rage within me... The raw desire to repay them in kind, to settle the balance..."

"The problem is," Kal said, "the more you feed revenge, the more ravenous it grows. It is like a beast within your breast. Its hunger is never sated. And, Devved"—Kal laid a hand on the man's shoulder—"if you commit yourself to the path of revenge, you'd best dig two graves." Devved glanced at Kal. "Aye, for sure as night follows day, the path of vengeance leads to two graves, your enemy's and your own. It is a course that will be the death of you, even as you mete out death upon your enemy." Kal paused a moment and glanced over the water to the other sloop. "And in this particular course, if you choose to continue down it, you'd best be digging a third."

"A third grave?"

"Aye, a third grave, and a generous one at that... for your friends."

Devved looked taken aback and scratched his head, brows knitted and face pensive. "I-I'm sorry, Master Kalaquinn. I haven't been thinking straight. My head's been in a fog, in a storm of my own making. I've let my passion get the better of me."

"Your baser passions are the issue, Devved. Not your grief. Nor your love for those you've lost. The strength of your grief and love is good. It marks your depth and measure as a man, a Holdsman stout and true. Why else, do you think, did I choose you as a companion for this journey?" Kal pressed the big man's shoulder.

"I hope you've haven't chosen amiss, Master Kalaquinn. There were others... Others might have served you better."

"No, no, Devved. It's you that I've chosen, and you that I need—that we all need, for we rely on one another."

Devved bowed his head. "Many thanks, young Master Hordanu. I pray I will not fail you again." Even as he spoke, the blacksmith's stomach growled in protest of the morning's hour and its emptiness.

Kal smiled at his companion and nodded. "Now go quell that angry stomach of yours, Devved. You'll find the galley well-provisioned."

Devved bowed his head again, and politely took his leave, his courtesy not disguising the struggle the man fought within himself, a struggle that revealed itself in the dark expression that had settled on his face. The big smith turned away and strode back to the quarterdeck.

Kal glanced over to the other sloop. There Gwyn stood on deck, waving in greeting. Kal lifted his hand in brief reply, then moved back to the rail, where he leaned, looking pensively over the gunwale. His eyes drifted upriver to a barge laden with lumber, its mainsail taut against the rising wind, which was freshening from the west. The stiffening breeze caressed his face and hair. In the sky above the barge, a gull struggled against the gust with fluttering wings. Suddenly, it stopped resisting and turned, so that it flew now without effort before the wind, its wings outstretched and graceful on the draft.

Clever creature, Kal mused, choosing not to spend itself fighting a facing breeze but rather to use the opposing winds to its own advantage. *And so shall we*—he smiled wryly at the thought—*so shall we not fight the winds of fate's caprice that have driven us from our intended course, but harness them, and so tame them to our own purpose!*

It had been a good decision, a natural decision to improvise, to seize upon and exploit the new circumstances into which they had been thrown. Kal's thoughts turned to the evening before, to the bizarre twining string of events that left them shipboard and bound downstream towards Dinas Antrum, the very heart of Arvon—and the very heart of danger.

Straightaway, as breeze and current carried them downriver into the night, he had held hurried conference with Galli and Gwyn, Devved having stolen away below deck in stony silence. The events that had befallen them at Woodglence presented them with an opportunity, Kal averred, and though it meant changing the course of action they had agreed upon at Aelward's Cot, they would have been foolish not to use it to their end. Galli had been of the same mind, as was Gwyn.

Then, even as the Holdsmen whispered one to the other, Uferian had approached. He had been profuse in his gratitude. He had claimed that he stood now in great debt to Kal twice over—not only for his own life, but for that of his daughter. In words of sweeping generosity, Uferian had laid his every resource at Kal's disposal. Though unspoken by Uferian, it had become evident to Kal that the king had recognized in him something more than an itinerant and seafaring highland bard.

Kal had asked leave of Uferian to continue downriver with the king and his retinue, and allowed that he and his fellows had intended to head north through the Marchlands to the Dumoric coast. Uferian had been more than delighted to accede to Kal's request and had agreed to carry them however far they wished along the river.

Later, it had been a growing excitement that blunted the edge of Kal's anxiety as much as the Arvisian wine that the king had insisted upon sharing with his guests and new companions, in token of their agreed-upon arrangement. Bethsefra had been in attendance, her face radiant in the lantern light, her green eyes luminous, as she, time and again, regarded Kal with a steady gaze. The evening had slipped away as the Winfarthing's waters slid beneath the ship's hull. Too soon, it seemed to Kal, had the companions been compelled to bid good-night and retire for the night, Gwyn and Galli to the other sloop for reasons of space and lodging, and Kal to a private berth below deck, in which he had tossed and turned, resolving a new plan in his mind.

Now the two boats rounded a steep bluff. Kal started from his reverie. He found his eyes fixed in amazement on the starkly changed landscape that now marked their passage. Crude hovels sprawled across dust-ridden fields right down to the banks of the river. Ill-clad women milled about the decrepit buildings, children in tow, carrying water pots or tending open cooking fires. Kal wrinkled his nose. The air had turned acrid. A massive building came into view, its walls uneven with roughly dressed stone, the roof covered with grimy slate, belching smoke from half a dozen enormous chimneys. Around it thronged a busy hive of men, countless in number, shirtless and smeared with toil. Some were loading donkey carts with ingots of metal, hoisting them on wooden cranes and tackle from huge piles in a sprawling work-yard. Others drove the loaded carts into the dark recesses of the building. At a wharf before the building, a barge, dangerously overladen with slabs of wood, was only just docking. Before it had even come to rest, a caravan of wagons descended upon it, and a small army of men began to strip it of its cargo.

"Welcome to Medue, Kalaquinn."

Kal turned at the sound of the voice.

"My lord Uferian, good morning." Kal inclined his head in greeting to the king, who wore a cloak against the coolness of the morning, his thick silver hair framing a face as weathered and austere as his home seat at Swanskeld.

"It wasn't long ago that it used to be one of the most charming towns on the Winfarthing, believe it or not. Not long ago at all. When I was a lad, in fact."

Kal's eyes strayed back to the industry and squalor that spread in seemingly equal proportion along the riverbank.

"What happened, you ask?" Uferian said, a half-smile on his face. "The Mindal, that's what happened. That's an ironworks"—the king pointed to the towering edifice—"and there, a smelter, just ahead of us around this bend in the river. It provides the raw iron blocks you see laid up there. They decided to build them here, using forced labour—forced mostly from any folk impolitic enough to grumble against their policies, and those that have been taken off their land on account of the mines."

"The mines?"

"Aye, iron mines. It was discovered that the land north of the Winfarthing close to Medue was rich with ore. The people were driven from their farms. Good dark soil it was, too. Fed half of Arvon. But that didn't matter to the Mindal."

"And close enough to the river for ease of shipment," Kal said.

"Aye, that and with wood enough to feed their furnaces from the vast forests of Rootfall Frith. They lie near to hand as well. The manufactories make mostly armaments—swords, shields, pikes, armour, anything you care to name—and send them downriver to Dinas Antrum for their own lowland levies. For Ferabek's armies, as well."

"And make a tidy profit for themselves in doing so, I'd wager," Kal said.

"Aye, that they do. It is the perfect place for their schemes." Uferian watched the foundry loom over them and slip past as the ships glided along the Winfarthing. "And speaking of schemes, Kalaquinn, have you given further thought to your own plans, and where you might want to be disembarked? I was thinking myself that Queen's Hythe would serve you well, if you want to travel overland to the coast—plenty of wild, hidden country around the Lake of Swallows for you and your companions to pass unnoticed to the north."

"Actually, my lord, I've been considering another way."

Uferian looked at the Holdsman with open curiosity.

"I've been thinking long this past night," Kal said. "I think that we will remain with you on board all the way to Dinas Antrum. That is, if you'll have us."

"To Dinas Antrum? But that's madness, Kalaquinn. Much as I'd like to prolong the pleasure of your company, you'd be marked as a highlander—as a probable enemy—the moment you stepped foot in the city. You'd be entering the very lair of the Boar."

"With all due respect, so will you, my lord. These days a seaholdsman's hardly more welcome than a highlander to them that hold the reins of power."

"But I am King of the Oakapple Isles, a thane of Arvon. I and my retainers enjoy immunity of person under the Truce of Convocation that holds force in Dinas Antrum. Not Gawmage, nor even Ferabek himself, dares break faith with the custom of the Truce."

"Which makes this plan of mine all the easier."

"Easier?" Uferian's face furrowed in a frown, his brows knit, shadowing the crow's feet that spread in deeper lines around his eyes.

"Aye, easier, my lord, much easier than travelling roundabout over hard terrain to the Dumoric Sea."

"But how so then easier, man?" The king scowled.

"Forgive me, my lord Uferian. I do not mean to speak in riddles. It's just that I balk at my request for fear that I should impose more than is meet upon your goodwill. I would not have you add kindness upon kindness to friends such as we that are but newly met and untested."

"Untested? Having twice rendered me life-saving service?" Uferian clapped a hand on Kal's back, and his bearded face broke into clean lines of laughter. "For a highlander bred far from the smooth-tongued arts of the city, you are the very soul of subtle court craft, Kalaquinn. Come, out with it then! Tell me your plan, and tell it to me plain."

"If my companions and I ... If we were to wear your livery, my lord, and make as though we are of your court, we'd share in that protection provided your entire retinue under the Truce of Convocation. We would have the freedom of the city. It would afford us a way to quietly gain passage on one of the many vessels that are sure to be bound for Gorfalster by way of Lake Lavengro."

"Ah, so it's to Gorfalster you're bound?"

"Aye, my lord." Kal's heart beat faster, and he took a breath, trying to assuage the recurring twinge of fear and doubt that he had revealed too much. In the assurance of his heart, however, he knew that the man before him was a man he could trust. "It is to Gorfalster that we—"

Uferian raised his hand to stop Kal, turning his head to the side. "Say no more, Kalaquinn. Your argument carries much force. Sometimes it's to one's best advantage to be bold and so hide in the plain sight of one's enemy." The king stroked his beard and nodded with decision. "Yes. Good," he said. "Consider the matter settled between us. I'd be honoured to have you wear the silver swan of the Isles. We have court garb to spare in the locker. The ship's master, Voiquan, will see to your apparel."

Once again, Kal expressed his thanks to Uferian. The king demurred, saying that it was but a little thing in balance of the debt he owed Kal. Then, pleading the infirmities of age to excuse himself, he withdrew to his cabin, leaving the young Holdsman to his thoughts.

A strange uneasiness had settled over Kal, prompting him to doubt the soundness of the line of argument he had used with Uferian. There were deeper motives to his decision, he realized, veiled motives he had not ventured to voice aloud. Most immediate was a sense of responsibility and protectiveness towards Uferian, born of the possible repercussions arising from Devved's vengeful slaying of Lysak. The venerable seaholdsman might have need yet of their four stout sword arms in his defence, for Kal wondered how much stock could wisely be placed in the Truce of Convocation in a world roiling with the faithless intrigue of power politics, a world increasingly bereft of loyalty and honour. And if Uferian were to stand pressed and in need, beleaguered in Dinas Antrum, so, too, would his daughter, Bethsefra.

"Stand by to gybe!" The words rang out across the deck. Kal looked up from the glistening ripple of the water. Before them, a headland loomed over the river, forcing a turn to starboard. With questioning eyes, Kal turned from the rail and looked to the seaholdsman who had given the command. It was Voiquan, the man whom Uferian had mentioned, and he had noted Kal's glance.

"We're running before the wind, lad. A stiff river wind. We

must trim sails and make ready our helm," the seaholdsman said. "In mainsheet!" he cried again.

One of the deckhands pulled on the line that controlled the mainsail, bringing in the boom amidships, letting the great spread of canvas go slack. Kal glanced back to the steersman, who bore away, putting up the helm. For a moment the sloop drifted dead before the wind. The boom wavered listlessly until wind caught the other side of the sail and Voiquan shouted another command. The mainsheet was played out, and the sail billowed again.

"Opposite helm!" At Voiquan's words, the steersman put down the helm, and the sloop veered past the jutting point of land into the middle of the Winfarthing.

"Ah, *Gloamseeker*. She's a fine ship. Handles like a charm," said Voiquan, standing above the main hold hatch. He beamed at Kal.

"*Gloamseeker*?"

"Aye, that's her name. Uferian's father had her built. Years ago, when Uferian was still a youngling. Kept her berthed at Wood-glence for trips downriver to Dinas Antrum. Used her any time he crossed the mountains from the Isles. Old Nastraf named her *Gloamseeker*. He meant it to have a double edge—the name, see?" Voiquan nodded and winked at Kal knowingly. "*Gloamseeker* . . . Aye, it's a word on the state of affairs in Dinas Antrum. Even back then, he had a low opinion of the way things were unfolding there. He could see the signs, right enough, he could. It turns out there was more than ample reason for his fears." Voiquan wrinkled his nose and looked away towards the riverbank at another building, one even more immense than the forgeworks, belching huge clouds of black smoke from its chimneys, the sur-rounding landscape bleak with misshapen heaps of slag skirted by milling swarms of sweat-grimed men and draught animals.

"A smelter?" Kal asked.

"Aye, that it is, a smelter. Provides the iron for the forgeworks just back of us," Voiquan replied, then turned to face Kal again. "Well, it was Nastraf's son, Uferian, who put the craft to good use. Drawn to the bustle of Dinas Antrum was he. As you'd expect from a young man. As for Nastraf, he came to avoid the lowlands. Preferred the measured peace of Swanskeld and the waters around the Isles. Spent his days exploring. Now there was a sailor bred to the bone. Loved the sea. So my grandda told me, when I was a lad. He was Nastraf's ship steward. Performed service like mine. On *Gloamseeker* here, same as me. Ah, but she's a well-built ship, a ship that trimmed well in my grandda's time. Trims like a beauty now."

"Could she use another hand, *Gloamseeker*?"

"How do you mean, Master Kalaquinn?" Voiquan asked.

"I mean, can I be of any help with the shipboard tasks? I've a mind not to be idle, to stretch my limbs and work up a sweat. Perhaps earn my passage."

Voiquan grinned widely, dark shocks of hair fluttering in the breeze.

"There's no doubt, nay. You've earned your passage and more in the saving of milady. That was right bold, the way that you turned the tables on Lysak. It's just as well that eel is dead, elsewise you'd be forever minding your back."

"All the same, I'd like to help, if you don't mind teaching the art of sailing to a ship-ignorant landsman."

"Aye, then, Master Kalaquinn, if you will it. We'll put you to work and make a sailor of you. The river's a fine place to start."

The morning hours melted away in peace as the two sloops glided along the Winfarthing River. Voiquan taught Kal the ways of the *Gloamseeker* as much by example and gesture as by spoken word. Kal relished the simple monotony of the tasks, a gentle rhythm that soothed his worried mind.

Once, at midmorning, when he was on the foredeck stowing cordage, his ear caught the indistinct sound of a woman's voice. He glanced up to see Bethsefra emerge into the sunshine from her cabin, shielding her eyes with her hand as they adjusted to the bright daylight. She was deep in conversation with her father, who came up behind her, only his head visible at the opening of the hatch. Kal averted his eyes and fell back to the task at hand. As he coiled the lengths of rope, apparently absorbed in his duties, he strained to hear what father and daughter were discussing, but to no avail. When the sound of the voices subsided, he ventured to glance up again and realized she had descended below deck, leaving Uferian to speak to his ship steward, who glanced repeatedly in Kal's direction, as if in earnest explanation.

Devved returned to the deck as well, stormy-browed and taciturn, offering little more than a sullen look at one of the seaholdsmen who dared to greet him. The blacksmith's eyes met Kal's, but the big man broke his gaze and stared instead out across the river's surface. There was more pain in Devved's eyes than ire, Kal thought, and it was obvious that the man's thin veneer of surly ill temper overlaid a battleground of confusion, fear, and anxiety that plagued and rent the poor man's heart.

Suddenly, Devved turned and looked across the deck, distracted from his worried ruminations. Galli had hailed from the other ship, and now called again, waving in greeting. The blacksmith ducked his head and retreated below deck, scuttling away like a recalcitrant badger, disturbed by the merry approach of revelers, to its den. The other river sloop was pulling up alongside. Bethsefra must have nearly collided with the blacksmith, for she now stood on deck again, dressed casually in a simple blouse and skirt. When the two vessels were grappled, Voiquan helped Bethsefra board the companion ship on a makeshift gangway that had been laid between the two vessels. Once safely aboard, Bethsefra thanked the steward and cast a glance at Kal, who nodded in return. The two ships disengaged from one another and soon resumed their separate positions on the river.

"My lady Bethsefra's decided to spend the day aboard the *Pelidore* with her maid," said Voiquan with a smile as he stepped towards Kal. "Makes for a welcome change from all this rough male company." The steward chuckled as he turned back to his station on the aft deck.

The day wore on, and Kal lost himself amid the lines and sheets, occasionally asking the advice of the sailors, but, more often than not, quietly regarding them as they went about their tasks, allowing his mind to wander in the gathering summer heat. He again considered the name of the sloop—*Gloamseeker*! How aptly it described him and his own daunting mission to the shad-owedland hundreds of miles beyond Arvon's eastern boundaries. But first they'd have to manage getting out of Dinas Antrum in one piece. He sighed.

By late afternoon, though still strong, the sun had slipped far from its midday height, losing much of its intensity. Once again, the other sloop swung alongside, and Bethsefra returned to the *Gloamseeker*. When she set foot back on deck, Uferian was there to greet her. From the corner of his eye, Kal caught her discreet searching glance as she drew away from her father's affectionate embrace. Then she bent over and whispered something in the old man's ear.

"Ah, yes, yes, of course," Uferian said, nodding to his daughter. "Come along, Kalaquinn. Leave aside your tasks." He beckoned to the young Holdsman. "You are our guest, and it is the time for supper. A late supper, I must apologize. I don't know about you, but I'm famished. Must be the river air. Foul though it is, it still braces a man's hunger."

"Or it may be your healthy constitution has given you a trencherman's appetite, Father," said Bethsefra, standing next to him.

"Thanks to Kalaquinn here," Uferian said, nodding.

"Aye, thanks to Kalaquinn, whom you're keeping from being fed. In payment for the boon of good health, you'll make a starveling out of him," Bethsefra said, a laugh in her voice, having begun to descend the stairs of the hatch ahead of Uferian.

In the relatively tight quarters of the galley, they sat down to a simple but hearty meal of stewed beef, turnip, and onion, washed down with a rich brown ale. At Kal's bidding, Devved had joined the party and seemed in a somewhat more mollified state of mind, entering into good-natured, albeit reserved, conversation with the others. Kal ate with an air of contentment, realizing only now how hungry he had been. He watched as the company and the fare further softened Devved's demeanour.

For her part, Bethsefra picked at the meal like a sparrow, not speaking much but glancing now and again at the others at table. Uferian, however, grew effusive and regaled them with stories of his childhood in Swanskeld, calling on help from Bethsefra or Voiquan when his memory failed him, for they had heard these same accounts many times over and knew them nearly as well as the old man did himself. Over a dessert of honeyed pastries, sipping on a glass of sweet red wine, Uferian waxed sentimental and talked poignantly of his long-dead wife, dwelling at length on her youth and her beauty. She had died, he explained, his eyes welling with tears, of a fever when Bethsefra was born, after a furious late-winter storm had lashed the Isles. While he spoke, it grew darker, the failing light of dusk on the river darkening the single window of the cramped galley. Voiquan rose to light another lantern, one which hung on a chain over their heads. It swung gently with the movement of the ship, the mellow light pooling on the table. Finally, stifling a yawn, his glass empty and himself drained of words, Uferian announced he was retiring for the night. Bethsefra, too, excused herself and offered to see her father to his cabin.

Restless, urged by the need for open air, Kal returned above deck. So, also, did Voiquan, to check on his men and the trim of the sloop. It was twilight, and the riverbanks on either side loomed dim and indistinct in the offing. The *Pelidore* appeared as a ghostly presence on their port quarter, the white of her sails proof against the failing light. A gentle breeze riffled softly over the water.

"Well, Kalaquinn, here's the moment of her contentment," said Voiquan, his hand gripping a sidestay. "She's found what she was seeking."

"Who? What do you mean?" Kal said, startled by the unexpected remark.

Voiquan smiled. "*Gloamseeker*. She's found what she's sought— the gloaming, a time between the strife and toil of the day and the unknown terrors of the night."

"An all too brief respite, I'm afraid," Kal said as his mind drifted back to his earlier bodeful musings.

"Aye, that may well be so. But for all the dark-edged misgivings, it can be a good time, a time for taking stock and rest." Voiquan stifled a yawn. "And speaking of rest," he resumed, "the hour has come for me to turn in as well. It's been a long day, kept more than busy by two jobs."

"Two jobs?" Kal said.

"Aye, one more than my usual quota—keeping *Gloamseeker* in trim and teaching a landsman his knots." Voiquan's amused eyes wandered to the stern of the boat, even as he let go of the sidestay and made to return to the hatch on the quarterdeck. "I see that your black-humoured blacksmith has found a friend," he added as he left, nodding towards Devved, who had followed them on deck and was standing now by the tillerman, a lanky, clean-faced sailor, deep in conversation with him.

After the ship steward had disappeared, Kal made his way forward past the fluttering jib to the foredeck of the boat, absorbing the stillness that had settled over the river with the onset of night. Mercifully, the rising tide of darkness now cloaked the blighted riverbanks and their burden of human misery, leaving him once again to thoughts of the future and the possibility that one day harmony might be restored to Ahn Norvys and that, beyond all the expectations of his upbringing in the remote little clanholding of Lammermorn, he was destined to play no small role in this enterprise. He sighed and lowered himself to sit, leaning against the capstan. He sat for what seemed a long time, his eyes closed, his head resting against the heavy coils of rope, lulled by the gentle rush of water cleaved by the progress of the ship's bow. At length, he roused himself, leaned forward, and pulled the Pyx of Roncador, in its case, from his night pouch. He unfastened the buckle of the case and gingerly slid the Pyx out, its delicate chain playing out between his fingers. In his hand, the half-moon face glowed softly green against the deepening murk of evening. The reassurance of its gleam recalled to Kal the time it had served him as a torch and beacon, the only hope he could cling to deep in the lightless caverns of Thyus.

In an instant, Kal was stirred from his thoughts, aware at once of the quiet tread of footfalls on the deck behind him.

"What have you there?" A quiet voice broke the stillness.

Kal slipped the Pyx back into its case and stowed it in his codynnos. "Oh, nothing. You startled me, my lady," he said, clambering to his feet.

Bethsefra stood nearby, draped against the chill of the evening in a long hooded brown cloak. "How do you mean 'nothing,' Kalaquinn?" she said. "Whatever it was you were holding, it was glowing. Strangely so...a soft light...and unnatural."

"It's just something a friend gave me once. A special keepsake."

"You make it sound so long ago, Kal. And yet we are of an age, you and I. The seasons' wheel has not turned that many times on us." Bethsefra took a step closer and now stood next to him beside the capstan and drew her hood back. Her face was pale in the soft radiance of starlight, and Kal could detect the look of curious inquiry, a barely perceptible glint in her eyes.

"In truth, it seems like an age has passed," he said.

"And what he gave you, your friend—you treasure it?"

"That I do. He was a bard."

"Like you?"

"Aye, like me."

"But, this friend, he is dead, if I guess aright?"

"Alas, yes, he is."

Bethsefra reached out and brushed the fingers of his hand. "I'm sorry," she said.

Kal bent his neck back, lifting his face to the night. His eyes wandered across the star-bejeweled sky. To his mind drifted images of Wilum, the Great Glence, Wuldor's Howe, the lake-set valley, and the encompassing Radolan Mountains. Unthinking, as if by instinct, his right hand lifted to cup the pios at his throat. He laid a finger with feathered lightness across its small strings, their thrum faint and scarcely audible. "He was a good man...," he said in little more than a breath, still staring into the starlit blackness.

"Look at the Shepherd," Bethsefra said softly, her head lifted as well. The light of the summer constellations cleared the shadows from her face and served to highlight the elegant sweep of her features. "Re'm ena, look how bright, how clear he shines tonight."

"Aye, there's no mistaking him.... Those other stars, they're like sheep in his fold. He's a good guide to them."

"And to the wayfarer," Bethsefra added.

"Not to mention the lonely farm lads. I can't tell you how many nights I would step out from our farmhouse and wander through the night, watching the stars, until I'd sit—just like now, here—musing upon the constellations caught in the dark night waters of Deepmere—" Kal faltered; his stare fell to Bethsefra as he realized suddenly the import of what he had let slip, wishing he could take the words back. "I...I...uh..."

"Did you say Deepmere?" Bethsefra asked, her eyes wide and fixed on Kal's face. "You did say Deepmere...You're a Lammermornian! You're from the Stoneholding!" Bethsefra's voice rose with excitement.

Kal bowed his head in mute resignation.

"But I thought you were all massacred by the Boar," the woman said.

"Most of us, yes. But not all."

"How many of you survived? And how...With only the Wyrd-laugh Pass, and Ferabek's...?"

Kal sighed and lifted his eyes to meet Bethsefra's. For some reason, his mind felt easier, as if a burden had been lifted from it.

"Aye, it seemed there was no escape. But in Wuldor's keeping, a way opened to us, and we fled underground. Not more than a handful of us. Thirty-four in all."

"And Wilum the Bard?"

"He is dead."

"He is dead...," Bethsefra echoed softly, her eyes widening in an expression of dawning comprehension. "Your friend...And you are a bard...." Kal's heartbeat quickened as he gazed steadily into the young woman's pale face. "But you—you're more than just a bard, aren't you? Kalaquinn, you are Hordanu!"

Kal closed his eyes and inclined his head to her. There was no point in denying it.

Hurriedly, the young woman drew her cloak around herself and fell to her knees. "My-my lord Myghternos—"

"No, Bethsefra, please...." Kal lowered himself to a crouch, placed his hand beneath her chin and lifted her face. "You're a hard one to keep secrets from," he said.

"So my father tells me." The hint of a smile played on Bethsefra's lips.

"Aye, Wilum perished," Kal continued, "but not before he accomplished his last duty as Bard, which was to pass the office on to me."

"But the Talamadh?"

"Lost to us. Lost and in the clutches of the Boar." A sigh escaped Kal as a groan, and he sank to the deck to sit leaning once more against the capstan. "But that is not the greatest concern," he continued. "The Sacred Fire of Tramys is extinguished and must be rekindled. What you saw in my hand was the Pyx of Roncador, given me by Wilum, the only vessel that can contain the spark necessary to rekindle the Fire. Only it is not I who can get the spark, and the one who can...I know not where he is."

"Kalaquinn, these are heavy burdens—"

"Aye, they are, very heavy. But they are burdens I must bear."

"Surely there is some way I can help you." Bethsefra's voice was soft and coloured with concern. "Is...is there any way I may help?"

Kal looked at Bethsefra again and smiled. "You've already helped us, greatly, when you arranged for passage from Swanskeld, and you help us now by letting us sail down to Dinas Antrum with you and make pretense that we're your father's retainers."

"Aye, sail into the very lair of the enemy, where they would like nothing more than to lay their blood-stained hands on you. That's a poor measure of friendship, I'd say. Surely there is more we can do. What about after Dinas Antrum? Where are you bound?"

"To Gorfalster, that much I've told your father, but more than that I cannot tell you. Our plans and where we are headed must remain privy knowledge, both for your own safety and for mine. It would be more than dangerous for you to know. You must understand that."

"Is there no way I can help you? Please, let me help you!" Bethsefra's voice rose in pitch, insistent, pleading.

Kal grew silent and shook his head, his features stern.

"No, Bethsefra," he said at length. "The best way you can help is by keeping your own counsel. Forget that you know what you've learned tonight. Or even that you know me. If you don't, you risk putting us both in peril, and far more besides."

"What about my father? Surely I can confide this to my father?"

"You don't understand, Bethsefra." Kal shook his head again and glanced sharply at the woman. "Nobody must know. Nobody. There's so much that hangs in the balance, so very much—everything!"

"All the more reason for you to gain the Isles as a knowing ally in your struggle." Kal's fierce stare was mirrored in the face of Bethsefra. It was an expression he had seen her wear before—resolute, implacable, and commanding—when she had first taken him captive.

"No, Bethsefra. This is a struggle that we will never win by matching force with force. Rather, our success depends entirely on stealth and secrecy."

"All the same, Kalaquinn, you can't expect to accomplish your mission without the benefit of friends. Please! You can trust my father as you would me."

Again Kal shook his head, but more slowly and less emphatically.

"Please! I tell him everything. My heart is his heart."

The Holdsman brought his hand up and rubbed his temples, frowning.

"Please, Kalaquinn, if you can't trust me...?"

"All right then, if you must. But mind, Bethsefra, just him, and him alone. No one else."

Bethsefra reached out and took his hand into hers. "Thank you, my lord Hordanu," she said and lowered her face to press her lips to his hand. "Thank you for your trust. The House of Uferian is highly honoured." She raised her eyes to meet his. "Rest easy in your mind, Kalaquinn. Uferian is still awake and reading in his cabin. I'll go speak with him now, before he retires."

Kal got to his feet as Bethsefra stood. The woman bowed her head and turned to go below decks, leaving Kal alone. He stared up at the night sky, entranced once more by the unwavering brilliance of the Shepherd. The bright summer constellation put him in mind of Aelward, and he wondered how, for their part, he and Broq were faring. With a pang of compunction, Kal realized that he had, yet again, betrayed the man's sage counsel to guard his identity, and in so doing had squandered his most precious commodity—anonymity.

He shook his head ruefully. "Yet hope . . . Yet hope . . . Yet hope . . . ," he heard himself mutter. And then, as if from a spring welling up from his heart, the words became a whispered song into the night.

> "Yet hope! For hope is life's bequest,
> Emboldening the meekest breast,
> To which the stars above attest.
> Doth not the faintest light shine best
> Amidst night's darkling veil?"

Presently, Kal's fingers strayed to the flap of his night pouch. Again he removed the Pyx of Roncador and held it out before him, letting it dangle for a moment from the end of its chain, his eyes fixed on its steady glow. For some while, Kal considered the gentle tug of its pendulum swings. Then, on an impulse, he placed the chain over his head and around his neck and tucked the cool stone vessel against his chest, beneath his tunic. He stood gazing downstream into the heavy blackness of the night, lulled by the churning splash of river water against the bow. The Pyx's weight reminded him of the burden he bore, his burden as High Bard of Ahn Norvys, as Hordanu. How much of that burden had he now shunted onto the shoulders of Uferian and his house, he wondered. What weight of danger and woe had he brought down upon the old king and his daughter?

TWENTY-EIGHT

Kal stared out into a steady grey drizzle from Uferian's apartments. It had started to rain the morning after they had arrived and had continued solidly for two days now. Under the scudding shreds of cloud, the vast paved courtyard below him stretched between long and ornately dressed grey-stone buildings flanking the Silver Palace. The grounds were expansive, to say the least, and Kal had never thought, even in his wildest imaginings that a place of such somber grandeur could exist in Arvon. Indeed, even the glories of Sterentref in Magan's underground domain paled in comparison to the ancient and stark beauty of the Silver Palace, with its filigree of manicured gardens woven in and around the seemingly endless succession of turreted, gargoyle-encrusted, and ivy-clad edifices, shadowed cloisters, and cobbled courtyards. At the centre of the complex of buildings, more than two hundred paces away to his right, at an angle across the court from the very window in which he stood thinking, rose the spire of the Palace itself, home to the high king and queen of Arvon from the years immediately following the reign of Ardiel himself, when the edifice had been first constructed.

With the protection offered him by Uferian's livery and the Truce of Convocation invoked by Gawmage for the gathering of Arvon's thanes and earls in Dinas Antrum, Kal had spent much of the past three days exploring the palace grounds despite the weather. He returned more than once to the quay where the two river sloops lay berthed, moored among a small fleet of similar ships, each flying the colours of one of an assortment of Arvonian lords. There the Dinastor River edged the grounds, its brown waters curling along the base of a high cliff over which the Palace towered before crawling away downstream to Lake Lavengro. Devved had remained aboard the ships with the seaholdsmen who minded the vessels. His humour had not improved, and, though he greeted Kal civilly, he remained aloof and had not but once or twice ascended the long flight of steps from the moorage to view the royal estate.

The wonder of the capital had been much diminished, however, by the single foray Kal had ventured into the streets of the city itself. The infinite labyrinth of squalid alleys that comprised Dinas Antrum made Woodglence seem like a quaint country village. It became quickly apparent to Kal that neither the Truce of Convocation nor the livery of the Oakapple Isles would afford him even a mote of protection outside of the palace grounds. The garb, in fact, served more to attract that seemingly large margin of the Dinasantrian population that sought easy prey for their malfeasance. Kal had returned to the Silver Palace bereft by a pickpocket of his purse and the small amount he had taken in it, and would have lost Rhodangalas and his hunting knife also had he not kept a firm hand on the hilt of each for the brief time he had walked the capital's streets. By dint of luck as much as good foresight, he had left the Pyx of Roncador in Gwyn's silent keeping, locked within the chambers allotted to Uferian and his retinue.

On the whole, Kal realized, they were a broken people. Such was evident in their eyes, hollowed by hunger and hopelessness, a hopelessness bred of their own impoverishment and the rapacity of the merchants and guildsmen, all Mindal-minded, who, though they battened themselves upon the labours of their countrymen, barred the doors of their ears to the pleas of the same without concession and dared not step foot in the streets of their fellow citizens.

He had first seen the brokenness of the people from a distance, when the ships had sailed through the river gates of the city three days ago. Weary faces appeared, like those of timid mice, lining the long banks inside the river wall to watch the two river sloops as they glided into Dinas Antrum between one of several immense pairs of wrought-iron portals that stood open in the city's ramparts. As they passed, the faces vanished, the people scurrying into the shadows of overhanging buildings, up narrow streets that dribbled filth into the already-fouled waters of the Dinastor. But faces that disappeared were replaced by other faces that peeked out for a moment at the ships and their passengers before fading back into the wretchedness. Deeper into the city they sailed, until the sea of decay broke against the stone-and-iron-grilled walls of mansions and town estates—somber, still, and lifeless—that themselves skirted and pressed against the Silver Palace.

Bethsefra had been affected by it, too, silently withdrawing into her shipboard quarters, where she had stayed with her handmaid, preferring the familiarity of her austere cabin to the foreign opulence of Uferian's assigned lodgings in the Palace. Only once, on their first day and at her father's express bidding, did she venture to walk among the gardens of the Palace with Kal. But she had been ill at ease the while and, after no more than half an hour, had begged Kal's forgiveness and slipped back down the steps to the quay, the ship, and her cabin. Kal had not seen her since, even when he visited the ships' moorage, though his thoughts had turned to her more often than he cared to admit.

At Uferian's command, the ships lay ready at berth, prepared to set sail on a moment's notice should the need arise. Uferian was a man to be prepared, and he had confided to Kal more than once that he harboured grave misgivings about the gathering, despite the tone of merry celebration that was being set for the event by the endless string of lavish banquets, entertainments, and festivities that were already well underway. Even upon their arrival at the Silver Palace, he had pressed Kal to take one of the ships and two of his men as her crew. He had urged Kal to take the vessel and, under the colours of the Oakapple Isles and the pretense of making a short sailing jaunt on Lake Lavengro, leave Dinas Antrum with his companions and make for Gorfalster. Kal had thanked Uferian for his generous offer and had been sorely tempted to take him up on it, indeed would have, had it not been for the burden of responsibility he felt for Devved's actions and the consequences that they might bring upon Uferian's house. In the face of Uferian's protests, Kal had decided to remain with him until the matter was resolved for better or for worse; then, Kal said, he and his companions might avail themselves of the king's kindness.

Indeed, rumours had begun to swirl around the halls of the Silver Palace as the retinues and courtiers of the various Arvonian lords met and mingled. There were many travellers who had passed through Woodglence in the wake of their confrontation with Lysak, and stories abounded, as witnesses, often of dubious credibility, offered the latest variant account of the crimes committed against the young Melderenysian lord and his house. Uferian had taken to remaining in his rooms at all times, other than to present himself at the offices of the Proconsul of Arvon, a man reputed to have the ear of Ferabek, in order to gain an audience to plead in his own defense against the accusations, rumoured or otherwise, that had been brought against him. For two days now, his attempts to speak with the proconsul had been unsuccessful, thwarted, as he was jockeyed from one underling to the next. In the meantime, more and more nobles arrived at the Silver Palace, rumours grew more swollen, and the ships remained in a state of constant, though unobtrusive, readiness.

Uferian, it became obvious, was much mollified by Kal's presence and had taken to keeping his company and seeking his counsel as the days of the Convocation approached. He was a good man, Kal discovered, a quiet man of keen mind and resolute will who had a mien of gentle if unbending authority and who enjoyed the complete loyalty and allegiance of his men. As the days passed, Kal, too, had grown fondly respectful of the man.

Across the broad courtyard, Kal watched three men clad in black step out of the adjacent building and stride towards him, their black cloaks billowing behind them as they hurried over the wet cobbles. They looked like a storm-tossed ravens, Uferian leading the way, his silver head bared, the attendants in his wake pulling their hoods against the cold rain. The king's face was set and his gait purposeful. There was news, Kal thought to himself as he stepped away from the window and closed it on the dampness outside.

A few minutes passed before Uferian and his men entered the chambers, shaking the rain from their cloaks and handing them to a footman.

"Kalaquinn?" Uferian called, then spotted the Hordanu standing by the hearth, where a small fire burned brightly in the grate. "Ah, there you are. We have won a hearing before the proconsul." Uferian approached the fireplace and stood rubbing his hands together. "There is an uncommon chill in the air. I am of a mind that it bodes no good. And it's not just the air that's chill. No." He chuckled without humour.

"Aye, my lord. You've heard the old malediction—'May you live in interesting times'?"

"Hmm, would that our visit to Dinas Antrum be filled with boredom." Uferian smiled ruefully. "But, sadly, such is not our lot."

"But you have gained an audience?"

"Yes, indeed, before the Proconsul of Arvon, on the morrow."

"Do you know what kind of man he is?"

"No, no, I do not. But he is Ferabek's man, so I'll not hold out much hope for mercy. I dare trust, though, that justice will be given its due."

"But he is Arvonian himself, is he not, the proconsul?"

"Aye, and recently elevated to the post by Ferabek for the occasion of the gathering. So much I've heard, but no more. Handpicked from the Mindal, no doubt, for his rare and notable virtues—avarice, connivance, treachery, self-interest, murderousness..."

"Well, you shall know him soon enough—"

"Me? No, I say, rather, we shall know him soon enough. I would sooner have you attend me at this hearing than any other, Kalaquinn. You will come with me? I will rely on your prudent judgment and counsel."

"I am bound by duty and honour to attend you in this and would do so even if I were not." Kal fell silent for a moment and walked slowly to the window again. He looked down on the courtyard outside, then gazed to where the Dinastor lay hidden behind the buildings of the Silver Palace.

"I think it wise to have the ships ready, as you have done, my lord," Kal said. "But I will have to make more preparations myself before tomorrow. At what hour do you stand before the proconsul?"

"Not 'til after midday, although, if experience speaks, I doubt we'll see anything of him much before supper. His offices seem to keep their own time."

"Good. Then, my lord Uferian, by your gracious leave, I'll accept the ship you have offered and the men to crew her, and now I shall excuse myself to attend to my own needs in preparation for tomorrow. I doubt that I will linger in Dinas Antrum any longer than to learn what judgment is made against the accusations you face. Now, I must speak with my companions."

"You have my leave, Kalaquinn, and my ship, both with my goodwill."

✧   ✧   ✧

Morning found Kal on the deck of one of the river sloops. It had stopped raining during the night, and dawn had broken gently, a silver light seeping through the thick overcast that yet obscured the sky. His fellow Holdsmen had removed themselves from Uferian's rooms the night before and settled into the cabins of the ship. They worked now with him, as did the two crewmen promised by Uferian, ensuring that the vessel was adequately provisioned and ready to set sail downstream the moment he returned from the offices of the proconsul.

The two seaholdsmen obeyed Kal's every direction as they would orders given by Uferian himself. They had doffed the habit of Uferian's court in favour of the sailor's loose blouse and trousers and padded barefoot and cheerful over the wet planks of the deck, seemingly impervious to the dank chill of dawn on the Dinastor that gnawed at Kal. The black leather jerkins, the leggings, and the cloaks of the Isles' livery lay ready to hand, however, a suit for each man on board, and would be put on just prior to their sailing from Dinas Antrum—they were, after all, sailing as a visiting party of the Convocation with the desire to witness, firsthand, the splendour of a sunset on the shining waters of Lake Lavengro. It was a sight worth seeing, or so they had been told, and so they would tell any of the Mindal's river patrols should they be challenged in their flight from the city.

For now, only Kal wore the black garments, Rhodangalas slung at his hip, the silver swan on his chest glistening feebly in the wan morning light. His own clothes were stowed below deck with the Holdsmen's weapons and the Pyx of Roncador. Kal had taken Gwyn aside, holding the Pyx in its leather case fashioned by the hammerfolk of Nua Cearta. He impressed upon Gwyn its importance and swore the mute Holdsman to guard it as he would his own life. Were they to lose the Pyx, he had said... Well, it was beyond thinking. Their mission and purpose would be forfeit, as would be all hope for Ahn Norvys.

Kal left Gwyn to weigh the burden of responsibility that had been placed upon his shoulders and slipped away from his river sloop and onto its sister ship. On its deck, he met briefly with Bethsefra. He told her of his intentions to leave Dinas Antrum after her father's audience with the proconsul, averring that the accusations against him would most certainly be dismissed. Despite his assurances, she appeared withdrawn, troubled, as if intuiting that danger lurked on the fringes of the not-too-distant future. Kal sensed her foreboding and attempted to assuage her fears, but she said little, and soon they had fallen into an uneasy silence. They stood leaning on the rail for a long while, looking out at the other ships moored in the palace harbour and the wide expanse of the Dinastor behind them.

Bethsefra relieved the tension, placing her hand on his. As he looked at her, her gaze drifted from their hands on the rail to his face. She held him in her green eyes, unblinking and expressionless, wisps of sable hair straying across her brow, teased in the river breeze. Then she leaned forward and, lifting her face, pressed her lips to his cheek.

"Go now," she whispered into his ear after a long moment, then lowered her eyes. "My father needs you again." She stepped away from him. He bowed his head stiffly, turned, and left.

It was late morning by the time Kal walked up the stairs from the quay. A breeze had risen, breaking the overcast and permitting the sun to shine intermittently through rent clouds with a cold and stark light that belied the fact that it was turning summer. He looked down on the small fleet in the harbour. There, Bethsefra stood at the rail of her ship, looking up at him. Kal raised his hand, and she, he saw, smiled and half lifted hers, then slipped away into her cabin. There was a finality about the leave-taking that Kal felt like a cold weight in the pit of his stomach. Her scent lingered with him, as did the warmth of her face on his cheek. He wondered if he would ever see the princess again and was surprised by a tightness in his throat at the thought. He turned quickly and climbed the remaining stairs two at time.

He crossed the palace grounds at a stride, politely nodding to any he met as he wended his way to the central courtyard and Uferian's lodgings. Outside the chambers, he caught the attention of a footman and bade him bring hot water, food, and ale to the privacy of his room. In short order, Kal was fed, bathed and clean-shaven, and once more dressed in Uferian's livery. He sought out the king in his chamber and found the man pacing the room, attended by two liveried retainers. The two seaholdsmen flitted about the margins of the room like black wrens, tending to meaningless tasks obviously meant to accomplish nothing more than to keep them from drawing upon themselves their lord's ire in his disquieted state.

"Ah, Kalaquinn, there you are," Uferian said, crossing the room to seize Kal's forearm in one hand and his shoulder in the other. "I thought perhaps you had—"

"Forgotten? Left already? No, my lord Uferian, I am ever at your service." Kal smiled in an attempt to calm the man.

"Yes. Yes, of course." The king forced a smile as well. "And I at yours. Come, the hour is upon us." Uferian released his grip on Kal. "Let us see what kind of a man the Proconsul of Arvon is."

The four men left the residences and made their way across the courtyard. Dark wet patches mottled the cobblestones, now awash in sunlight beneath a blue sky. Kal looked up and hoped that their plight might enjoy the same turn of fortune that the weather had—dismal prospects turning sunny.

They entered the offices of the proconsul and were met by a secretary who greeted them perfunctorily. The man ushered them through double doors into a large, high-ceilinged room hung around with ornate tapestries and furnished with upholstered couches and chairs, along with a broad table of gleaming wood. The secretary stood between the doors, a hand on each, bowed his head slightly and exited, pulling the doors closed.

On the table stood a pewter flagon and several small goblets. Kal lifted the flagon, sniffed its contents, and, satisfied with what he discovered, filled two cups. He handed one to Uferian and said, raising the other, "And so, we wait."

But the wait was not overlong. Within a half an hour, the secretary had returned.

"His Excellency, the honourable Proconsul of the Gharssûlian Vassalage of Arvon, will see you now." He half bowed; then, eyeing Rhodangalas at Kal's side and the dagger hanging from Uferian's belt, he said, "Your weapons, sires, you may leave with me."

Reluctantly, Kal unbuckled the belt from his waist and handed both his sword and his knife to the secretary. Likewise, Uferian and his men surrendered their weapons to the secretary, who, at a word, summoned a hitherto unseen lackey to his side. He burdened the man with the pile of weapons and dismissed him.

"If you would follow me," the secretary said, lowering his eyes. He led the way out of the room, along a wide hallway, past a pair of pikemen standing on either side of a massive set of doors, and directed the group into another great chamber. The pikemen wheeled in behind Uferian's party as they entered. The guards stationed themselves at the men's backs, in front of the doors, which were closed with a low thud as the secretary left. On either side of the group, a second and a third pair of guards took two firm paces forward from the walls of the room and stood, stiff and without expression, staring straight ahead. Kal glanced at Uferian, his concern reflected in the king's own look.

Nearly a dozen paces in front of them, an enormous table of deeply carved oak filled the centre of the room. At the table stood a man bent over a sheaf of papers neatly stacked in front of him, beside a quill and a gilded inkhorn. His hair fell over his face, veiling his features. He lifted a page from the top of the pile, scrutinized it, then exchanged it for another, not lifting his eyes, not facing the men who had been brought before him. The man wore a chain of office around his neck. It pressed into the thick fur of his collar and dangled from his chest, glinting in the light of the myriad candles that lit the chamber. The minutes stretched on interminably. Beside Kal, Uferian shifted his weight.

"My lord Proconsul, I—"

"You will not speak unless you are asked to do so," the man stated in a flat tone, not lifting his eyes from the paper in his hand.

Uferian's neck reddened, and a vein in his temple stood out and began to throb. Kal placed a hand on the king's arm and said under his breath, "Peace, Uferian, wait." But something in the proconsul's voice had taken Kal off-guard, too—something he recognized yet could not quite place. Whatever it was, it made his heart pound and his mouth go dry. To their left and their right, the guards remained unmoving. Kal felt the unpleasant, yet increasingly familiar, sensation of imminent danger.

At length, the proconsul exchanged sheets again, still not lifting his head to look at the men brought before him.

"So, Uferian of the Oakapple Isles, vassal to the high king of Arvon and so also to His Illustrious Majesty Ferabek IV, you come to worry me with your trifling grievances over the seaholding of Melderenys and its lord..." He dropped the sheet he held and studied another on the table. "Torras, is it? Or Lysak, that you killed? Or was it both?"

Kal's mind raced. That voice—where did he know that voice?

"My lord Proconsul," Uferian said, stiffening. "The accusations

levelled against me are false. I killed neither the Lord of Melderenys, Torras, nor his son."

"Hmm." The proconsul was silent for a moment, then said,
"Yet your army now occupies Tarkhuna."

"B-but, I—" Uferian stammered, aghast.

"And both lords of Melderenys are slain."

"Yes, yes, they are. But not by my hand. Lysak slew his—"

The proconsul lifted an open palm, silencing Uferian, and said,
"Whether by your hand or not matters little. Either way, we find our
Melderenysian problem solved." Finally, the proconsul straightened
and lifted his eyes from the pages on the table. Kal's heart leapt in
his throat, and he felt his head spin. The proconsul looked first at
Uferian, then glanced at Kal. There was a flash of recognition in
the Proconsul's steel-grey eyes, and the slightest hint of a smile
played at the corners of the thick lips that grew from his oval face.

Kal tried to marshal his wits, collecting thoughts that slewed
about like a team of startled horses running wild. So, the man's
seeds of wild ambition had borne for him a bounty of glory, Kal
thought. And here, by the questionable graces of the Boar, the
traitorous Holdsman stood as Proconsul of Arvon, now more
powerful even than Gawmage himself. Uferian glanced from the
proconsul to Kal and back again, visibly confused.

"Yes, indeed." Enbarr leered at Kal. "Yes, yes, indeed."

There could be no escape from this predicament, Kal thought,
glancing again at the guards to left and right and sensing the
presence of the two others behind him who barred the door.

"Ferabek appreciates a man of action," Enbarr continued, turning again to Uferian, "and your actions do you credit. You do
realize that I enjoy Ferabek's favour and have the power to show
you his partiality?" Enbarr looked down to the table again and
reached for a clean sheet of vellum and prepared it to receive
ink. "So, I ask you, do you recognize and offer allegiance to the
high king of Arvon?"

Uferian was silent a moment, then said, calmly, "I will recognize
and offer allegiance to the high king of Arvon."

"Gawmage?" Enbarr glanced up at him.

"I will recognize and offer allegiance to the high king of Arvon."

"You are a sly one, Uferian." Enbarr grinned and cast a brief
look at Kal. "But you have rendered a great service to my lord
Ferabek. He will be greatly pleased. Yes, very pleased, indeed."

Enbarr picked up the quill, dipped it in the inkhorn, and wrote on the vellum. A minute later, he dusted the sheet, rolled it, and sealed it, affixing a red ribbon with wax and impressing the warm wax with a signet.

"The seal of Ferabek himself," Enbarr said, "acquitting you of any charge that has been or may be brought against you pertaining to the past lords of Melderenys, and granting you title." He handed the document to Uferian. "The seaholdings are yours, Uferian, Lord of the Arvonian Isles. You are free to go." Then, turning to the guards at his left, he said, "Sergeant, have your men escort Lord Uferian and his retinue back to his lodgings and search his rooms for any sign of my fellow Holdsmen. If you find them, place them under arrest.

"And, Sergeant, have this man"—he looked at Kal with a grin— "taken to Tower Dinas."

TWENTY-NINE

The tongue of flame borne ahead of him on the stairs wavered, oily and weak, as it licked at the dead air of the stone passage. He fixed his eyes on it and tried to focus his attention, but it slipped from his mind's grip like an eel from the cold fingers of an old fisherman. The sight of the torch swam before his eyes even as his toe caught the lip of a step and he stumbled once more, the chains clanking from his manacled wrists. He fell against the wall of the passage. He was utterly spent. Exhaustion, like lead in his veins, weighted his limbs. He rested his forehead on the damp chill of the stone, his breaths laboured and catching in his throat. A hand from behind snatched at his shoulder, seizing the crumpled black cloth of his cloak and tunic, and pulled him away from the wall. Someone barked an order, another swore an imprecation, and Kal lifted a foot to the next step and blearily raised his eyes once more to the torch.

It was the sixth or seventh time he had been moved in half as many days, or so he supposed, for he could not be certain how long he had been kept captive after his arrest. The passage of time had become a blur to him, difficult to mark in the dark recesses of the dungeons, where he had been left alone to his gnawing doubts and fears. Indeed, he could not even be sure he was still in the grim confines of Tower Dinas, where he had been taken by boat under heavy guard. The portcullis of the Tower's watergate had closed behind him like the mouth of a ravening creature. After that, he had been led down deep into the bowels of the Tower and locked in a dank cell bereft of light and crawling with vermin, where the echoes of Uferian's remonstrances against his arrest faded from his mind, and a creeping despair began to take possession of him. In a stupor, he had been moved to another cell, then another, and another, his fitful sleep interrupted over and over as he was brusquely awakened and ushered from one stinking hole to the next, until he had lost count of them and was far beyond caring.

Kal glanced back over his shoulder, down the steps to the open door below him. The door belonged to the cell from which he was now being escorted between the rancid bodies of a pair of sullen turnkeys, fore and aft, who took turns swearing at him. It had been a room less foul than the others, though still damp, lit feebly by a single lantern hung from a bracket set high on the wall. The gaol cell had in it a straw mattress, a basin for water, and a bucket by way of a privy—but he could not remember how or when he had gotten there. He did, however, have a vague recollection that, barely conscious, he had been bundled for a second time onto a boat and had been transported across the wave-chopped waters of the Dinastor River under cover of night. The bitter-tasting wine they had pressed on him, with a crust of bread and some mouldy cheese, must have contained a sleeping draught. Either that or his senses had been dulled by a despondency made all the worse by the head-clouding vapours that seeped into the ancient riverside fortress from the vast network of caves and sewers which underlay it. It hardly mattered anyway. Kal had failed—he had failed miserably.

"Come on now, pick up your heels, worm, or you'll be late," growled the man in front of Kal, scowling over his shoulder. Both guards were Gharssûlian, grim-faced, coarse men who spoke Arvonian but with the distinctive accent of the Boar's countrymen, guttural and choked. Although unhelmeted, the guards were clad in mail from head to knee, and they were well armed, like all the guards and gaolers Kal had encountered from the moment of his arrest, even the Telessarians, whom he was more used to seeing in subtle woodland garb.

The other guard prodded Kal roughly from behind, but Kal was too tired to object. He lifted a foot and stumbled again, but braced himself against the stone-block wall. He winced as a manacle bit into a wrist already chafed raw and bleeding. Pushing himself off the wall, he continued to climb the stairs. This time, at least, they had removed the leg shackles.

Soon, the gloom became increasingly dispelled by natural light from narrow openings set into the stone, until, finally, the staircase came to an end at a landing that led into the middle of a long hallway, paneled in oak, with a marble floor. Farther down the hallway, from a broad open doorway on the right, there flowed a wide pool of sunlight. Kal squinted at the brightness and raised his manacled hands to shade his eyes. From a place close at hand, Kal heard a hum of commotion, low and indistinct, the sound muffled and skewed somehow by the walls of the building.

"Get on with you, slug! You'll have time to gawk soon enough. This way." The guards shoved him away from the sunlit doorway and down the hall into a large drawing room, richly furnished, its far wall bright with an open casement window, which was edged by furled drapery fluttering in a slight breeze. A murmuring buzz of voices grew louder.

"Hold out your hands." The guard stepped up from behind him and unlocked the iron cuffs that fettered Kal's arms. Blinking in the light, he rubbed at his wrists and flexed his fingers, easing back the circulation of blood. Kal's eyes strayed to the window of the chamber—the painful blessedness of light! Kal winced and closed his eyes.

"Don't you take to any notions of escape now," the guard holding the chains said. "There's Scorpions at every door and beyond, by orders of my lord Ferabek himself. And even more of them in the square below, watching the windows—make you no mistake."

Kal nodded mutely. He was back, he realized, in one of the many buildings that were clustered around the Silver Palace.

"In there with you." The man lifted his hand towards the open door of an adjoining chamber, the chains clanking in his grip. Kal obediently shuffled forward. On a bed against the far wall, there were clothes neatly laid out. A water basin with ewer stood nearby on a side table beneath a shuttered window. "Take off those rags and wash yourself. See that you shave. Dress yourself with those clothes."

"Yes, be dressed proper, grub," said the other man. "They're right fine clothes. Fit for a king." The man sniggered to himself.

"There is no time for a bath, but mind you make your appearance presentable—clean-faced and shaven. You cannot be late for the Convocation, so you had best be ready when we come for you in a moment."

"Else we will have to turn you out dressed proper ourselves, worm."

"And that is not something you would want us to do, you can trust me. Now, take off those rags." The guards stood waiting, the one leering at him with an ugly sneer on his face, as Kal hesitantly pulled off first his boots and then his tunic and hose. He let the clothes fall to the floor until he stood stripped naked in the middle of the room. The pale silver swan lay crumpled, half hidden in the folds of filthy black cloth at his feet.

Without another word, the sneering Gharssûlian snatched up the discarded clothes from the floor, and the pair left the bedchamber, swinging the door closed on Kal. A key rattled in the lock.

Kal stood motionless for a long moment as if bound by a spell, then turned slowly and went to the basin and filled it with water. With bemusement, he regarded his haggard features in a small mirror above the side table, blinking at the image in the glass as if it were beyond recognition. He broke the gaze and shook his head. He lifted a razor and looked again in the mirror to scrape away his growth of beard. The water was warm. He finished shaving and began to wipe his face and body clean with the sponge he had found beside the basin. It was little enough, but for the first time in days he felt refreshed, even somewhat relieved. He towelled himself dry. For the moment, at least, he was not languishing in a damp, dark cell. All the same, he shivered again, and apprehension clenched at his gut, as he turned and saw the clothes set out for him. Reluctantly, he approached the bed and examined the finely tailored clothes spread out on the counterpane. They were the formal garb of a courtier or a nobleman, stiff and impractical, not at all what he was used to. Beyond a doubt, something was being planned for him by the forces of the enemy, something that was sure to be unpleasant, even deadly dangerous—a final dashing of all his hopes and plans.

Lifting up a high-collared white-linen shirt, he fingered it; then, with little choice but to stifle his reluctance and obey the guards, who would return all too soon, he slipped his arms into the sleeves and buttoned it. He pulled on close-fitting cream-coloured hose, together with loose thigh-length breeches and a padded jerkin with hooked ivory fastenings. Both jerkin and breeches were beige in colour and heavily embroidered, with jewels stitched in between the slashings. Around his waist Kal buckled a tooled leather belt.

Outside, the hubbub of voices swelled and grew increasingly louder, even through the shuttered windows of the bedchamber. He let the hem of the surcoat that he had lifted fall back to the bed, he stepped towards the window, lifted the sash, and eased open the shutters. Below him stretched the Great Square, the familiar broad span of cobblestone that fronted the Silver Palace and its sprawling collection of royal chancery offices and lodgings. The open space that lay spread out before him buzzed with a growing throng of people who milled about and jostled one another, most of them facing a spot situated on his end of the square, off to his right. Many of them pointed and gestured, as if in expectation, while many more folk continued to trickle in from the surrounding maze of alleys. Sprinkled through the crowd were the dread Black Scorpion Dragoons, each standing alert and stiff-backed, each afforded a wide berth by the massing press of people. Kal realized now, with certainty, that he was in an apartment of the Silver Palace itself. Just out of sight below him, he remembered, was a portico fronting the main palace building, from which a broad flight of steps descended to the square and from which, in the past, royal proclamations had been issued.

A couple of hundred paces away, on the far left side of the open concourse, there stood a building from which banners hung fluttering beneath the windows. These bore the emblems of many of Arvon's lords, marking their lodgings for the Convocation. Even though he could not make it out from this distance, the three black banners at the leftmost corner of the building, Kal knew, showed a silver swan. It was from the window above the middle banner that Kal had looked upon the same courtyard, then rain-washed and empty, perhaps three days ago. Kal's mind strayed to Uferian and Bethsefra. He wondered how she was faring now that he had been caught out and his plans had come so unexpectedly unravelled. He knew himself to be a danger to those associated with him. Happily, though, Enbarr had allowed the seaheld king to leave, pardon in hand, albeit under heavy guard. In truth, there was little that the Boar and his minions had to fear; the world was theirs, and all in it. At least, Uferian and his daughter should be safe, or so Kal assured himself.

Startled from his thoughts by a key rattling in the lock, Kal turned, and the door of the bedchamber burst open.

"What's this?" the first guard through the door demanded as he drew his sword. "What are you doing at the window?"

"Nothing—nothing at all," Kal said, raising his arms in a gesture of peaceful surrender.

"Stay away from the window." The guard sheathed his sword and lumbered across the room to slam the shutters closed. "You will have your look outside soon enough," he said as he turned to face Kal again. "Go on. Finish dressing."

The second guard stepped into the doorway, his face still contorted in sneering contempt. Under their watchful eyes Kal put on the surcoat—a billowing robe of red velvet edged with sable and stitched with gold cord—and slipped his feet into the soft calf-leather shoes that had been placed beside the clothes.

"What now?" He stepped away from the bed, holding himself stiffly in the strangeness of his new garb.

"The cap, too. And pendant. Be quick about it." The guard pointed to the items of attire that remained on the bed.

Kal placed the chain of the pendant around his neck and regarded the round gold medallion in the palm of his hand. On the face of the medal was etched the outline of a hind. Then, with studied diffidence, he took the black felt cap in hand, frowned at its white plume and its jewel encrusted turn-up, and placed it awkwardly on his head.

"Now you're a picture, worm," the guard in the doorway said. "A perfect picture of yourself, I'd say."

"Make way! Move aside! Into the light, closer to the window." a man issued gruff orders in Gharssûlian as a handful of Black Scorpions moved in. "Right there. Put it there!" One of the guards grabbed Kal's arm and pulled him roughly to the side. "That's good. Now we have a chance to compare him with the original."

It was a commanding voice and familiar, all too familiar, now that the man had switched to speaking Arvonian. As Enbarr stepped in front of Kal, a couple of Scorpions placed a large frame covered by a cloth beside Kal.

"Do you like art? Take a look," Enbarr said with a sly grin on his face as he unveiled the large painting.

Kal's eyes widened in stark surprise. From the painting, an image stared back at him. The young Holdsman's first thought was that he must be looking at himself in a mirror. The attire, the face, the figure were his. So, too, were the facial expression and pose. Knitting his brow, he took a hesitant step forward, his hand raised as if to test and explore the painting.

"Aye, take a good look, my slippery Master Kalaquinn Wright," said Enbarr, drawing out the syllables of Kal's name in lazy mockery. "It is you. You, sure enough, in all your regal glory. Your spitting image, anyway." Enbarr nodded, his thick lips pursed knowingly, his arms folded across his chest. "Aye, who'd have thought? Your very self! And you, like a picture sprung to life. A sight for sore eyes, too, I might add." A wry smile softened Enbarr's cold features.

"That—it has nothing to do with me. You know it's not me. It's—"

"Colurian, yes. A painting of the young king from the Stoneholding. Been gathering dust for years in Owlpen Castle. But it might as well be you. A remarkable likeness, wouldn't you say? I would. Like father, like son, I'd say, one a mirror of the other."

"No...No!" Kal's voice rose in stern protest as, clenching his fists in frustration, he stepped back from the picture and shook his head. "You're wrong, absolutely wrong. I'm no king's son, I tell you. Frysan Wright is my father. Frysan, the wheelwright of Lammermorn. Ask anyone. Anyone!" He looked around in desperation. From everything he had learned at Aelward's Cot, he understood the long-hidden reason for the likeness, that it was not as one of father to son but a chance likeness that had arched like a stray bolt of lightning over the several generations that lay between him and his royal ancestor—scarcely more than an accidental quirk of bloodline, like a harelip or lefthandedness, or the streak of white growing at the nape of his neck that blazed his otherwise sable hair. "It is no more that a strange resemblance—"

"Proof positive, I'd call it. Proof enough for me and for my lord Ferabek that you, my fine young Holdsman, are the long-lost Prince Starigan and none other, stolen, secreted into the Stoneholding as a babe, and nurtured as a commoner's son." Enbarr paused to adjust the gold-embroidered deep crimson cloak that was draped over his simple white tunic, brushing some dust off his sleeve. He looked up to the armed escort that surrounded them. "See that you guard him closely," he said, "with your very lives. Guard him...like royalty." Enbarr turned on his heel and began to walk away.

"No!" Kal cried out. "Here, take back your trappings! Do what you want with me. I don't care!" He tore off his cap and lifted the pendant on its chain. "Take it back!"

Enbarr stopped in his tracks. Slowly, with an air of studied indifference, he turned. His gaze sought out Kal again. His eyes narrowed into piercing little gemstones that flared with anger like cool points of blue flame in a face that had hardened like granite.

"Put that back on. Now!"

Kal let the pendant fall back around his neck and for a moment stared down at the feather-topped cap clutched in his hands.

"Let me make something clear to you, young Master Wright...." Enbarr wagged his forefinger in admonition and then paused, cupping his chin with the same hand as if pondering the words to say next. "Abundantly clear, in fact. You will do as you are bidden, or it will be the worse for your friends from the Isles. You have little idea how much worse. Uferian will die, and his daughter..." Enbarr's eyes narrowed as he watched Kal's reaction. "As I thought. She will spend years ruing the day she met you, begging us to put her out of her misery. Do I make myself understood?"

Kal nodded in mute acknowledgment and replaced the cap on his head, his bid at resistance thwarted by a deft counterstroke—a counterstroke that went straight to the heart.

A guard placed a hand firmly on Kal's shoulder, wheeled him around, and pushed him towards the door. Acutely aware of the conspicuous figure he cut, Kal stepped in behind the guard at the door, as one of the Black Scorpions recovered the painting and fell in behind him. They threaded their way through a maze of galleries and stairs, descending to the main hall of the Silver Palace, a grand chamber filled with paintings that dwelled in vivid detail on the theme of hunting, a relic of the reign of Colurian.

From the main hall, they passed through a set of stout oaken doors flanked by a detail of soldiers who gazed ahead soberly with seeming inattention but bore the dread Scorpion insignia, a warrant of their efficiency and discipline, and emerged into a covered arcade soaring with white marble columns and arches. The space bustled with soldiers, liveried servants, and attendants, many of whom stopped to look, some discreetly pointing in Kal's direction.

This made him still more uncomfortable. Like a cornered animal, his eyes darting, he sought for an avenue of escape—any avenue. If only he could bolt from this place, reach the warren of alleyways surrounding the square, and lose himself, evading pursuit in some way. His mind raced. He gauged his chances, but almost immediately a dozen Dragoons fell in beside him and his two Gharssûlian keepers. They marched him to a shaded wing that adjoined the unroofed part of the portico. From the portico, a broad and gentle flight of steps fell to the Great Square below. He caught a glimpse of the growing swarm of people gathered there. A dais and high carved chair stood empty in the portico. These had become the focal point of the many eyes in the milling crowd below. Before the stage, a row of heralds in dark livery stood, staring blankly out over the square, waiting. Each held lowered to his side a long silver trumpet decorated with coloured bunting that stirred and fluttered in the breeze.

Kal remained hedged in by his escort. Around him, other armed men moved with purpose, most of them Black Scorpions and Gharssûlian footsoldiers. There was little more than a sprinkling of the usurper Gawmage's own mastiff's-head troops, the voices of these nearly drowned in the harsh foreign sounds of Gharssûlian that filled the area around the dais and the shadowed coolness of the portico.

He spotted Enbarr engaged in an animated conversation with a lean middle-aged man who was overseeing the preparations for the Convocation from a central spot behind the dais. Quick and birdlike in his movements, the man bore a marked air of authority as he looked aside from Enbarr and crisply issued orders to various soldiers and attendants, after which he returned his attention to his master.

Kal glanced at the painting that had been set on an easel nearby. Then turned away from it and pushed forward in an effort to take in his surroundings from a better point of vantage. He remained flanked by guards, and when he moved too far out towards the stage to gain a better look at the square below, they quickly closed ranks and pressed him back to the shadows. Still, he was able to tell, even at a glance, that the square was filling rapidly. Indeed, he thought he had seen Uferian's silver swan standard in the array of banners fluttering before the steps that led up to the raised stagelike platform that was being prepared for the Convocation of Notables. Of course, as a vassal, the old king would have to be present here for this event; an event of this magnitude and moment occurred only once or twice in the span of a century.

Forced to retreat into the wings, Kal noticed on a tall hooded figure clad all in black, wearing a sleeveless leather jerkin, gauntlets, and hose, standing square-shouldered beside a pillar a scant few paces away from him. There was a sinister aloofness in the man's mien and stature, the way he held himself unsmiling, as he looked out on the square, bare arms folded across his chest, his grey hair cropped short under his upraised cowl and a scar running down his cheek from the corner of his eye.

Kal's attention wandered again. While Enbarr had left the scene, the overseer to whom he had earlier been speaking remained near the dais, still issuing orders and sometimes checking the sheet that he held in his hand. Glancing up from his parchment, he marked the arrival of an attendant gingerly carrying something wrapped in a black cloth with an air of hesitation and inquiry. Immediately, the overseer directed the attendant, ushering him towards the black-clad man. The sombre man took in hand the object now proferred him by the servant, who retreated like a startled rat back into the safety of the Palace, and tore away the cloth.

Kal swallowed hard. The taste of bile rose sour in his throat. The man held a scabbard and slowly drew out the sword that it enclosed, his fist clenching the weapon's hawk-shaped hilt. He pulled the length of blade clear of the scabbard and held it up before him, flexing his gauntleted wrist, testing the sword's weight and heft. He nodded in approval of Rhodangalas, admiring the smithcraft, the temper of its steel. Then, after laying aside the scabbard, two-handed he brought the blade around in a whirring arc that sliced the air before him at a sharp angle. He straightened and held Rhodangalas in front of him. His lips curled in the faint makings of a smile, all the more fearful in a face so wanting in emotion. Again he swung the sword, and again. The blade whistled through the air, the man taking grim pleasure in his practiced strokes. Now all eyes in the vicinity of the portico were trained on the man. Kal caught his breath. It was a pointed choice of instrument, Kal thought. There had to be a reason. Now that he thought about it, it was obvious. His knees felt weak and his stomach churned as waves of fear washed over him. The headsman glanced at him unsmiling, then returned to his measured evaluation of the sword.

In the distance, a horn blast rose above the din of the crowd. At once, in reply, there erupted a deafening blare of trumpets from the heralds ranged high above the people in full view. The overseer summoned Kal and his escort closer to the dais. He had the picture of King Colurian brought forward, then hurried to make last-minute adjustments and dispositions in a quick series of orders accompanied by sharp gestures. Kal was now afforded a clearer view of the enormous crowd that had gathered before the steps. All heads were craned towards the back of the Great Square. Kal looked to the standards arrayed below and spotted Uferian and several of his men. The king faced him, his head lifted, gazing up towards the raised platform. From this distance, though, it was impossible to make out his facial expression.

At a discreet remove from the contingent that had come from the Oakapple Isles were the obvious figures of Gwyn, Galli, and Devved. Kal felt a warmth that dispelled some of the gnawing fear. His friends had risked everything to be present.

An expectant hush fell over the crowd. Out of a wide boulevard that formed the main entrance to the square, a small handful of riders appeared—cavalrymen mounted on great warhorses, the grim silhouette of a scorpion emblazoned on each of their tabards. This was how the Black Scorpion Dragoons had started out—as an elite group of armed horsemen, taking for their own the heraldic sign of Ferabek himself. These would be the elite of the elite.

The riders pressed forward into the square. Scrambling out of the way, the crowd parted before them, making way for a carriage drawn by six horses that followed, its large curtained windows and gilded trim gracing a black chassis so highly polished that it gleamed in the strong afternoon sun. When they reached the steps of the portico, the mounted men drew aside to the edge of the crowded concourse, leaving the carriage to pull to a stop amid the banners that represented the foremost vassals of Arvon's high king, not just the leaders of clanholdings, counties, and keverangs, but guildmasters, too, from Dinas Antrum, many of them members of the Mindal, gathered with the members of their fraternity under pennants that showed the emblems of their craft.

A footman, dressed in a mastiff's-head tunic, stepped forward to open the door of the carriage. The first of its occupants stooped his head and set foot on the ground of the square. A man of imposing build and height, with a strong jaw and guarded eyes, he wore an ermine cape over a purple doublet. The devious usurper Gawmage, Kal surmised. He bore a gleaming silver mace, and a simple gold coronet wreathed his full white head of hair. He took three strides to the bottom of the stairs and turned to face the carriage and the crowd beyond it.

A second figure descended from the carriage, this one younger, but more stooped and decidedly nervous, his hair thinning, draped in a long brown bard's cloak tied about the waist with a white sash and bearing in his arms a harp—a golden harp. Kal's eyes widened as he beheld the Talamadh, clutched by somebody who could only be Messaan, the onetime merchant trader falsely installed by Gawmage and the powermongers of the Mindal as Hordanu, in defiance of all custom and usage, in an attempt to undermine Wilum. Messaan moved to stand beside Gawmage at the base of the stairs.

Another wave of numbing fear washed over him as the next figure emerged from the carriage in all his exotic garb, complete with black leather cap and ungainly chin flaps, set off by a white beltless robe embroidered with strange devices: Cromus. Kal fought to stifle the chill that prickled his spine as he remembered with alarming vividness the role that the Thrygian magician had played as Ferabek's soothsayer and conjurer of spirits on that fateful day when Kal and Galli had stumbled on the enemy camp in an upland meadow and had barely escaped with their lives.

Behind Cromus, the door to the carriage gaped empty and black. A stillness had fallen over the entire square. Some time passed before there was a movement in the shadows of the carriage's compartment. Kal was beyond shock or surprise, when, tossing back his long mane of jet-black hair, a short but imposing figure disembarked, a figure whose thick, bearded features and manner would be forever associated in Kal's memory with the terrible destruction of the Stoneholding. The dread Boar of Gharssûl turned from the carriage to the sea of onlookers and raised an arm in greeting, his personality a raw force of nature that seemed to draw all irresistibly into its sway.

"Hail, Ferabek!" Close-packed in the square, its instincts spontaneous and violent, the crowd erupted into a loud cheer that was marked by an eerily hypnotic rhythm, repeated again and again, carried on its own swell like a chant—"Hail, Ferabek! Hail, Ferabek!"

Ferabek quelled the noise of the crowd with a broad gesture of his hands and then turned to mount the staircase, drawing in his wake the other three dignitaries. Now the young Holdsman had a full-frontal view of him and recognized, suddenly, the way in which he was attired. He swallowed hard against the bile rising in his gorge as he took in the crimson velvet robe and heavy golden chain and pendant. It was a deeply disquieting sight. Ferabek was dressed from head to toe exactly like Kal, even to the soft leather shoes and the feathered cap with jewelled turn-up, which was handed to him now by Cromus.

With a rough energy, Ferabek tramped up the steps, ascending towards the portico that overlooked the concourse and its throng, its open forecourt surmounted by the raised structure of the dais. Cromus remained just a step behind him, while Gawmage and Messaan followed even farther behind, their bearing more irresolute and uncertain than that of the Thrygian. Messaan seemed particularly discomfited, holding the golden harp as if it were a useless appendage, like a person ignorant of music, unschooled in the use of the instrument. For his part, Gawmage, who had been a guildsman, a silversmith, appeared to be somewhat more comfortable with the mace, which looked decidedly more than ceremonial, a wickedly lethal club with an orblike head, prickling with long metal spikes.

When they reached the top of the staircase, Ferabek, still accompanied by Cromus, continued his progress across the stone forecourt towards the farther set of steps, which led to the heavily carpeted stage. At the top, flanked by the magician, he turned his back to the ornate high-backed chair that dominated the raised platform and, arms folded across his chest, bowed to the crowd below, which erupted once more into a thunderous chant of "Hail, Ferabek!" Meanwhile, Gawmage and Messaan remained standing at the foot of the raised structure, facing the Boar, raising their arms in acclaim, adding their voices to the din.

Again, with a confident motion of his hands, Ferabek quieted the throng in the square. "Greetings, distinguished citizens of Arvon—kings, thanes, vassals, subjects," Ferabek said. "Loyal subjects, all."

Kal's memories of his first encounter with the Boar stirred to life again at the sound of the man's voice—deep and mellifluous, unique in its power, its lulling resonance belied by the thick lips and the dour cast of his face. It rang out clear over the hush, reaching even the farthest corners of the square, perfect in its pitch and range. Except that today he spoke in good, clear, near-perfect Arvonian, tinged with just enough of an accent to make him seem evocatively foreign and intriguing.

Ferabek cast his gaze over the assembly. Calmly he moved his head around, first away from Kal and then towards him, so that his cold green eyes locked with Kal's, lingering on him with a menace that was almost palpable. Kal flinched at the malevolent air of power exuding from the man, but held his gaze, nervously whispering supplication to Wuldor under his breath, refusing to avert his eyes and be cowed. It was Ferabek who broke the fetters of what seemed like an endless moment, shifting his eyes, turning them to the headsman, beside whom a good half-dozen armed Scorpions had quietly taken station. Almost imperceptibly, Ferabek nodded in acknowledgment of their presence, even as his lips twisted in the slightest of smiles.

"You have been summoned to the Great Square for the Convocation of Notables," he said, returning his attention to the crowd. "I hardly need tell you, an event so rare signifies that momentous events are afoot, that decisions of the highest import are required, that strong action must be taken. The old order is dying, but, even in its death throes, it obstructs the march of peace and order within the kingdoms and principalities of Ahn Norvys that destiny has laid within my charge. The old harmony has been faltering for many years, over a span of time that is measured now in generations and centuries, withering to a shrivelled husk, weak and outworn, with only a small cankerous body of adherents, most of them here in Arvon, its birthplace and cradle, resisting what in the end must come to Arvon and to all of Ahn Norvys without fail, as surely as the sun will rise tomorrow." Ferabek paused as his words echoed over the square and faded away. The assembled people waited, the silence crackling over the square, until the Boar spoke again.

"As you well know, from Gharssûl a new order has come—vibrant, living, powerful, a new order not to be gainsaid by brain-addled simpletons who place such undue stock on living in the faded glories of the past. No, we have a glorious new order that has stepped into the breach. Its power is beyond resistance, and it is taking the place of the old. All the peoples of Ahn Norvys now receive it with the acclaim and gratitude it deserves.

"Except here in Arvon," Ferabek continued, his voice grown somber, "where grave and contentious afflictions beset the body politic, afflictions that hinder the inevitable course of our new Gharssûlian order, afflictions that beg a purgative remedy. My faithful subjects and vassals, let me not mince words. I speak of treason, a nefarious breaking of faith that wears many deviously subtle guises, but none more subtle than what I have found here in Arvon.

"I am Autarch of the Gharssûl Confederacy." Ferabek raised a clenched fist, his hand trembling with anger. "I, constituted by right of main force and natural order as liege lord of this kingdom. I am the bearer of a new dispensation, and I am here to apply my sovereign remedy to Arvon's cankerworm of conniving treachery." Composing himself, he turned suddenly to his left and nodded to the soldiers beside the headsman. They advanced to the foot of the dais, where Gawmage and Messaan stood rooted to the spot, a look of shocked surprise on their features.

"Seize them! Seize the traitors, who lay false claim to crown and harp!" Ferabek bellowed, his arm extended as he pointed directly at the two most eminent members of the Mindal.

"H-how so, my lord? What I have done, I have done on your sufferance." Gawmage turned to look up at Ferabek. "What have I done to cause offence? This?" He raised the spiked silver rod in his hand. "I willingly surrender to Your August Majesty." The silver mace fell to the flagstone at Gawmage's feet. He reached to his head and removed the golden circlet. He let it fall to the ground as he lifted his eyes to meet the gaze of Ferabek. "I surrender the throne to you." The Dinasantrian climbed the first few of steps of the stage, head bowed and hands clasped in deference, even as the soldiers advanced in a tightening half-circle below, their swords drawn.

"I-I-I, too, my lord," stuttered Messaan, ashen-faced, behind Gawmage. "Ever only acting by your leave and in your grace—on your sufferance, like my lord the king, ever only on your sufferance, Lord Ferabek." The man stooped, as if bowing, and placed the harp on the ground, then inched cautiously away from it, as if the thing bore contagion. The soldiers closed behind him, and in an effort to evade them, he scrambled up the steps off balance, jostling with Gawmage.

"Seize them! Now!" Ferabek shook with fury, his finger still extended in accusation. Black Scorpions now jumped ahead onto the steps and drew around Gawmage and Messaan, forcing them back-to-back.

The black-clad executioner strode forward, Rhodangalas held lightly in hand, his forearms as powerful and heavily muscled as Devved's. Now, however, he presented an even grimmer figure, for his head was covered with a hood, its slits for eyes giving him a fiercely impassive air.

With little show of resistance, his chiselled face twisted in a scowl, Gawmage was pushed roughly down to the foot of the stairs. Two soldiers sheathed their swords, then grabbed his arms, while a third stood ready with a length of cord to bind his hands behind his back. In a burst, Gawmage flew from the hands that restrained him and made a mad lunge for the mace that remained lying close by. Seizing the haft, he swung it wildly around and struck the nearest Black Scorpion a wicked blow across the side of the face, just below the protection of his helmet. The man screamed, then slumped down writhing in pain, his head crumpled to a mass of blood and pulp by the wicked spikes. Before Gawmage could free the weapon from the man's face, another soldier sprang forward and brought his sword down full on the mace, knocking it from Gawmage's grasp to the flagstones. Dragoons surrounded him again and pressed him to the ground, pinioning his arms behind him and binding his hands. Struggling against the hands that held him, he was dragged to his feet, wheeled around before the headsman, and forced to his knees. Three soldiers held him fixed in place by the shoulders and arms, as another, facing him, grabbed two fistfuls of the man's white mane and pulled his head forward and down, exposing the back of his neck.

Rhodangalas whistled through the air in a full arc barely slowed by flesh and bone. The severed head was lifted high, the face twitching, eyes wide and mouth agape in a noiseless scream of horror. The Dragoons drew back smartly, and the headless body slumped sideways to the ground. Kal winced, but could not look away. Blood pooled on the flagstones and ran away from the corpse in crimson fingers down joints and runnels in the pavement, one such finger meeting and encircling the discarded coronet of the king of Arvon that still lay where it had fallen.

The shocked silence that had fallen over the Great Square below, as the scene unfolded, gave way to an uproar of approval as the crowd was swept up in the bloodlust and the shifting tide of power. Many, however—Uferian and his retinue, among them, Kal could see as he strained to look, as well as his own companions—stood silent, wide-eyed and incredulous, struck dumb by the stark display of cruelty to which they had just been witness.

The Dragoon holding Gawmage's head handed it to an attendant, who scurried away with the trophy, careless of the blood and gore as he clutched it to his tunic. Other attendants rushed in to remove the rest of Gawmage's corpse, leaving a broad smear of crimson on the pavement before the dais as they dragged it away.

Ferabek now inclined his head towards Messaan. The craven man had been held in tight check, whimpering and without a struggle, cowering, his eyes darting back and forth but averted from the bloody scene, his mind become unhinged by the sudden turn of events. Slowly, sensing that his time had come, Messaan opened his eyes and stared up at Ferabek even as his captors pressed him forward to where Gawmage had just stood. His foot slipped in the blood, and he fell to his hands and knees. Urine pooled around him, staining his brown robe and streaking the crimsoned stones a lighter red.

"No! No, my lord! You c-c-can't. I've done nothing! N-n-nothing. No treason. You are my master, I tell you, my one and only master." Messaan craned his neck, seeking Ferabek's eye, his soft, pliant face contorted with fear. "I will do your bidding. Believe me! You must believe me! Whatever you want! Believe me! Believe me!"

His mewling rose to a scream as he begged for his life. Kal stifled a strange admixture of pity for the pleading figure and raw contempt for his display of cowardice. At least Gawmage had died as a man—not so Messaan.

Once again, Rhodangalas came hurtling around in a smooth death stroke in the hands of the executioner. This time there was no triumphant display of the head, which was removed quickly and unceremoniously along with the body in its long bardic cloak, now sodden and dripping.

One attendant stepped forward and gathered up Gawmage's crown, cleaning it of gore on a cloth that he carried, then setting it on a cushion of blue velvet held by a second attendant. Yet another had picked up the harp Messaan had left on the ground near the executioner, who remained standing at stiff attention, holding Rhodangalas point down before him, both hands on the pommel, ready for whatever grim new task might be required of him.

The attendant who bore the slender golden coronet on its cushion ascended the stairs of the dais and held it out to Cromus. The magician had remained unmoved throughout the happenings, a look of supercilious disinterest on his face, except for the long glance he cast at the patterns of blood on the pavement below, which he studied with the hint of a smirk teasing the corners of his mouth. He now turned to the attendant that had come to his side and lifted the coronet without a word.

Having doffed his bonnet, Ferabek turned to face the crowded square. Cromus moved behind him and held out the slender crown with both hands, tall and gaunt, like an ungainly bird of prey.

"Vassals and loyal subjects of Arvon, know you this." Cromus let the words ring out slowly and then paused. "The age of Ardiel has ended. The ploughman's seed is no more. A new order rises in its place." He paused again. "A new order demands a new king. Fresh bloodlines sprung from the soil of Gharssûl. Behold!" Cromus cried, his voice rising and becoming shrill as he placed the crown on the head of the Boar. "Behold His Royal Majesty Ferabek, High King of Arvon! Ruler of the world!"

Ferabek stood looking over the crowd, his powerful earthen solidity strangely magnified by the symbol of kingship he now wore on his brow.

"Hail, Ferabek!" Cromus intoned, as he moved to stand at the Boar's right hand.

"Hail, Ferabek!" The crowd took up the refrain again and again.

Though much shorter than Cromus, Ferabek dominated the stage, lifting his arm in acknowledgment of the crowd's approbation. His thick lips stretched in a smug grin. The crowd cheered for long minutes without abatement, until, at last, he quieted them with a lifted hand. Now the other attendant came forward, holding the Talamadh, and mounted the steps of the dais. Ferabek beckoned him forward and took the golden harp from his hands.

"Now, by the power that is vested in me as high king of Arvon—first in a line of blood that will stretch through the ages from generation to generation—I give Ahn Norvys its new Hordanu—its true Hordanu—keeper of the Talamadh, keeper of the earthborn harmony, first in a line of bards that will sing the glories of this new order." With that, Ferabek pressed the Talamadh into the hands of Cromus, who bowed. "Cromus, Lord of the Harp, will usher in the new order in song on this auspicious day, this day which has been known as the Summer Loosening but shall be no more, for just as the infancy of spring yields to the ripeness of summer, so does the futile promise of the old harmony submit and yield to the new order. And so, this high feast of Ahn Norvys shall no more be called the Summer Loosening, but shall be called henceforth the Day of Triumph!" Ferabek raised his hand to Cromus, who bowed again and lifted the Talamadh. Eyes agleam, Cromus sought the strings of the harp.

"Hold, Cromus!" Ferabek commanded. "Before you usher in this new order, before you sing the Day of Triumph, one last affair of state remains. There remains one last bit of sordid treachery we must uproot, yet one more false claim of kingship we must rebuff." Ferabek turned to where Kal stood in the shadows below the dais and lifted an upturned palm. "Bring him forth, our so-called king, along with the portrait of his late, lamented sire."

Kal took a breath and tried to calm himself as his guards herded him to the front of the dais. He cast a fearful glance at the hooded executioner. Above him, Ferabek had seated himself on his chair of state.

"To us, to us, let him come to us, our esteemed royal personage. Stay, stay!" Ferabek bade the guards hold back, even as other servants placed the easel with the portrait of King Colurian in full view of the crowd. "Yes, without his courtiers, himself alone, so that we may admire him." Smiling coldly, he beckoned the young Holdsman up the steps of the stage.

His feet leaden, stifling the lump in his throat and the churning of his stomach, Kal plodded his way up the stairs unaccompanied, closing the distance between himself and the Boar, who hovered over him on his thronelike seat, dark and threatening, as inevitable as a looming storm. Fighting his dread, Kal came to stand before Ferabek, the man who as Autarch of the Gharssûlian Confederacy had brought so much of Ahn Norvys under his sway.

In a sudden display of agility, Ferabek leaped from his chair and strode up to Kal, stationing himself within arm's length of him, looking him over with a quizzical and malicious eye, taking in the young Holdsman's dress and features from top to bottom with an exaggerated attention to detail. For long moments, not a word passed the man's lips. So close that he could almost smell and feel the Boar's feral energy, Kal struggled to stave off his feelings of hopeless fear.

Finally Ferabek spoke.

"Well, well, well! What have we here? Yet another king for Arvon? It seems that Arvon has a surfeit of kings."

"I am not a king," Kal said, suppressing the quaver in his voice.

"Ah, but your clothes betray you." Ferabek pinched the sable edge of the red velvet surcoat. "Why, you're the very picture of your sire."

"You're mistaken."

"How so? Have you not heard the common wisdom in that far-off highland haunt of yours? Clothes make the man. Look, look how royal we are, the two of us vying with one another for overlordship of Arvon. So nobly attired, the both of us." Ferabek indicated his own identical garb with a flourish of his hand.

The crowd had fallen still, utterly still, hanging on every word of the conversation, its sharp clarity of tone causing it to resonate throughout the square in echo from the surrounding buildings.

"You're mistaken. I'm not who you think I am. I am not Colurian's son. I am not Starigan. He remains lost. I'm no king."

"Well, of course you're not. How could I be so terribly simple? You'd think I was a highland yokel born and bred." Below them, the crowd twittered at the jest, and Ferabek smiled appreciatively before returning to Kal. "Why, of course you're not Prince Starigan," he said. "The very thought is absurd." Ferabek's tone took on a harder, ironic edge as he brought one arm across his chest and used it as a rest to cradle his forehead in the palm of the other hand, caressing the coronet that circled his brow, his features creased with an exaggerated frown.

"Why, that's it! I've found the very answer! Such an easy conundrum to solve—why it is that you cannot possibly be the long-lamented King Starigan!" His mouth grew slack with a mocking smile as he lowered his hand, gazing spellbound at the splayed fingers and open palm as if they were an oracle that held the solution that he sought.

"Why, a king is not a king without his crown!" the Boar cried out even as he tore the bonnet from Kal's head and cast it off. "A king's but a common knave, the shadow of a man without the glister of gold on his royal brow!" With two hands, Ferabek lifted from his own head the regal circlet of gold that he had stripped from the ill-fated Gawmage. "I crown thee King Kalaquinn Wright." Kal flinched as the Boar placed the circlet on his head. "Hail, King Kalaquinn! Hail, Your Royal Highness!" Ferabek stepped away and bowed in false obeisance, then fixed a steady, pondering eye on the young Holdsman again.

"Has a fine ring to it, does it not? King Kalaquinn Wright, foremost of my vassals. Or should it be King Starigan? No, no, High King Starigan rather, so near to the throne, so desirous of my royal estate that he mocks me with his garb, makes mimicry of my kingship, my high kingship over Arvon." Like a rising storm, Ferabek now ground his teeth in a sudden manifestation of anger, which seemed to subside almost as soon as it began, replaced by a tone more sinister for all its wheedling softness. "Ah, but let us leave aside rancour, King Kal. Cromus, pray, what do you think? May I be so bold and so familiar as to call our royal personage King Kal?"

"By all means, my lord, he has earned your honour and your respect," Cromus said, tipping his head ever so slightly toward Kal.

"Good King Kal, king of the old and the moth-eaten, the pride of Ardiel's long and illustrious line. Come, I have a notion to be festive. Let us celebrate our discovery of the lost prince and his crowning." Ferabek clapped an easy hand on Kal's shoulder. Kal bristled at the intrusive shock of the man's touch, but did not speak. "It's a pity, though, that he wraps himself in silence, our good King Kal. I've a notion that he might be stirred to speech by song. Cromus, what say you hand him the Talamadh for a spell? Don't worry, you'll get it back soon enough."

The Thrygian magician proffered the harp to Kal, grinning rapaciously, his half-lidded eyes looking down his aquiline nose.

"Take it!" Ferabek ordered curtly, his voice rising to a surly growl at Kal's hesitance to reach out and accept the instrument. "Or do we need to punish your friends for your unwillingness to cooperate?"

"Come, play us a jig, O king of what is past," Cromus urged, lifting the harp higher. "Or better still, a lay for your crowning."

"Very good, Cromus! We need a lay for his crowning.... It will be his dirge."

THIRTY

The fog that had clouded Kal's thoughts cleared like the mists of a summer's dawn retreating before the sun. Below him, the crowd had fallen into an uneasy quiet, anticipating the next gruesome event in the day's spectacle. Cromus's raptorial form still loomed to Kal's right, holding out the Talamadh. The arched swan's neck and golden strings gleamed in the sunlight. Kal traced its gentle curve with his gaze, but did not move. Behind him, the Boar grunted his encouragement and patted Kal on the shoulder. The Holdsman bristled again under the touch.

"Not in the Harp, but hands that play . . . The one who sings, and not the Lay . . ." Like the thought of a thought, words drifted to Kal's mind. *"Mark, it is he who sings today . . . For I Hordanu am . . . for I Hordanu am . . . Hordanu am . . ."*

He let his eyes fall to the press of people filling the square below him. On their faces, in their eyes, he perceived the breadth of human emotion—passion and hope, expectation, fear, elation and sorrow, grief, anger, joy, despair, indifference—all were laid out before him. In his breast, his heart skipped a beat.

"For I Hordanu am . . . I Hordanu am . . . Hordanu am . . ."

The crowd shuffled and murmured in the cobbled courtyard. To Kal, the colours of the lords of Arvon's retinues seemed to grow in vividness, as if the sun had begun to shine brighter. Somewhere, a young child cried with the choking sob of protest over a whim not catered to by his parent. A breath of breeze teased a stray lock of hair at Kal's brow beneath the circlet of gold, and he heard the soft rustle of a banner hung from the walls of the palace towering behind him. Cromus rocked almost imperceptibly back and forth, still holding out the Talamadh, gloating over his prize, his dark mirth catching in his throat as a muted cough. Ferabek's hand now rested on Kal's shoulder. He felt its prickling heat.

"Come, come, King Kalaquinn." The Boar spoke in a low voice, its spell binding, its power palpable and absolute. "Come, my lord, you bear the crown, now take up the harp, your precious token, and play for us. Come, here"—Ferabek lifted his hand from Kal's shoulder—"take our seat as your own, as your regnal throne. Rule over us in song, O king of an age now spent, now ended. Come, play!" He shoved Kal stumbling a step toward the Thrygian magician, who pressed the Talamadh into Kal's hands, spun him around, and pushed him in the direction of the chair.

"For I Hordanu am ... I Hordanu am ... Hordanu am ..."

Kal felt the cool weight of the Talamadh in his hands and the familiar chill that ran up his spine at the otherworldliness that emanated from the object. Its presence seemed to stave off and repel the seductive lure of Ferabek's voice.

Without taking his eyes from the harp, Kal stepped to the ornate seat and turned toward the crowded square. Slowly he lifted the harp, his gaze following it, until he held it high over his head.

"For I Hordanu am ... I Hordanu am ... Hordanu am ..."

"Yes, yes, sit! Play for us!" Ferabek's thick lips quivered in a sneer. "Play!" he barked, "Play!"

"I give thee thanks, O Wuldor," Kal whispered, still looking at the raised harp, its frame flashing with blinding auric light reflected from the sun. Ferabek continued to speak, malice and contempt seeping from his words. From the corner of his eye, Kal saw Cromus ape his master's scorn as he lifted his head and gazed down his long nose, disdain pulling at the corners of his mouth. A breeze rose. The unfastened flaps of the magician's black leather cap lifted and fell, making it look as though a large raven had come to perch on the Thrygian's head. The banners above Kal snapped in the stiffening breeze.

"Yes, yes! Play! Sing!" the Boar cried. "Sing to Wuldor, who was and who is no more! Sing, yes, sing!" Ferabek's laughter rose maniacal, feral, resounding from the dais like the howl of a beast. "Enbarr!" he called, looking into the portico for his proconsul. "Enbarr! This is your countryman! This is your doing! Come and witness his end!"

"Thou, Wuldor, in the beginning hast laid the foundations of Ahn Norvys unto all its furthest marks," Kal intoned, his voice rising with the wind. "All within the compass of the rising and setting of the sun thou hast laid and even beyond these boundaries all is of thy founding might. When the sum of the ages shall be filled—"

"Hail, king of yesterday!" Ferabek howled. "Sing of that which is no more—"

"—and century upon century shall lie in the procession of the years, these mighty works of thine shall march darkling into night, but thou shalt endure." Kal's voice grew steadily stronger, even as the rising wind buffeted him and made the crimson cloak press to his side and tug, flapping, from his neck. "All these shall wax old like a garment, and as a vesture shalt thou change them, and they shall unto harmony be restored for the span of a Great Year, until chaos doth rise afresh from gloom-darkened fields—"

Ferabek threw back his head in laughter. "A new day dawns!" he shouted "Yes! Yes! A new day dawns!" The Boar continued to laugh, and Kal saw Cromus slip a long dagger from the sleeve of his robe. The Thrygian's eyes narrowed, and he took a half-step towards Kal.

"Though these works of thine wax old," Kal continued, closing his eyes and lifting his face to the raised harp. "Thou art ever the same, and thy years shall not fail, from generation unto generation, though they be as countless as the leaves of spring."

Even as the last syllable was spoken by Kal, the wind blew still harder.

"Yes! A new day! A new age!" Ferabek said. "Cromus, do not even the elements attest to it? Yes! Yes!"

In that moment, there rose from the Talamadh a whisper of a sound. It grew steadily stronger, louder, a resonance encompassing all tones at once, from the deepest earthborn boom to the thinnest trill of birdsong, rising, growing, deepening. Kal felt the Talamadh vibrating in his hands. In the harp's song he could hear lines of melody, dozens of them intertwined, woven together without any dissonance. He heard phrases of tunes he knew. One would rise above the others, then fall back into the harmonic tapestry of the whole, even as two others swirled up above the rest like swallows in chase of one another.

Kal opened his eyes slowly. The sun blazed in the deep azure field of the sky. As he lowered his gaze, Kal was startled to find that the sea of faces in the square, the soldiers closest to hand, even Enbarr, Cromus, and Ferabek, had all disappeared. No longer did Kal stand on the raised dais at the foot of the Silver Palace. He stood at a seashore, its vast, gently undulating surface stretching out uninterrupted to the far horizon, a barely discernible line where blue ocean met blue sky. Then a rank of mountains rose up out of the sea, obliterating the horizon and encircling a portion of the water with their stony fastness. Footing the mountains was an expanse of deep green forest, broken here and there by cleared fields and pastureland that swept down to the water's edge. Steadings dotted the open land, and, far to his left, Kal could see the clustered buildings of a large settlement like a dark grey smudge on the shore. To his right, on the opposite end of the small sea, an island sat in the mouth of a bay. A castle stood on the island, and behind the island, small in the distance, Kal saw the tall domed form of the Great Glence.

The Stoneholding lay spread out before him, pristine in its wild beauty, ringed around by the snow-capped peaks of the Radolans, Deepmere sparkling beneath a cloudless sky. From the surface of the lake, a great flock of white geese lifted in a cloud of flashing wings. They banked away, steadily climbing, then wheeled around, until they were flying directly toward the Great Glence.

Kal looked again toward Wuldor's Howe, protected by the island. Before Kal's eyes, the form of the Great Glence began to shift, as if somehow being wrested from the ground on which it sat. It grew larger, slowly at first, the granite dome swelling, until it seemed that the distance between him and the structure was rapidly closing. Kal felt a sensation of weightlessness and was unsure if the building was flying towards him or he towards the building. The stonework of the Glence had lost all appearance of solidity as it stretched, filling Kal's entire field of vision. The massive dome loomed over him, and its great oaken doors flew open, revealing nothing but shadow-cast blackness. The opening grew wider, like the maw of a ravening beast, and Kal was devoured by the edifice to the sound of a howling wind. The doors slammed shut behind him. There was silence and utter darkness.

Kal felt the raw surge of fear consume him. His heartbeat throbbed in his ears, and he heard his fitful, sucking breath catch in his throat. His fear enveloped him and coalesced, covering him like another skin that painfully peeled away from him and slipped, a formless vapour, into the darkness. Fear was replaced by doubt, which crept over him, heavy and clinging, until it, too, was rent from his frame and flew off unseen. He would have cried out from the agony that wracked his being, had he the breath to do it.

Now anger filled his veins and seeped out his pores, condensing on his body like a heavy sweat that trickled and ran cold from his brow, his chest, his limbs. His strength ebbed with it as it pooled at his feet and purled away into the blackness.

Pride swelled in his chest, expanding his lungs until he thought his distended torso would tear apart, rib from rib. His head jerked back, and his mouth gaped open. In a silent scream, a torrent of black smoke spewed from his throat and swirled up into the void above him.

Wave after wave, his viciousness manifested itself in violent, wrenching forms—resentment, a leaden weight that bowed him over nearly to the ground; envy, an icy chill in his marrow; disdain, contempt, and scorn contorted his features and made his eyes burn like metal orbs in the belly of a forgeman's fire, until he would have torn them out himself. Avarice, malice, ill-will, and meanness, every trace of corruption or aberration of his character appeared to him like another self and tore at his very being, leaving him weak and empty, like a vessel drained, a shell, thin and brittle.

Kal had fallen to his knees, leaning on the knuckles of one hand, gripping his stomach with the other. Around him he could see all his maleficence, every flaw of his character, depicted by the vague shadow forms of his intemperate nature, as on an invisible stage, black on black, with himself at the centre. These same amorphous, miasmal shapes that swirled around and surrounded him now mocked him, condemned him in voices from his past—his own voice and his own past. Kal buried his head in his hands, sobbing noiselessly, too feeble and frightened even to lift his eyes.

He gradually became conscious of a faint light in the abyss of darkness that enshrouded him, but, peering between his fingers, he saw only blackness and shadow. Still, Kal sensed the light growing stronger, and a calmness overcame him, a calmness that blossomed into a deep peace. Kal lowered his hands from his face and looked with shocked bemusement at his fingers and his palms.

They glowed dimly, as if he held light cupped in his hands. The gleam grew steadily brighter. The brilliance, it occurred to Kal, came not from his hands at all, but was reflected by them. He moved his hands away from his face, and they dimmed. Drawing them closer to his face, they became brilliant again. Around him, the shadows gave way to the mysterious candescence, and he rose to his feet. Courage possessed him, and he laughed aloud. He stood in the centre of an ever-widening sphere of light, around the vague margins of which shrieked and thrashed the shadow-shapes of his faults. These retreated from him, shrank back into the failing shade of darkness, until the grey stone walls of the Great Glence appeared, and the shadows were no more.

Like a wave erupting from the surface of a still pool into which a stone is thrown, an intensity of brilliant light burst from Kal, and he could see nothing but whiteness. From the depth of brilliance, the faint form of an immense block of stone resolved, upon which stood the Talamadh—luminous, marvellous, glorious! Kal's eyes were fixed on it, and it alone. The Talamadh consumed his entire attention.

Staring at the harp, Kal became slowly conscious of a single line of melody carried by a single human voice singing in a language foreign to his ear, woven into the now gentle sonority of the harp. The Talamadh glinted in the sunlight, its golden form framed once more by the blue Arvonian sky. Kal lowered himself, still singing, to the throne in front of which he had been standing, and, as he drew the harp to himself, the wind music faded and was replaced by the fanned thrum of rising and falling arpeggios as his fingers moved over the strings.

The wind had subsided to little more than the waft of a warm summer's breeze. The breeze carried a clamour of fear, panic, grief, and sorrow mixed with laughter and cries of elation to his ear. It dawned on Kal that there were people nearby. It struck him as bizarre, this eclectic jumble of expressed emotion. Close at hand, someone screamed, "No! No! Stop! Take it from him! Take it! Take it! Take it!"

The melody was complete, and Kal let his palms rest on the strings he had been plucking. He raised his eyes from the harp and looked to the square below. The expanse of cobblestone was in a state of near-complete chaos. A press of people fled from the square up every avenue and alley that led away from the

Palace. Others stood fixed in place, scattered across the square, staring up, enraptured, at Kal holding the sacred harp. Some stood staring with blank, expressionless faces; some seemed caught up in what appeared to Kal like uncontrolled giddiness. All around them, banners and pieces of clothing lay strewn over the cobbles.

And there were bodies. Some writhed in convulsive anguish. Others lay motionless. Whether these were dead or alive, Kal could not be sure. Many of them were Black Scorpion Dragoons or Gawmage's dog's-head troops. In a far corner of the square, a lone soldier tried to restore some order and rally the few of his compatriots who were still standing.

"Cromus! Take it from him! Stop him! Cromus!"

Kal looked to his left, where Ferabek was on all fours, his back arched, snarling over his shoulder at his Thrygian magician. Slaver and vomit stained the Boar's contorted face and pooled on the flagstone and over his fingers and hands.

"Cromus, you wretch, do something!"

There was the sharp clatter of metal on stone. Kal looked at his feet, and there lay a bloodied dagger, the one the Thrygian had drawn from his robes. Kal lifted his gaze to where Cromus stood motionless, little more than an arm's length away, his expression wooden and inscrutable.

"Cromus! Cromus!" Ferabek cried.

The Thrygian blinked once, heavily, and opened his mouth as if to speak, but no sound came out. He lowered his eyes to where his hands pressed against his lower abdomen. A red stain crept from behind his hands, drawn, as by a wick, by the white fabric of his robes. As Cromus lowered his hands, a mess of mottled pink viscera slipped from a long tear in the cloth at his belly, spilling into his hands, overfilling them and falling to the ground. The faintest hint of a smile teased the Thrygian's face, and he sank to his knees and closed his eyes.

"Cromus! Crom—Proconsul!" Ferabek screamed, clawing at the soiled flags with his nails. "Stop this from happening! Proconsul! Enbarr! Enbarr! Enbarr! Enbarr!"

Kal glanced into the wings of the portico. There were no soldiers or guardsmen to be seen. The headsman had fled, leaving Rhodangalas lying on the ground where it had fallen from his hand. Only the unmistakable figure of Enbarr remained, aloof and cringing, clinging to the shadows of the portico. He clutched his robes about him, and a look of strained confusion etched his dimly lit features as he looked at his liege lord groveling on the dais atop the Great Square. Enbarr shot a long glance at Kal, his expression unchanged, then turned and fled into the Palace.

The Boar raved, shaking his head from side to side, then began to pound it on the wet flagstones. A spurt of blood flew from his scalp, and just when it seemed that he would split his skull open, Ferabek slumped to the ground. His limbs twitched, and then he fell still.

"Kal!"

Gwyn came bounding up the steps two at a time towards him. "Kal!"

Galli and Devved were running up behind Gwyn. Both were shouting as they ran. As Gwyn approached the top of the stairs, a soldier appeared from the palace and ran to Ferabek. Kneeling beside his master, the soldier glanced up at Gwyn but offered him no challenge as he ran past. Another soldier appeared but ignored the Holdsmen altogether, coming to the assistance of his comrade and his lord.

Kal looked up at Gwyn from where he sat. The young Holdsman's face was placid, but his eyes betrayed an insistence and an urgency of purpose. Galli and Devved now flanked Gwyn.

"Kal, are you all right?" Devved said. "Get up. We must go."

Kal remained seated, motionless. Gwyn reached forward and gently shook Kal's shoulder and nodded to his friend.

"Uferian and his men have left for the ships," Galli said. "I sent them ahead while we came to get you. Everything's in confusion. What happened, Kal? Did you see it? I'm standing there watching the Boar and his Thrygian pushing you around, and all of a sudden—"

"Galli, leave off," Devved said. "We have to go, Kal."

"All of a sudden, I'm in my beeyard," Galli continued, "at the Burrows, nice and peaceful, until the bees all start to attack me. But it's not the bees attacking me, it's me attacking me! It was the strangest—"

"And I was afire in my own forge, and we'll talk about it later, so stop nattering, Galli," the blacksmith said. "Now we must run. While we have a chance."

Kal smiled. "It's all right, friends," he said and stood up. "All is well. Come, let us leave as Devved bids us." Kal walked past the soldiers still crouching over Ferabek's inert body without looking at them. "Galli, my sword, get it for me, please. And the scabbard..." Kal cast a glance to one side and the other, until he saw Rhodangalas's sheath and the sword belt lying on a table within the portico. "There." He pointed.

Led by Kal, the group turned and descended the stairs to the square. A knot of soldiers on the far side of the square had seen them and raised the alarm. "To arms! To arms!" The cry echoed off the surrounding buildings as the small cohort began to run across the cobbles toward the stairs, swords drawn.

An alley branched off the square skirting the foundation of the Silver Palace. Kal glanced at his companions. "To the moorage. To the ships," he said. "Now we run, friends! Now we run!"

Devved balked, hesitated and looked at Kal, then stooped to the prone figure of a fallen soldier, his mastiff's-head tunic crumpled over him, and drew the man's sword. "I stay here," he said. "You all go."

Kal placed a hand on the blacksmith's chest. "Hold them off as long as you can," he said. "We'll wait for you as long as we can. Briacoil, Devved. May Wuldor hold you in his eye."

"Go, Kal. Go now. Briacoil."

As Kal skip-stepped backwards away from Devved down the alley, the blacksmith turned to face the square. Kal spun around and ran after the two other Holdsmen, clutching the Talamadh to his breast. In but a moment, Kal could hear behind him the grunted exertion of Devved swinging the sword and the ringing clash of metal on metal. As their way cut to the right around a corner away from the Palace walls, Kal glanced back up the alley. Devved fought three soldiers. Two more stood ready behind them, and still two others lay on the cobbles nearby.

"May Wuldor hold you ever in his eye, Devved.... Friend," Kal whispered, then turned the corner, and Devved was lost to his sight.

The three Holdsmen ran through the grounds of the Silver Palace, heading for the quay down alleys and bypaths that were all but deserted. Those few people whom they did chance to encounter either ignored their passage or looked at them with the blank stare of utter confusion. Through it all, Kal tried to push the thought of Devved from his mind. He had sacrificed himself for the sake of his friends.

Once, as the Holdsmen slowed their pace to get their bearings, a man appeared from an adjoining alley and pulled up short at the sight of Kal, blocking the way. Dressed in common garb, coarse and well-patched, the man clearly belonged to the outer streets of the city. The stranger's eyes settled on the Talamadh, then searched Kal's face. A look of dawning comprehension quickly passed over the man's face, replaced almost at once by a queer admixture of pain, intercession, and a profound joy. Kal pulled the velvet robe over the Talamadh, concealing it from view. The stranger fell to his knees and grabbed Kal's hand and pressed it to his brow. The man muttered something that Kal could not make out. Then, lifting his face to look at Kal, he said, "Thank you, my lord, thank you. I am one of... There are others, many others. Ardiel's breath still fills the breast of many in Arvon, even here in Dinas Antrum. I-I could not see you..." The stranger's voice caught in his throat. He coughed, then continued, "B-but I heard you. I was beckoned...drawn, somehow...I can't explain, but I came days ago to wait at the Palace gates. Then I heard your voice. And the music!" The man threw his head back, still clinging to Kal's hand, and laughed. Kal glanced at his companions. Gwyn nodded and smiled, looking at the kneeling man.

"The gates were left open after the music.... Oh, the music!" he said. "Many fled, but I found you! I found—" The sound of cries echoed from the stone walls crowding the narrow street, and the man glanced down the alley behind the Holdsmen.

"Kal!" Galli tugged on his friend's sleeve and shot a glance back down the way they had come. "Kal, we must go. Now!"

The stranger let go of Kal's hand, stood and bowed stiffly. "Yes, go, go ...," he said as he stepped aside. "I will tell the others. Go, now, and thank you, thank you, my lord Myghternos Hordanu." He bowed again.

Kal stared at the man, who remained bent over, looking at the cobbles at his feet. Galli grabbed Kal's arm and tugged him away. Without glancing up, the stranger turned and retreated back down the alley from which he had emerged.

Kal was shaken by the encounter but doggedly followed Gwyn and Galli in their flight to the ships. "How had he known me?" Kal puzzled aloud to himself. "And the music? How had he—"

"Kal, this way!" Galli called. "We'll throw them off our path!"

They crossed a small enclosed courtyard and slipped beneath an archway into a narrow passage, then another, and out onto an expanse of manicured lawns that overlooked the Dinastor River. Kal's thoughts turned again to the strange man, but there was no time to think further. They had reached the top of the long flight of stone stairs leading to the quay.

Below them, the two sister river sloops from Uferian's fleet sat amid nearly forty similar ships moored to stays along the quay or lying at anchor in the harbour's sheltered waters. Save for the seaholdsmen standing ready to sail on the *Gloamseeker* and the *Pelidore*, not a soul stirred on the decks of any of the ships. On the *Gloamseeker*, a sailor bent over the hatch and straightened again even as Bethsefra appeared from belowdecks and looked up the steps. She waved excitedly, then turned back to issue orders to her men on both the ships. Her voice drifted up the stairs, but was unintelligible, lost to the Holdsmen in the breeze.

Kal sped down the stairs and stepped onto the quay by the sloops a moment later. Bethsefra stood waiting for him on the deck of her ship. The fear and expectancy that etched her gentle features softened into relief as she ran down the gangplank and threw her arms around Kal's neck and buried her head in the folds of cloth on his chest. Just as suddenly, she withdrew, staring at the golden harp that poked out from beneath his cloak.

"The Talamadh?" she said in barely more than a whisper.

Kal drew back his robe, revealing the harp. Bethsefra stared at it, her hands covering her mouth.

"Oh, Kalaquinn," she said at length. "I heard it! Oh, it was the most beautiful... Was it you? Oh, yes! Yes, it was! Oh, Kal!"

"You heard the music, too?" Galli asked, drawing up beside Kal. "How could you? You were here, weren't you?"

"Yes, Galli, yes. But there was such a wind. We thought the ships would be lost, even tied to the docks. But then the sound... I've never heard anything like it."

"What happened then?" Galli asked, pressing closer.

"What happened?" Bethsefra glanced up at Galli. "Why do you ask, Galligaskin?"

"Something happened, didn't it? What happened after you heard the music?"

"I was not here."

"You weren't here?"

"I mean, I was here, but I somehow found myself in the castle court at Swanskeld. I know, it sounds absurd!" She shook her head and glanced at Kal again.

"No, it doesn't," Galli said. "Tell me what happened, Bethsefra."

"I was fighting. I-I fought myself.... I mean, I was at practice with my sword, and I ended up sparring against myself. But... it wasn't me...."

"It was everything wrong in you?" Galli said.

"Yes...somehow," Bethsefra said. Her brow furrowed in thought. "And it was more than sparring. It was a fight to the death, but I won.... Somehow, I won." She looked exhausted and confused, but beneath that there was a look of peace. Kal placed his hand on hers.

"Galli, Gwyn, we must leave. Go, ensure that the *Pelidore* is ready to sail." The two Holdsmen turned away and bounded along the quay and up the plank to the second river sloop. Kal turned again to the woman. "Where is your father? Has he arrived yet?"

"No. I don't know where he is."

"Galli told him to make for the ships from the Silver Palace," Kal said. "He should have been here by now."

"No doubt he would have to gather his effects from his lodging. I'm sure he will arrive soon. But where is Devved? I do not see him with you."

"No." Kal shook his head and looked out across the river. "No, Devved is not with us. He is dead. He gave himself up to let us escape. But Uferian," he said, looking back at the young woman, "he will escape the city without any trouble, and when he arrives, you and he will have to set sail for Woodglence immediately. Given the turn of events, there will be no suspicion at your leaving so abruptly."

"And you...?"

"We will avail ourselves of Uferian's generosity and board the *Pelidore*. We sail for Gorfalster."

Bethsefra's green eyes searched Kal's face.

"No," he said, "I know you would join us, but your father needs you. And I have something that I would have you do for me. There is none other that I would ask this of."

"What, my lord?"

"The Talamadh..." He glanced down at the harp he held under his crimson cloak.

"I-I don't understand."

"It is not safe for it to be with me, not with me where I journey," Kal said. "I have lost it once before. I will not risk it again."

Bethsefra made to protest, but Kal lifted his hand to stop her and shook his head slowly, then placed his hand in the crook of her arm and directed her away from the sloops.

"You must take it, Bethsefra. Take it to my people in the Marshes of Atramar. You must tell no one, not even your father. Such information could well place his life at risk, even as I place yours at risk by asking you to do this. But, even so, will you? Will you do it?"

The woman's eyes narrowed a moment in thought as she looked into Kal's face. There was such a strength within her. Kal had never seen the like in any woman before.

"Tell me," she said. "Tell me what I must do."

"My people are hidden deep in the Marshes of Atramar. Thurfar is their chief. Give him the Talamadh. He must place it in Aelward's Cot."

The young woman nodded. "But . . . but how am I to get to the Marshes, Kal?"

"The Asgarth Forest. The old trackways lead deep into the heart of it. Be careful. The folk there are friendly, but very wary and suspicious. Ask for Old Jock. They will take you to him, and he will take you to Aelward's Cot."

He quickly went over his instructions again, asked Bethsefra to repeat them, and then swore her to silence. He shot a glance up the steps from the quay. "The moment Uferian comes, you must leave. And if he doesn't arrive in the next quarter hour—"

"He will come," the woman said. "He will come."

Kal quickly unfastened his cloak and wrapped the golden harp in the heavy crimson fabric. "You will need no more token than this to prove to Jock that you are who you say you are. He is the first one to whom you may show the harp, and the last, until you reach Aelward's Cot and give it to Thurfar. And this too"—he removed the golden circlet from his head and folded it in the velvet robe—"in warrant of the success of my journey." He handed the bundle to Bethsefra, holding onto it after she had reached out to take it. "Stay there, Bethsefra. Stay there in safety until I return."

She looked into his eyes, then leaned forward and pressed her lips to his for a lingering moment. They parted and looked at one another again.

"Stay at Aelward's Cot until I return."

"My lord," Bethsefra said, "I will do your bidding as regards the Talamadh, but whether I stay there or not... My duty is to my king and my country. I must return to Swanskeld." She turned from Kal. "So, to our ships."

"Aye, to our ships.... Bethsefra?"

"Yes, Kalaquinn?" The woman stopped and turned.

"Ah... ah... Y-you will be very careful?" Kal's face crimsoned. "I mean to say, travel safely. I will see you again, Bethsefra."

"Yes, Kalaquinn," she said and smiled. "Until we meet again."

"May you be held in Wuldor's eye."

"And you, Kal. Briacoil."

Kal watched Bethsefra climb the gangplank to her ship, before he turned to his own.

"Milady told us to obey you as we would our lord Uferian. Such was her command, such is my will." The sailor and his mate bowed their heads smartly, then straightened as Kal stepped onto the deck of the *Pelidore*. "What is your command, my lord?"

"We sail downriver to Lake Lavengro and then up the Parwyden River to Gorfalster."

"Aye, good, my lord... and, my lord..." The seaholdsman held out a white cloth wrapped around a small object. "Milady Bethsefra asked me to give you this."

"What is it?" Kal asked, taking it from the man.

"I don't know," the seaholdsman said. "It never occurred to me to ask her." He winked at Kal and turned away to issue a series of soft-spoken directions to his fellow sailor as they cast off the lines.

In a moment, the *Pelidore* was under sail and moving away from the quay, gently making her way through the cluster of moored river craft. Bethsefra stood on the deck of the *Gloamseeker*, watching the ship retreat. She raised a hand, then let it fall to her side. Kal felt the Dinastor River catch the sloop and pull it into its grip. The current favoured them, as did the breeze. The *Gloamseeker*, however, would have to fight to make her way, but Kal knew her master to be a more than capable sailor. The voyage upstream would prove little challenge to him. Bethsefra and Uferian would make it out of Dinas Antrum without difficulty, if Uferian ever managed to get to his ship.

At that moment, in the growing distance, figures clad in black appeared at the top of the steps descending to the quay. They made their way quickly down the stairs. Bethsefra had seen them, too, for she slipped away from the rail of the sloop to meet the party on the quay. She threw her arms around one man. No sooner had the group boarded the sloop than it pushed off from the quay to follow its sister ship out of the Palace harbour and onto the river. The sails of the *Pelidore* billowed, and the sloop increased speed. In no more than a minute, the sloop was rounding a bend in the river, and, even as it began to make its first tack across the river, the *Gloamseeker* was lost to sight.

Kal looked at the white cloth he held in his hand. Gently he unfolded it to expose the delicate image of the Talamadh—his pios! He had carried it in his pocket, he remembered, when he accompanied Uferian to the chamber of the proconsul. But how had Bethsefra retrieved it? Well, it mattered little whether by guile, by charm, or by bribe, she had restored it to him, and for that he was grateful. He turned the pios over in his hand. Beneath it was a small silver pendant in the shape of a swan affixed to a chain. There was also a folded slip of paper. This he opened to find words written on it in a fine hand: "Friend of Uferian, Friend of the Oakapple Isles, my lord Myghternos Hordanu, you will never be far from my heart. B." Kal slid the handkerchief, pios, and paper into his pocket. The pendant he studied for a few moments before gently hanging it around his neck on its chain.

Kal fell to pondering what lay behind, and what lay ahead. He could find no reasonable explanation for what had so recently happened—the wind music, the visions, the resultant panic and mass chaos. But he had escaped. Bethsefra and Uferian would be safe. The Talamadh, by Wuldor's care, would also be safe, placed in the keeping of the Holdsfolk at Aelward's Cot. Devved, however, was lost, and for the first time since their flight from the city, Kal felt a deep pang of realization. The big blacksmith, one of the precious few left of the Clanholding of Lammemorn, had perished to preserve Kal's life. Kal's eyes clouded as tears welled. He quietly sang verses of the prayer of passage for Devved and watched the river banks slip away.

The river was almost empty of watercraft. There were no river patrols to be seen, and, other than a few odd boats that kept their distance, most of the vessels that they passed seemed to be abandoned, drifting along the river or caught up along the reedy banks. In all, it was a strangely quiet voyage, the ship passing without challenge quickly down the Dinastor River and out onto Lake Lavengro.

Kal had not moved from the rail of the ship through the whole journey. Now, to the west over the placid waters of Lake Lavengro, the sun blazed in its dying colours, glorious as it illuminated the sky and fell slowly into the waters. Truly, it was an incredible sight, and Kal became aware of the silent presence of his companions by his side. Kal pushed himself away from the rail and turned to the other side of the ship. There, to the east, purple twilight crept up from the horizon. Clouds were gathering. Heavy anvil thunderheads stained the already dark sky, and forked tongues of lightning chased the blackness in flickering silver. Kal pondered the display and mused to himself, a grin creasing his features. There, he thought, lay his path, there his future, and there his hopes—for there lay Kêl-Skrivar.